Jenny T. Colgan

RESISTANCE
is
FUTILE

orbit

www.orbitbooks.net

ORBIT

First published in Great Britain in 2015 by Orbit
This paperback edition published in 2016 by Orbit

1 3 5 7 9 10 8 6 4 2

Typeset in Caslon by M Rules
Printed and bound in Great Britain by
Clays Ltd, St Ives plc

Papers used by Orbit are from well-managed forests
and other responsible sources.

 MIX
Paper from
responsible sources
FSC
www.fsc.org FSC® C104740

Orbit
An imprint of
Little, Brown Book Group
Carmelite House
50 Victoria Embankment
London EC4Y 0DZ

An Hachette UK Company
www.hachette.co.uk

www.orbitbooks.net

This book is dedicated to my wonderful father, who introduced me to Isaac Asimov, Close Encounters, Robert Fisk and all the rest. Although don't read Chapter 18 (just Dad – the rest of you can). Erm or, actually, Chapter 19. But apart from that, enjoy.

I like mathematics because it is not human and has nothing particular to do with this planet or with the whole accidental universe.

BERTRAND RUSSELL

At first glance, the dead hand looked almost beautiful. Outstretched, thrown open and perfectly clear. Transparent, as if made of resin or glass or ice: a piece of sculpture.

If you weren't heading that way – and only six people on the planet were authorised to be heading that way – you could have missed it entirely.

Missed the soft, puffy, empty flesh behind the lip of the spotless desk, in the room with no wastepaper bins; no dust, no papers or bags or mess: nothing at all. Apart from the completely drained, clear, plasticised, beautiful corpse.

It would start to break down soon, and then the sensors which detected movement and dirt and scents would all spring into action. But for now, all was quiet. The CCTVs scanned over the area again, then stopped, whizzed, burred and back, again and again. But their eyes were as sightless as the colourless man who lay, bloodless, vacant, on a spotless floor, underneath the spotless desk in the pure, white room.

Chapter One

Mrs Harmon wasn't particularly pleased to be forced out of her cosy caretaker's cubby-hole to show yet another newbie around, and she wasn't afraid to show it.

'Here's the main office,' she said with bad grace. So far this week it had been generally polite young men with shy smiles or clever, blinking eyes.

This lanky girl with bright red hair didn't fit the pattern at all, so she wasn't going to waste half her morning in the freezing corridors pointing out toilets.

She sniffed, regretting as she did so eating her lunchtime KitKat at 9 a.m. again. At least when she worked in a prison there had been a bit of banter from time to time. But academics – bloody hell.

How was it a job anyway? Sitting around, drinking coffee and leaving their cups unwashed for her to collect like some kind of cup fairy. And they got paid way more than her, she was sure of it. For scribbling their funny signs everywhere. Sometimes Mrs Harmon wasn't entirely sure academics weren't just all pretending, like a very elaborate form of benefit fraud.

It would have surprised her to know that Dr Connie MacAdair, PhD in probability algebras, Glasgow, post-doctoral scholar in probabilistic number theory, MIT, tipped as a possible future Fields medallist and with an Erdös number of 3, sometimes felt exactly the same way.

Connie blinked.

'Sorry, did you say *this* was the main office?'

If asked to describe what she was looking at, the first phrase that would have occurred to her would probably have been 'bunker, following a nuclear attack'.

'Open plan,' sniffed Mrs Harmon, as if this were an excuse.

The grey room was beneath ground level in the ugly modern block; its few bolted windows showed people's feet tramping to and fro in the rain. It was large and dark and square, very gloomy, lined with tables like a primary-school classroom.

There were no computers, just rows of empty plug points. The most overwhelming impression was of balled-up paper and wadded, overflowing bins. Blackboards and whiteboards lined the walls. Several of the latter had print-out facilities, and great curls of paper rolled across the floor like unfurled tongues. Connie has seen pictures of the maths department: it was beautiful. This was clearly some overflow holding area.

There were paper cups and paper plates, often holding the traces of previous meals. It smelled of mathematics, which felt comfortingly familiar to Connie: a mixture of dusty, crumbed calculators; hastily applied deodorant; old coffee with, underneath it, an unlikely yet undeniable whiff of Banda paper ink.

It was currently empty. And not at all what Connie had expected after the flattering interview, the amazing offer of a post-doc fellowship in her very own specialty, in one of the most beautiful academic cities on Earth, digs included, no teaching, just pure freedom to work for the next two years.

4

This, she reminded herself, was a dream job, an unexpectedly amazing opportunity in these days of cut research budgets and straitened universities. She'd been on cloud nine since she got the letter.

'So, here you are,' said Mrs Harmon, pointedly looking at her watch.

'Oh yes,' said Connie, her heart suddenly beating a little faster. She'd thought this job was too good to be true. Maybe she'd been right. 'Um, yes, I suppose ... is there a desk for me?'

Over in the far corner was a small cleared space, with one dead pot plant sitting in the middle of it.

'Okay,' said Connie, turning round, perplexed. 'I just have a few more questions ... '

But Mrs Harmon was gone. She moved, Connie noticed, surprisingly fast for someone with such a low centre of gravity.

Connie glanced around, just in case her new colleagues had decided to hide under their desks and jump out and throw a surprise welcome party for her that would then go awkwardly shy and wrong. It had happened before.

But the room was deathly silent. She crossed it and looked up at a window and the grey paving stones. Then she pulled up a little chair and hauled herself onto it. Well, that was better, if still not the beautiful book-lined office in an ancient sun-dappled tower that she'd allowed herself to imagine.

Just beyond the pathway that bounded this big, ugly building was straight countryside: they were on the very verge of the campus. In the distance, nearly hidden by the drizzling rain, were the rolling gentle fens that surrounded the college town; closer in, a patch of grass criss-crossed with muddy paths gave way to fields – real live fields with sheep in them.

After three years in a grey, sooty, vibrant Glasgow faculty, it was a revelation. Connie looked for a window to open. They didn't.

The rain was coming down stronger and stronger, although through the distant low hills, the occasional slant of sunshine was visible. Suddenly, at the end of the far field, she made out something through the rain. It was moving very slowly. Very slowly indeed. At first it looked like some kind of odd, slow-moving square robot, lumbering under its own steam, but she realised it couldn't possibly be. For starters, it was brown. Who would ever make a brown robot? Eventually the visual clues coalesced: what she was in fact looking at was a piano. A piano moving across a field. In the rain.

Was this rag week? Had they motorised the piano? Was this some kind of ridiculous stunt? Connie had been in academia long enough to have seen them all and wasn't really in the mood. She was about to turn away when the piano trundled forwards a little more and she realised that there was some-body out there. Someone – a slim figure, tall and lanky as a Giacometti – was pushing the piano. He – it appeared to be a he – was absolutely soaking wet. His white shirt clung to his back and he was wearing a pair of thick-rimmed glasses which were dripping.

But she knew for a fact that pianos were heavy instruments. They weighed a ton, there was nowhere to get a grip and they were resolutely unwieldy. Yet this big, scrawny drink of water out in the field by himself seemed to be hoofing it along absolutely fine.

Drama soc., she thought with a sigh. There was probably a drunk medical student inside shaking a bucket for rag week. The setting of her new university might be very different, but students didn't change much.

*

6

She turned back round to the room. There was a large unsolved equation on the massive whiteboard at the far end, and a brand-new whiteboard pen laid out temptingly. Unable to help herself, Connie went forward and deftly and tidily solved it. Until it came to putting up the solution of 8.008135.

'Ah,' she said out loud. 'Very funny.'

She re-solved it to 04.0404 just as the door creaked open tentatively.

Connie smiled patiently, although inside she still felt nervous. Since she was six years old, at the mathlete-for-tots conference, she was used to being the only girl, or thereabouts. It still boiled down to people at parties introducing her as some kind of perpetual student, or her freaking out men who, when she told them she was a mathematician, tended to stutter a lot and talk about their GCSEs as if her job was a direct challenge to their masculinity.

And here she was again, the new kid, in another classroom, in another town. It was meant to get easier, but it didn't, particularly.

A large man entered. He had frizzy hair, glasses and a huge beard, and resembled a friendly bear. He glanced around nervously, then smiled as his eyes rested on her.

'Whoa,' he said. 'You.'

'Hello?' said Connie. She didn't recognise the man at all and wondered who he was looking for. 'I'm Dr MacAdair.'

The man's large brown eyes widened.

'And they keep on coming. Nikoli puzzles, right?'

Connie stiffened.

'Might be. Who are you?'

'I'm Arnold,' said the man, not at all put out by the brusqueness of her question. His accent was American. 'Arnold Li Kierkan.'

7

'Oh, I've heard of you!' said Connie, relieved. They shook hands. 'The cake cutter. *BM Monthly*.'

He beamed.

'Oh great! Want me to autograph that for you sometime?'

'Uh, I'm not ... oh. Right. I got you. Very funny. But hang on.' She paused. 'We're in the same field.'

'Yeah, actually I've seen you at about nineteen conferences.'

Connie went a little pink. Being a female mathematician in an unusual field was a little like being famous, except without the money, adulation and free clothes.

'Uh, yeah,' said Connie. 'But ... I mean, I don't understand ... I mean, I thought this was a statistical analysis fellowship. Like, *one fellowship*.'

Her heart suddenly plummeted like a lift. She couldn't have misunderstood, could she?

'I mean ... I thought I passed the interview. I mean, I've given up my car ... I've moved out of my flat ... I mean, if we're in competition now—'

'Uh, do you want to breathe into a paper bag?'

'What? No! I want someone who can tell me what's going on.'

'Calm down,' said Arnold. 'It's all right: we're all here. Nobody knows. Evelyn Prowtheroe ...'

'You're not serious?'

He had named the acknowledged leader of the field, whose last job as far as Connie was aware was Professor Emeritus at the University of Cairo.

'Ranjit Dasgupta ...'

'Cor!'

Then it struck her.

Connie took a deep breath before she mentioned the next name herself. As it happened they both said it at the same time.

'Sé Weerasinghe . . . '

'Oh, you know him?' said Arnold pleasantly.

Connie gave him a narrow look.

'Well, so obviously, you, Complete Stranger, already know that I do.'

Arnold raised his large hands in a gesture of appeasement.

'No, no, no.'

His round smiling cheeks went a little pink, and Connie looked around for something to else to do or, if all else failed, fiddle with.

It had been the pairs conference in Copenhagen. There had been something local and revolting called eau de vie. And dancing. Mathematicians dancing was rarely a good look, so there'd been more eau de vie to make the dancing better, which also somehow improved the taste of the eau de vie.

And then . . . a very tall Sri Lankan boy with cheekbones that could cut glass and a charmingly deep voice. A primes race which had ended up upstairs. The seduction had taken place in front of everyone she'd ever collaborated with in the history of the world.

But that was not the worst of it. The worst of it was, when she left his room the next morning and went back to her own to change and wash her face, by the time she got down to breakfast it was entirely clear from the looks everyone gave her and the large collection of guys round Sé's table that he'd already told everyone.

But he did not stand up to greet her, nor did he say anything.

She had looked at him and he had blushed to the roots of his dark hair. She had simply turned around and left the dining room. He had contacted her later to try and explain, to apologise, even to ask her out again, but she had never replied:

9

the awful humiliation of walking into that room full of everyone discussing her was behind Connie's deep and utter
commitment to never ever dating other maths people, even
though it was four years ago now and they were still the only
people she ever met.

She still flushed bright red to think about it, which she tried
her best never to do. And what had been huge anger at Sé's
behaviour had mellowed now, of course – but she wasn't keen
to be working with him again, not a bit.

'Beautiful country, Denmark,' mused Arnold.

'Hmm,' said Connie.

Grinning (and, Connie suspected, getting his own back for
her not recognising him), Arnold extended an arm around the
room.

'Well, anyway,' he said. 'Welcome to the bunker.'

'How long have you been here?'

'Um, three ... four days?'

'Fast work.'

Arnold nodded.

'It is a bit of ... well, totally ... a bunker,' Connie went on.

'I know,' he said. 'Those bastard physicists get all the
good stuff. Did you see their new facility? Ludicrous big
white thing, looks like they all work in a gigantic Apple
Mac.'

'Haven't seen a thing,' said Connie, yawning. 'I took the
sleeper. I haven't even found my rooms yet.'

Arnold cheered up a little. 'Oh, they're a lot nicer than
this.'

'Less nice than this is quite a concept. Seriously, everyone
thinks I've moved to some kind of amazing castle. With a
portcullis in it. And battlements.'

There was a sudden shouting down the hallway, and a large
banging noise.

10

'What's that?'

Arnold popped his head back out the door.

'Hey! You can't bring that in here.'

'Well, obviously I *can*,' came a laconic voice. 'The real question is, how far?'

Connie followed Arnold out of the bunker and into a corridor, where a large grand piano was tightly wedged. Standing in front of it, dripping wet but seemingly completely unperturbed by this fact, was the exceedingly tall, slender man she'd seen in the field.

'Uh, hi?' she said tentatively. The man stared at her curiously. His eyes were dark and intense, behind thick-framed glasses.

'Oh yes,' said Arnold. 'I knew I'd forgotten someone.'

'You have ...' The strange man made a gesturing movement to the side of her head. He seemed to be groping for the word, and Connie wondered where he was from. The amount of people who felt the need to point out that she had bright red hair never ceased to surprise her. '... hair,' he settled on finally. He couldn't seem to take his eyes off it.

'This is Luke,' said Arnold finally. 'I'd like to say he's not normally like this, but so far ...'

'Hi there,' said Connie politely. 'What's your field?'

Luke squinted at her, like he was trying to take his eyes off her hair but couldn't quite manage it.

'Oh, this and that,' he said vaguely.

'Luke, you're wet,' said Arnold, changing the subject quickly. 'You need dry clothes. You'll freeze.'

Luke glanced down as if he'd just noticed.

'RIGHT,' he said. 'Clothes. Yes.'

And he turned around and marched off, ducking under the piano, which he left wedged in the middle of the corridor.

11

'Mrs Harmon isn't going to like that,' predicted Arnold. 'Particularly after the whole ... nest incident ...'

Connie blinked.

'This isn't going to be like other maths departments, is it?'

'No,' said Arnold sadly. 'Cardiff's got a lacrosse team.'

Chapter Two

Connie quickly ascertained two things amid her shock at being in a group rather than this job being just for her: one, that no one else appeared to have the faintest clue as to what was going on either – Arnold explained he reckoned some dodgy billionaire wanted to be the world's foremost number theorist and was simply rounding up the rest of them to lock them away a dungeon – and two, that there was a 'faculty meeting' at 9 p.m. that evening which would hopefully clear things up a bit.

Before then she decided to go and check out her new digs, assuming they were unlikely to be worse than the office space.

The rain had finally stopped and a watery sunlight had appeared across the smoothed-down cobblestones. Leaving the low, ugly, modern building behind, Connie walked down the street and headed to the old college buildings where her rooms were. The old colleges and golden libraries gleamed in the weak light, as timeless and unchanging as the rain itself.

This was more like it, she thought. Her college building was hundreds of years old, with different turrets, stained-glass windows and bits and bobs seemingly bolted on from different historical periods around a medieval core. A wooden porter's lodge stood at the entrance, keeping out tourists and the unwary.

'Hello,' said Connie, slightly nervously. The golden stone seemed to glow with its patina of years; the perfectly green quad beyond designed to invoke awe. It was working.

'Uh, hello. Dr MacAdair?' said the man.

She smiled. At least somebody was expecting her.

'Hello?'

'Hello. Robinson.'

She wondered why he was saying Robinson, then realised it was his name.

'Oh! Hello. Hello, Robinson. Uh, am I … in the right place?'

'Of course, Doctor.'

He handed over a large, ancient set of keys. 'Do you need a hand up with your luggage?'

Connie shook her head. 'Nope, thanks.'

She'd travelled down with just a suitcase; her parents had the rest, and would drive down with it later. She was a bit embarrassed at still having to get her parents to drive her to college at twenty-seven years old, but she had left her little car behind. Cambridge wasn't going to be about getting out and about, or driving up and down to London. It was an extraordinary opportunity, a jewel of a job, a chance to bury herself solidly and fully in work, just the way she liked it, and she was intending to take it. Which meant she didn't need much.

She followed the signs to her set of rooms: P14. The buildings around the square of grass were fifteenth century in pale ancient brick with high mullioned windows. It was very different from the old grey tenement she had left behind.

Inside, the corridor was absolutely silent, rugs positioned along the black and white tiled floor. She pushed open a heavy, studded, wooden door and quietly slipped inside, up the narrow, polished wooden staircase just at its entrance and into the main room.

Connie gasped. They must have got it wrong.

She was standing in large, corner, oak-panelled room. Huge, high windows looked out over the quad. There was a square rug on the dark oak floor, patterned with little birds, and rows of empty bookshelves just waiting to be filled. A large chester-field sofa had plump, comfortable-looking cushions on it. Through the back was a small, pristine kitchen and a bath-room behind it that, with a large clawfoot bath on black and white tiles, Connie looked at longingly. Then, of all things, in the bedroom off it, which had a view over the low-lying hills, was an actual four-poster bed.

Connie laughed out loud, and walked over to it wonder-ingly. The curtains, hanging on ancient wooden poles, were soft, clean, blue velvet, unimaginably old with plant and flower embroidered fringes. She shook her head in amaze-ment. This was ... well. It was something else.

She tentatively sat on the side of the bed, wondering what on earth she'd let herself in for. And – if she were completely honest – feeling a bit odd and lonely in this strange place, even with such a spectacularly amazing apartment. In fact, that almost made it worse, having no one to share it with. No, it didn't make it worse, she rapidly decided. But still.

Of course she had friends – but it was harder in her world that she'd have supposed. She didn't have a lot of school friends, seeing as she had skipped two years ahead. Then going so early to university had meant she had missed out on a lot of the fun everyone else was having. Amid her small cohort of chums, the girls used to make jokes about how many men she had access to. But Connie didn't want to disabuse them of this without referencing how very introverted many mathematicians were, and of the ones that weren't, a lot of them didn't really want to talk shop after spending all day on it: they wanted to go out and get drunk and party with the gorgeous female drama students like everybody else.

And even when she met someone and it got more serious, there was always some debate about who got shortlisted for which grant and who was on the list for which prize and Connie wasn't just a mathematician, she was an unusually good one, so hearing remarks about tokenism and political correctness and quotients always got her more than a little wound up. Not to mention the havoc it could cause in highly-strung, delicately balanced departments. Engineers for sex, she always maintained – they knew where everything went and had a tendency towards patience – and maths for work, and, well, maybe when she got around to the love part, she'd know what she was after. They did say you just knew.

Sometimes Connie worried that she wouldn't know. That all the stuff she did know – Planck's constant, Brouwer's fixed-point theorem – might not leave room for the other stuff.

She remembered again that Sé was there. Oh lord.

There came a knock at the door. Connie jumped up from where she'd been napping, startled. Her first thought was that it must be the bursar come to tell her there'd been some sort of mistake with the rooms, and actually she was in the shared dorm down the road.

'Hello?'

'Uh, yeah, hello?' came back an impatient, accented female voice.

Connie pulled back the heavy wooden door. Standing there was a small, defiant-looking woman, a little stout, her hair braided tightly back from her head.

'Professor Prowtheroe!' said Connie, slightly starstruck.

She'd seen her lecture as an undergraduate, and had been blown away.

'A WOMAN,' said Evelyn Prowtheroe crossly.

'So they say,' said Connie, a little taken aback.

'I can't believe there's another WOMAN on this corridor. Who *isn't* here?'

The woman rubbed her chin thoughtfully. She barely came up to Connie's neck.

'Can you count?' she said.

'That's an arithmetic test?' said Connie crossly. She was tired and a little on edge, and hadn't come all this way to be yelled at by a small person.

'Have you got any tea?'

'No.'

'Come next door. I have tea.'

'I don't . . .'

'You don't want tea? You're British, aren't you? What is the matter with you? It rained today and it's three o'clock in the afternoon. You don't have tea, someone is going to come along and arrest you and give you a French passport.'

'All right, all right,' said Connie, wondering if Professor Evelyn Prowtheroe would at least know more about what was going on than she did.

'Right. Good. Come on then,' said the woman, and Connie stepped out the few paces down the long, panelled hallway. Suddenly the woman stiffened and turned back.

'You are a mathematician, aren't you?' she said in an accusatory tone. 'I mean, you aren't some kind of a physicist?'

'Do I look like a physicist?'

'You look like a red setter,' said the woman, continuing onwards. It was useful that Connie was truly desperate for a cup of tea.

*

17

The professor led her into a very similar set of rooms, equally beautiful, but these looked over the great, round library on the other side of the college, rather than the quad, and had a lovely view of the fields beyond from the main sitting room. It also had a little scalloped balcony Connie hadn't noticed in her own set, that you could sit out on on sunny days, something they would come to use often as Evelyn liked to smoke but had lied and told the bursar she didn't.

The rooms were already beautifully furnished, the bookshelves full: there were lovely soapstone carvings, and exquisite rugs – Evelyn had worked all over the world and had brought back many lovely, intriguing things which made the room homely and charming. A fire was already going in the little grate, smelling beautifully of burning cedar, and an old-fashioned teapot was on the stove.

Evelyn added milk, then poured out their tea into delicate, blue and gold cups through a tea strainer.

'Raisin cookie?' she said.

Connie took one. It was the best cookie she had ever eaten in her life.

'That's amazing.'

'Precision,' said Evelyn. 'That's what most people skip in recipes. They pretend it's flair, or creativity. But it isn't.'

She sighed, took another bite and looked back at Connie.

'So, Ron Weasley,' she said. 'Have you got the faintest idea what's going on?'

'I don't understand,' said Connie. 'I thought ... I thought it was newly created fellowship posts. A place to think, and so on. That's how they sold it at the interview. I thought it was just me. I didn't realise there'd be ... so many of us ... '

'Well, quite,' said Evelyn. They both looked at their teacups.

'I mean ... they can't mean to choose only one of us, surely?'

'Well, if they do ...'

'I built a lot of my PhD on your work ...'

'Good,' said Evelyn complacently.

'It's ... it's so elegant.'

'Thank you.'

Then Evelyn turned to her.

'So why on earth would they employ both of us?' she asked.

'Um, so we could collaborate?'

'Actually, they invented this thing called the internet that's very handy for that. I don't know if you've heard of it.'

Connie looked at her.

'I know.'

'And you've met the others?'

Connie nodded.

'Yes. Ranjit seems enthused.'

'Arnold ... Ranjit ... Sé ...'

'Um,' said Connie, going pink.

'Hang on,' said Evelyn. 'Weren't you in Copenhagen?'

Connie stared at her tea.

'With the eau de vie? And the primes?'

'Can we change the subject?'

'Actually I should probably ...'

There was a loud knock at the door. Evelyn rolled her eyes and got up off the sofa.

'3.07 every day this week. Just when they've cooled down to the exact temperature he likes.'

'You make cookies every day?' said Connie, perking up slightly.

'Nature,' said Evelyn, moving towards the door, 'is an endless combination and repetition of very few laws.'

*

19

Entering via the few stairs through the narrow hallway, and still, to Connie's surprise, wearing the same, damp clothes, was the tall, thin young man she'd seen that morning pushing the piano. Luke.

He stared at her again.

'Hair,' he said again.

'Could you stop doing that?' said Connie, as politely as she could manage. 'It's really creepy. My name isn't "Hair".'

His eyes widened behind the black-rimmed spectacles.

'Oh. Seriously? Creepy. Whoa. Sorry. Creepy?'

Evelyn came forward.

'Yes. You're freaking people out, weirdo.'

Luke nodded.

'And that's bad.'

In Connie's experience, nothing was more tedious than non-mathematicians asking her if everyone she met was autistic or Aspergers-y or weird. There were plenty of delightful, sociable mathematicians, and plenty of introverts too, which was quite nice back in the day you were just allowed to be a bit quiet without everyone slinging a bunch of labels at you all the time. People she met who might have been on the spectrum tended to be both exceptionally high-functioning and very, very happy to be doing a job they loved, so that wasn't problematic either. Unbelievably stupid Hollywood movies helped nobody: a certain amount of eccentricity in the work environment didn't bother Connie one bit.

This chap, however, seemed a little more that way than usual.

'So you've met Luke,' said Evelyn.

'At 10.22,' supplied Luke helpfully. 'Umm ...'

He looked thoughtfully in the direction of the raisin cookies. There was a pause.

'Would you like to come in and have a raisin cookie?' said

Evelyn. Luke suddenly beamed and stepped across the threshold. His smile transformed his whole face.

'Yes!'

He ate two cookies enthusiastically, then looked fixedly at a third.

'Two is polite,' said Evelyn warningly, pouring him a cup of tea. 'It's like living next door to Winnie the Pooh,' she added to Connie. 'Except without Pooh's rigorous, analytical brain.'

Connie looked at him curiously.

'So where did you apply from?'

Luke waved long hands about.

'Oh no, I was here already,' he said.

He glanced up at her.

'The university is very good to me.'

'He's brilliant apparently,' said Evelyn crossly. 'Never published. Never taught. They just let him hang out.'

'Really?' said Connie. 'You've never *published*? Wow.'

Luke smiled quickly and looked slightly embarrassed.

'So have you published a lot?' he asked slightly distractedly.

'Here and there,' said Connie, although she was fiercely proud of the papers that had appeared in academic journals, even if her mother had looked at them as if it wasn't very much to show for her supposedly incredibly clever daughter and all those years of supporting her through ever more advanced degrees.

'Not as much as me,' chipped in Evelyn. 'I kind of wrote the book. Oh no, hang on, I *actually* wrote the book.'

'So tell me about your universe,' said Luke, ignoring Evelyn. 'How probable is it?'

'Oh, you know,' said Connie. 'Four elephants on the back of a giant turtle, then just turtles all the way down. I'm not ... I'm looking for real-world solutions, that's all. Practicalities. I'm a rational person.'

Luke looked amused.

'In an irrational job?'

'Why, because I'm a woman?'

'No,' said Luke slowly. 'Because it's an irrational job.'

'So why are you here?'

'Because the irrationality is the fun bit,' said Luke. 'Everything else is just slide rules.'

'Slide rules took us into space,' reminded Connie. 'Don't underestimate the slide rule.'

Luke smiled.

'But they don't write poetry about slide rules.'

'Well, maybe they should,' said Connie. 'An ode to those of us slogging away in the foothills instead of messing about with stardust.'

'An unfoolable fool,' said Luke.

'What?' said Connie, prickled.

'... with a slide rule. A poem about slide rules, there we are. I would also have mentioned your hair, but I couldn't fit it in.'

'No,' said Evelyn, glancing at her watch.

'What?'

'This is the time you ask me for a cookie to take away and I say no, then change my mind.'

Luke frowned. Connie suddenly glanced at the heavy, old-fashioned watch on his wrist. It was telling completely the wrong time.

Luke blinked twice rapidly.

'Can I have some more cookies for later?'

'No.'

'Okay.'

Luke got up to go. 'See you later,' he said. He looked at his dysfunctional watch and frowned a little more. 'At the weird meeting thing. I don't really understand meetings. I don't understand when everybody says, "Yabba yabba yabba," and everyone says, "No," then somebody taller says, "But no, what about—?" and then they just repeat, "Yabba yabba yabba" again and everyone says, "Oh yes, THAT'S the 'yabba yabba yabba' we meant." I really don't understand them at all.'

Evelyn spun three cookies into a freezer bag and handed them over.

'And then a tall person says, "Thank you for coming," even though you have to go and it's miserable and nobody wants to be there and so it's a lie.'

He made his way to the door.

'It just seems such a very time-consuming way of telling lies.'

'Bye, Luke,' said Evelyn, rolling her eyes at Connie.

'Now,' she said when he'd gone. 'How many years have you been working in maths departments?'

'Uh, six?'

'Have you ever met a mathier specimen?'

Connie simply shook her head.

Connie took a nap, then wandered back down to what she was already thinking of as the bunker. Having a meeting at night was odd, but this whole thing was odd.

The weather had truly warmed up though, and the evening was practically balmy for spring. Crocuses and daffodils lined the edge of the quad as she walked out and down, past the student union, loud with the noise of incredibly intelligent, self-confident undergraduates, the cream of Britain's youth, balancing pints of cider and black on their chins and hollering about snooker.

She had taken a luxurious, foaming bath – she could very much, she had decided, get used to this; it was like the nicest hotel she'd ever lived in – put her clothes (not very many) away in the big, heavy armoire, selected a floral dress and leggings, then changed and stepped out into the lovely spring evening, the scent of early hyacinths and heavy blossom in the air. It was delicious after smoky Glasgow, although that had a charm of its own. She lingered, the cobblestones of the old streets gently lit by wrought-iron lamps overhead, then moved out of the noise of the students and past the ring road and it really was wonderfully quiet in this little town on the edge of the fens.

She saw the dimly lit maths and sciences building ahead and stopped. There were a few people entering, looking furtive. Her new colleagues. Her work ahead, in this new life, this new job. She bit her lip. She just had to get on with it. If she wanted to do real work – proper work, work that could be built on and remembered – then she just needed to focus on the job. Whatever that was.

At the doorway the security guard checked her new ID very carefully, shining a torch in her face and scanning the barcode. That was a little odd, but Connie was too preoccupied to notice. The door was unlocked for her – possibly they had security issues at night. Although unless someone was very good at getting high on whiteboard pens, she wouldn't have thought they had much inside anyone would want to steal.

She followed the long corridor down to the bunker. The piano, she noticed, had vanished. She wondered where it had gone.

Nervously, she pushed open the door and stepped indoors.

Friendly Arnold immediately gave her a wave, as did Evelyn.

'You missed dinner,' said Evelyn. 'They got the roast potatoes wrong again.'

Evelyn was sitting next to Luke, who was staring out of the

window, but at a nudge from Evelyn, turned his head. His eyes looked huge behind his horn-rimmed glasses; a deep brown with a sharp line of sooty, long, very black eyelashes across them. His gaze seemed to slip off her face and onto her hair, but his pupils were large dark holes. For a second, Connie thought he looked blind. Then, with effort, he wrenched his gaze onto her face and gave an apologetic movement of his lips she took for a smile, and mouthed, 'Yabba yabba yabba.'

She glanced around the room. Arnold said, 'Hello! Is your apartment nice? Surely they wouldn't put us in an awful joint if they were going to *Hunger Games* us?'

He looked pensive.

'Or, like, that's exactly what they would do.'

But Connie wasn't listening as her gaze had fallen on Sé. He was as rangy and handsome as ever, his skin a coppery colour, an old soft-looking plaid shirt. She bit her lip, aware that the rest of the room, including Ranjit, were all watching them, except for Luke, who was staring out of the window again.

'Um, hello,' she said awkwardly. 'Hi, Sé.'

'Hey, hi there, uh, Connie. How you doing?'

Sé said this in such a studiously cool way – and his high, fine features, long mouth and almond-shaped eyes did always give him a look of distance – that Connie was slightly mollified, as his gaze slid away from her face. He was obviously just as uncomfortable about this meeting as she was, which somehow made her feel a little better.

'Good,' she said. 'Good, thanks. A surprise to see you here.'

'A surprise for all of us to be here,' he returned in his deep baritone.

It was true: they felt like anxious children waiting in a classroom for the new headmistress. Evelyn was strictly ticking

25

things off on a to-do list. Luke was drawing fractals on a piece of paper with his left hand. Arnold was watching an episode of *Futurama* on his iPhone. But no one could quite hide their nerves.

At 9.15 p.m. precisely, the door slammed open in a dramatic way. In marched three figures, all men. Connie felt Evelyn give a 'hmmm'.

The first was a tall, broad-shouldered figure. He had thinning blond hair, expensively trendy, very thin glasses and was wearing a pale blue shirt with a pastel cashmere jumper knotted in a studiously casual manner around his shoulders. The other men with him were wearing suits. He gave a nonchalant look at the mathematicians – Connie suddenly felt very scruffy in her floral dress, and she was reasonably sure Arnold had something from his dinner on his Time Lords Lego T-shirt – and sat up a little straighter. Sé was, as always, immaculately neat in a brown checked shirt on his lean form. Evelyn was wearing black trousers and don't-mess-with-me biker boots, and Luke was wearing – what was he wearing? It was an old corduroy jacket with elbow patches, and a soft old jumper over a worn shirt, which looked incredibly faded. Clean, just very worn, yet obviously they matched and were made to go together. Ranjit was wearing a polo shirt which looked like his mum had ironed it.

'Ahem,' said the blond, confident-looking man, giving a smile that showed his teeth, but didn't quite reach his eyes.

'Welcome. Welcome, all of you.'

One of the men in suits shuffled an entire sheaf of papers he was carrying. Connie realised he had also carried in two boxes, and both of them were entirely full of paper too.

'So, welcome and congratulations on your fellowships. We at the university feel that as you are at the very top of your fields; you should be proud of your hard work and success.'

Something didn't ring quite true about this, but Connie damped it down as insecurity and paid close attention.

'Although if anyone would like to tell me why there's a grand piano in the gents, I'd be delighted.

'As I'm sure you know, I'm Professor Hirati, head of the astrophysics institute and overall dean of science. 'Now, there is no teaching, no seminars, no students as part of your conditions here.'

He gave his odd smile again.

'But of course, don't think we're letting you off that easily!'

Evelyn glanced quickly at Connie. The man holding the papers stepped forward.

'So, guys.'

The man rolled up his sleeves in a faux-casual gesture.

'Here's the deal. We over at the physics department—'

Evelyn made a quiet tut.

'We were just kind of looking for your help on a small thing here ...'

There was silence in the room.

'We just need you to look at this thing for us ... it's no biggie.'

'What *thing*?' said Arnold.

'We just ... We just want you to run some numbers on a thing we're working on.'

'I knew astrophysicists couldn't add up,' said Evelyn.

'Can't you run them through the state-of-the-art computers Geneva keeps buying you?' said Arnold. Professor Hirati smiled his tight little smile again.

'Well, actually that's what we want from you. No computers. We just want you to ... to have a look for some stuff here. Patterns. That's all we want from you guys. Just think of it as an intellectual exercise.'

'Without running it through a computer?'

27

'Nope.'

Professor Hirati had turned rather pink. 'Just good old pure maths brain power.'

'But ...' said Arnold.

'So,' said the professor. 'That's the job. No computers. We've got you here in this nice, cosy location ...'

'This is why I couldn't get a Wi-Fi signal,' said Sé.

'And we're going to give you these ... just these numbers we've been looking at. And we're just interested to see what you guys come up with.'

'Slide rules!' Luke muttered to Connie.

'But—' said Arnold.

'And the rest of the time,' said Professor Hirati, 'you'll be free to pursue your own research, in your own time, in the lap of luxury, with everything taken care of.'

The six looked at one another.

'But—' said Arnold.

'So, I know this sounds very cloak-and-dagger, guys. It's just a thing, part of our work, no need to worry about it at all, just ruling out something, nothing really, barely worth mentioning. You'll probably find it fun. So.'

He cleared his throat.

'I can't wait to turn all this over to you; I really can't. I just need you to sign off on these contracts, just to let me know you're on board for this ...'

He held up some papers.

Arnold squinted.

'Hey, is that the Official Secrets Act? No way, man!'

Professor Hirati sighed.

'Really, before we go any further, I just need everyone to sign this ... just this piece of paper. A disclaimer, that's all. People need to sign this to go to the loo these days; it's everywhere.'

Arnold looked unconvinced. 'Hey, man' he said. 'I, like, I don't think so, okay?'

Professor Hirati gave a too-wide smile that didn't exactly inspire confidence.

'It's really nothing to worry about,' he said. 'You know, in our line of work, we often take on bits and pieces for the government ... nothing sinister, just standard practice.'

Connie looked at Sé out of the corner of her eye: he was rifling through the large leather bag he carried everywhere, overflowing with papers. Sure enough, there was the contract she'd received – Connie was ashamed now to think of how she'd been so delighted and exuberant at having been accepted as a fellow; she'd signed it in double-quick time and sent it back the same day. It had simply never occurred to her that it could be anything other than problem-solving: how could it? She blushed, thinking how flattered she'd been. And now, what were they doing? Sé found the relevant paragraph, buried late in the boilerplate, and read it to himself, nodding solemnly.

'You see the thing is,' Arnold was going on, 'it's like, man, you brought us here to be smart and now it feels to me like you're treating us like total idiots.'

Professor Hirati nodded thoughtfully.

'Yeah, yeah, I see how you might feel that.'

He looked around. Outside, it was very dark suddenly. He held up the papers.

'I'm afraid this is all I can tell you. Apart from that it is probably nothing, and that it is Her Majesty's Government asking you, and that this is a national security request.'

There was a silence in the room. Except for a slight humming. Connie realised it was Arnold doing the James Bond theme.

Nobody moved. Then surprisingly, someone jumped up.

'I'll sign it,' said Luke. He fished out an antique fountain pen from his coat pocket, then shifted it from hand to hand nervously, as if not quite sure what to do with it. The professor looked at him sternly.

'Thank you ... there and there ... '

Professor Hirati peered at the rest of them over his fashionable glasses.

'Your country really does need you, you know,' he said, and Connie, despite herself, felt an odd thrill go up her spine. What could it possibly be? Some of her physicist colleagues had gone to work for defence companies and become very tight-lipped about what they actually did for a job, and GCHQ had a large team of code-breakers often taken from her specialty, but she had happily expected to fill out her career working on her beloved probability, teaching students, supervising exciting new work – this was taking an unexpected turn. She didn't think much of this chap. But her country needing her ... she stood up.

'I'll do it too,' she said nervously. Professor Hirati gave her the same, slightly over-wide smile.

'Thank you,' he said. 'Thank you. You are doing us a service.'

After that, all the boys and Evelyn followed suit, leaving just Arnold sitting there crossly.

'This is invasion of privacy, man. You don't know what our security services do with this stuff. Can't trust anyone these days. The NSA will be all over all of us, do you know what I mean? Never sign anything.'

Professor Hirati frowned. This looked much more like his more natural expression.

'I'm sorry about that, Doctor Li,' he said, glancing at another pile of papers on his desk. 'I truly am sorry about that. In fact, I think if you don't take up our offer and therefore the fellowship ... Well, I think that means your position in this country becomes untenable.'

Arnold's normally friendly face was horrified.

'You mean if I don't join up for your bullshit operation you're going to *deport* me?'

Professor Hirati shrugged.

'I think, Doctor Li, if you can't be for this country we have to assume you're against it.'

Arnold was gobsmacked. 'Are you *shitting* me? I can't believe this ...'

Sé came over to him. 'Calm down, man. Calm down. It's in the contract, man. You've signed them already. Just do it.'

'But they're saying they're going to take my job away—'

'Ssh. Look, you don't know. It might be something cool!'

'How can it be cool, man? Look at his sweater!'

Sé patted him on the shoulder.

'You can go away and think about it.'

'I'm afraid he can't,' said Professor Hirati briskly. 'We can't risk further discussion among you. If Doctor Li, or anyone else, wants to leave, they leave right now.'

The mood in the room had changed very fast, and nobody knew quite what to do.

After a long pause, Arnold looked at everyone round the desks, looked at the professor and swore profusely. Then he paused.

'Fine,' he said. 'Give me the goddamn piece of paper, you bunch of little rat fink spy asses.'

He sat sullenly and scribbled his signature on it in tiny, messy handwriting, then threw it back across the desk without getting up. Professor Hirati picked it up solemnly and gave Arnold a long look. Arnold's chubby cheeks had gone very pink, but he didn't glance up.

'Very good,' said the professor. 'And now, we shall hand

over the rest of the papers in the morning and you can begin. No computers. No internet. No mentioning it to anyone. This work has already been filtered in every obvious and possible way we can think of. Now we need something direct from your perhaps slightly less obvious brains. Then we can rule it out, go on our way, and you can enjoy the rest of the year in the nicest surroundings we can think of. All right? You can talk about this to one another but absolutely nobody else at all. Nobody. We will find out, okay?'

The meeting broke up after that, a security guard closing the bunker door behind them. They walked back together, slowly down the cobbled roads.

'What a dickwad,' said Arnold, his heavy brow furrowed.

'What do you think it is?' Connie asked, but he shrugged, even as she went on.

'Nuclear bomb threat statistics? Some hideous global warming maths they need done to check whether the world's got five months to live or seven, and how many million people it's worth saving to eat tins in a bunker? Something they don't want the Star Boys to grubby their little paws with.'

Arnold shook his head.

'Has to be cryptography, remember Hardy? Economy runs on the damn thing. Probably trying to stop the robots taking over. Skynet, man.'

Connie frowned. Evelyn caught her up.

'What do *you* think?' she said to her.

Evelyn just shook her head.

'In my country, when government men turn up and want you to sign stuff, I can tell you it's a one-way ticket to pain right there.' And she walked on in silence.

'OOH, sweepstake!' Ranjit was saying, hopping up and down.

Connie suspected he might be having the most exciting night of his life. 'Let's have a sweepstake! Winner buys pizza!'

Evelyn rolled her eyes. 'It'll be a frequency. Some kind of sunspot frequency. They're going to want us to track it down, figure out what they can use it for. Microwave ovens, probably.'

'Would they make you sign the Official Secrets Act for a new kind of oven?' said Arnold scornfully.

'They might,' said Evelyn. 'The college is probably owned by an oven manufacturer anyway. We probably just signed the Bosch Official Secrets Act.'

Connie felt slightly disappointed. It was true and entirely possible that it was something along those lines: a commercial – or worse, weaponisable – emanation along the wavelengths, and they were there to crunch the numbers before the head honchos brought in the engineers to manipulate it. Seemed a touch theatrical, but then Professor Hirati appeared to be a theatrical kind of a chap. Although why no computers?

'Codes and crypto,' Arnold said again. 'Something a computer can't break. And if we don't give them the answer they want ... Guantanamo Bay.'

'You'll never fit the jumpsuit,' said Sé.

'Shut up, Skeletor.'

Sé had up until now been walking along quietly, but he turned to them now.

'Actually, did you not see where the paperwork was from?'

'Go on then,' said Arnold.

'Area 51!' said Ranjit excitedly.

'Put the Haribo away, Ranjit,' said Evelyn sternly.

Sé shook his head.

'Not exactly,' he said. 'Mullard.'

Chapter Three

Having got undressed and managed the slight trick of getting up onto the astonishing four-poster bed, Connie lay on it, shifting about, completely unable to sleep. Why on earth hadn't she smelt a rat before she took this job?

Because she had wanted to believe they wanted her, that was all. And maybe for this, she could be perfect. After all, computing power would only be helpful to a point. They could find regular patterns; sort and arrange and classify. But to draw out something beautiful, or pure, or new ... this was beyond a box of circuits. She tossed and turned.

Mullard. The huge astronomical facility that could pick up signals from deep in space. Why would it have a stream of numbers it couldn't make sense of? She thought of a storm somewhere, a huge sunspot interfering with radio waves, a massive cataclysm billions of kilometres away, entropy, many years ago, acting on something they could only sense the tiniest trace of now. The thought of it made her feel very small suddenly, and rather lonely: the concept of an entire galaxy, burning up, with no witnesses and nobody to care, except thousands of pages of slightly anomalous megahertz printout.

Eventually she gave up on sleep altogether and went to one of the windows to look out on the quiet rolling hills beyond.

The evening was still warm, and there was a clear spring smell of turned earth and early green in the air. She threw on a huge, old fisherman's jumper that had belonged to a man she had once known (and liked less than his jumper) laced up a pair of old Converse trainers but left on her old flannel pyjama bottoms, and crept out quietly into the night.

The ground was damp with dew, but the air was fresh and sweet, softer than she was used to. The traffic noise was far away in the distance, but the bells of the ancient town chimed the half hour as she passed. The night porter stood up to check her out, but as soon as he realised she wasn't an undergraduate, waved her past with an admonition to watch out for herself.

Three streets and she was at the edge of the hills, a full moon lighting up the world. There was nobody there at all, not even a late-night dog-walker or two. Feeling jittery, full of a strange, unnerving excitement that would not dissipate, she decided to walk it out and, under the bright light of the moon and stars, she marched onto the pathway off the road and up the low fen. The grass was wet brushing across her ankles; there was scuttling and scuffling from little paws in the undergrowth and, as she left the lights of the town behind, her eyes adjusted and the sky ahead of her was larger than ever as she gazed up, wondering at the endless sub-stratum commotion taking place in the vast silence of space.

She nearly tripped over the body lying on the hillside.

'OH MY GOD!' Connie yelled, coming to a sudden standstill, her hands fleeing to her mouth.

The figure uncoiled languorously, as if not entirely surprised to be tripped over in the middle of the night. Connie was about to jump backwards, when she realised who it was.

'Bloody hell!' she said. 'What are you doing here?'

Luke was lying stretched out on his back, staring at the sky.

'Luke?'

'Hair,' he said dreamily, as if half asleep, not turning his head. He had taken off his glasses, and again those large eyes were dark shadows in his face. Connie followed his gaze. He was staring intently at the clear sky, the stars overshadowed by the moonlight.

'Is it wet down there?' she said.

Luke wriggled.

'Ish. Yes.'

'Do you just like wet stuff?'

Luke didn't answer.

'What are you looking at?' she asked.

He didn't answer this either.

'I just like looking at the sky,' he said finally. 'The motion over there by Regulus. And Alphard, and Hydra. It looks pink to me. Which do you like? Come and lie down.'

'In the wet grass.'

'Wet-ish.'

She looked at him for a moment. And although it was very unlike her, she lay down near, but not next, to him, not touching, following his gaze.

'I don't see any motion,' she said. All she could see up there was black and navy blue and the bright white pinpricks of the brilliant stars. She started calculating their vectors in her head out of long habit, then stopped. 'Or pink.'

'It's not really pink,' he said. 'Pink ... ish. Except you know, I'm not entirely sure. I'm a bit colour-blind.'

'Okay,' said Connie. 'Well, that explains it. You're colour-blind?'

'Well. Yes. I can't see a lot of colour.'

'Doesn't it just mean you mix up a lot of colours?' said Connie. 'Like red and green?'

'Not me,' said Luke. 'I can't ... I can't see many at all.'

'Except up there?'

He nodded.

'Yes. I see more colours up there. I see ... I see a lot up there. I find it soothing. Here, down here, everything is just rushing shadows. But up there, there's space. I can see clearly. There's room to fit everything in. And it moves at about the right speed, don't you find?'

An aeroplane, destined for Stansted, sailed over their heads.

'Well, some things do,' he said. It was very quiet up on the hill, just the whisper of wind in the long grass; the occasional rustle of a field mouse going about its business; the gentle hooting of an owl.

'And I can work there,' he added, raising his hand with its graceful, long fingers connecting the dots. 'The graph of it. It's like, finally, a large enough canvas.'

'Like a giant iPad,' said Connie, watching as he traced patterns across the sky.

'What's that?' he frowned.

She turned to look at him.

'You've never heard of an *iPad*?'

'Of course I have,' he said swiftly. 'They're ... awesome?'

Connie smiled.

'Totally.'

They lay there, watching Saturn inch its way across the night sky. Connie wondered if he'd fallen asleep. She didn't feel sleepy at all.

'When I was little,' she began. She hadn't thought about this for years. 'When I was very small I was in the car, with just my dad – I don't know where the others were.'

Luke didn't move, so she continued.

'And I was kind of asleep against the window, then I woke up and I saw ... I saw a UFO.'

He looked at her then.

'*Really?*'

'Yes! Well, no. Not REALLY. It was a huge, round shape, half the size of the sky, with lights twinkling all round it in a circle.'

'And?'

'And ... it was amazing. I was kind of terrified and really excited all at once. This is it, I thought. They're here. My dad ... my dad took me to see *Close Encounters of the Third Kind* when I was little. And when we came out, he said to me, "You know, if aliens came for me, I would go straightaway. I would love that. I would walk straight into that space ship." And I said, "What, without us?" and he looked a bit strange and said he would miss us a lot, but, you know. Aliens!

'And I said, "Me too!"'

Luke smiled.

'I take it that didn't happen?'

Connie fell silent.

'He did leave us,' she said eventually. 'But not for aliens. For some stupid woman who lived down the street. Mum never got over it. She'd much rather he'd have been kidnapped and painfully probed and experimented on.'

Luke blinked in the darkness.

'I am sorry about that.'

'It happens a lot,' said Connie swiftly. She hated to dwell on the pain of those years; had dealt with it then by burying her head in her books and studying until she couldn't hear the shouting and the fights any more. In mathematics, where the numbers did interesting things, but they were reliable. They behaved in comprehensible ways. $2x$ was always more than x, if x was a natural number. You could start from that, from the very basics, and end up anywhere you liked.

'So, what was it?' asked Luke eventually. Connie had lost her train of thought.

'What ... oh, the spaceship?'

'The spaceship.'

'It was the lights of the cars on the next hill,' she said. 'On the road round the hill. The hill was round and dark and the red lights were going one way and the yellow lights were going another way.'

'Aha,' said Luke. 'Well, we've all done it.'

'Mistaken some cars for a spaceship?'

'Maybe not *all* of us.'

'What if ... I mean, what if,' said Connie. 'I mean, I've heard rumours about these secret tasks, but I never thought I'd be caught up in one.'

'I doubt that's our job,' said Luke. 'You have to remember how those scientists think. Disprove, disprove, disprove. They want us to come back and tell them it's nothing.'

'I suppose,' said Connie.

'If you think about it too much,' said Luke. 'It might get in the way.'

'They can't stop speculation.'

He looked at her. 'From the looks of that little display of intimidation tonight, they can stop a lot of things.'

'But ... you know ... '

Connie cast her hands to the sky.

'What if ... what if it was a message, from further away than you can imagine? On a different wavelength?'

She thought of the rows of numbers again.

'What if it was a song?'

Luke looked at her.

'You think an unimaginably faraway species in an unimaginably faraway universe, probably on a dimensional axis to us, and with goodness knows what kind of spatial relationships to us, nano or vast ... you think they'd send us "Orinoco Flow"?'

Connie stared at him.

'Seriously, that's the first song that came to mind?'

'It's a pretty song,' said Luke defiantly.

'I just . . . I just don't know.'

Luke held up his hands towards Polaris, just visible to their right, and moved his right over his left to form an oval.

'What are you doing?'

'First principles,' he said. 'What's the time?'

'Five past twelve.'

'Exactly?'

'Yes.' Connie always knew what time it was.

'Well, we'll start from here,' said Luke. '52 12 0 0 7 0.'

Connie looked at him.

'Is that . . . ? You did not just work out the latitude and longitude? Are you dead reckoning? You must know them off by heart. Where are we . . . ? North and east.'

Luke shrugged.

'I'm a stranger here myself,' he said. 'Sorry. I was just meaning we should just deal with what we know, okay? In this job.'

Connie nodded, then sat up.

'Oh,' said Luke. 'Are we going?'

'Do I need to take you through this "wet" thing again?'

As he stood up, Connie noticed that underneath his coat he too was wearing his pyjamas; incredibly old-fashioned cotton pyjamas with a very faded pink stripe.

'Are those pyjamas?'

He frowned.

'It's night-time isn't it?'

'Yes.'

'And you're wearing pyjamas.'

'Girls look cute out in pyjamas,' said Connie. 'Boys look creepy.'

'I have a lot to learn,' said Luke, looking down awkwardly.

'A lot to learn about what?' said Connie.

'Um . . .' Luke looked abashed.

'Have you never worked on a mixed team before?' she teased him. So many of these boys who grew up in maths found women an alien species, particularly if they'd been to all-boys schools. Luke must be another one.

Luke's face lit up.

'No!' he said. 'That's probably why I keep making stupid ... pyjama-based mistakes.'

Connie smiled.

'That's okay,' she said. 'We're not that frightening.'

Luke raised his eyebrows but didn't say anything.

'Right, we'd better get back. Now they're watching us and everything. God, I really believed him when he said that. I guess the real work begins tomorrow.' Connie realised she was babbling as they started down the path.

'Looking for the cars driving round the hill,' said Luke.

They reached the main road and turned off into their quad, bidding each other good night.

The man who had followed them up and into the undergrowth quietly continued on the same way, nodding quickly to the night porter as he passed.

Chapter Four

They sat as a group at breakfast, all anxious about the day ahead, reluctant to speak to one another. The refectory was a riotous affair: long, wooden benches where students bolted endless rounds of toast and drank unspeakable coffee. Evelyn had brought her own flask from the espresso machine she kept in her little kitchen. It was to become their new obsession, until every morning there were four – Luke and Ranjit didn't drink it – big thermal cups lined up before they left for the day.

Because the days were long.

It reminded Connie of Rumpelstiltskin; of trying to spin straw into gold. The reams and reams of numbers never seemed to end; they spilled out of box after box. Everyone started at the beginning – if it was, of course, the beginning; that was not at all necessarily clear – and did everything with the numbers they could think of. It reminded Connie of the tests the school psychologists had given her when she was very small when they pulled her out of class, and all the grown-ups had looked at her and made her feel a freak.

They calculated entropy and plotted on graphs, broke down algebraically, counted, squared, triple-rooted, divided, stepped – all by hand, all on paper.

This was effectively what had happened: all large planets and stars gave out a background frequency, a low-level hum that simply indicated that they were there. According to the Mullard cosmologists, these were the frequencies of a sudden, mysterious radio signal from deepest space, pumped out with more energy than the sun could manage in a million years. Then it had immediately stopped.

They had run frequency analysis, SETI had got involved– briefly, rather over-excitedly – but the more computer simulations they ran, the less they learned. This little band, and their pencils and calculators, were the line of last resort.

'This is like one of those awful spot quizzes where they called you out of class,' grumbled Connie on the fourth morning. Luke was building an astonishing complicated origami pyramid of folded discarded paper. Connie hadn't seen him do any work at all. What he did do was come by looking at the rest of their work, and immediately point out its flaws, sometimes writing them rapidly up on one of the blackboards. This was dispiriting, but incredibly impressive. Connie had never met a more natural-born mathematician in her life: his talent was fluent, completely innate. But he seemed completely uninterested in developing any theories himself.

'But those bits were awesome!' Arnold had said immediately she mentioned the quizzes. 'The only times you didn't have to take constant ritual abuse from the rest of the class! A quiet corner of the teachers' staffroom and a stopwatch. And lots of attention!'

Ranjit sighed a happy sigh at the memory.

'Did you ever get to go to those American mathematics conventions?' said Arnold as he deftly multiplied three enormous numbers on his fingers, moving them like a speeding abacus. 'Oh man, those things were heaven.'

'I once did fifteen hours on the free Dance Dance

Revolution they set up there,' said Ranjit, sighing. 'That was the best night of my life.'

'The best night of your entire life?' said Evelyn sternly. Ranjit blinked behind his glasses.

'I'm a very good dancer,' he said.

'Man, the free snacks ... nothing to do all day but beat the other guy. Or, erm, woman,' said Arnold, to be polite.

'Stupid show-off competitions,' said Evelyn. 'Mathematics is about investigating the subtle beauty of patterns hidden in rules, not showing off.'

'Which is why,' said Arnold, holding up a pile of paperwork, 'they've given us this pile of stinking pig knickers to work with.'

'Arnold, what do you think "knickers" means?' asked Sé.

'I'm enjoying you guys pretending you've ever seen a pair,' snorted Evelyn.

'Okay, come on, guys, let's get on,' begged Connie, as Luke came round again with his mantra: disprove, disprove, disprove. Although she was full of admiration for his methods – or would have been, if she could have figured out his methods at all – it was still rather dispiriting: the sense that you might be, in the end, working on nothing at all.

Still, they worked on, through the nights, eating together, discussing possibilities, but it was like knitting stars together: there were no threads they could tease out, nothing that made the numbers seem random, or deliberate, or anything other than, almost certainly, what Occam's razor suggested they were, and Luke agreed: an inexplicable radioactive interference, a nothing from Kepler-186f.

Every so often Professor Hirati would bustle in, immaculately dressed, huffing and looking at his watch and mentioning other meetings he absolutely had to get to, and had they found anything? No, very good, that would be all.

By day nine, they were all heartily sick of it. Connie was dreaming in megahertz, the six digits, non-repeating, non-anything: 145.786; 120.634; 389.544. Plotted on a graph, they went up and down and round in completely random swathes, meaningless, simply patterns you could make with any numbers at any time, signifying nothing at all. Ranjit filled scratchy notebooks with lines of thick, black algorithms, playing with the numbers, twisting them, turning them, breaking them down and down again and again.

Arnold used the blackboards to work them in different dimensions; treat them as the lengths of great, hundred-sided, multidimensional shapes that cavorted uselessly up the dirty walls in marker pen. Luke drew two eyes and some teeth on one particularly dragonish extended shape, a polytope unfolded from four dimensions down to two.

One morning Connie came in after a night full of tumbled dreams in the four-poster bed, when the numbers had swelled up as great waves and threatened to pull her down, down beneath them and drown her. She felt tired and grumpy and unutterably fed up with the bunker, and the security cards, and getting cramp in her hand from trying to work out sums that had no solution or any solution.

Now, she turned up to see that Luke had managed to bring the piano back in and, not only that, he was lying underneath it, tightening and loosening strings in a way that was making it sound absolutely dreadful.

'Stop torturing that instrument,' said Connie, pushing her hair behind her ears. 'It's cruel. AND unusual.'

The two booted feet sticking out from underneath the stringed section of the piano failed to move. Instead, a long, pale hand appeared, groping at the keys from underneath and played a great crashing handful of discordant notes.

'Sixth and a half,' said Arnold without looking up from his

mass of paper. 'Luke, man, that's a sixth and a half interval. You're going to have to stop this. It's like you're weaponising the whole concept of music.'

'You are. You're breaking it,' said Connie, as the hand went on, feeling its way around, and the tone of the notes went up and down like shrieks as he loosened and tightened the springs.

'ARGH!' she yelled finally, throwing down her stylus. She went and stood by the lid of the piano, holding it up. Over on the other side of the room, Sé was still working away quite happily. She shook her head in amazement.

'I see more fingers, I am dropping this,' she exclaimed loudly. 'I mean it.'

The boots moved then, and Luke emerged smoothly into the room. He was lying on his back on a skateboard. The large, dark eyes behind the thick, dark-rimmed glasses were puzzled.

'I'm just de-tempering the piano,' he said.

'Yes, well,' said Connie. 'You're also de-tempering the maths department.'

'I don't mind it,' said Sé mildly from the back of the room.

'That's because years of heavy metal have burned out your soul,' said Connie. 'And *you* can go and make horrible noises in the rec.'

'I don't like it in there,' said Luke, patting his piano as if reluctant to leave it. 'I feel sorry for the vending machines. And as I am 99.974 per cent convinced now that our work here is completely futile. I thought it was time for a little musical entertainment.'

'ARGH!' said Connie. 'We have been cooped up in here for too long. Seriously. Hasn't anyone got a home to go to? Arnold, aren't you married?'

Arnold looked slightly less jolly than normal.

'Uh, no, well, not exactly . . . I mean, not as such.'

'You don't *know*?'

'Uh, well. No. But I have, you know . . . a very busy avatar.' His voice trailed off.

Connie turned to Evelyn.

'What about you?'

'I'm married to mathematics,' said Evelyn stoutly. 'Also, that cow left me back in Cairo. Witch.'

She scored her paper so hard with her pencil it tore. Sé raised his eyebrows.

'Seriously, we're *all* single?' said Connie, aghast.

'I'm engaged,' volunteered Ranjit surprisingly. 'What? I am! Since I was eleven. My parents were thrilled; she's my second cousin, so it's cool. Just waiting for her to turn twenty-one. She's good at maths too.'

'But she doesn't live with you?'

'What, before we're married? Ha!'

Connie shook her head. 'Amazing. You'd almost think they did this on purpose.'

'You didn't ask me,' said Sé. Connie went slightly pink. She didn't really want to know if Sé had a girlfriend.

'Um . . . ' she muttered. 'Do . . . ?'

'No,' said Sé, looking down.

'Nobody asked me either,' Luke was complaining to Evelyn. She patted his hand. 'That's because you're so weird,' she said reassuringly. 'Also, because your music is so horrible.'

'I like it,' said Luke, sidling back towards the piano.

'I think I might have to give you a massive punch if you start making that noise again,' said Arnold. 'Sorry in advance.' He held up a large, meaty knuckle. Luke's forehead furrowed.

'But,' he said, 'to propel that fist with the necessary force to injure me, you'd unbalance your height–weight ratio. Gravity wouldn't cover it.'

'Are you calling me fat?' said Arnold, standing up.

'Yes,' said Luke, looking confused.

'You come over here and I'll solve that for you.'

'I get that,' said Luke wonderingly. 'Because you wouldn't want to expend any extra energy in moving. Exothermically it would be disadvantageous, plus your lung capacity—'

'Okay,' said Connie, standing up between them. 'Enough. We need fresh air. And this room really, really, *really* needs fresh air. Mrs H is refusing to clean up any more, says we're like a big bunch of monkeys.'

She tried not to look at Arnold, who was sadly examining his hairy knuckles.

'Come on! Out! You can do more maths walking in the fresh air anyway!'

It was, they discovered to some surprise, the most beautiful spring day. The trees were full of blossom that drifted beneath their feet, the sun was warm on their backs and, as soon as they got moving out of the town, crossing the road heavy with bicycles, and set out on a trail that led to the woods, Connie took a deep breath and thought about what a good idea this was. Get everyone moving; stop them being so cranky and dependent on coffee all the time. Perhaps they'd find a country pub at the end of their walk, bond a little rather than fractious bickering as they each raced to prove something before the others; to solve a puzzle that perhaps could not be solved.

'What do you think?' she asked Evelyn as they walked together, scattered circles of daffodils lining their way.

'Oh, we're probably trying to fix somebody's broken fricking telescope,' said Evelyn, who was glancing at her watch and frowning. She liked to cook and eat her lunch at the same time every day, and this was it. 'I don't know why they're making such a big fuss.'

'What are you doing?'

'I'm calculating the subword complexity, looking at how often each possible pair of numbers is used, each triple and so on.'

Connie nodded.

'But nothing, right?'

'The weird thing is,' said Evelyn, watching a wispy cloud disappear high in the sky. Ahead of them, Sé and Arnold were walking together, Arnold struggling a little to keep up with Sé's lanky stride. It was odd, Connie reflected, to see Arnold outdoors. He didn't belong outside; he was an inside cat, with a can of cola surgically attached to his left hand. Ranjit was scurrying along behind them, occasionally making a remark that the boys batted away like a fly. Luke, Connie noticed, had surreptitiously picked a daffodil and was looking at it curiously. 'I've started to think it might be anything. Votes cast in the last Eurovision Song Contest. Stock market trades. Freckles per person. Stuff it couldn't possibly be.'

'I know. I know what you mean. Just seems so . . . ' Connie smiled. 'I quite like it. Just the purity of digits, repeating, turning upside down. It's like playing in a sandpit. No rules.'

'No rules because we don't know what they want,' said Evelyn. 'I like solving problems because I can kind of normalise the concept of an answer. Here . . . *pfff*.

'It's a far-off exploding sun,' Evelyn went on, 'sending random blazes across a distant galaxy. They're just pissed because their stupid hyper-expensive telescope can't pick it up. It's probably incredibly beautiful. It's a dying star: it's even sad. But it doesn't *mean* anything.'

They had reached the top of the hill. Everyone had taken their coats off except Luke, who was still wearing the worn-in cord jacket with the patched elbows that was slightly too big for him.

From there they could see a long way across the flat countryside, all the way down to the river flowing through Ely and on towards the sea. Connie watched it wind its way across the flatlands, patchworked with green and great, tended hedges; sheep dotted here and there; cows burying their heads in the fresh, spring, green grass, the sweet, scattered daisies. It was a beautiful sight: England in all its calm and spectacular beauty. Steeples were dotted here and there, tiny clusters of towns. In the distance, a silent train slid past, bearing passengers to the great machine of London, sixty miles below.

Everyone stretched out, sat down. Sé lay down entirely, pulled out his sketch pad and started drawing the cloud formations overhead for a project he had in mind. Evelyn took out a small, filthy-smelling, brown cigarillo and lit it up defiantly.

'Way to totally like ruin the moment,' said Arnold, coughing dramatically.

'Or massively improve it,' said Evelyn. 'I always stand upwind of you, so now may I suggest you do the same?'

Connie stared at the river, her gaze following two lazy terns circling overhead. It was as difficult to imagine the pounding, roaring energy, noise, traffic and people of London – only a hundred kilometres away, nothing in spatial terms, not really – as it was to imagine a dying sun spurting out its final embers across a distant star, confusing the tiny signals only a rudimentary Earth device could pick up . . .

'It's all perspective, isn't it?' said a low voice, echoing her thoughts. She turned, startled. Luke was standing there.

'From up here, everything looks far, even when it isn't. It just depends where you're standing.'

Suddenly Connie was conscious that Luke was standing very close to her. He wasn't touching her, but he was uncomfortably close; she could hear his breathing, smell a light smell she couldn't identify but later struck her as something not unlike salt water. His long, thick eyelashes were casting shadows on his pale cheek. She blinked. His eyes really were incredibly large. She had noticed – she didn't know if the others had – how bad his eyesight really was. He got by on familiar routes and, she had also noticed, he had taken to checking out where she was in the room by her hair.

'Luke!' shouted Evelyn. 'Personal space.'

'Oh lord,' said Luke, moving back a step and wobbling slightly. Connie put out a hand to stop him from falling, but he avoided it and successfully performed an awkward back-hopping manoeuvre until he'd stopped himself. 'Sorry. Evelyn keeps telling me off for it.'

'That's all right. I ... I don't mind,' said Connie, almost before she realised what she was saying. Then she flushed a dark red, her cheeks growing hot. I've been trapped in that room too long, she thought to herself. I'm going nuts. Too much time enclosed and indoors. Too long without ... I mean, not that ... I mean, Luke was pretty ... too pretty, she told herself. Too pretty for a boy. Although his strong shoulders under that jacket ... and his long, elegant fingers ...

'THAT is BEAUTIFUL!' shouted Arnold suddenly, and she turned towards him, conscious of being pleased at the distraction.

'That is the most BEAUTIFUL thing I have EVER SEEN.'

Everyone followed where he was pointing. Just down the hill on the other side, slightly hidden from view along the path, was a little sign for a pub.

They sat outside, the sun warm on their backs, pints all round, enjoying the odd freedom; not, for once, panicking and worrying about the work they had done and not done; about who was watching them. They were just a group of colleagues, friends almost, sitting like normal people, having a pint in a pub, just like normal people did on Fridays or whatever day it was (actually it was a Wednesday, but none of them had noticed a weekend for three weeks now).

The unexpected loveliness of the afternoon, and the unexpectedly strong local cider, acted on all of them quickly, and soon the noise levels round the table rose with a great deal of banter based around which of them was the biggest loser: Sé getting upset at the others ridiculing his attempt to make fractals out of empty crisp packets; a very awkward interlude when Ranjit jumped up and showed them his immaculately worked out and extremely sexually explicit dance routine when 'Blurred Lines' came on the radio; a fight between Evelyn and Arnold on a subject nobody could remember afterwards but was either the oppressive nature of the Catholic church or the correct way to cook a chicken ballotine.

For the most part, Connie was happy to sit, soaking up the atmosphere, laughing at the stupid jokes, enjoying the fresh air and the sunset as the pub filled up with farmers and local people, not the students they were used to; and the garden, with its wooden trestle tables and many dogs, turned on its fairy lights, and moths fluttered around them, and the scent of meadow grass mingled with pear cider and Evelyn's filthy little black cigarettes mixed and descended with the dew, and the evening took on a slightly hazy feel of laughter and noise and all of them together.

Later – much later – Connie was wondering about how exactly they were all going to stagger their way home, particularly when there seemed to be twice as many sheep in the fields than before – she found this thought highly amusing and started to giggle. When she came back from the loos she noticed that Luke was standing on the table, shouting about star signals.

She looked around. He was obviously talking too loudly. The other tables were pretending not to hear him, but she still had the idea that he shouldn't be speaking aloud about their project. They shouldn't mention it outside the bunker at all. Surely that was the deal? Even through her slightly befugged state, this seemed very wrong.

'Come down,' she hissed urgently, threading her way through the other tables. 'Luke! Get down from there!'

Luke frowned at her.

'I'm not "up" anywhere.'

'You're "up" on the table.'

He glanced at it.

'This is "up" relatively speaking. It's actually nothing at all in real terms.'

'Well, can you get down off nothing then, please.'

'All I'm saying is ... '

'All you're saying is something you can say very quietly, in private in the bunker,' said Connie. The others were watching both of them, eyes fixed on one another.

'We don't need a bunker,' said Luke. 'That's the point. We've all looked at it properly. Except for you, Sé. Your investigation into the hierarchical structures of the sequence is flawed. You're not considering the fact that we can apply any semantic interpretation to derive meaning: we're looking for a natural interpretation, and yours isn't it. Just because a structure is delightful doesn't mean you can jam the data in.'

'That's absolute ... ' Sé thought for a moment and stared into his glass. 'Oh yeah. Yeah. Fair enough. Why didn't you tell me before?'

'Doesn't make any difference,' said Luke loftily. 'You could

53

substitute a small rhesus monkey for the 120-cell for all the usefulness you'll add to the work.'

'Oh well, thanks for that,' said the normally unflappable Sé.

'No, listen,' said Luke, waving his long hands about in agitation. Evelyn tugged his jacket so he stepped down off the table, but he stayed standing up. Several of the nearby tables were looking straight at the madman. Connie found herself wishing they'd get thrown out, but she couldn't see any staff nearby.

'Listen to me!' said Luke. 'It's been fun ... um, well, I'm not sure what fun is, but I think we should say, "It's been fun," and anyway. We can see. These mean nothing. They are futile streams of nothing, probably the last gasps of a dying supernova. We need to tell them, "Take your ridiculously expensive satellite telescopes and point them somewhere else. You're doing nobody any good and wasting all your money and stuff." And then we can go back to doing whatever we like to do instead of trying to solve stupid Sudoku puzzles and calling it a job. I say we tell them tomorrow.'

'Do you reckon a month is enough, bud?' said Arnold, frowning.

'You could spend a hundred years on this,' said Luke. 'You'd get nowhere. It's nothing. Nothing. And it's wasting our time.'

Evelyn nodded.'I wouldn't mind putting a book together with the rest of my fellowship year.'

'I want to visit home,' said Sé.

'I'm getting married!' said Ranjit happily.

'I'd be delighted to fuck off that professor guy,' said Arnold.

Luke looked at Connie. She stared straight back at him.

'No!' she said.

'What?'

'No! I'm not done!'

'Not done doing *what*? Long division?'

'I don't know,' said Connie, conscious of her tongue feeling thick in her mouth. 'I'll know it when I find it.'

'You'll never find it.'

'You seem very sure of that. Don't you want me to find it?'

They locked gazes for a long time. Luke dropped his first. Eventually Arnold stood up.

'Ach, Connie's probably right,' he said. 'Can't give up on sucking the government teat quite yet.'

Evelyn sighed. 'Killjoy.'

'I'm quite liking it,' said Ranjit.

Connie looked at Luke's face. For someone so mild-mannered, he didn't look like a man who had just lost a work argument. Suddenly, he looked pale, and completely and utterly heartbroken.

Arnold didn't notice, and heaved his hefty bulk off the bench.

'Right, I'm gonna turn in. I know we're in Britain and all that, but I don't see why I should have to drink till I'm unconscious just because it's local.'

The others muttered agreement and everyone gradually stood up, moving slightly unsteadily up to the crest, over the hill and back down to the lights of town, all now on and shining in a comforting fashion.

Only Luke stayed where he was, still standing behind a sea of empty glasses, the stricken look still on his face. Connie stayed behind for a second, feeling bad to have upset him so much.

'I'm sorry,' she said. 'I just ... I just don't feel I'm done yet. I feel there is something in it. Something connecting it. Something just out of reach that I can't see. I know it sounds crazy. Call it my Spidey sense.'

Luke looked confused, then, once again, completely crest-fallen.

'I understand,' he said. Connie couldn't understand why he was so miserable about it. It was only a job, after all. A job they were being contracted to do.

She offered him her arm jauntily to walk down the hill with, but he looked at it as if he had no idea what to do with it, so she took it back, embarrassed with her forwardness for the second time that evening. Remember Sé, she told herself. Don't make a total idiot of yourself. At least Sé was interested at the time. Stop it.

She set off down the path.

'I'll ... I'll see you in the morning,' she said when he made no move to follow her. Instead, he was gazing into the night sky, where the stars had just started popping out. He nodded.

'I'll stay a while,' he said.

They got back to the college, full of bonhomie, although Connie was still worried about Luke. So she didn't notice as the others said their goodnights and went to their own sets that she was left alone in the corridor with Sé.

'Goodnight,' she said pleasantly, feeling in her bag. Sé looked uncomfortable.

'Actually,' he said. 'Actually.'

He moved a little closer.

'I wondered if, maybe ... you might like a nightcap or a coffee or something.'

Connie looked up at his handsome face, completely taken by surprise. Their relationship had been – the occasional ribbing from the others aside – entirely professional since their paths had crossed again and she had ceased to think of him as anything other than a quiet, serious colleague.

'Oh,' she said. 'Oh, Sé, I ...'

His high-cheekboned face was a very awkward mix of nerves and hope. She cast her eyes down.

'I think with us working so much together ... it would just get complicated ...'

He gave a short nod.

'Plus, you like that other guy.'

'What other guy?' said Connie, colouring.

'What other guy?' mimicked Sé crossly. 'Arnold? Uh, no. That moony-looking guy with the big cow eyes? You're always looking at him.'

'I'm not always looking at him!' said Connie. 'I'm always looking at nineteen thousand pages of senseless printout, like everybody else.'

'Which is why you need to do something to take your mind off it.'

Connie had a quick flashback to Sé's long, almost hairless, beautiful, brown-skinned body but shook her head.

'No,' she said.

'Because of him?'

'Because of all sorts of things,' she said. Sé blinked slowly, his face slowly closing up.

'Well, if you change your mind, you know where I am.'

'Thank you,' said Connie. He waved an arm at her and sauntered off down the corridor, leaving her standing alone, feeling very peculiar.

Chapter Five

It almost certainly had a lot to do with the cider – and Sé's very awkward proposal – but Connie slept badly. She tossed and turned under the covers, finding the night stuffy, the curtains of the four-poster oppressive. She couldn't get a comfortable spot, feeling like she was in a ship on the sea, tipping in and out of an uncomfortable half-sleep, thirsty, that image of Luke's devastated face coming back to her again and again, even though it was not in the least clear why he was so upset.

Finally, at just before four, she gave up. The ancient oak floorboards creaked under her feet, which were still unaccustomed to such luxury, and she wobbled over to the little kitchen where she drank a glass of water so fast she forgot to turn off the tap. The water pounded down in the sink and, a little befuddled, Connie watched it for a while, blinking. Then she leaned over and turned it off.

She put on the kettle and made herself a cup of tea, but didn't put any lights on. The moon was shining brightly through the windows, and she didn't think her eyes were up to it. Instead she took the tea, pulled a blanket off the sofa and wrapped it round herself, and headed to the large window.

Sure enough, although she didn't quite have a little balcony like Evelyn, she did have a tiny bit of space between the window and the crenellations; just about enough to squeeze herself out, and up and over the roof. She did so now, gazing out over the rooftops of the ancient buildings, and beyond, to the gentle rolling hills, the stars blazing away overhead. She fancied she saw someone walk up one of the hills, but she couldn't have done; nobody would be out at this time of night.

Instead, she drank more of her hot tea and gazed out at the skyline, half asleep, half awake, wondering when the fingers of dawn would arrive. Somehow it seemed at this time that they never would; that they would be dark for ever, nothing but the faint light of distant stars to guide them; nothing but eternal nightfall.

She must have fallen asleep properly then, partly because when she awoke, the stars were fading, and, more pressingly, she found herself falling – lurching to one side. The shock woke her instantly and she cried out, grabbing onto a crenellation, convinced in her dream traces that she was falling overboard from a boat.

When Connie realised she was in no danger of falling off the room but had merely moved in her sleep, she was cross with herself, but still shaken up. There was no boat, no sea, no . . .

Connie froze.

Dawn was just beginning; straight ahead, she was facing the east, and the first streaking of pinks, purples and yellows were starting to shoot out. But mostly the sky was still dark, and the gently undulating hills looked more like . . .

Connie shot up, still in her pyjamas, pulled on a jumper and ran to the bunker. She didn't realise she was in bare feet until she was nearly there.

She didn't expect anyone to be around, but a security guard – not like the normal, heavy chaps she generally saw there, but a young, smart man with a very short haircut – was awake and alert, ticked off her name and let her through the door.

Connie went straight to the piles of paper, grabbed a stack, stole a big fresh whiteboard pen off Sé's desk (Arnold's were always running out; Sé's desk was always immaculate and his stationery pristine) and started on the far left of the room, the whiteboard nearest the door. Pulling her hair off her face with a rubber band, she rubbed the sleep from her eyes and began.

Four hours later, the others crawled in, in various degrees of messiness: Arnold with bags under his eyes, Ranjit yawning, Evelyn looking pristine as always. Luke was nowhere to be seen.

'Whoa,' said Arnold, pushing open the door with the hand which wasn't holding his enormo-cup into which he religiously emptied Evelyn's special coffee at breakfast every morning.

Connie didn't even look round. Every single centimetre of every single whiteboard was covered top to toe with pen. She was stretching up to the top of one with a set square, almost out of breath. The pen was nearly run out.

'Is that my pen?' said Sé. It was as if last night hadn't happened; he was completely back to his normal self.

'What is this?' said Arnold quietly. Evelyn had already stepped forward and was examining one of the boards intently.

'Oh my God,' she said. Then she said it again. 'Oh my God.'

'What is this?' said Arnold again.

He stepped closer.

The normally unshakeable Evelyn had sat down. She kept looking at the whiteboards then looking at the floor again as if when she looked back up, something would have changed.

'Only, it was quite a new pen,' Sé was saying.

'Because, these are just, like, random wave flows,' said Arnold. 'We've been through this.'

Each of the whiteboards was covered in undulations. Some had peaks; some of the lines curved over themselves. Some were big; some were small. It looked completely random, line after line after line of it, none of it consistent in shape or height.

It looked like the ocean.

'I ran sine, cosine, blah blah, the whole business,' said Ranjit. 'Which by the way is VERY HARD TO DO without a computer. Nothing, just random. Like this, in fact. Connie, have you gone completely crazy maybe? Cool. You do *look* a bit sticky.'

'Shut UP, you idiots,' said Evelyn, sounding as if she were having difficulty breathing. 'Connie? CONNIE?'

Connie couldn't stop, couldn't even hear them or focus. She was miles away, tossed on a far distant sea, where the waves were all around her, higher and higher, the spray blowing in the wind, the great pull beneath her of a great and legendary ocean, its mighty power pulling her down, pulling her ...

'Look to her!'

Suddenly, Luke was in the doorway from nowhere: now, he was tearing across the classroom floor, incredibly fast, just as an exhausted Connie misstepped abruptly from the high desk she was tiptoeing on to reach the very last corner of clear whiteboard, and slipped off altogether.

Just in time he darted over as she slumped down, and he caught her easily.

'Whoa,' said Evelyn, getting up as the others moved forward and turned round.

'She's not very good at holding her drink,' said Sé, voice of experience.

Connie was profoundly agitated and unbelievably embarrassed to find herself in Luke's arms. He set her down gently on the sole large chair in the room, gazing at her intently. For the first time that morning, Connie realised she hadn't had a shower or washed her face. She wished she had. Then she blinked and looked round and round the room again, at the waves the numbers had brought.

'It's real,' she said. her heart pounding.

Luke didn't say anything, but gazed at her fixedly.

'It's real, isn't it?' she persisted. 'You knew, didn't you? You knew it was real. You've known all along.'

'I ... I have to go,' said Luke. 'Are you all right?'

Connie found herself nodding, although in fact her stomach was doing somersaults and her brain appeared to be cracking.

'Um ... yeah. Fine.'

And he was gone.

'Right,' Arnold was saying. 'Now, I have to tell you right, I got into Caltech when I was fifteen, yeah? And, like, I came to England on like a Google Genius grant, okay? Right? And you know I'm an Epic Secundus but I don't like to mention that.

'Anyway, seriously, girl dudes. What the fuck is going on?'

Evelyn brought Connie over some water, which she swallowed gratefully.

'Can you really not see?'

Connie had filled the whiteboards so fully it was as if they were all on a boat and each of them was a window, showing the waves beyond.

'I see ... a load of wave shapes, some peaked, mostly barely related to one another,' said Arnold. 'So it's a Fourier sequence ... wave shapes, some decaying in amplitude, some staying stable: just your common or garden set of boring periodic functions. They even all look smooth. So when you superimpose the figures like you have ... where does this get us?'

'Yeah, also I totally waved it out before,' said Ranjit. 'So I knew it didn't work. And I did it by hand. Did I mention that?'

Everyone ignored him.

'Christ, you guys are THICK. What are you *looking* at?'

'Unrelated waves,' said Arnold.

'That's right,' said Evelyn. 'Or, as most people would call them, waves.'

There was a silence.

'It's brilliant,' said Evelyn crossly. 'She interpreted the data as ideals of rings, and plotted the corresponding algebraic curves – making this.'

'What the hell do you mean?' said Arnold eventually.

'Oh, for heaven's sake, Arnold. What is mathematics?'

'It's a way of using abstract rules to describe the world.'

'The exact world?'

'No, an approximation of the world, using only necessary factors to . . .

'Oh,' said Arnold.

'Uh-huh,' said Evelyn.'

'This isn't mathematics.'

'No,' said Evelyn.

Connie weakly put her cup down.

'It's art,' she said, as the others goggled at her.

'What, like drawing and stuff?' said Ranjit sceptically.

'But if it's art . . . ' said Arnold.

Connie looked at him, her face weary, blue shadows smudged beneath her eyes.

'There's an artist,' she said.

Chapter Six

They sat in silence. Ranjit was wriggling. Every so often he would say, 'But!' and then trail off, or 'So!', then start playing with his fingers again. Evelyn was swearing under her breath. Arnold marched around the room, holding up sheafs of paper against the results, shaking his head then scribbling.

'You can do it as often as you like,' said Connie in a hollow tone, staring listlessly into space. 'They've sent us a picture of the sea.'

'No fucking way, man,' said Arnold. 'This is totally randomised . . .'

He got to the final board.

'Fuck me,' he said.

Every single line of converted numbers ended in a crest, a crescendo, with the final coordinates in the sequence coming down to land . . . on a beautifully executed, smooth curve, which perfectly resembled an inclining shore.

'I'll go and get Professor Hirati,' said Sé, standing up, brushing down his immaculate shirt, and swallowing loudly.

'I'll do it! I'll do it!' said Ranjit, sticking his hand in the air. 'I'll tell him.'

'What precisely are you going to tell him?' said Arnold promptly.

'That there are aliens who do swimming!' said Ranjit.

The room stared at him. Evelyn, who had started ripping up pieces of the printout paper, smiled wryly.

'Maybe you should just go,' said Arnold to Sé. Sé nodded and made his way to the door. There, he paused and turned back.

'You know,' he said. 'The second I step through this door . . . the very second . . . the entire world will change.'

'We could be wrong.'

'That won't even matter once it gets out,' said Sé.

They were silent as that sank in.

'I'm going to be famous!' said Ranjit. 'This is brilliant.'

'No, you won't,' said Evelyn shortly. 'That's why they made us sign all that shit. You breathe a word of it to anyone and you'll find yourself in a blacked-out plane in about ten minutes flat.'

'True dat,' said Arnold.

Sé put his hand on the door again.

'I'll just get the professor,' he said. It was at that precise instant that they heard the sirens.

Nobody spoke while Sé was out of the room. Arnold carried on trying to follow Connie's workings, occasionally letting out great sighs. Evelyn smoked a cigarillo, which nobody even commented on. Ranjit took out his phone, then put it away again at a fierce look from Evelyn and Arnold muttering, 'Orange jumpsuits, Ranjit, orange jumpsuits."

Connie just stared straight ahead, her conviction so fierce it was overwhelming: she was right, she knew. But Luke had already known. And where the hell was he now?

'Where the hell did Luke go?' said Arnold, echoing her thoughts exactly. 'Some people just cannot bear being proved wrong. Sore loser.'

After forty-five minutes – although it felt like much, much

longer as they sat like condemned criminals in a cell – there was a commotion outside and a crashing through the door. As they were the only team that used the bunker they looked at each other in consternation. It sounded like Sé shouting, but he was not someone who ever raised his voice.

Evelyn crushed out her cigarillo and stood up just as Sé banged open the door, his normally implacable face contorted, his eyes wide.

'Ben Hirati . . . Professor Hirati. He's dead.'

'He's what?!' Arnold stood up

'Before I got the chance . . . he wasn't in his office, apparently he was up at the Mullard SCIF . . . '

'The what?' said Connie.

'The SCIF . . . oh, I'll explain later. But . . . he's . . . dead. And . . . I mean, not just dead.'

Ranjit perked up.

'No, I mean . . . I mean, he's . . . it's gruesome, man. I heard.'

There was a long pause.

'Whoa,' said Arnold.

Connie felt her heart suddenly pound rapidly in her chest like she couldn't breathe.

'What, like somebody did it?'

'They don't know.'

'I don't like today any more,' said Ranjit, his mouth a wavy line.

Connie stood up. She tried to keep her voice calm.

'Did you see Luke?' she asked. Sé looked at her as if completely confused by the question.

'No. But . . . '

Three men in suits walked into the room. They had obviously been there the entire time.

'I think these men want to talk to us all together.'

*

'Who the hell are you?' said Arnold rudely.

'We don't have to answer that,' said one of the men.

'Uh, yes you do. In, like a democracy, yeah?'

The man sighed and glanced at his partner, who had picked up a whiteboard eraser and was cleaning Connie's drawings off the whiteboards round the room. The third man was picking up the boxes and boxes of papers.

'Well, you can come with us or you can wait for the police,' said the man. 'I promise you'll probably find it easier to explain to us.'

'Why would we need the police?'

'Your boss is dead,' said the man. 'Or didn't you get that? Bit of a coincidence, timing-wise, wouldn't you say?'

Sé looked stricken as the ramifications of what the man had implied sunk in.

'You've been spying on us.'

The man rolled his eyes.

'Look, we're the goodies.'

'Also, that fat one picks his nose a lot when you aren't here,' said the second man. The first man silenced him with a look.

Now they were truly frightened.

'Honestly, we are the good guys.'

Arnold started humming something Connie later recognised as 'Cloudbusting' by Kate Bush. More sirens started up outside, and the man raised his eyebrows.

Sé stepped forward.

'We need to go and sort this out,' he said.

'We do,' said the man. 'But I'm afraid I'll need your phones.'

They were escorted out of the bunker one at a time, into the back of a van like criminals. Connie thought people would notice them, but nobody batted an eyelid; around them, the bustling, self-absorbed life of an academic town continued unnoticed. It was the most stunning spring day as they sat, looking at each other in the back of the van – Connie wanted a shower more than just about anything in the entire world – as it drove them back up the hill, towards the astronomical facility, Mullard, where Professor Hirati had had his office.

Built in the nineteenth century, the observatory had spread since then thanks to the highly popular physics and astronomy departments. There were several exquisite, historical telescopes that had been gifted to the university, as well as the state-of-the-art Cambridge Low Frequency Synthesis Telescope, and the great satellite domes which collected signals from deepest space. Connie glanced round the van. Everyone was lost in thought. Ranjit was jiggling up and down, bouncing on his hands. Arnold looked like he wanted to kick him.

The gates of the facility were, they were surprised to see, locked, with what looked like soldiers manning the guardhouse and a large, heavily barred gate with barbed wire in front of their way. This was new.

A man alighted from the van as they stopped, opened the back and, with a torch, shone a light alarmingly into all of their faces. Connie felt her heart race like never before. He ticked them off on his sheet.

'Is that the last of them?' said the guard.

'Not quite,' said the man who was travelling upfront. 'There's one more we need to talk to.'

The large barred gates opened, and the van drove slowly forward.

Chapter Seven

The facility was absolutely full of people, bustling past here and there. Nearly all of them, Connie noticed, were men. The van drove to a low building and then stopped, and they followed the men carefully, like a crocodile of school children. They stopped in front of a low door, in a brand-new, all-white building Connie hadn't seen before on her one trip to visit the observatory four or five years ago as part of a summer course.

Once they'd been checked over yet again, the door opened and they were admitted into the astonishing building.

Everything inside it gleamed, a stark contrast to the mathematics department. The tiles on the floor, the walls, the bright lights set into the ceiling, all glowed white. It felt like being inside a television set.

'This is the SCIF,' announced the man.

'Sensitive Compartmented Information Facility,' said Arnold instantly. The man nodded.

'Secret Crap In Fact' said Arnold again. The man ignored him.

'This is a sterile facility,' he went on. 'It is completely isolated from the outside world. No noise, no internet, no unauthorised entry, no comms except an internal camera loop which records everything that goes on in here. It is bombproof and infiltration-proof. And, er . . . be careful using the loos. It has infiltration-proof sewerage. So don't flush anything but paper.'

Everywhere, lights and sirens were going off. Nobody was walking.

Connie and Evelyn swapped looks.

'Once you all get changed and scrub down, there's something I want to show you.'

'No way, dude.'

Arnold could only just squeeze his wide American bulk into the white suits provided.

'You look like a snowman,' said Connie.

'You look like a lit match,' retorted Arnold sharply, and she smiled at him.

'What are these *for*?' said Ranjit, who was still beside himself. 'Do you think it's like, totally an alien autopsy?'

'Yeah, that's right, Ranjit. It's an alien autopsy and all the biologists and coroners and veterinary surgeons and speciologists and chemists on Earth are busy tonight,' said Arnold.

'I think they'll want to stop us contaminating the area,' said Sé.

'Well, in that case, you need a bigger suit too,' said Arnold. It was true: the ridiculous baggy shoes that went over their shoes and the white scrubs they'd been given to wear didn't come anywhere near covering Sé's long legs, and he had ten centimetres of golden-brown ankle sticking out the bottom.

Evelyn sniffed.

'And nobody,' she added, 'nobody has asked us about the work. Nobody at all.'

'Maybe they've got more pressing matters,' pointed out Sé. Evelyn shook her head.

'No,' she said. 'Well, they must have had an inkling before they even let us on to this shit. So, what time did you get up?'

Connie felt weary and powerless, shepherded about when all she wanted was to sit somewhere dark and quiet, and process her discovery.

'3.55.'

Evelyn nodded.

'I wonder when the professor died. But I would put a bet on it being some time after 4 a.m.'

'Why would anyone want to kill a physics professor?' said Arnold. 'Unless ...'

'Well, we were just about to tell him what we'd discovered,' said Evelyn. 'Maybe somebody didn't want him to know.'

The five gazed at each other.

'It's a conspiracy,' gasped Ranjit.

'Ranj, this isn't James Bond, man,' said Arnold.

Ranjit looked around them at the blinking pure spotless room and looked back at Arnold.

'It's not Ranj.'

But no one else was quite so certain, and sure enough, after the bare minimum of time to get dressed, the door opened and a man entered and led them out into a pristine white lift, which immediately descended.

'No, this isn't at all like James Bond,' Ranjit muttered.

A long corridor lay ahead, with doors off it on both sides. They were led individually through separate ones. Connie found herself in a small, plain office lined with astronomy text-books. Sitting there was the man who'd addressed them in the bunker – and indeed, had been there originally on the night they'd met Professor Hirati – who introduced himself as Nigel. He was dark and smartly dressed, and looked like he spent a lot of time in the gym. Someone looking less like a

71

Nigel Connie couldn't imagine. He had a lot of hair on the back of his hands.

'So,' said Nigel, looking down at a sheaf of paperwork. 'You're our little Einstein.'

He had brought her a cup of coffee. She wanted not to drink it, but it smelled surprisingly good. She looked at it then back at Nigel. She was overwhelmed suddenly with the desire to call her father.

'Are you the police?'

'No,' said Nigel, smiling slightly. 'No. Seriously, you don't like my suit?'

'Don't I need to speak to a lawyer or something?'

'Why, what have you done?'

'Nothing. Nothing!' said Connie, feeling a ridiculous sense of guilt suddenly. 'Nothing! What happened to Professor Hirati?'

'Well, that's what we're endeavouring to establish.'

'But I thought you were spying on everybody?'

'Well ... it happened very quickly. In our top-secret, clean facility. We don't know ... yet. But the footage was paused.'

'But you check everyone in and out.'

'Yes. Usually we do,' said Nigel, looking grim. 'This morning ... this morning has been a little busier than most.'

'Because of us.'

'Yes,' said Nigel. 'Because of you.'

He leaned forward and folded his hands on his desk.

'There's no point telling you I'm not a bad guy,' he said. 'But if I can put it this way: what you have figured out, what you have learned ...'

'It's true.'

'We thought it might be.'

'Christ,' said Connie. 'I mean, bloody hell. I mean, I'm only an academic. I've got nothing to do with this kind of thing.

You've got whole teams of people who do nothing else but look for stuff like this. I'm just the maths girl.'

'Well, turns out we needed a maths girl,' said Nigel.

'Are you from the government?'

Nigel didn't answer.

'Was he?'

Nigel shook up his papers. 'That's not important. It's done now. And my job is to stop all hell breaking loose. More than it already has done.'

He put his papers down again.

'If this gets out, Doctor,' he said slowly. 'You have to think. Stock markets. Looting. Jobs. Panic. Take any stupid film you've ever seen and multiply it by a million. People behave the way they've been taught to respond by films.'

'Is that why you've rolled up your sleeves?' said Connie. Nigel glanced away for a second and she noticed his lips twitch.

'Well, quite,' he said. 'But don't worry. You're not under suspicion.'

'I'm glad to hear it,' said Connie.

'We did see where you were this morning.'

Connie tried to retrace what she had done in that room in a panic. So they'd all been there in the morning . . . or nearly all of them.

He looked up at her. His eyes were a penetrating grey.

'Tell me about Luke Beith.'

Afterwards, Connie worried whether her face gave her away at the very first moment: the bright red cheeks, the stuttering. She was, she realised, not entirely cut out for a life of secrecy.

'I don't know him,' she muttered. 'I don't know anything about him.'

'Well, you've been holed up 24/7 together for over a month,' said Nigel. 'You must have learned a bit.'

Connie shook his head.

'He's . . . he's *s'enfermé*, as the French say,' she said. 'He's not . . . he's just closed in on himself. A little distracted. A little strange. But not really that strange in mathematician terms.'

'Because we have very little information on him.'

Connie looked at him.

'What do you mean?'

'He claims to have been born in the former Yugoslavia, before the war; smuggled over here when he was very young. No birth certificate, no passport. Brought up in a Barnado's home, where nobody still works.'

'Oh,' said Connie, suddenly filled with pity for the quiet little boy he must have been.

Nigel regarded her shrewdly.

'A wounded bird?' he said. Connie shrugged.

'He seems very . . . lonely.'

'Odd? Bit of a loner?' said Nigel, leaning forward.

'What are you getting at?' said Connie.

'Nothing,' said Nigel. 'I just want to have a word with him, that's all. He wasn't with you this morning, was he?'

'He was!' said Connie, protesting. 'He was! He came in the classroom. I . . . I had a bit of a wobble. He helped me. So. He was with us.'

'And then he hung around?'

'Well . . . I mean you were filming us, right?

'Man, I have had some boring surveillance jobs before,' said Nigel quietly, shaking his head. 'Yes. We were. And he left. And then we lost sight of him.'

Connie brightened.

'Well, obviously he can't have come to you, can't have come

here. You'd definitely have seen him. You must have cameras all over this facility.'

Nigel cleared his throat.

'Well, no,' he said. 'Not all over. We don't know where he went. He didn't sign in with a security pass, but, well, I assume if you wanted to do someone some harm you might not walk in the front door.'

Connie shook her head.

'That's not Luke,' she said. 'That's not him at all.'

'I thought you said you barely knew him.'

Connie stared at her hands and sighed.

Nigel got to his feet. He was taller that Connie had expected.

'Come with me,' he commanded. Connie stiffened, but found herself getting up to follow him.

They left the room and entered the corridor. The others were already waiting there, looking anxious.

'Just tell them you're called Spartacus,' Arnold hissed to her as she passed behind Nigel; the rest followed in her wake, each accompanied by a serious-looking man with tidy hair. Ranjit was still chatting to his.

'Anyway, so, you know, he doesn't really eat, you know? And he wears the same clothes every day. He's really weird.'

'Shut up, Ranjit,' said Arnold.

'Why couldn't you have just told us all this?' said the one accompanying Sé. Sé gave a silent shrug.

'Didn't notice.'

The lift ascended three floors, above ground again, and into another startlingly white corridor. Here there were real police-men, one each on either side of an office door. The door itself was behind a thick Flexiglass electronic gate. Nigel pressed his finger in a scanner to the side. A small 'ooh' could be heard from Ranjit. Nothing happened. He swore and did it two more times, pressing his finger very hard against it until it finally relented and slid apart, juddering as it did so.

The two policemen nodded to him respectfully, handed them all masks and pushed open the office door.

Fiddling with her mask, the bright sunlight coming through the windows came as a shock to Connie, and she blinked. The idea that outside, in the world, it was still a sunny, bright, spring day was extraordinary. Out there in the world – the world people thought was still the world – people were just going about their business, falling in love, booking holidays, eating cupcakes, falling out with their mums.

But they didn't know. They didn't realise.

She was so caught up that she was moments behind the others as their gasps filled the room.

'What the actual fuck?' said Arnold. She followed where they were looking, and she too had a sharp intake of breath. Lying curled up under a spotless white desk, with nothing on it apart from a state-of-the-art computer with a huge screen, was a body. A corpse. Connie hadn't realised until that precise moment that she had never seen a dead body before: not her grandmother's, nor an accident. This was the first time she had ever seen anybody dead. But she was pretty damn sure they weren't meant to look like this.

Unavoidably curious, she knelt down.

'Don't go any closer,' growled Nigel.

The body – corpse – thing was in the shape of a person. But . . . but it was impossible. It was translucent. Completely see-through, like a jellyfish. The skin, liquefying, dripping out . . . the smell wasn't everywhere yet, but it was tactile, traceable on the air, the very taste of something beyond awful, beyond imagining; a smell that would never leave you, that would become part of you, just like you would

76

never be able to unsee this: the drained remains of Professor Hirati.

His hair now was no longer suspiciously tinted gold, but colourless, pure white. Clothes covered most of his body, but Connie found herself utterly fixated on the veins, traced everywhere, as if the corpse were made of lace; the discernible shape of the eyeball behind the socket; the glinting, visible bones of the ear. It was like a medical lab, an exhibition – not a person.

'How ... I mean, *what*?' Arnold was saying.

'The good thing is,' Ranjit was saying. 'I am totally not going to be sick.'

He promptly threw up into a bin, adding to the unpleasant aromas in the room.

'Oh,' he said. 'Sorry.'

'What happened?' said Connie, her voice trembling. 'What happened here?'

Nigel shook his head.

'As soon as the forensics guys stop having a little-girl attack and come back in the room again we might be able to find out. But at the moment I think ... it appears his skin has lost all its pigmentation.'

Connie shook her head.

'What does that mean?'

'What makes your skin a certain colour—'

'Could that kill you?'

'Hey, I don't have a pigmentation division, okay?'

'You should,' muttered Arnold.

'Yeah, all right, Captain Right-on,' said Nigel. 'More pressing matters, yes?'

He looked at them. A couple of terrified-looking scientists, also in the white hazmat suits, began inching their way back into the room.

'Pussies,' said Nigel, none too quietly. Then he turned to them again.

'Did somebody do it?' said Evelyn.

'We don't know,' said Nigel. 'We're also testing for pathogens. Hence the jumpsuits and the masks and so on. Now, we'll need DNA samples, obviously.'

'Seriously?' said Arnold. 'It seems to me you've been examining everything, including our crap, for weeks.'

Nigel stopped him with a look.

'A man is lying here dead,' he said, 'on the day of the most important scientific discovery of our time. Is that funny to you, big man?'

'No,' muttered Arnold.

'Good.'

Nigel looked over them as if they were a crowd of naughty schoolchildren.

'And I really do need to talk to your colleague. I can't imagine why that is difficult for you to get your heads around, with all your huge brains and everything.'

'You can't think ...' burst out Connie. Nigel opened his hands.

'Something has happened. And a man is dead. Isn't your job looking for patterns?'

'The only thing Luke could murder was Debussy,' said Arnold.

'Who?' said Nigel.

'Never mind,' growled Arnold.

Suddenly, there was a rush of people past the door and a red light went off above their heads. Professor Hirati's computer, which one of the forensic team had been picking up gingerly, suddenly turned itself on.

'What's going on?' said Ranjit. The noise of feet stamping down corridors could be heard. Nosy passers-by were suddenly staring at their phones.

'You know if *I* were running a top-secret facility,' observed Arnold. 'I'd probably not have all those big, flashy, red light things.'

Nobody paid any attention to him. Nigel stared at them, then glanced at his phone.

'Stay here,' he growled.

'Not with the dead body thing?' said Ranjit nervously.

'Well, not in here. Out in ... here, in one of these offices.'

'All together?' said one of the aides.

'What, in case they plot a graph?' said Nigel. 'They're not under suspicion. They're helping us.'

Everyone else had turned and gone already, wherever their phones and alarms were summoning them, pulling their masks off as they went.

'Uh, yeah,' said Arnold as they were leaving, and they were ushered back into a different room, more like a staff room with, Connie was relieved to see, both a bathroom and a coffee machine. 'Uh, excuse me, but seeing as someone might be feeding on, like, the academic staff, can you leave us some big guy with a fighting stick, please?'

Nigel turned around, surveyed the situation then nodded.

'Yes. Brian, stay here.'

Brian had a thick bouncer's neck and a slit for a mouth. He nodded importantly.

'Are you going to lock the door?' said Arnold.

Nigel looked at them.

'Look. You're not the bad guys. We're not the bad guys. Can we just get that straight?'

'Who are the bad guys then?'

Nigel's eyes rolled.

'Can you just stay here and try not to get into any more trouble?'

*

There was coffee, which they all partook of, and food in the fridge which nobody wanted. The idea that the little pot of cottage cheese might have belonged to the despoiled body lying a few feet away through a wall was unutterably depressing.

'I'm having a very strange day,' said Ranjit, pacing round the room. Connie glanced at Sé, who was plucking at his hazmat suit. As soon as he realised she had noticed him doing it, he stopped, only to start again moments later. Only Evelyn was calm, making coffee for everyone, very carefully measuring the water into the jug, running the steamer for a precise amount of time.

'How are you so calm?' said Connie, who had thrown water all over her face and head in the little attached bathroom and felt slightly better, if still completely shell-shocked.

'I grew up in a civil war,' said Evelyn simply. 'I learned a bit earlier than you lot that the idea that you control your environment is nothing other than a ridiculous charade. You control what you can control – this is good coffee, by the way – and everything else you try and let wash over you.'

'Like a wave,' said Connie.

'Man, I hope Luke shows up. For his own good,' said Arnold, passing his hand over his bald head. 'They know it wasn't us. They're going to be looking for someone to pin this thing on. Odd math geeks who can't answer straightforward questions are going to be right up their list.'

'Could have been one of his four ex-wives,' observed Evelyn.

'He had four ex-wives?' said Connie.

'Don't know,' said Evelyn. 'But you have to admit he looked the type.'

Ranjit couldn't hold it in any longer.

'OR THE ALIENS!' he said. 'THEY'RE ALREADY HERE! They . . . jumped out of the sea and did this.'

Everyone looked at him.

'Would you like a tinfoil hat?' asked Arnold politely.

'How did they get in?' said Evelyn. 'Fishbowl?'

Ranjit pouted and folded his arms.

'Look,' said Arnold. 'We've got a signal – possibly. Some kind of a signal from deepest space. That doesn't mean they're going to turn up and invade us on, like, the same day.'

'In movies that's totally always what it means,' said Ranjit. 'And maybe beautiful alien girls.'

'We've been sending signals out for years,' said Arnold. 'It's just exploratory. Possibly amazing. Incredible. And the chances of us having evolved in a remotely compatible fashion are insane: natural selection and all its little accidents, on a different time-scale, in a totally different environment . . . '

'Or: conditions to support life are always the same on the same universe–length time-scale . . . ' mused Evelyn.

'Don't *think* so,' said Arnold snootily. 'We've got sixty-seven thousand different types of bug, remember?'

'And every single one of them likes to overrun other bugs' territories,' said Evelyn.

They didn't say much after that.

After a couple of hours, Nigel marched back into the room. He looked harassed.

'You know all that stuff?' he said. 'Well. There's more. A *lot* more.'

The five of them sat, grubby, anxious, behind a long desk on a stage in a huge lecture theatre in a far corner of the compound in front of at least a hundred scientists. Connie did her best to stumble through what she'd discovered and how, but she could see from the sceptical looks on the physicists' faces that what she'd felt was closer to creative inspiration than anything else.

'It's not possible,' a large, Scandinavian man with incredibly up-to-date glasses was saying. 'There's no way ... Kepler-186f is so far away, learning this information ... I mean, it couldn't travel fast enough. They couldn't know. It's way, way beyond the speed of light. I mean, by *factors*. So, it can't be anything to do with that.'

Arnold leaned back. He was enjoying this, Connie could tell. She suspected him of pretending to be on a panel at ComicCon.

'Yeah, right, but of course we don't give a fuck about that.'

'Well, maybe you should,' said the sarcastic Scandinavian. 'It's science.'

'Quite. It ain't maths. Maths don't give a shit what your ideas are. Hundred years ago you thought an atom was an indivisible rock. Forty years ago you didn't think little bits of quarky shit could travel backwards in time. Three hundred years ago, you thought the stars were God's heavenly pinpricks. Doesn't mean shit to us. Gravity could reverse tomorrow, you guys are all out of a job. But the maths stays exactly the same.'

The busy room fell silent.

In the end, after a long, long day, they were allowed to return to their college rooms. Everyone was made to sign a lot of paperwork, although how they expected to keep a secret among a team this large, Connie could not imagine. 'It's all right,' Arnold had said. 'Physicists have no mates.'

They were to report to the bunker again in the morning, keep working on the message – because they were messages, clearly now. They were to talk to no one. They were to expect visits from the police. And they were to tell someone the second anyone saw Luke Beith. They weren't getting their phones back, but there would be a man posted. Partly, Nigel explained, to wait for Luke. Partly in case what had happened to the professor wasn't an accident, and wasn't an isolated case.

None of them mentioned Luke as they ate a late supper which had been left for them, isolated and alone in the huge, echoing refectory, students long cleared away, the smell of gravy lingering over everything. They could barely speak at all; all trapped in their private imaginings.

It couldn't be odd, quirky Luke – God knows what it was at all. Connie was hoping for a bug: what else but a fast-acting bacteria could have wrought such devastation? Some bug, she thought anxiously, that wasn't infectious. But why didn't he come? Why didn't he show himself? Where was he?

And the little doubt that was in everybody's minds and nobody mentioned out loud for fear of sounding either ridiculous or terrifying: if an alien life-form had sent Earth a message, had an alien life-form started to kill?

Chapter Eight

As the others said their goodnights, Connie sidled along the end of the opposite corridor – there was a small flight of stairs, then she and Evelyn were to the right. Ranjit and Sé were the same a floor above them, and to the left on the same floor as Connie and Evelyn's rooms were Arnold and Luke' sets. Arnold had already knocked on Luke's door, of course, but to no avail. After everyone had retired, though, Connie went across the stairs too.

It was very quiet in the stairwell, and ill-lit. No one was about. Connie approached the door – another old heavy, wooden-panelled thing, with the number '24' written on it. She knocked quietly, then slightly more loudly. There was no response.

'Luke?' she whispered. 'L?'

Nothing. She crouched down, then blinked. There was an old bolthole from the original door, but none of them had the large keys any longer; everything was locked with a Yale. She looked at the Yale lock. It was covered in dust; sticky. She put her finger to it. It looked as if nobody had put a key in there for a very long time.

Connie blinked. Very quietly, desperate not to creak, she glanced behind her. Still nobody there. Dare she? Could she?

Her hand, trembling, rested on the dull brass, round handle. She clasped it firmly and, no longer entirely sure what she was doing, turned it clockwise. It gave a faint, rusty, squeaking noise as it turned, which sounded incredibly loud to Connie's ears. But nobody stirred.

The door slowly opened wide and she gazed in, her hands at her mouth.

'Luke?'

Still nothing. The vestibule was exactly the same as hers except reversed: a coat rack, and a small set of steps up to the sitting room. There was a faint chalky smell in the air, nothing more. Moonlight was flooding through the high, mullioned windows. No lights were on. Glancing behind her, Connie thought the hallway looked very dark. Swallowing carefully, she realised that obviously he wasn't here – but why the unlocked door? Had someone else already been through here? Was it just Luke being absentminded? She certainly wouldn't put that past him. She shouldn't be in here; she shouldn't be looking through his stuff.

But where *was* he? Would he have left a clue?

She was up the steps before it occurred to her that the reason the door might be open might be because somebody was already there.

'Hello?'

Her voice suddenly was quavering. She did the first thing she could think of and turned on the large overhead light, which hung down on a long chain from the ceiling.

Instantly the room normalised; the moonlight and the shadows were gone and she could look around at the mirror image of her own home: the fireplace, the tiny kitchen, the room leading into the ... the bedroom.

Nothing stirred. There was not the sense one got that somebody was in a space even when you could not hear them. But

still, Connie was absolutely ready to turn around and retreat ...
until something caught her eye.

At first she couldn't work out quite what she was looking at.
The room was exactly the same as hers – shabby sofa, fireplace, tables – with the same inability to decorate it given
their fourteen-hour working days (although Evelyn's
remained a haven and was where they generally hung out).
It lacked the enormous piles of speculative paper Connie
tended to scribble on, unable to get the numbers out of her
head even when she did collapse back home, but apart from
that, it was identical. Except ... what was it? What was different?

She looked around. There were two coats hanging at the
little entrance: one old and tweedy, one an expensive-looking,
very old-fashioned raincoat. She had never seen Luke in a
coat, regardless of the weather. But that didn't mean he didn't
own some. No, it was something else ... her eyes scanned the
room. What was it, what was it ...?

Eventually she realised. Where were all the books? There
was no personality in the room at all; no pictures on the wall,
no rugs. Why were there no books? she wondered. She had
never met an academic with no books, never ever.

Something caught her eye suddenly, on top of the empty
shelves. There was one thing and one thing only there; something lying discarded ...

Connie reached up to the highest shelf to the small, dusty
object and grabbed it with her hands. It was just what she had
thought it was: a photo frame.

She looked at the old picture for a long time. At first she was
disappointed, assumed it was exactly what it looked like: an
overlooked picture from the last inhabitant. The frame was an
old, dark wood, then there was an insert and a small faded

photograph that was not, as she had first thought, black and white; instead it was from the seventies – must be – overexposed and very faded. It was a bunch of happy-looking young men outside the college, clutching some publications they were showing off proudly. The men were skinny, mostly bearded.

But what she noticed most about it was the young man second from left who was prominent in the shot. He had a lean, handsome face and heavy-rimmed spectacles. But it wasn't that which caught her attention. It was the jacket he was wearing. It was obviously a cold day. The man was wearing what looked like – if she squinted – a checked shirt and a brown cord jacket with patches on the sleeves. Nothing too unusual about that in the sartorial academic scheme of things, she supposed. But clearly visible over his arm was – she turned back to check. Yes. It was the same. It was the Acquascutum raincoat currently hanging up in the vestibule. And although the colours were faded, she was reasonably sure the cord jacket had elbow patches.

Suddenly, Connie was very frightened. Her heart was beating so hard in her chest she was sure it must be audible to Arnold next door. But she couldn't not see. She couldn't not look. As if sleepwalking, barely able to breathe, she moved very slowly towards the bedroom.

The door was open. Connie didn't allow herself to think what she would say if Luke walked in right now. She didn't allow herself to finish the thought ... whoever he was.

She put the light on straightaway. Same room but in reverse: four-poster, large old wardrobe by the door. She inched forward to the wardrobe and, carefully, desperately trying not to catch a glimpse of her reflection in the mirror, of her deeply guilty face, she pulled it open.

Tweed jackets; one corduroy. Checked shirts. Just as she'd

seen. She picked up one of the jackets and looked in the inside. Sure enough, under the Turnbull & Asser brand name, were three initials: JMC.

Luke was wearing another man's clothes. A man who appeared to have lived here before – for a long time, with his once fashionable clothes, and when he had finally had to leave, had done so in a typically scatty, academic way. Then Luke had moved in ...

And then there appeared – she glanced around the bedroom now – no books, no papers, no clothes, no computer, no ... no *nothing*. There seemed to be absolutely nothing of the man she knew as Luke Beith at all.

Connie was glad to escape the set, to creep back across the corridor, leaving the door open behind her. Now she understood why Luke didn't bother to lock the door. He had literally nothing to lose.

In the bathroom of Luke's set, the figure stayed absolutely still.

Chapter Nine

Connie took a bath, then fell into bed and was asleep in moments, her mind blank, overstretched; too much to take in.

She woke in the very darkest hour of the night, her heart pounding, no transitional period before being asleep and being absolutely alert. At first she thought a noise must have woken her, but there was nothing and nobody there. The entire city was asleep.

She crept over to her little nook behind the crenellations. From up here, nobody would guess she was there.

She looked out across the fens, over the small, rolling hills.

Just like last night, she thought she saw a figure. It wasn't possible.

Then her heart began again to beat incredibly quickly in her chest. She clambered out of the window. Across from her was an old elm tree. She looked at it. Then she glanced down, into the street. Sure enough, there was a man standing there. He must be stationed. Looking out for them, yes, but she was pretty sure if she walked through the front gate, he would have something to say about it. She glanced over his shoulder. There was a glow, sure enough. Seriously, no way. She looked at her watch: it was 3.45 a.m. The deadest part of the night, and he was obviously freezing, knackered and trying to keep himself awake, till his relief came – at 6 a.m., she guessed. Although she didn't know quite how this worked. Then presumably there'd be guys round the other side of the building, at its only entrance – maybe in a car? But nonetheless, there he was: absorbed, swiping one finger across a row of coloured sweets on his phone screen. Playing a game. Oblivious to the rest of the world.

She swallowed hard and weighed the odds. If that was a man out there, it was Luke, she was sure of it. If she was caught climbing down a tree to get out, she would be in enormous trouble, no doubt about it – immediately under suspicion. But if she did nothing . . .

Doing nothing didn't even figure as an option. She pulled on her old jumper and her soft-soled Converse. She had never been the most outdoorsy of children; had never revelled in climbing a tree, or shinning up a rope. But she needed to do it now, and with a slight quiet 'yikes' and an exhalation of breath, she swung herself, feeling horrendously exposed, out of the crenellation and onto the top branches of the tree, which swayed to her weight as if a recipient of a mysterious breeze. She froze, expecting the guard to immediately look up, but she could still see the light of his phone, the pink and yellow candies moving about.

The tree's trunk came out from the side; she ought, if she climbed down the right-hand side, to be invisible to him.

As long as she was very, very quiet.

She felt her hands grow slick with sweat as she wobbled slightly at the top of a tree. Surely you couldn't get down a rustly tree without someone hearing you? At this, she heard the ping from the man's phone, and felt a genuine breeze ruffle through the branches; a wind coming in from the east and the distant sea, for which she was intensely grateful. She stopped a moment more, then, when the next gust came, descended a few branches. And, holding on tortuously, sure at any moment she'd be spotted – by him, by the night porter, by any passer-by, by someone on the floor below, by the police who were presumably crawling through the town – she descended, slowly, slowly, slowly, until eventually her trainers softly padded on the ground and, hugging the wall closely, she sidestepped until she had made it around the corner into the shadow of the alley that separated their college from the great library, and then could patter forward quickly until she moved, back alley to back alley, across the town and hit the little path that led up into the low hills.

She didn't need a torch – could not possibly have carried one in any case – and was grateful for the huge moon and the fact that she was wearing a dark sweater. The only thing she could do nothing about was her hair, but at least Luke would know it was her. There was not, strangely, the slightest doubt in her mind that it was him. It was as if he had called to her and all she had to do was follow. And, even more strangely, she was not afraid any more. In all of Connie's organised, determined, motivated, intellectual life, this was very new. She had thought she would be more afraid: she was not.

He was lying in the same spot as she had encountered him before, flat on his back on a bed of gorse, looking contentedly at the moon.

'Hair!' he said in delight as she loomed into view: out of breath, wide awake and alert from the strangeness and beauty of the evening, and the new nearness of the stars. Alive.

Chapter Ten

Connie sat cross-legged on the damp grass, staring at Luke. He had smiled and been pleased to see her, but his large eyes were straying, clearly, to the sky again, and his temperament was distracted.

'Luke!' she hissed. 'Where were you today?'

He lifted his hands and shrugged at the same time with his shoulders. It was an odd gesture that he didn't pull off terribly well.

'I ... I was. I don't know. Thinking about things.'

'You heard what happened? It's so awful.'

Luke looked at her in surprise.

'No,' he said. 'Tell me what happened. I heard music in the street though. Very loud. Intermittent. Not bad.'

'Sirens,' said Connie. 'Sirens. They're called sirens. Didn't you know that?'

Luke shrugged.

'I ... I don't always know the names for things.'

'And why not?' said Connie.

Her heart was pounding in her chest; he was making her very anxious all of a sudden. Why had he known about the message? Why? Her brain was telling her one thing, deep inside like a tolling bell: her eyes, her consciousness, her experience were refusing to accept it for an instant.

'I don't know,' said Luke.

He looked up at her, perched on the grass.

'So. Do they know? Do they know what you know?'

Connie nodded.

'What you knew already,' she said softly.

There was a long silence. He did not deny it.

'And the professor?' Connie said eventually when she couldn't wait any more.

'Who?'

'Professor Hirati?'

Luke looked puzzled.

'Who?'

'The man, the man who leads the programme. With the yellow hair? The man who comes in every day and asks us if we've found anything? Ben Hirati? Professor Hirati? The guy who runs the programme who comes in every day?'

'Tall,' said Luke. 'The tall ... sorry. I find it ... I find it hard to tell people apart sometimes. Everyone is kind of the same colour.'

Connie was gesticulating with exasperation.

'The man who came in every day! Luke, he's *dead*. He *died*.'

Luke sat bolt upright.

'He's *dead*?'

His face was genuinely and totally surprised. Connie had watched it very closely. Luke was difficult to understand, but he was not hard to read, and she could not see him as an actor. He was shocked to the core.

'How?' said Luke, agitated. 'How is he dead? How was he killed?'

'They don't know for certain he was killed,' said Connie. 'But he was found ... in the lab ...'

She felt her voice wobble.

'And he didn't have any . . .'

She stopped, suddenly frightened. Above them, the faint trail of a plane's lights fell in the slipstream over the flat east of a darkened, quiet England, where everyone, it felt, slept the last peaceful gentle sleep of their lives; the last night they could ever believe themselves alone in the universe, apart from, perhaps, a god who didn't truly concern himself in their daily affairs nearly as much as they would like him to.

Connie and Luke looked at one another.

'Colour,' said Luke slowly. 'He didn't have any colour.'

Connie could barely speak, couldn't swallow at all. Her heart was banging in her chest. She nodded.

'Yes,' she said. 'He didn't have any colour.'

She looked at him.

'And . . . you knew that. Were you there?'

'What? No, of course not. Of course . . .'

Luke was looking very puzzled suddenly, stopped and touched his fingers to his eyes.

'What?' he was saying. 'What is this?'

He pulled his fingers away. They were wet. He took an exploratory lick of his fingers.

'What's happening?' he said to Connie, fear in his voice. She looked at his face.

'You're . . . you're crying' she said, completely confused. Luke looked at his fingers, then touched them to his eyes again.

'*That's* crying?' said Luke in a quiet voice. 'Oh,' he said. 'I didn't know.'

'Have you never done it before?'

There was a long silence.

'Yes,' said Luke, suddenly very weary. 'I have done it before.'

Connie's hands were trembling.

'Luke,' she said, 'you have to tell me. Whatever it is. Can you ... can you tell me – please – who you are?'

Luke took a large, old-fashioned handkerchief from the top pocket of his jacket, and gently wiped the moisture from his long fingers.

'There was no colour left in him,' he said again.

'No,' said Connie. 'They think someone might have done that to him.'

Luke nodded.

'Yes,' he said. 'I'm afraid somebody did.'

'Do you know who?'

They were now standing, facing each other, under the clear night sky.

'They're here,' Luke said.

Connie swallowed. The way he said it – calmly, matter of fact – set a bolt of fear through her.

'Who's here? Who's here, Luke?'

Luke tilted his head as if distracted.

'Hair.'

'Connie.'

'Names are hard for me,' he said. 'What does Connie mean?'

'It's short for Constance,' said Connie. 'I've always hated it.'

'Constance?'

'Like constant. You know. Do make the hilarious maths joke; I've only heard it nine thousand times.'

'You are a constant.'

'Well, that's what the name says. I change my lipstick some-times.'

'You are always the same.'

'People are never the same, Luke.'

There was a long pause.

'Luke?'

He ran his hands through his thick, dark hair, making it flop shaggily on top of his head. It made him look very young suddenly. She held his gaze.

'Luke,' she said again. 'Are you people?'

He took a deep breath, and then another. Then he exhaled very slowly, as if laying down a burden that he had been carrying for a long, long time.

'Well,' he said, 'that really rather depends.'

Connie looked at him, holding her breath.

She couldn't believe that yesterday she had been just a normal girl, like everyone else. Her job was a little unusual, but no biggie in the scheme of things. And today everything had changed so fiercely and dramatically she had absolutely no idea what her place was in the universe, nor who else was in it. She had no scheme of things.

'On what?'

'Well, do I consider myself a person: of course. Am I a human person?' He looked up. 'Not exactly.'

'Ha!' Connie couldn't help it: it just burst out. She suddenly found herself holding back an unexpected desire to laugh. 'Ha!'

She swallowed the urge before she collapsed in utter hysterics.

'Because ... because you're from ...' She choked again, pointing at him. '*You're* from ... the place that sent us the picture.'

He nodded slowly.

'Kepler-186f.'

'That's not what we call it.'

Connie laughed again. She couldn't help herself.

'No. It wouldn't be. What do you call it?'

He didn't answer. She moved closer.

'But ... But I mean, *look at you*,' she said. 'I mean, the real you ... is this what you look like? Do you *look* human?'

She felt an urge to put out a hand, touch his face, and an equal, opposing urge to take off screaming for the nearest airport and buy a ticket to New Zealand.

'Because to me you look really, *really* human.'

Luke nodded.

'I know.'

He glanced down at his body.

'No,' he said simply. 'No. I don't. No. It takes a lot of effort to live like this. I can't ... I can't quite get used to it.'

Connie flinched backwards. She remembered again the terrible empty visage; the clear, drained corpse.

'Where ...?' she said. 'Where did you get ...?'

She swallowed, rubbed her eyes very hard with her hands, as if this would help.

'The body you are in,' she said, 'is it yours? Did you take it?'

Luke shook his head.

'No,' he said. 'It was given. And the body is mine; please don't worry. The pigment was given.'

He looked at her. 'You think you were the first,' he said, 'but you weren't. A young boy ... a brilliant ... he was brilliant. Very sick. Not well at all. But he found me first, the first of all your species. In Belarus, in a bed, with a tiny computer.' He shook his head. 'Brilliant.'

'What happened?'

'He was sick,' said Luke. 'There was nothing I could do, nothing anyone could do. But he helped me. He was ... He was very excited to meet an alien.'

He looked at Connie, who had managed to regain control of herself although she was still trembling. 'Well, put it this way, he didn't fall about laughing.'

'I'm only doing that because I don't believe you yet,' said Connie. 'Also I need to work out whether you're going to suck out all my juice so I'm half listening and half wondering who's the fastest runner.'

Luke blinked.

'But I would never ... I would never do that to anyone.' He hit his fist with his other hand. '*Práklon*! GOD, who is it? Who found me? So quickly ... '

'How long have you been here?'

'6.49,' said Luke. 'Four years. His – sorry. He had a name. And I do know it. It was Artem. And it was his last ... gift to me. So I could live ... so I could pass ... '

His voice turned harder, but Connie didn't notice.

'Somewhere far away from the sea.'

Connie was reaching for her smartphone then cursed when she remembered they had been confiscated.

'You're saying a kid died?'

Luke nodded. 'Nothing to do with me. He was born in a radioactive wasteland. He started to die from the second he was two cells in the belly of his mother.'

He glanced down at the handkerchief.

'Why now?' he said. 'Why could they not just let me be?'

She looked at him.

'What do you actually look like?'

He shrugged.

'Well ... we don't ... we have no colour, so ... '

'Yes, I get that,' said Connie. 'But are you a biped ... I mean, do you walk on two legs and stuff? Or are you like a jel-lyfish?'

Luke didn't smile. He looked straight at her.

'A jellyfish is a good ... it's not a bad way of thinking about us. Yes, we are bipeds, but ... ' He extended his arms. 'We have more practical arms that can get places. I mean, seriously, how do you manage with these?' He waggled his hands. 'Oh, these things are useless. And these ridiculous bones. These bones! How on earth do you get about with great, big, breakable – and I will tell you, I have broken a lot of them finding this out – bits of stick inside you? How do you get through doors and around things and climb things without these stupid, big, heavy, internal logs?'

He looked crossly at his long legs.

'And short legs. It takes *so long* to get anywhere. All this bloody gravity. So much stupid bloody gravity. Which is why you need sticks in your arms. Because everything, everything is so, so heavy, and you don't even know and you need to be heavy too to deal with it. And people walk around with great sorrowful expressions and such sadness and worry inside and they think it's because of weird things like handbags and whether they'll go to a noisy party and whether they should have more stick leg things only smaller.'

'You mean children?' said Connie.

'Uh-huh, yes, them. But it's not that. It's because they're being push-push-pushed down to the earth all the time; oppressed by very weight of the air that you breathe.'

'Why, what, do you live underwater like Ranjit thinks?'

'Sometimes,' said Luke. 'Some do.'

He looked up.

'That's ... that's our problem. The tides ... the tide groups. There is ... Our planet has problems.'

Connie stood up, shaking her head, and started to back away.

'No,' she said. 'No, this is ridiculous. No. No, no, no. You're as real as I am.'

'Of course I am,' said Luke in some surprise.

'You were born in the former Yugoslavia ...'

'That was Artem's idea. So I wouldn't need documents. Although I had to pretend to be quite young.'

'How old are you?'

'Four hundred and seventy-nine. Earth years, about three hundred. It is quite young.'

Connie looked away, swore and wished she had a cigarette even though she didn't smoke and had no intention of ever doing so.

'Prove it,' she said suddenly.

Luke turned his dark eyes on her.

'No!' he said straightaway. 'I don't want it. I don't want to prove it, and I don't want it to happen. I'm just a guy who was born in an orphanage and has stupid ideas about things. That's all. Just another eccentric academic. Possibly insane. Forget we had this conversation.'

'And who's wanted by the police.'

Luke's face grew wary again.

'They think . . . they think I did that to the tall man?'

'They think somebody did, and let me say you're the only one who vanished for the entire day.'

'Because you've just got in touch with my home, which, I will tell you now, is not good news for anyone. But it is very particularly very, very not good news for me.'

He turned the whole depth of his black eyes on her. Suddenly, in the moonlight, Connie found herself staring into them. She found them fathomless: a different world, a bottomless sense of something other than what he appeared to be.

'Can I touch you?' she found herself asking.

Luke nodded.

'I can't remember which bits are the naughty bits though,' he said. 'Artem told me, but I can never remember. Also he was only ten – I'm not sure he was totally clear himself.'

'Which bits are the naughty bits in your other shape?'

'Oh, all of them I think,' said Luke carelessly.

'That must make commuting very difficult,' said Connie.

Nervously she took a step towards him. They were standing very close now. She remembered his inability to respect personal space, the lack of normal physical cues she often caught from him. But his little oddities, his strangeness, they couldn't possibly add up to . . .

But they were in a new world now. A new existence; a new something she knew to be true, however difficult it was to countenance, to believe.

'Bloody hell,' she said suddenly. 'I can't believe David Icke was right all along'

The stars blazed overhead as she very gently stretched out her left hand (it was an old – and a bad, she admitted – habit to tend to think of right-handed mathematicians as not quite the real deal, but it persisted). Luke, she noticed, lifted his own left arm in response. Carefully, terrified, she extended her hand . . .

She touched his forearm, between his hand and the faded olive check of the cotton shirt he was wearing. His skin was soft, dry, warm. It felt like . . . just . . . just skin. Not sweaty, not clammy; nor, as she had slightly expected, dry and powdery as a dead leaf.

She smelled the scent again she had smelled before: a faint whiff of the sea, of shells and salted wind.

'Is there the real you underneath this?' she whispered.

He lifted his other hand and gently touched her hair.

'You know,' he said, 'in this particular spectrum galaxy, this is almost the only colour I can see.'

He laced it between his fingers thoughtfully; moving slowly, unhurriedly, interweaving his fingers patiently in and out; drinking it in; feasting on it with his eyes; holding it up, closer, to his face, as if he'd forgotten everything else that was going on. Yet oddly, Connie felt her pulse slow at last; after everything, after all the tension and horrors of the day gone by, she found herself now more relaxed; was somehow happy to let him touch it with his strange, long fingers.

'Is there a real you?' he said. 'Underneath this?'

The sudden noise of the sirens cracked the skies.

'Oh God,' said Connie, glancing down the rolling hillside. 'They know. They're looking for us.'

'Music,' said Luke.

'It's not music!' said Connie in exasperation. 'That isn't music!'

There was no point in trying anything ridiculous this time: it could only end very badly. This time they walked back in the front door, together. Robinson the porter blinked twice when he saw them and glanced quickly at his phone. Connie nodded at the old man to let him know she didn't think it was his fault that he had to do what he was going to do.

'We don't have much time,' said Connie, knocking on Evelyn's door. Evelyn opened up immediately. Evidently she wasn't getting much sleep either. Connie woke the boys too; Arnold rubbing his eyes from too much time in front of the computer; Sé sombre in a pair of dark pyjamas. Only Ranjit had been fast asleep, his hair sticking up from his head.

'Where were you, dude?' said Arnold. 'They think you killed that other dude.'

Luke didn't say anything.

'Did you?'

He shook his head wearily.

'Do you know who did?' said Sé. 'Or, like, what?'

Luke hesitated as the others stared.

'I think . . . I think it might be somebody just like me.'

'What, an extraordinarily talented and really lazy mathematician who's never heard of Bart Simpson? Or, like, *cheese*?' said Arnold.

Luke shook his head.

'Not exactly.'

Outside the sirens started up again. He glanced over at the window.

'The thing is, I'm different.'

'We noticed,' said Evelyn.

'We need to protect him,' said Connie fiercely.

There was the sound of boots in the hallway, and a banging of doors in the other wing.

'Why, because he killed the professor?' said Sé, a shadow passing across his face.

'Because he's an *alien*, you twonks,' burst out Connie in frustration. 'It's actually perfectly obvious when you think about it.'

There came a heavy knocking on the door. They all stood in a circle and stared at him. Luke rubbed the back of his neck, profoundly uncomfortable under the scrutiny.

'Yay!' said Ranjit. 'But don't death-ray drain me like you did the professor.'

'I ...' Luke shook his head. The pounding came again.

'Professor Prowtheroe? Are you there?'

Evelyn stood up and looked around.

'Ah,' she said quietly. 'The knock on the door in the middle of the night. I know it so well. One reason I moved to Britain was that I thought that this was a country where the knock on the door in the middle of the night did not come. Apparently I was wrong.'

She looked at Luke.

'They are coming for you.'

He nodded numbly.

'Is it true what she says?'

He nodded again.

'You look real enough to me,' she said.

'I *am* real,' said Luke. 'I keep saying.'

Arnold's mouth was gaping.

'Can you, like, make yourself invisible?' said Ranjit excitedly. 'Or beam yourself up? Or fly?'

'We would never have met if I could,' said Luke. Connie suddenly found herself glad, even though it was so very bad.

'I'm coming, I'm coming,' shouted Evelyn to the door in a sleepy voice. She turned back to Luke.

'Don't tell them anything. Nothing. Don't let them suspect. If they suspect – if ANYONE says anything . . . '

She glared round the room fiercely.

'They'll chop him up for parts, you understand?'

Arnold nodded dumbfoundedly. Ranjit bobbed up and down. Sé was impassive as ever.

'Not a word. Not a word from you to them. Not a word from us to anyone until we figure out what to do.'

'I have too many secrets to keep,' said Ranjit wonderingly.

'Well, welcome to adulthood.'

And Evelyn went and opened the great oak door before Nigel and his men splintered the four-hundred-year-old wood to pieces.

Nigel was as dapper as ever, even at 4 a.m. He nodded.

'Bit of a conference going on?' he said.

'Well, seeing as we're not allowed to talk to anybody except each other, it's either this or sit in your room on your own in your underpants,' said Arnold.

'Do much of that, big man?' said Nigel pleasantly. His gaze rested on Luke. 'Ah. Doctor Beith. We just wondered if we could have a word?'

'Of course,' said Luke, looking at his shoes.

'Did you really need to have all the sirens and heavies?' said Connie. 'We don't live in a police state.'

Nigel looked at her.

'Well, the Queen has taken it pretty well, all things considered. But I don't think anybody quite knows what kind of a state we are living in,' he remarked. 'Not after what you chaps have come up with. Therefore we need to make sure everyone is safe.'

Everyone thought about Ben Hirati. It barely needed Nigel to add, 'But they weren't, were they?'

After the men had taken Luke away, they sat there in silence. Dawn was breaking outside the windows, but nobody could have slept in any case.

Evelyn, as always in times of emergency, went and put on some coffee. Then she took large amounts of dried fruit and grains from her small kitchen store cupboards and set about making homemade muesli. It was surprisingly reassuring to watch.

'I can't believe Luke is an alien!' said Ranjit excitedly. 'I can't believe I've met a real-life alien! I wish I was an alien.'

'You are to him,' pointed out Arnold. Sé frowned.

'Do you think ...' he said. 'Do you think what's happened ... I mean he's always been a little peculiar. Do you think he might be ... catastrophically mentally ill? I mean, if he's had some sort of psychotic break, some kind of episode ... the way Hirati was killed was really unpleasant.'

'Luke didn't kill him,' said Connie fiercely. 'I think ... I looked into his eyes. I believe him.'

'Maybe they're not eyes,' said Ranjit thoughtfully. 'Maybe they're tiny feelers painted to look like eyes.'

'Oh God, it's such a mess,' said Connie.

Evelyn brought over five bowls of muesli and set them down with spoons tidily placed at right angles.

'A mathematical truth,' she said, 'is neither complicated nor simple in itself. It simply is.'

'Well, Occam's razor says he's a homicidal nut-job.' Arnold frowned. 'Which is annoying, because I really liked him.'

And it went on. It did not stop: not for sleep; not for the chance to take the implications in; not for a break; not even to mourn the man they barely knew. They were servants of a government power now, and it went on, and on, and on.

There was more information sputtering out, great screeds that needed decoding, worked up, laboriously unravelled. Arnold had tracked down the hidden microphones in their room, and had sat next to one of them an iPod playing continuous Justin Bieber straight down it, so they could talk quietly, reasonably confident they wouldn't be overheard, and also it would make whoever was spying on them want to kill themselves.

Connie's head was spinning; she was a constant mix of feeling utterly on edge and entirely exhausted, and was terribly worried about Luke. She didn't see him all day, and wondered whether they were holding him up in the SCIF. She worried about DNA. Did he have any? Would it help or not help? Would he tell them? Surely not. Would they believe them? It was a stretch: from some distant signals from another galaxy, to an alien walking among them.

And of course, if they did, the consequences would be even worse.

Instead she buried her head in the numbers. It was slow going, very slow. Something round was emerging, but very tentatively. She could only imagine there was some way to communicate and codify within it: an internal key that would make her read more fluently, but she couldn't sense what it was.

And it was hard to concentrate anyway, when all her thoughts were of Luke – who he was and what was happening, but it was more that, and she knew it. The way he had wound her hair around his fingers as he stood so close, as she gazed into his deep eyes.

'Oh crap,' she thought, getting herself another cup of coffee. 'This is worse than that time with Sé.'

'Hmm?' said Sé who was in the way. She looked at him, startled.

'Sorry, was I talking out loud? Sleep-deprived.'

'Oh no,' he said, filling her cup for her. 'No, you just looked a million miles away.'

Connie inadvertently let a half-smile cross her lips, her gaze out the window and far across the field. Sé watched her, but she didn't even notice he was there.

It was like a mirage when Luke re-appeared two days later, Connie thought through her exhaustion: her dream become reality when he appeared back in the room at five in the evening after two days where they had got no further than the endless waves and the curves of a shoreline and something that appeared to be a line. It was a huge map. But to where? What of? Why?

When Luke walked in, alone, everybody froze at first. Then Arnold's face broke into a huge smile.

'Seriously, dude, no handcuffs?'

Luke held up his hands.

'They couldn't hold me,' he said, looking down. 'Apparently the DNA machine isn't working.'

'That's weird,' said Ranjit. They gave him a second to get it.

'Seriously, dude, you broke the DNA machine?!' said Arnold. 'Whoa!'

'I'm not allowed to travel anywhere. But they didn't find

any evidence that I *was* there, I don't think. That Nigel, he asked and he asked and he asked, over and over again, the same things, all the time.'

'But they can't prove you weren't?' said Sé. Connie looked at him in surprise. His tone was hostile.

'Sé?'

'What?' said Sé. 'I can tell you that I didn't kill him. But it certainly looked like somebody did.'

Luke blinked.

'I don't have any interest in trying to change your mind,' he said, and turned away. Connie walked over with a pile of printouts and cleared her throat.

'Um' she said. 'I was thinking.'

Arnold watched her out of the corner of his eye.

'I mean, obviously ... you can read these, right? If they're from your people.'

Everyone was watching openly now. Luke bit his lip.

'Mmm,' he said.

'Well, can you or can't you?' said Connie. 'Because it's going to take us for bloody ever.'

'If he just translates it straightaway, they're going to suspect something's up,' said Arnold.

'Rightly,' said Evelyn.

'Well, we'll just pretend it took a bit longer and play Jenga,' said Connie.

Luke nodded sadly.

'Don't you want to read it?' said Ranjit.

'I don't really have to,' said Luke. But he picked up the first of the printouts and read it intently; then the next and the next. He sat down heavily, ignoring the rest of them, even as Evelyn demanded, 'What does it say?'

Ranjit, meanwhile, was behind Luke's back, surreptitiously sniffing him.

'Stop it,' hissed Connie as she saw him lean in.

'He smells like the sea,' whispered back Ranjit. 'Like the sea that you saw in the designs.'

Connie didn't want to say that she already knew that. Luke didn't notice at all: he ran his hands through his thick, curly hair, his expression intent and very serious.

'Have you got feet? Have you got toes?' Ranjit was saying. 'Does your hand turn into a gun? What are the ladies like on your planet? Are you actually blue?'

'Shut up, Ranjit,' said Sé, who had taken up another pile of the paperwork and had started to work on it after Connie and Evelyn had given them a quick seminar on how Connie had solved the signal two days before. But he was only pretending to work, Connie could tell. She was surprised he was so hostile. She ignored the little voice inside her telling her that Sé perhaps had very good reasons to be afraid that someone from another world might be walking among them.

'Yeah, shut ... Hang on, are you actually blue? And what about the ladies? Are there ladies? Are you a lady? Oh. That would be disappointing. Because you're quite good-looking,' said Ranjit. 'But not for a lady.'

Arnold looked down at his pen and paper.

'I shall now prepare a four-hundred-point questionnaire of all the things I want to know about aliens, alien planets, alien ladies and there's another bit about alien ladies, which you can either read, or mind-meld with me later. But no probes. But if you own a probe, I would really like to see it.'

Sé tutted loudly.

'I want a probe,' said Ranjit. 'But to probe other people with, I mean. As a noun. I don't want, like, "a quick probe".'

Luke was still ignoring all of them and instead picked up another printout, but was saying something under his breath. When he finally turned around, his face was grave.

'What does it say?' said Arnold. 'Are they going to blow us up in, like, four minutes? Because if they are ... '

He looked sorrowfully at Evelyn and Connie and batted his eyelashes.

'Don't even think it, big man,' said Evelyn.

'Are they going to make us their slaves and force us to do things with their ladies?' said Ranjit.

'I need to get out of this bunker,' said Evelyn, putting her hand over her eyes, 'before you all turn into sex pests. Also, I can't believe there's the existence of an entire, new, intelligent species in the galaxy and all you think about is rubbing your groins up against it.'

'Or a ton of shit getting blown up,' said Arnold. 'Also we think about that.'

Luke shook his head. 'No, nothing like that,' he said. 'No. It's just what I thought. They're coming for me.'

Chapter Eleven

There was silence.

'Oh, it's all about *you*,' said Sé, not pleasantly. 'Is that nice?'

Luke stared at him, blinking repeatedly. 'Not particularly,' he said. 'Not at all, in fact.'

'He's being sarcastic,' said Connie. 'And he's going to stop it right now. Seeing as we are looking at the first ever trans-latable signals from the other side of space, maybe you could put down the scepticism and aggression for two seconds?'

Sé stood up. His face was drawn and furious.

'Prove it.' he said. 'Prove it to us. We're all sitting here, in fear of our lives either from some ... some ... sky-ray gun or from some psycho loose in the facility, so it might be helpful if we knew a little bit about what we were dealing with rather than taking Luke's airy-fairy word for it.'

Everyone was very tense now, looking at each other. Finally Luke sighed. 'This is why I had to move from Belarus. I don't do well with wild temperature fluctuations. And I can't be too near the sea. Too tempting. So here was by far the best option ...'

'What are you talking about?' said Ranjit. 'Do you melt?'

'Does anyone know where to get some ice water?' said Luke quietly. They thought for a second.

'Biology lab,' said Evelyn. 'Ninth floor. I'll defrost one of the rat biopsies. The animal cryogenics girl fancies me bad.'

'Well, you're a lot more attractive than what she spends most of her day looking at,' pointed out Arnold.

'That'll do it,' said Luke, as she left the room at high speed.

'Where are those cameras?' said Arnold. 'I saw them in the SCIF.'

He screwed up his eyes and marched around the room.

'Here,' he said finally, glancing down an angle. He pivoted up. Sure enough, there was a slightly larger hole in the pinboard tiles that covered the walls. 'And the same on the other side ...'

'Or we could just go out to the cupboard,' offered Ranjit. 'Get cosy.'

'No, if we all disappear, they'll get suspicious,' said Arnold. 'We'll have to just find a blind spot for Luke then pretend we're doing something else.'

He moved up to the mike and switched off Justin Bieber.

'Okay, you guys, time to discuss the cleaning rota once again. Evelyn's going to show us how to scrub everything down properly to stop all that mould stuff getting about ...'

Arnold droned on, while Luke, his face pale and tense moved towards the back of the room. There was a cupboard lining the wall, filled with textbooks, and he sat cross-legged in front of it.

Arnold took a look at the angles and deemed him probably okay as Evelyn came in bearing a large washing-up basin full of ice.

'I took the rat out,' she said helpfully. 'That girl really does like me.'

Arnold kept up a plethora of drivel about washing-up liquid as Luke sat next to the basin and plunged his hand into it.

For a long time nothing happened, just Arnold reading out

a long list of ingredients from a box of laundry detergent he'd found.

'So, right. Modern detergent formulations – the entire product versus just the surfactant – contain several components. Three main ingredients are builders (fifty per cent by weight, approximately), the alkylbenzene sulfonate surfactant (fifteen per cent) and bleaches (seven per cent).'

Time seemed to slow. Connie looked on, her heart full of confusion. What if it was a trick or a mistake or simply not true? What if she had been wrong; that she had been taken in by his odd charm, and by the strange things that appeared to be happening; that were undeniably happening all around them? That they were all having some kind of collective hysterical breakdown brought on by the death of their boss and the alien signal? Sé was leaning against the far wall with his arms folded. Ranjit was jiggling, saying, 'I don't see anything. What's happening? Why isn't anything happening? Is this a joke?'

'Now one thing you don't want to do when you're building a cleaning product,' Arnold droned on, 'is get one with too much – or too little – surfactant. The exact correct percentage in fact is slightly less than fifteen per cent, which reacts perfectly with imbedded grease.'

'Oh my God,' said Ranjit.

'I know, that's right,' said Arnold quickly. 'Thank you for having a proportionate response to the importance of our cleaning rota.'

Connie crept a little closer and took a sharp intake of breath.

Luke's right hand – still wearing the old-fashioned gold watch that didn't work – was changing. The fingers were lengthening, unfurling from the hand, the forearm growing wider and stronger-looking as the colour came and went, fading in and out: in its place there was a startling clear phosphorescence, glistening, the long, long fingers – there were three, and one very long thumb – sparkling; they were, as he had said, not unlike a jellyfish, but the flesh was illuminated, glowing underneath, with an odd, colourless sparkling flickering up and down.

They all stared. Arnold's recitation faded away. Sé came over from his standpoint, looked and cursed softly and long under his breath in his own language. Evelyn swallowed. Ranjit turned away and quietly threw up in the wastepaper bin again.

'Fuck the fuck-fuck,' said Arnold. 'And, erm, don't forget to use a finishing glass polish.'

Connie gazed, hypnotised.

'It's beautiful,' she said. Luke lifted his head, his eyes full of pain, and held her gaze.

'Have you got a tail?' said Ranjit excitedly, seemingly entirely recovered. 'Have you got a tail though? How many legs have you got? Eight? I bet it's eight. And a tail!'

Luke lifted his hand out of the water and clutched it, in obvious pain, to his chest. Gradually the lights began to fade, the fingers began to furl themselves up; the colour gradually returned. He winced, his face creasing.

'Does it hurt?' said Connie.

He nodded.

'All the time,' he said quietly.

'Your tail must *really* hurt,' said Ranjit.

'I don't have a tail, Ranjit.'

'Hmm,' said Ranjit. 'Have you got fins?'

'So I believe we're coming to the end of our cleaning seminar for today,' said Arnold, a hiccup in his voice. He couldn't tear his eyes away from Luke's body. 'Please just remember: be safe out there in Cleaning World.'

Evelyn was the most surprising of all. Having sat watching

the display in total silence, she got up suddenly, her little solid body moving swiftly across the tiled floor, put her arms round Luke's neck and, in a completely uncharacteristic display, gave him a swift hug.

'Welcome,' she said quietly. Luke looked completely surprised.

'You are totally like X-Men!' said Ranji. 'This is amazing. What can you do?'

Luke shrugged.

'Well, mostly mathematics.'

'No way! You must have superpowers.'

'Well, if you call sitting with your arm in a bucket of ice water for half an hour a superpower, then I suppose so.'

'Really, dude? You don't have superstrength or anything?' said Arnold, having put Justin Bieber back next to the microphone the expectation that their watchers would once more see five not terribly well-dressed mathematicians sitting doodling on pieces of paper.

'You can move a piano!' remembered Connie suddenly.

'Um, yes,' said Luke. 'There were a lot of complaints about that, I remember.'

'But most people would find that too heavy to move.'

'Yes, I have some muscularity advantages, I think,' said Luke. 'Although everything on your planet is heavy to me.'

'Pick me up,' said Ranjit. 'Pick me up and throw me across the room! No, hang on, don't pick me up. Or pick me up and gently put me down again.'

'Yeah, guys, don't forget the cameras,' said Arnold. 'Maybe just pick up a four-poster bed later.'

They sat in silence. Evelyn took out some delicious-looking chicken mayonnaise sandwiches and handed them round. Then it was slightly awkward as everyone watched Luke to see if he ate anything.

'I don't ... I mean, I can eat,' said Luke. 'But I couldn't eat another animal. There's an animal in there, yes?'

'Yes, but only a little one,' said Ranjit.

'What have you been eating?'

Luke showed her a sachet of Soylent.

'It seemed safer. I don't know what I'm doing otherwise,' he said. 'Plus, your cookies. Your cookies have been very help-ful. Thank you for those. The other stuff tastes like ... '

He shook his head.

'Well. I could not eat a living thing: I am a living thing.'

Nobody felt much like the sandwiches after that.

'So, tell us about your world, man,' said Arnold. 'Have you got, like, three moons?'

'No, just the one moon,' said Luke. 'A lot like this one. Having a single moon is very, very useful if you want to sus-tain life. Tides, and so on.'

'And you live in the sea?'

'We're amphibians,' said Luke. 'Me, personally, I'm mixed, which is, um, unusual, so I don't mind really. But I like to sleep in the water if I can. I don't like being so dry all the time.'

'Do you have houses? And the internet? And families? And chocolate? And Sellotape? And war?'

Luke blinked. 'Thanks, Ranjit. Can I answer those later? But we have society. Not family in quite the same way.'

'Oh my God, do you spawn?'

'That's a very personal question,' said Evelyn, batting him down. There was a pause. 'Do you spawn though?'

'I don't ... One doesn't really talk about spawn,' said Luke.

'Well, I'm taking that as a definite yes,' said Arnold, and Ranjit nodded his head.

'What does it say?' said Sé, who was still leaning against the wall, unwilling to join their group. He had, though, eaten the sandwich. 'The message. They're after you. Why?'

'We have a problem,' said Luke. 'It is a struggle. There are those who think we should be only water-based, and those who want to spend more time on land. And those who want to be free to go wherever the hell we damn well choose. Some propose partition. Some want to build a great big wall between the land and the sea.'

'Good luck with that,' said Evelyn.

'So we tried,' he went on. 'Tried to find a way to keep the two sides together, talking, rather than apart, consolidating their differences. I'm a genuine ...'

There was a pause.

'What?' prompted Arnold. 'And what are you anyway? Like, Klingon? Or Gallifreyan?'

Luke shook his head. 'I'm just a mix.'

Sé shook his head. 'I don't understand. How many people live in this civilisation?'

Luke shrugged. 'On the planet? Ninety billion, give or take.'

'And they came after you? What's so special about you?'

'Are you, like, a really terrifying warlord in your own culture?' said Ranjit. 'OOO – or a goodie? Are you Optimus Prime?'

Luke shook his head.

'No,' he said. 'I'm just a mathematical engineer.'

'So what's so special about you?' said Sé.

Luke sighed. He waited a little and then began.

'I don't believe in walls and I don't believe in enforced separation. But I was working on the project. The land–sea project. So I sabotaged it.'

'Just like you tried to sabotage us,' said Connie. Luke

nodded. He looked at her. 'Yes,' he said. 'I genuinely didn't think you'd figure it out. The astrophysicists got nowhere near. Engineers neither. I reckoned without you.'

'Hang on, they asked us *third*?' said Arnold. Luke ignored him.

'What did you do?' said Sé. 'Did you kill a bunch of people?'

Luke frowned.

'No,' he said. 'Why would I do that?'

'Well, I think there's quite a lot we don't know about you,' said Sé. 'So it seems like a reasonable question.'

Luke paused. 'Caused a bit of fuss of course.'

'So what did you do?'

'Well, I have a friend who's a space engineer ... local stuff, of course, just mining and a bit of star power exploitation. Ninety billion is quite a large energy ask.'

'He gave you a rocket?'

'Yes,' said Luke. 'I don't know when he's going to get it back ...'

'But that's not possible,' said Arnold. 'How long did it take you to get here?'

'Forty years,' said Luke.

'It took you forty years sitting in a rocket to get here?'

Luke shrugged. 'I'm a patient man.'

'Hang on, doesn't that mean they'll be following you?' said Ranjit. 'I mean, why are we hearing from them now?'

Luke nodded.

'Because they are close at hand,' he said simply. 'And at least one of them is here.'

Chapter Twelve

MI5 field agent Nigel Cardon's alarm went off at 5.30 a.m. every morning, but he didn't need it this morning. Hadn't needed it in the last two days, ever since the young technician had grabbed him and taken him into the Mullard SCIF suggesting there was something he needed to see.

He lay wide awake, looking at the dawn starting to push its way into the room. Beside him was his wife, fast asleep. She slept daintily, a single, perfectly highlighted blonde lock strewn across the pillow. He looked at her and sighed. She was gorgeous, Annabel. Beautiful and classy and elegant; kept a lovely house. His mates all envied him. They would never know how much of an animal he felt next to her; too masculine and hairy and unworthy of her delicate attentions.

In his turn, he would never know how much of the beast she had wanted when she had agreed to marry him; how much his delicate, polite enquiries and the way he treated her like a princess bored her halfway to tears. They had no children.

Nigel rolled out of bed. Normally he would hit a power circuit now, as much to clear his head as to keep himself fit – he found being intimidatingly fit a useful psychological tool in his job. But there was no time for that now. Even though his phone had been on silent throughout the night, he had never hit a level of sleep deep enough that the blink-blink-blink of the tiny red light hadn't haunted his dreams.

He showered downstairs; Annabel, bless her, had laid out his clothes the night before. She was a dab hand with the iron. 'I like doing it,' she always insisted as she stood in front of her soaps, ironing away while he worked late again, night after night; she would fall asleep under a perfectly uncreased coverlet and he would watch her in the darkened hallway when he finally got in, shoes off at the door.

He took his coffee outside. It was going to be a beautiful day, astonishingly lovely for so early in the year. Their little chunk of English paradise, Nigel thought to himself briefly, and somewhat wistfully. Then he glanced down at the phone which was going crazy underneath his big hand; blinking, vibrating and twisting like it was alive: his day had begun.

In the car, Nigel laboriously stabbed his way through the four layers of security on his large, chunky, non-standard-issue telephone, checked his newsfeed – it was fine, though the fact that run-of-the-mill coups and murders were his new idea of 'fine' struck him rather forcibly – then hit the A46 with other men whose jackets were hanging on the hooks behind the driving seat. He put on his ridiculous Bluetooth earpiece, about which he had long ceased to feel self-conscious, and took his calls in order of importance. First, the Cabinet Office.

He disliked the silky tones of the Prime Minister's chief of staff: she sounded constantly rather fed up and condescending. That the most astonishing of events was upon them and she still refused to drop the froideur he had found counter-intuitively reassuring. She was undoubtedly shitting it just as much as the rest of them; you wouldn't be human if you weren't. The fact that she still couldn't let it show meant it was all an act after all, so he could almost certainly get behind it.

'Anyali.'

'Mr Cardon.'

He half smiled.

'How is he this morning?'

Anyali sounded impatient.

'He's fine.'

'Come on, darling,' said Nigel, knowing how much this riled her. 'You're talking to me, and I'm talking to them, and I need to know. I'm not the fucking *News of the World*, am I? So, can I ask again? Because the calmer and quieter he is, the more time I have and the less we all turn into chickens chasing our own fucking tails. How. Is. He?'

'Chickens don't have tails.'

'Yeah, they do. Big feathery tails. I've seen 'em.'

There was a slightly exasperated noise on the other end, and the sound of a door slamming and background noise being cut off. Then a pause before she spoke.

'He's ... he's still delighted.'

'Oh, for *fuck's* sake,' swore Nigel. 'What is WRONG with him?'

'He's over the moon. Polls are absolutely desperate, people are out of work, nothing good is happening overseas, we don't even have a nice, distracting war. This really couldn't have come at a better time.'

'Fuck's sake. Tell me he hasn't spoken to the Americans.'

'It's all we can do to stop him speaking to anyone.'

'And you're lecturing *us* about containment,' said Nigel, exasperated.

'How are you doing at your end?' said Anyali, changing the subject.

'We're fine,' said Nigel. 'But my lot are all nerds. They've

121

got no mates. Who are they going to tell? Your lot get taken out to lunch with journalists all the fricking time. How far has it spread?'

'We managed to persuade him not to tell his kids.'

'Oh, thank God for that.'

The Prime Minister's kids were famous in certain circles for behaving so appallingly their security detail spent most of the time apologising to Topshop. At the moment there was a standoff between the PM's office and *The X Factor*, to which the eldest daughter had applied in secret and who were understandably anxious to have her appear. The PM was pretty happy with his life, on the whole, but he would have preferred Barack Obama's daughters.

'But I believe his mood could be characterised as positive.'

Her voice lowered a little, became uncharacteristically confiding.

'You know what he said?'

'Oh God,' said Nigel. 'Tell me.'

'He said, "If it was between this and the zombie apocalypse, I'm so glad we got this one."'

There was a long silence.

'Zombie fucking apocalypse?' said Nigel eventually. 'Zombie fucking *apocalypse*? God, Anyali, I think I want these aliens to come and take us over. Save us from the bunch of utter fucking idiots we all apparently are.'

'I can't comment on that,' said Anyali. 'Where were we?'

Nigel shifted the gleaming car into sixth gear, overtook a salesman's Galaxy in the fast lane and took a sip of black coffee from his brushed-steel cup.

'Contained,' he growled. 'More or less. But this Ben Hirati thing . . . I can't. I can't get a handle on it. It's too coincidental to have happened on the day. It just points to one of the six, or someone at the facility who wanted to stop what he was doing.'

'Or just didn't like him. Or it really was natural causes. How on earth did you get the wife to identify him?'

'Didn't,' said Nigel briefly. 'Brought out his watch and rings. Told her someone at the office had already done it and it wouldn't be necessary. Then I offered to let her see the body and, thankfully, she said no.'

'And she believed that? She just swallowed it.'

'Look, I know you're a weird, emotionless robot, but she was pretty cut up about everything and barely took a thing in. So let's say yes.'

'But why would your spods kill him?'

'Dunno,' said Nigel. 'Maybe they knew they were getting close to the truth and didn't want it to come out.'

'But then why not kill the girl? She's the one who figured it out.'

Nigel shook his head. He couldn't understand that either. He'd had his own men on all of them for seventy-two hours and – nothing.

'My money's on the weird, wimpy guy,' he said, rubbing his head.

'I thought they were all weird.'

'Oh, they're a frog box. But the skinny one has a way of looking at you ... like you're not there at all.'

There was a rustle of papers.

'Do you mean Luke Beith?'

'That's the one.'

'I thought he had problems with his eyesight.'

'Hmm,' said Nigel.

'Wouldn't it be rather tricky for someone with vision problems to sneak past all your detection systems ... plus isn't he rather ... ?'

She coughed quietly.

'What?'

'. . . um, noticeable? Wouldn't someone remember seeing him?'

'What do you mean by that?'

She coughed again.

'I mean, he's . . .'

For the first time he could remember, Nigel detected a note of softness in her voice.

'What?' he growled, his lips twitching for the first time that day.

'Well, he's rather . . . I mean, *I* don't of course, but he could be considered . . . rather . . .'

Nigel left her hanging on the end of the line.

'. . . handsome?'

He smiled to himself.

'Really?' he said.

'It's just a professional observation,' said Anyali tightly. 'I just thought that might make him more likely to be noticed. Like your girl with the bright ginger hair.'

'They'd notice her,' said Nigel. 'There are barely any girls there. I doubt they'd notice some scruffy chap.'

'No,' said Anyali hurriedly. 'Of course they wouldn't.'

There was a silence.

'Wouldn't it make more sense,' said Anyali, 'just to keep them all in custody? I don't like the idea of them all running free. It's an uncontrollable variable.'

'Well,' said Nigel. 'We've considered this. Firstly, they're they only ones who can translate the data. Or rather, they have been so far. I am in no mood to open the data setup to anyone else right now, even if I was allowed to, which I'm not.'

'No,' said Anyali. 'Quite.'

'So it makes sense to have them together. Their phones have been removed and their passports are being monitored,

124

except for young Beith, who doesn't appear to have one. Or a phone in fact.'

This made Nigel cross. There were so many things about that man that didn't add up.

'They can get on with their work. Or having long, fucking boring meetings about cleaning products, which seems to be about all they're doing at the moment.'

'Fine, good, I realise we need them,' said Anyali. 'I just wondered if it wouldn't make more sense to have them all together in custody.'

'Perhaps,' said Nigel. 'Unfortunately it's against the law.'

'I don't think the PM and COBRA are going to have much problem with suspending habeas corpus under this particular set of circumstances,' said Anyali stiffly. 'We'll be lucky if we can avoid a state of emergency. We've already informed the top brass to stand by for a potential large-scale military exercise.'

'Have you now?' said Nigel, watching a truck pulling into a service station and wondering how his mind could hold both the concept of a military state of alert in the UK and wanting a muffin at the same time.

'So the least you could do is pull them in. And make them work at the same time. Tell them it's for their own protection.'

'Okay, two things,' said Nigel, conscious time was rushing on. 'They're better like this. They don't feel too much under suspicion, they can move about – they know they're being watched, but they can do it within limits. They're still pretty relaxed. They're working for us. If they decide they're being persecuted, or unjustly imprisoned – and I'll tell you now that fat American is fairly well-briefed on his human rights – they could shut up shop in two seconds, seal their mouths and then we'd have a whole new set of problems on our hands, do you understand? Involving starting all over again from the beginning, getting a clutch of Bletchers in, and if you think mathematicians are difficult to work with, wait till you meet these guys.

'We're far, far better keeping them onside and cooperative and aware that this is for the good of the country, and possibly the world. Which it is. Plus, if we're all nice and friendly and gentle and there is a rotten one in the middle, it's going to be a much better way to flush them out, letting them gradually relax until we know exactly what the hell is up.'

He thought about it. 'Unless of course the message is, "We're coming next Tuesday to blow up the planet, have a nice day, goodbye."'

Anyali sniffed dismissively.

'Well, if we all thought like that, there wouldn't be much use in us carrying on at all.'

There was a short pause.

'Right, well, I have to go and brief the PM. I need results, I need exactly what is in those messages and I need them soon.'

'Fine,' said Nigel. 'But you have to let me handle them my way.'

'All right,' said Anyali. 'For now. Try not to let them kill anyone else, will you?'

Nigel let out an irritated sigh and went to hang up the phone.

'Oh – you said there were two reasons we shouldn't put your group in custody,' said Anyali suddenly, just before his finger hit the off switch. 'What was the other one?'

'Because it's wrong,' growled Nigel, and hung up.

The SCIF was at its quietest at just before seven, which was exactly how Nigel liked it. The men on the door snapped to attention – they had been bollocked to within an inch of their lives and interrogated back to front. Everyone now wore a paranoid, worried expression every day; Nigel was pleased to see people stiffen as he went past. Nothing wrong with a little alertness in the workplace.

His own office was at the very top of the building, in a turret. It had once been used by Arthur Eddington, although this meant little to Nigel. There was also a stunning view across the ancient buildings and libraries which made up the town – this morning rising up out of a warm, early summer mist. There was only one way up – up a creaking staircase in fact – so if anyone was coming to see him he knew all about it. Apart from that, he had perfect privacy. His subordinates downstairs knew he was exasperated when the floorboards creaked over their heads as he marched up and down.

He sat down, got his assistant Dahlia – who as usual scuttled in and out of his room like a rabbit – to get him more coffee. She was Civil Service Fast Stream, off-the-chart clever, posh and completely wasted making him coffee, the only fact they could both agree on. She sidled in now. She was the only person whose tread was light enough on the two-hundred-year-old wooden staircase not to alert him. Every scientist in the building was quite disastrously in love with her.

'What?' he said.

'Oh yah, also, the police are here.'

Nigel looked up at her.

'The what?'

'The police are here, yah? After, you know. The thing with the professor.'

'The death you mean?'

Nigel frowned. He assumed Thames House would have smoothed all this over by now. The last thing he needed was some clumsy plod marching round the place, asking questions about why so many of the rooms had such strong locking capabilities.

'Did you tell them we weren't very interested in plods?'

Dahlia shrugged.

'It's not in my job description to be rude to Her Majesty's police force,' she said.

'It's not in your job description to use powdered milk in my coffee, but somehow you manage it,' said Nigel, looking down at his cup with distaste, a slight scum floating on the surface.

He sighed. Probably best with a bit of mid-level charm. Give them a bit of a kick out of the spying thing, sort out the mix-up, get them on their way.

'Send them up,' he said. He'd go to see the six afterwards.

The two policemen entered the room five minutes later, their tread heavy on the steps. Nigel sighed. He didn't have time for this, really didn't. One sat in the corner with his hat on his knees; the other stepped forward.

'Do you want coffee?' asked Dahlia offhandedly. The policeman looked at her as if sizing up whether she meant it or not, which was wise – she didn't.

He was thickset, grey-haired, comfortable-looking.

'DCI Malik,' said the man, putting out a hand to shake.

'Nigel Cardon,' said Nigel. 'Sorry, I don't quite understand what you're doing here.'

Malik gave him a long policeman's stare, but that didn't matter to Nigel; he was king of the long stares. He could sit here all day: rank was with him.

Nigel drank some more of Dahlia's deliberately terrible coffee and glanced at his encrypted emails. He didn't need to decrypt them to know exactly who they'd be from: Cabinet Office, Home Office, Thames House. Every single one of them asking, 'Exactly what the fuck is going on in the skies above our heads?'

'I'm sorry,' said Nigel. 'Only, I'm very busy.'

Malik cleared his throat.

'Too busy to notice a dead body in your laboratory?'

'No,' said Nigel, 'and we're all beside ourselves with horror at what's happened, for our facility and for his family. And as soon as they release the body, well, we can have a funeral.'

'The family is complaining, saying the body isn't local.'

'No,' said Nigel.

'They've taken it away somewhere.'

'We just need to make sure we work everything out properly and do the best for the family,' Nigel said, as he'd already said before.

'And you seriously think it's natural causes?'

'We're not ruling anything out.'

'So there are grounds for a murder investigation?'

Nigel looked at Malik coolly.

'Do you listen to a lot of gossip, DCI Malik?'

'Why didn't that body get to the local morgue? Death in the workplace? I believe that's standard procedure.'

Nigel leaned forward. 'Forgive me, DCI, but as far as I understood, we thought the Cambridgeshire Constabulary also understood that this case has been deemed classified Top Secret and is now in the hands of ... my colleagues and myself.'

'Well, so they say,' said Malik. 'But I have to tell you that we're the ones who have had to speak to his wife and his family, and I'll tell you they're beside themselves. And I haven't seen much classified investigating going on. So I thought I'd come up and take a look, seeing as this is my town, as it were.'

'Much obliged,' said Nigel. 'But don't you have several acres worth of equal opportunities paperwork to be getting one with?'

Malik shook his head.

'Not when there's a murder, sir.'

'I realise that,' said Nigel. 'But I'm telling you we have it all under control.'

'You have a suspect in custody?'

'We have some people under observation,' said Nigel, irritated despite himself. 'And besides, this is a matter of national security . . . '

'I'm sure clearance could be arranged,' said the policeman, sitting back comfortably on his large haunches.

'And I'm equally sure it couldn't,' said Nigel.

'All right,' said the policeman, standing up to leave. 'Well, I thought I'd check. I'm sure my tiny uniform brain wouldn't understand anything anyway. But I have to tell you: we're the ones the family are coming round to see, hurling themselves on us. We've got his wife down the station every day, and all we can say is, "Sorry, luv, apparently it's Top Secret"? It's not good enough, sir.'

The policeman looked straight at Nigel, who sized him up. He wondered if it would actually not be very useful to have a time-served copper onside. He knew absolutely how good the bullshit radar of your average copper was; how good they were at spotting lies – their average working life consisting of nothing but – and their ability to focus on one problem at a time, like a dog with a bone. If he could put a lid on this, it might help him get on with a lot of the other stuff without bringing too many more people into the loop.

'Can you keep your mouth shut, DCI?'

The man looked at him.

'I have photographs of the dean you wouldn't believe.'

Nigel's lips twitched. He wondered if he could wangle a bit of help without telling Malik what was really going on, and decided that he could. He seemed old school. Nigel liked old school. He liked by-the-book decent plod work – no mavericks. Nigel had never met a maverick who had been anything

130

other than the most gigantic pain in the arse and who could hold up perfectly straightforward investigations for months on end purely by being a prick. As soon as Nigel saw a whiff of a leather jacket on a police officer, he automatically zoned out. But Malik seemed more his sort.

'Go do your due diligence on these guys,' he said, scribbling down the names of the six mathematicians. 'And I'll meet you at the Watson building at eleven. Introduce you to Professor Hirati's original team.'

Malik nodded and took down the details in his notebook.

'Be nice to have this cleared up,' said Malik. Nigel didn't mention that the death of a physics professor came extraordinarily low on his list of priorities now. However, he would be extremely interested in Malik's opinion of Luke Beith.

Nigel strode down to the maths department just after nine. It was a couple of miles, but he could use his phone without being overheard on the way, and it was still a lovely day. He knew from the overnight feeds that none of them had gone home the night before: they had ordered pizza, which security had checked out (and then, Nigel noticed from the log, ordered some for themselves), and stayed up all night working on the papers. Nigel tried not to get increasingly nervous as he neared the Watson building. When it had been one piece of potential evidence from space, he could just about manage it psychologically.

What the hell they had now he didn't even want to think.

But it was his job to get on with it. He made his face impassive, trying to prepare for any eventuality; anything they could possibly say to them.

'This is amazing,' Luke was saying. 'It's just completely unbelievable ... I ... I don't have the words.'

'Get your head out of there,' said Arnold. 'Seriously, you look like a greedy dog.'

'How can you not have eaten pizza before?' said Ranjit, puzzled.

'Because – alien?' said Evelyn tartly. She was bored out of her mind. Having to sit up all night pretending to work while Luke translated had been incredibly tedious. She glanced at Connie, who actually had worked, but was still on the first page when Luke was through a bookful.

'Yes, but you've been here for years,' pointed out Ranjit. 'And it's not like the world has a great pizza shortage. God, that would be awful if they came and took away our pizza. That would be absolutely the worst thing.'

'Yes, Ranjit,' said Arnold. 'The worst thing. Absolutely.'

Luke shrugged. 'I don't know. It just always looked like something too big for a human to eat.'

Everyone studiously avoided looking at Arnold's impressive stomach.

'Anyway, shut up,' said Arnold.

'Okay,' said Luke.

He looked longingly at the last cold slice of pizza in the box.

'You never take the last slice,' said Evelyn sternly.

'No, I know,' said Luke, giving it a last glance. Then he looked again at the pile of papers and let out a heavy sigh.

'What does it say?' said Connie. She touched him gently on the arm. She could tell from his face how worried he was.

Luke picked them up. Arnold, conscious of the cameras, picked up a pile of papers too and shook them officiously. Then he said loudly, 'We're not discussing this out loud so some spoddy intern can tape it and leave the tapes in the back of a taxi. We're taking the mikes out now, and we'll report back later, and if you don't like it, unleash the hounds or the smoke guns, or any other hilarious things you've got planned.'

He unceremoniously unplugged the two mikes he'd uncovered, hoping against hope that any other recording equipment he couldn't find would be too far away to pick them up. There was a general sigh of relief in the room.

'Fuck every single fucking asshole last one of you,' said Arnold loudly, then paused.

'You know, Arnold, you were actually holding up your middle fingers,' said Connie. 'Which they can probably see.'

'Oh yes,' said Arnold, putting his hands behind his back.

'You cock-sucking bunch of motherfucking pricks,' he whispered into his beard. Then he straightened up.

'Good to get that out of my system,' he said. 'Pricks.'

'Also,' he continued, looking round the room, 'is any of us wearing a wire? I mean, is anyone trying to grass anyone else up?'

'If I was going to grass anyone up,' said Evelyn, 'I'd have at least made sure they sent in the good pizza.'

'Not in a million years,' said Connie defiantly.

'I didn't understand the question,' said Luke. Connie explained.

'Why would I want to turn myself in?' Luke asked, perplexed.

'We assume you wouldn't,' said Arnold. 'It was a general question.'

'I have no idea what's going on,' said Ranjit.

They looked at Sé.

'What?' said Sé. 'I don't think we should be doing this project alone because it's patently crazy, and I'm worried we have an alien murderer in our midst. Why does that make me the bad guy? Can no one else see what a risk we're all taking? Am I the only grown-up?'

Evelyn shook her head. 'But are you ... are you going to report back what we're saying?'

Sé looked at her levelly. 'I hope we all are. Or are we going to cope with an alien threat on our own? Is that the plan?'

'Yes, but when we've decided ... what's best for all of us.'

'I don't see an "us",' said Sé. 'I see some humans, and I see something else.'

Arnold sighed.

'Well, are you relaying what we're saying *right now*?'

Sé shook his head. 'Of course not. I'm not a spy. Or a twat.'

'I loved that film,' said Ranjit. '*Spy Twats*. Hang on, was it *Spy Twats*?'

Arnold blinked.

'But you won't promise to stick with us afterwards.'

Sé looked pained and glanced at Luke, who was staring at the papers in total misery.

'I don't think this is about us all being best buddies, do you?'

'I think that might be all it's about,' said Arnold. 'In the end.'

There was a long silence. Finally Sé shrugged.

'I can't promise,' he said. 'But I will listen.'

'That's all we ask.'

Luke's heavy eyelids closed briefly as he lifted up the papers, tilting them slightly to the side so he could read them more easily.

'Well,' he said tentatively. 'It's quite a long message, with various polite expressions of solidarity and welcome.'

'How many intelligent planets are there?' said Ranjit suddenly. 'I mean, it can't just be you guys and us guys. I mean, if it's you guys and us guys, that must mean there's a billion guys. Stands to reason. Like if you see two cockroaches that means you've got a million cockroaches.'

Luke lifted his head.

'Of course,' he said briefly. 'Not many as odd as you lot.'

'We're not odd,' said Arnold. 'You're the one that can't do buttons.'

Luke's face took on a wounded expression.

'Evelyn doesn't mind doing my buttons,' he said quietly.

'I do not mind doing his buttons,' confirmed Evelyn.

'Go on, Luke,' said Connie. She could see he was not relishing what he had to read. Her heart quickened at the thought that what he held in his hands might be a death warrant.

'"Salutations, etc.",' Luke went on, glancing across. '"Normally, planets with interplanetary contact politely await contact from non-interplanetary neighbours, etc.".'

He looked at the others over the tops of his glasses.

'Which puts you guys about fifty years behind. At least.'

Arnold scowled.

'Don't be species-ist.'

'"... but in this instance we must make an exception. It is believed you have among you someone who is of interest to us. He is known as ..."'

Here Luke voice tailed off.

'Oh my!' said Ranjit. 'What's your real name. It isn't Luke, is it? That would be, like, a totally weird coincidence if your space name was the same as your Earth name. Or Skywalker. Obviously. What's your name? Is it, like, Zod? I hope it's Zod. Please be Zod. Zod Skywalker.'

Luke was embarrassed and rubbed his throat.

'I can't,' he said. 'Well, I can't make the noise with ... these stupid neck vibrating things. They aren't very useful. I don't know how you manage.'

'I can make a lion noise,' said Ranjit, and did so. 'Can't you make an alien noise?'

135

Luke shook his head.

'Not really.'

'Go on, have a shot,' said Ranjit.

Luke shook his head again.

'No,' he said. 'If there is some way people could still hear us . . .'

Connie nodded.

'Please, just go on,' she said, glancing at her watch. The sun was up outside; it was the beginning of another working day. Soon someone would be down to see how they were getting on: possibly that awful MI5 guy in the suit. Luke nodded hastily.

'If I am found – which is one thing. They don't know who I am.'

'Except you're exactly in the place where we found the message,' said Evelyn.

'Yes,' said Luke. 'Where I have always been. To stop you finding it. Thank you for reminding me of my failure to do so on this occasion.'

Connie flushed.

'I'm sorry.'

'Yeah, well, stop calling us backward, jellyfish boy,' said Arnold.

'". . . deal with him as our laws demand and we shall leave you in peace to continue your spiritual journey towards the universe alone. Keep this a secret from your populations if you can; uncertainty and fear are not the enemy of technological advance, but peace is better."'

Luke did something very uncharacteristic: he hit his fist heavily on the table, which shook underneath his force.

'They say that,' he said. 'They would cause war among their own people at any time they could.'

'What's the rest of it?'

'Coordinates, schematics, how they think I can be found.'

'How do they think you can be found?'

'They suggest freezing the world and seeing who turns transparent. I'm not sure they're very up on current world technologies.'

He turned over another page.

'Or taking everyone into custody. Politics either.'

'What on earth is it *like* on your planet?'

'Efficient,' said Luke. 'Past your first twenty billion, you have to be, really. That's why they're trying to stop the ...'

He twisted his mouth trying to think of a translation.

'The wets mixing with the dries, I suppose. Hence the wall.'

His face grew steely.

'There is no longer a wall.'

'What else is in the papers?'

Luke glanced down.

'They talk about the consequences of what I did.'

He went very silent and very still as the others looked at him.

'I do not want to talk about the consequences of what I did.'

'Well, I think you'd better start,' said Sé. 'Because do you want to know what you sound like to me? You sound like a ter- rorist.'

'I think ... the collateral damage was still better than the separation would have been,' said Luke. 'I am not the power that murders citizens for no other reason than the bad luck to be working next to them.'

He cast his eyes down on the page.

'Oh,' he said. His hand went to his mouth. Connie went to him. 'My friend,' said Luke. 'My friend, my brother; there is no distinction. Who gave me his ship. Who when I told him what I had done offered me his only ship, his pride and joy, without question, without even the faintest hesitation in doing so, who gave everything for me to escape. He did not escape.'

He swallowed.

'Saying it is harder than reading it. I could skip over the words when I read them.'

Connie nodded.

'We were ...'

'Did you seriously think you could blow up a wall and take a spaceship and run away and everyone else would be totally all right?' said Sé. 'Great planning.'

Luke stared straight at him.

'And I would do it again,' he said quietly. 'Because I believe all people should be free. Not just the wet or the dry. Not just the rich or the not-rich. You don't think it too? Your world is full of the oppressed. It is full of barriers and walls to keep people apart, to keep them oppressed. Or maybe you didn't notice?'

'There's pizza,' said Ranjit. 'There are consolations.'

Sé turned on Luke suddenly.

'Don't you dare talk to me about oppression. Don't you dare. Don't you DARE. My father was accused of betraying the Tamils when he was nineteen years old. They took two fingers from each hand so he could not work. Those are what rebels and freedom fighters do. That is what they do. You decide you're giving people freedoms that they may not even want.'

He banged his fist hard on the table.

'Don't you ever talk to me about oppression. Don't you ever dare.'

There was a long silence. Sé stormed towards the window; he was tall enough to look out. It was a beautiful day outside; the legs that passed by the basement window were bare, wearing sandals or flip-flops.

Luke lowered his head.

'It is clear,' he said, quietly. 'It is clear what they want me to do, and I will do it.'

'What is it?' said Connie, her heart pounding. He looked so pale and fragile for such a tall man. Sé looked stern and furious and would not turn round to look at any of them.

'They will take me back. Remove me. Take me home and ...'

His face twisted up. 'I think the expression is "make an example of me".'

'They'll kill you?' said Connie.

'Eventually,' said Luke.

He looked at Connie, then glanced at Sé.

'And I think that is right.'

'No way,' said Connie. 'No way, they're not having you.'

'They should have me,' said Luke. 'I ... I tried to act against cruelty and unfairness. I didn't kill anyone ... on purpose. Directly. You have to believe me – I would never do that. I'm only a mathematician. A mathematical engineer.'

'Why?' said Arnold. 'Seriously, dude, if you're just a little engineer who knocked down a bridge or a wall, or whatever, like you say ... why would they come all this way for you? Why would they break that weird interplanetary outreach code thing? For you? For knocking down a wall? People must do it all the time.'

'Not ... not quite like this.'

'You sound quite nails for a jellyfish.'

'With a tail,' added Ranjit.

'I don't have a tail,' said Luke.

'And neither do jellyfish,' pointed out Evelyn. 'Please calm down, Ranjit.'

Connie suddenly couldn't take it any more.

'SHUT UP EVERYONE!' she yelled at the top of her

lungs. She was trembling. 'They are not killing you. They are not taking you. You're not going anywhere.'

'Steady on, *Kick-Ass* girl' said Arnold, holding up his hands. Connie turned towards Luke.

'What does it say will happen after that?'

'They promise to leave Earth alone until you're ready to venture into the universe for yourselves,' said Luke.

'And if you don't get found?'

Luke blinked.

'It translates best as ... "consequences".'

There was a sharp rap at the door.

Chapter Thirteen

Nigel had wanted to knock. He wanted them onside; to believe he was helping them, being polite; doing things properly. Which he was, after a fashion. He glanced at his watch. He'd told DCI Malik to come and interview them in the afternoon. He'd be very interested to see the results.

'Hello,' he said, trying not to wrinkle his nose. He was a fastidious man. The room looked like a bomb had hit it. Papers and crumbs, empty cups and pencils were strewn everywhere. Under his foot were discarded sharpenings even though there was a bin less than a metre away.

'So much for all your cleaning meetings,' he murmured.

'Oh, is that what this is about?' said Arnold, gazing at him with open hostility.

The rest of them were sitting open-mouthed in a circle, all of them stiffening and falling silent as he walked in. The tension in the room was incredibly thick. Nigel felt his heart rate rise a little. They knew something: that much was obvious. If they hadn't managed to decode anything, they wouldn't have immediately stopped what they were doing and frozen in place.

The weird, gangly, specky one was obviously in the middle of speaking, but stopped abruptly.

'Please don't stop on my account,' said Nigel. 'We completely understood why you turned off the mikes; that's totally fine. But I can assure you I have the highest clearance.'

Sé snorted.

'Like that means anything,' he said. 'I expect Professor Hirati's was pretty high too.'

'We'll plug them back in now though,' said Arnold getting up. 'Now you're here. Just for insurance.'

He gave Nigel an extremely rude look, which Nigel ignored.

'Please carry on.'

There was a long, long silence in the room. Nigel let it play itself out. Silences didn't bother him. Although this one was certainly quickening his interest.

'Don't,' said Connie fiercely. 'Don't carry on.'

Evelyn shot her a warning look, then jumped up.

'Because,' she said, 'at the moment it's just gibberish. We've barely got anywhere with it. There's no point in saying anything about it, really; it would just be pure speculation.'

Ranjit chipped in excitedly.

'Well, the thing is,' he began, 'what you do is you start with the collections of numbers, they say, to start a polynomial. The next number gives the unit term, then x, then y, then x squared, y and y squared. You fill these numbers into a polynomial. Once you have the algebraic structure, you plot it over real numbers – whoa, man, it's the coolest! Do you see? Normally we can't do this over algebraically closed fields! Then this gives you a curve on the plane with Cartesian coord ...'

Nigel had stopped listening some time ago and now turned brusquely towards the whiteboard.

Connie moved anxiously.

'We do have some stuff,' she said. 'But we were just

discussing ... I mean, there's not much more we can tell you and we'd want to check it first ... of all things to get wrong.'

'I understand,' said Nigel smoothly. 'Of course. You're quite right. What is this please?'

Everyone in the room looked at Connie's latest drawing on the whiteboard.

Connie cleared her throat, deciding the best thing to do would be to stick as closely to the truth as possible without actually telling it. She noticed Luke's hand was resting over his mouth, as if he was trying to stop himself from speaking, from blurting it all out. She looked at him again, marvelling at how very human he appeared; but also, now she thought about it, not at all. Or maybe everyone was like that until you really looked at them. When they stopped just being one of the throng and became particular and specific to you. When they walked into your life and ...

She pulled herself back to the present.

'That's ... well, we think that's an illustration of their planet,' she said haltingly. Evelyn shot her another warning look, which she ignored.

'This is all we have so far.'

Nigel stood up to take a look at it.

'Wow, you got all that,' he said. Behind him the others looked at one another. Nigel stared at the planet for a long time, feeling the hairs on the back of his neck go up. Another world. Another world, with people – or whatever they were. Nigel wouldn't have admitted it, but in his head they looked like people, only maybe bluer. This was their world. And they had sent them a picture of it.

'What's this weird, jagged line?' he said. 'Is it a gas ring, like Saturn or something?'

Connie glanced at it. She knew it must be the wall.

143

'Well, that's a cool idea,' said Arnold. 'We never thought of that. Yeah, might be.'

Nigel looked at him quickly but Arnold's expression was totally impassive.

'Yes, or an equator or something . . . ' said Connie, trying to sound helpful.

Nigel took out his phone.

'I'll just take a picture,' he said, then noticed a button beside the whiteboard.

'Does that thing print out?'

'I know,' said Ranjit, unable to help himself. 'Cool, huh?'

He ran over and touched a button as Evelyn rolled her eyes.

Nigel snatched the paper that came out of the bottom, and tore it quickly from its roll.

'Good,' he said. 'I'll take this, I think.'

He stared at it.

'It really is a map, isn't it? Are they telling us where to find them?'

'We haven't got that far yet,' said Connie. Nigel nodded.

'Right. Fine. I'll pass this on.'

He looked around the room.

'I have to say, for a bunch of people working on the most exciting project of all time, you don't seem terribly excited.'

'That's because we're under house arrest,' pointed out Arnold. 'And one of us is dead.'

Nigel frowned.

'Yes, and we're working on that. But this . . . ' He held up the small piece of whiteboard paper. 'Another world! Another planet, of people who want to talk to us . . . don't you think it's utterly astounding?'

'Yes,' said Evelyn quickly. 'It's amazing.'

'Fish aliens!' said Ranjit happily.

Nigel looked at him quickly. This man misses nothing, thought Connie in dismay.

'What do you mean, fish aliens?'

'He's just speculating,' said Arnold quickly. 'We've all got a bet on. There's a lot of what looks like ... might be ... water on the planet.'

There was a pause in the room, as they tried to figure out whether Nigel had believed them. Ranjit had gone bright red. Connie hoped he wasn't going to throw up again.

'Yes, Arnold's bets all have gigantic boobs,' said Sé. 'Four of them. Five, sometimes.'

Connie looked at him gratefully as Nigel smiled.

'Well, be careful what you wish for,' he said. He picked up the paper.

'I'm going to take this to COBRA, okay?'

They nodded, just happy to see he was leaving.

'I'll be back this evening; see what else you guys have come up with. Good work, you guys. This is amazing. Keep at it. Anything else you need let us know.'

And he was gone.

Arnold grabbed one of Sé whiteboard pens and wrote in large letters YOU ARE A DICK and held it up, away from the cameras, in front of Ranjit's face. Ranjit looked like he was going to cry. Connie turned to Sé.

'Thank you,' she said. He shrugged and looked annoyed.

Nigel waited till he was in the corridor until he phoned London on the secure line.

'Yes?' said Anyali.

'I have a topography,' said Nigel.

'Okay, good, that's a start,' said Anyali. 'Anything else?'

'Oh, there's plenty more,' said Nigel. 'But tragically they appear to think I'm an absolute fucking idiot.'

Anyali sighed.

'I did tell you: don't give them any leeway to start conspiring to lie.'

'They can work the lies all they want,' said Nigel. 'Because here's the thing: why on earth would they lie to me if they didn't clearly have something to hide? They must know more, otherwise why the hell wouldn't they just cooperate?'

He hung up the phone and called the DCI.

'Hello. Yes. I think we've narrowed it down to one of the six. See if you can get a confession out of him, would you? And don't go too easy.'

Chapter Fourteen

'Thought you were going to turn yourself in,' said Sé.

Luke nodded.

'I was. I am.'

'Well, what's keeping you?'

'He's not turning himself in,' said Connie. 'He's not. They're not putting him to death. We're not. No way.'

'Well, if they nuke Tokyo we might have to,' mused Arnold.

'Are they going to blow up Tokyo?' said Ranjit excitedly.

'You mentioned ... consequences?' said Evelyn calmly.

There was a pause.

'It's possible, yes, and they have the capability, yes,' said Luke.

Sé gestured to the door.

'Been nice knowing you.'

'*Sé!*' Connie's heart was pounding and tears sprang to her eyes. She turned to Luke.

'You can't go.'

Luke nodded. 'I have to.'

They stared at each other. Suddenly, it was as if everyone else in the room had melted away. The messy surroundings, the cheap floor coverings, the dirty windows: all of it faded away, and all Connie could look at was him. Hypnotised, they moved closer to one another.

'The reason I didn't give myself up just now ... even though I have to, even though I will, I will ...'

Luke's gentle quiet voice was low and despairing. Connie held her breath. It wasn't possible he could feel the same way ... the distance between them was so far, so strange.

He shook his head and stretched out a hand.

'Oh, Hair,' he said. 'I will miss you so.'

Connie made a sharp intake of breath. It felt so wrong; everything was telling her this was wrong. But to hear at last what she knew deep down she had longed for; dreaded, shied away from but, in the end, longed for like nothing she had ever know ... suddenly, she felt her own hand go up to meet his; it was as if it was moving of its own accord. Everything around them slowed down, as the dust danced gently in the streaming morning sunlight.

'Oh, for FUCK'S sake,' said Arnold. 'You are shitting us.'

Sé sniffed very loudly. Evelyn threw her hands in the air.

'Luke, I warned you about personal space and boundaries! I told you. Get away from her. Get away from Connie.'

Connie shook her head. Her voice was shaking.

'No, Evelyn,' she said, wobbling. 'It's all right.'

'Oh, for fuck's sake,' said Evelyn, who never swore.

'Connie,' said Ranjit. 'Connie, you know, he has a tail.'

Arnold clasped his hand to his forehead.

'Well, this is excellent,' he said. 'What the fuck are we sup-posed to do now?'

'I know,' said Luke with uncharacteristically sharp tone. His hand was firmly in Connie's now: strong and warm. She squeezed it, astonished, utterly delighted to have him there by her side.

'I do know. And I will go. I am sorry for being weak.'

Connie shook her head.

'No,' she said. 'NO. No. They have no idea we've translated this thing, they have no idea who Luke is otherwise they wouldn't ask. We have time. We don't have to give everything up right away. There must be another way. There *must*.'

Evelyn looked up.

'You are a couple of utter bloody nutters,' she said.

'I know,' said Connie, still trembling.

'But,' said Evelyn 'I think you're right. I think you probably do have a little more time. I don't see why we can't fend them off a little longer. His people will be expecting it to take a while for us to get back to them. They probably think we're all just monkeys.'

'You are all just monkeys,' said Luke, looking confused.

'Be quiet, I'm trying to help you here.'

'You're just postponing the inevitable,' said Sé. 'If I was going to be killed, I'd probably want it done straightaway.'

'Sé, you're a psychopath,' said Connie.

'Yeah, well, he's a fish and you're holding hands with it,' said Sé, 'so I don't feel like I'm the one with psychiatric issues in this particular scenario.'

'I wonder what dying's like,' Ranjit mused.

'Can't you talk to them?' pleaded Connie, turning to Luke. 'Talk to Nigel and explain ... explain to your people that you're sorry.'

'I'm not sorry.'

'Okay then, well, just talk to them and ... ask them nicely ...' Her voice went quiet. 'Maybe ask them nicely if you can stay?'

'You *are* joking,' said Arnold. 'What do you think Nigel's going to do if we present that to him? They'll chop you up into tiny pieces. They'll run you off to the lab. You'll never be out of chains again. You'll wish you had died. They're all bastards, you know. As I've been saying all along.'

They looked at each other. Luke rubbed his neck thoughtfully.

'There is ... ' he began. 'There is ... when I arrived here. I crashed my ship. In Belarus. The ship doesn't work but ... it has a unit we could use to communicate. Possibly.'

'In Belarus?' said Sé sceptically.

'What's your better plan, Sé?' said Connie.

'How could you possibly get to Belarus? You've got no passports, and they're watching our every move,' said Evelyn.

'How would you even get out of the building?' said Arnold.

'I know,' said Luke. 'It's wrong.'

'NO,' said Connie again. 'If we just had some time ... they won't be expecting us to have worked it out so fast, will they? Just a little time. You can find it. Fix the comms unit. At least talk to them ... I can't think of a better idea at the moment. We can do something with it. Just ... just a little time.'

'Connie,' said Evelyn fiercely. 'Even if Luke did get out of here, there'd be a manhunt. He'd never get away. They'd kill him.'

'Well, according to this,' said Connie, grabbing a nearby pile of paper and shaking it furiously, 'they're going to kill him anyway.' Her voice shook. 'So I don't see how it can possibly be worse if we give him a chance.'

'Well, it'll be worse if they nuke Tokyo,' said Ranjit.

Connie was in tears now; needed a hand back to wipe her face. She wouldn't let go of Luke with the other one though.

'Time,' she said. 'Just a little bit of time. That's all. Then we'll go to them, tell them what we know. But just one little chance. Please. Just one chance. Three days?'

'He'll get stopped at the airport. Or the ferry terminal. Or the petrol station. Or the front door,' said Evelyn. 'And what if the authorities kill him and the aliens come anyway? What have you done then?'

'They won't kill him,' said Connie. 'They'll bring him back here to hand him over. Probably after doing all sorts of horrible stuff to him.'

There was a silence.

'Three days,' said Connie frantically, 'and we'll tell them then, we'll tell them. Rather than just sit here and wait for death. You can't! You can't let that happen to him. You can't!'

There was another long pause as everyone looked at the floor.

Evelyn looked levelly at Luke.

'You really want to risk it?' she said. He swallowed, glanced at Connie and gave a quick, sharp nod.

'Hang on,' said Ranjit. 'You can't just stroll out of here. There's a guy at the door. He'll just follow you out. He'll never let you steal a car! And that guy Nigel is just about everywhere.'

Luke nodded. 'I know.'

'We need a diversion,' said Arnold. 'Something that will distract them. Fire alarm?'

'When has there ever in the history of the world been a fire alarm anyone has paid the least bit of attention to?' snorted Evelyn.

'Okay, a fire then.'

'You want to set this place on fire?' she said. 'What is everybody's obsession with going to jail?'

'Just a little fire,' said Arnold. 'We'll light up a Bunsen burner up in chemistry, just let it go.'

'And when they pull all the bodies from the ashen wreckage, what's our strategy then?'

'We'll do it late at night, when there's nobody here.'

'How is that a distraction then? Anyway, there's always

somebody here ... and I don't think you've a lot of time to lose ...'

Evelyn's voice trailed off.

'What?' said Connie. 'What?'

Evelyn looked straight at Connie.

'I swear,' she said. 'I swear I never ever dreamed I'd get caught up in anything like this, and I never wanted to. You don't know what danger is, and you don't know what it's like. And it's not fun and exciting like an action movie. It's fun and exciting like shingles.'

'I know,' said Connie. 'I am so, so sorry.'

'I remember you from my graduate conference you know. Back in Hull. Couldn't miss that hair of yours. So smart, so timid, so quiet. There was absolutely nothing to you except numbers and hard work.'

She shook her head.

'Please tell me what you're thinking,' said Connie gravely.

Evelyn glanced at the discarded ice bowl. The ice had nearly all melted now, was dripping from the sides onto the carpet.

'We're not the only people in the building ... and we're not the only living things in the building.' Evelyn said. 'Six storeys up ...'

'The biology labs,' breathed Connie.

'And the hot-rat lady,' added Ranjit.

They took this in.

'What's up there?' said Arnold.

'Rabbits ... dogs ... some monkeys, I think.'

'You hold your fellow species up there?' said Luke in astonishment.

'We're going to keep *that* discussion for another day,' said Evelyn.

'It's all locked up and secure though, isn't it?' said Arnold. 'Precisely to stop people going in and freeing them.'

'Yes, but isn't there someone here strong enough to lift up a grand piano?' said Evelyn.

They thought about it.

'Okay, how about fire alarm first,' said Arnold. 'Then when the people are out . . . '

'Ooh!' said Ranjit. 'I'm fire marshall. I'll get to wear my hi-vis jacket.'

He grinned happily.

'I love being fire marshall. At least *something* good is going to happen today.'

Evelyn glanced at her watch.

'When?'

Arnold shrugged.

'Well, it might as well be now. There's no point going back and, you know, doing some packing. That might make them a little suspicious. And if time is what you want, Luke, then you need to get it. And fast.'

And Luke had nothing to pack, thought Connie.

Luke wrote something on a piece of paper and handed it to Arnold.

'What's this?'

'Memorise it, then eat it or something,' said Luke. 'It's a contact frequency Nigel can use. Give it to them in three days. Pretend I've gone on the run because they think I killed the professor, or just to get out of the space project or something, and nothing to do with Kepler-186f. Then pretend you've translated it on your own. There's not a lot more than what I've told you: the bulk of it is legal boilerplate.'

'There's *legal boilerplate* in space?' said Arnold, looking very disappointed.

'Legal boilerplate is practically a defining characteristic of all species evolved enough for interstellar travel,' said Luke.

Arnold's face looked sad.

'In the tiny possibility that this plan works, what next?' said Evelyn. They had thrown caution to the wind and were huddled by the cupboard, out of sight of the cameras. 'If the diversion works and you get away, what about after that?'

Arnold sighed theatrically and ferreted in the pockets of his enormous khaki shorts.

'Well, I sure hope no dickwad goes to the corner of Church Street and Station Road and steals my fucking white fucking car.' He threw the keys on the table, then slowly and meaningfully turned his back. Then he turned round again, more quickly this time.

'Can you drive?'

'I'm an engineer,' said Luke.

'Is that a yes?'

'I can drive,' said Connie.

Everyone looked at her.

'Yes, but obviously *you're* not going,' growled Sé.

Connie took a deep breath.

Her life, her entire life, she had been a good girl – studious, a little precocious, nervous maybe. But she had always coloured inside the lines. She had worked hard at school. She had a good job. She had paid her TV licence, and, aside from occasionally drinking too much at faculty parties, she had always, always behaved herself. All her life.

She swallowed hard.

'I am going,' she said.

There was consternation among the boys. Evelyn just nodded her head.

'It'll be far harder for the two of you to go.'

'No, it won't,' argued Connie. 'I'll dye my hair and I'll be able to sound less weird than him. And I can see.'

'But your passport, your bank cards ... they'll find you.'

Connie took out her wallet, took a deep breath, and handed it to Evelyn.

'I'll deny ever telling you I was going to do this,' she said. Evelyn took out all the cash that was in it. Then she opened her own wallet and took out all the cash in that – about fifty pounds – and handed it over. Then Ranjit and Arnold did the same. Arnold also insisted they take a gigantic sandwich. Ranjit's was mostly in change. Sé just stood there with a cross look on his face. 'I didn't bring my wallet.'

'That's fine, Sé.'

They all looked at each other.

'Seriously?' said Arnold. 'Seriously, you're doing this?'

'Three days,' said Connie. 'Three days. Then you can tell them everything you know. Please. Three days. Tell them we panicked and ran. That you knew nothing about it. That we stole your car and planned the entire thing. It's just a little time. It's just the tiniest of chances. If we can't get there in three days, we don't deserve the chance.' She shot Luke a very quick glance.

Finally, Arnold looked at her and nodded. Then he opened his arms and gave her a huge bear-hug, and suddenly they were all hugging, except for Sé. Evelyn took off her baker boy cap and wrapped Connie's hair up and under it.

Connie went up to Sé. The hat made her look like a small boy.

'Sé,' she said, 'I know you don't approve.'

'That would be understating the case,' he said.

'I know you're angry with me ... with everyone. Please. Please, please, I know you think this is wrong. But please, just don't ... don't give us up. Please. Please.'

Sé looked at her for a long moment then he sighed loudly.

'If it had been just him going,' he said, 'I would. I think having an alien at large in the world without people knowing is dangerous, unethical and wrong.'

He put out a long hand, with those delicate strong fingers and gently stroked a frond of hair that had fallen loose from her cap.

'But I could never hurt you again,' he said in a low voice. 'I could never hurt you, even when it hurts me more than anything.'

Chapter Fifteen

It had to be Connie and Luke at the lab so they would appear on the CCTV and avoid implicating the others. But they at least let Ranjit break the fire alarm out of the camera's eye, because he wanted to do it so very much. Evelyn took the opportunity to have one last cigarillo indoors.

'Okay, everyone,' said Arnold. 'Are we ready? Are we good for this? I would have preferred an elaborately-plotted *Ocean's 11*-style, super-organised plan with lots of clever alternatives for different eventualities and things that might happen but ...'

B B B B B B B B B B B B B R R R R R R R R R R R I I I I I I I I I I I - INNNNNNNNG!

Ranjit beamed happily and wished them good luck.

The noise of feet on the stairs hammering downwards gave them pause, but hand in hand, Connie's heart hammering in her chest, they continued upwards.

'We're just going to help the biologists,' they shouted loudly.

The lab had heavy, strong security doors to stop people breaking in, but it was being propped open as a stream of young people in lab coats came out, trying to look nonchalant about what was almost certainly an alarm, but aware that the fire alarm testing warning hadn't come round the intranet.

'Hey, dudes?' said one tall guy as they tried to take the door off him.

Connie flashed her pass.

'It's all right,' she said. 'It's just an drill, and I left my phone up here. And you know how long we'll be farting about outside till they sort it out.'

The guy nodded and quickly checked his pocket.

'God, I know.'

'I think we're sloping off to the union for a quick pint if you want to join us,' said Connie, trying her best to smile flirtatiously. 'Might as well make the most of it.'

The man nodded. 'Sure.'

'Great, see you down there,' said Connie, ducking under his arm.

The huge lab was empty. It had rows and rows of microscopes and an array of cabinets for specimens around the walls that made it look oddly like a kitchen.

'This is where you'd end up,' said Connie, startled suddenly. 'A smear of cells on a slide.'

She glanced up at Luke.

'If they discovered you.'

'So let's move fast,' said Luke simply.

Towards the end was a large locked door with a KEEP OUT warning in bright red. It was thick and soundproofed.

'Can you get through that door?' said Connie.

As if in answer, Luke pushed down heavily on the handle, broke it off, reached inside the hole and forced open the heavy lock.

Immediately a second alarm lit up, turning and whooping.

'I thought I liked you *before*,' said Connie, smiling despite herself.

But Luke wasn't listening. He was gazing straight ahead at the rows and rows of animals in cages: rabbits, guinea-pigs, lots and lots of mice. Further down the huge room, they could hear the startled yapping of monkeys, and woofing.

Luke turned to Connie, his eyes suddenly furious.

'If there's a fire, you leave these creatures behind? To die in a cage?'

He had to shout to make himself heard.

Connie blinked.

'It's ... it's a very complicated subject.'

'It doesn't look complicated to me,' said Luke. He moved forward briskly, and with a quick downward motion of his hand, knocked off the first of the locks from the cages. A massive commotion went up. He glanced back at Connie as if he couldn't believe she could belong to a species that could do something like that. For a moment, neither could she. She swallowed hard.

'Don't you ... I mean, doesn't that kind of thing go on where you're from?'

'Yes,' said Luke. 'That's why I left.'

He efficiently chopped all the locks. At first the animals were too traumatised, couldn't move out. Then they did the oddest thing: they jumped down and headed past Luke as if he simply wasn't there. The dogs, the guinea-pigs, the rabbits: they hopped curiously up to Connie, sniffing furiously; interested, frightened, engaging with her. But it was as if Luke was a pillar; they moved around him like a river.

The animals milled at first, confused. Then one followed by another guinea-pig bolted for the door. By the time they got to the dogs and monkeys, they were in absolutely no doubt about what direction they were going, and poured out and down the stairs. The noise was tremendous, and Connie could only stand straight in the current of fur pushing its way past

159

her. One dog stopped and looked at her sideways – its head was shaved; she couldn't begin to imagine what it had been through; it was trembling. The animal tilted its head. Unable to help herself, she caressed its shorn head, a lump in her throat.

'Run free, boy,' she whispered. 'Run as far as you can.'

The *whoop-whoop* security noise stepped up a gear, joining to the fire alarm, and redoubled the noise and the animals' panic.

'Come on,' said Connie. 'Come on – we have to go.'

Out of the lab, they turned right, reaching the main stairwell. Connie glanced down. Someone was already making their way up, in black boots which echoed on the staircase.

'Not that way.'

They turned, retraced their steps, darted across the lab again back to the fire escape downstairs, where they joined people from the higher floors of the building who were still on their way down, expostulating and pointing at the monkeys and dogs, all screeching and making a hell of a noise. It was pandemonium. Guinea-pigs were darting ahead of them in a waterfall; rats too, everywhere, instinctively making for the exit as Luke and Connie shoved them onwards. People ahead started to move quicker as they felt the array of paws coming behind them; one man screamed – and then they burst through the newly opened fire exit door at the bottom, round the back of the building and the fun really began.

There was running and shouting everywhere as the dogs started to go crazy at being outside again, setting up a huge commotion. The sheer number of rats and small rodents darting around made everyone start jumping up and down in derangement. Waves of screaming and panic manifested; once again Connie heard the sirens and caught sight of the back of the security man's head around the side of the building.

Arnold – God bless Arnold, God BLESS him – was haranguing him about something, shouting at him with wide gesticulatory arms, and the security man was trying to calm him down while also scanning the crowd. It was difficult to do both at once.

'Church Street and Station Road,' she said to Luke. 'Come now. QUICKLY!'

They ran through the pell-mell of the wheeling crowd, besieged by rabbits, and escaped down a small alleyway by the side of the cloisters. They flattened themselves against a wall as a fire engine went wailing past in a flash of red, then crossed over again around the back of the modern library. Connie looked around hopefully down Church Street, as the sirens faded behind them. Luke didn't really recognise cars as being particularly different entities and would have found it extremely difficult to tell a white car from a washing machine, but Connie saw it right away.

'Oh no,' she said, her hand flying to her mouth. 'Oh no.'

'What's wrong?' said Luke. 'What is it?'

Connie pressed the key fob she had taken from Arnold, just in case she was wrong – please, she must be wrong – but of course she was not wrong.

The enormous, roll-top, bright white jeep with the number plate ARLD 42, four huge top lights and, she could tell without even pressing it, a horn playing 'La Cucaracha', stood glistening on the street taking up two spaces, at least a foot higher than any other car around. It crossed her mind that it must be Arnold's pride and joy, and that he had given it to them without a moment's hesitation. Because, she also thought, had he had a moment's hesitation he would have realised this was the worst concept of a getaway vehicle in the history of the world; that it would never be forgotten by anyone who saw it.

She swallowed hard.

'Right,' she said. 'Right ...'

She looked around.

'Station Road. Station Road. Station. Quick. Let's go.'

They walked trying to look casual while going as fast as possible up the street, which was thronged with cheerful-looking tourists pointing out the punts going up and down the river, a possibility Connie considered then instantly discarded.

'Put your head down,' she said. 'These places are full of CCTV, full of it.'

She wondered how long it would take them to figure out what had happened. Half an hour, maybe, before the animals were back – the poor sods who hadn't had the chance to escape that was – and they realised that they were missing. Well, she would find out. There would be a hand on her shoulder any second ... she avoided looking at the guards, with their cheery peaked hats. Who was in on it? Who was looking for them? Soon, she thought, everyone – everyone would be. Whether they thought they were running away from murder, or running away to tell the world about their discoveries, or whether they even made the tiniest guess at the truth – they would be finding them anyway. There was no way they would be smarter or luckier than the manpower Nigel and his ilk could muster. But there was no going back.

Something touched her hand from behind, definitely and firmly. She moved away – and felt it again. She froze, terrified. Luke glanced at her to see what was up. Slowly, so slowly, she turned round, expecting to see Nigel or one of his henchmen.

Instead it was the dog from the lab, the one she had instinctively patted. He completely ignored Luke but instead came up and licked her hand in a hopeful fashion and wagged his tail at her.

'Oh GOD,' she said. She bent down and gave the dog a quick hug.

162

'Oh God,' she said again. She glanced around, then knelt on the floor.

'Look,' she said to the dog. 'If we make it back here – if I ever get to come back to this town again, I will come and find you. I promise. I promise.'

And with that, she took out Arnold's sandwich, let the dog sniff it, then gave it to Luke, who hurled it – with his considerable might – all the way up the street. The dog immediately pelted after it, whereupon they rushed away, heads down, and charged up the stairs to the station.

She bought two tickets to Aylesbury, it being the first alphabetical quick ticket that caught her eye, ran them through the barrier as they jumped onto a random very busy train at the last second, just as it was beeping its doors closed. A busier carriage was better, she thought. She looked at Luke, who was staring at her, his dark eyes luminous as ever. Without breaking their eye contact and – even though the carriage was full of cross, busy-looking people attempting to tap things on phones and read newspapers and shout messages and leaf through briefcases of paper and do all sorts of distracting things which made them feel less alone in the universe – despite all of this all around them, despite the risk that they would be seen and remembered, Connie moved forwards, very slowly, and put her head against Luke's chest, smelling again that fresh, airy, sea-salt smell he had. She brought her hand up to it and in return he – clumsily, nervously – put his arms around her, as if he were a coat, and pulled her close to him, tight, so tight she could feel his heart beating through his chest, just above hers. And paradoxically, even though she had never been so at risk, in such grave and real and terrible danger – in spite of all those things, she closed her eyes gently and, to her own surprise, felt herself safe.

Chapter Sixteen

Nigel was white with rage.

'What?'

Brian shuffled his feet and looked embarrassed.

'Well. Uh. Thing is. There was a fire alarm.'

'And what do you do when there's a fire alarm?'

'But, boss, there's four exits, and two of us.'

Nigel shook his head. He was absolutely flabbergasted. His hunch had been right: those bastards absolutely knew something. And he had absolutely genuinely believed that they would do what any scientist or mathematician would do: be delighted to be making an important new discovery. They had all been played for fools.

He hit his hand hard on the desk and swore madly. He was too late: Malik hadn't even made it in. But it was nobody's fault but his own. He should have done what the government had told him to do: he should have arrested them straightaway. Arrested them all on suspicion of murder and made them sweat it out in a cell.

But then, where would that have got them if they'd then refused to translate the data for him? And he still had four of them left who could do that. If he'd put them in jail, he'd have risked not finding anything else out. But now two of them had gone. One of them, presumably, the professor's killer. Statistically he had his money on the boy.

Nigel assumed that finding out what they now knew had just sent him temporarily insane and he had snapped – but why, why would they cover up for him? Help him escape? It didn't make any sense. Was the girl a hostage? He swore. That must be it. He must have got their cooperation for taking a hostage. Shit, this was absolutely the last thing he needed right in the middle of their investigation. That, and an outburst of people complaining they had monkeys in their back gardens. He sighed. This was a fiasco.

His phone had been ringing and ringing but he'd been ignoring it. Finally he glanced down and knew he had to pick it up. It was the PM's office. He doubted they were going to invite him to a garden party. First things first. Thank goodness, he thought, he'd already got the policeman onside.

Nigel had ordered them all back to the SCIF, back to the original interview rooms.

Sé stared. Arnold was trying to wind up the outdoor guard by shouting rude things about his mother. Evelyn was pacing up and down. Ranjit was fast asleep.

'Got them on the CCTV at the station, guv.'

Not for the last time, Nigel was to be relieved he'd extended a professional hand of courtesy to the local police force, as they repaid it in full.

With Malik's team leaping into action, within minutes there were more than fifty London Transport Police at King's Cross and Liverpool Street stations, all boarding and searching every train that arrived there; causing massive lateness, complaints, some hassle and much swearing as they moved through the carriages slowly, ignoring people's rude muttered remarks in their wake.

Nothing and nobody: they were on the lookout for red hair and dark hair and glasses, but red hair could be dyed or cut off or hidden under a wig, and every single man on the train had dark hair and glasses, even assuming Luke hadn't gone to the extraordinary, master-of-disguise lengths of taking off his glasses.

At Ely, they simply asked for ID at all the ticket barriers, politely. People weren't in such a rush, didn't mind so much.

At King's Lynn they shut the station doors. The stationmaster there was an ex-army man and he had been waiting for a manhunt like this all his life. He flattened down his moustache, and proceeded.

At Nantwich, they had unmanned the station in the latest round of cutbacks, and the APB messages filled up an empty answerphone line.

At Ipswich, Connie gulped, took in a deep breath, checked her hair was all up again under the cap, and ran up crying to the first ticket guard she could find, announcing that a red-headed woman and a dark-haired man had stood up next to her in the carriage and stolen her wallet and got out at Aylesbury. The kindly station guard, noting her distress, and wondering rather excitedly if this was a clue and might help the capture of the two fugitives that had just flashed up on his computer screen – suspected of murder no less – that they'd been told to watch out for, and whether this would mean a raise and possibly even a commendation, led her over to the far side of the barriers saying, 'There, there,' and turned round to make a phone call, whereupon Connie also turned around and said, 'It's all right, I've just seen a policeman – wow, there's lots of them, aren't there?'

She attempted a winning smile. 'I'll go straight to him and

save you the trouble! Thanks!' and, her heart beating like a piston, nonetheless attempted to saunter casually out into the concourse, where she disappeared into the throng.

Luke waited till everyone had left the carriage, then wrenched the door open on the other side of the train, dropped down to the live rail and walked unnoticed across the tracks and out through the goods yard.

He had slipped her a piece of paper with, written on it, in odd, square handwriting, each letter equally spaced, none touching: **QUEENSFLEET**. Then a latitude and a longitude (which made her smile at the idea she might be able to use it), then, on a glowing, silvery thread, a 3-D tracing of the topography from Ipswich which moved with her as she walked across the landscape. She had not the faintest idea how he'd done it. It was exquisitely beautiful and utterly impractical as she had to hide behind a tree whenever she consulted it to keep it from others' eyes.

She was to meet him there at nightfall. She would.

Chapter Seventeen

'Oh man,' said Arnold. 'I don't know nothing, man. Can't we just get back to work on this thing?'

'While you lie through your teeth at me?' said Nigel, his fury only barely controlled.

'Oh yeah, like the way you've been totally straight up with us this entire time,' said Arnold.

Nigel opened his arms.

'It's a matter of national security. Me, someone who works for national security. I'm sorry, Julian Assange, if my chitchat doesn't fulfil your every requirement for Wikipedia-editing purposes.'

Arnold shrugged.

'Well, where's my lawyer?'

'You went past the lawyer bit about three hundred infractions ago,' said Nigel, looking round the windowless room.

'Oh, it's Jack Bauer time,' mused Arnold. 'I have always wondered how well I would stand up to torture.'

He thought about it.

'That time I got my dick caught in my zipper probably indicates not very well. But I'm ready to try. Have you got the plastic floor sheets?' He looked around. 'Can I have the water one? Rather than the screwdriver one? I am totally scared of water, I promise. Definitely put me under water rather than gouge out my eye with a screwdriver. Terrified. Of. Water.'

'We're not going to do *torture*,' said Nigel, heaving a sigh. 'We're the British Government.'

'Ah, satire,' said Arnold knowingly. 'Like it.'

'Just tell us what you know.'

'I told you,' said Arnold. 'Not a darn thing until that guinea-pig bit me.'

Nigel rolled his eyes.

'So why did you keep messing with the mikes?'

'Because you're a bunch of spying bastards, and because we couldn't talk about what we were looking at if we didn't know who was listening. We care about security too, which you may or may not believe.'

'Was Luke Beith ... was he aggressive in any way towards Connie MacAdair? Intimidating?'

'Ha, Luke?' said Arnold smiling. 'No. Not at all. Just ... I mean, he was a bit strange, but I think that's all right. Or maybe it isn't these days.'

'Strange enough to abduct someone? Strange enough to kill someone?'

Arnold considered what he was about to say, then decided it couldn't do much harm. The smaller truth would hide the greater lie.

'I don't think he'd have needed to abduct Connie,' he said. 'I think she'd have gone pretty much anywhere with him.'

'Seriously?' said Nigel. He never understood what women saw in men. 'They were an item?'

'It was a surprise to us too, man,' said Arnold, picking up his baseball cap and scratching his head. 'We all thought she'd get back with Sé. Including Sé. Can I have some coffee?'

'No.'

'Only I've got slightly addicted over the last few months, doing your dirty work.'

Nigel rolled his eyes.

'Sue us,' he said.

He sat down in the chair.

'So they're in a relationship?'

This added a new dimension to it.

'They ran off together?'

Arnold shrugged. 'Can I get my wound dressed?' he said, revealing some tiny tooth marks on his stout, pale calf . 'You don't know what they've been pumping into those animals up there. Probably got anthrax. It's really sore. Torture.'

They both looked at the tiny scratch together. Arnold had the grace to look slightly shamefaced about it.

'Maybe he confessed to the murder and she persuaded him to go on the run,' said Malik in the hastily assembled incident room at the police station.

'She doesn't exactly seem like the Bonnie and Clyde type,' said Nigel.

'People do crazy things for love all the time,' said Malik, who did not look a crazy-things-for-love sort. He looked a going-to-the-garden-centre-on-a-Sunday sort.

'You've seen what comes in here on a Monday morning.'

Nigel shrugged.

'Where are we?'

Malik pulled up the CCTV footage of the vivisection lab. It was grainy, and both Connie and Luke had their backs to the camera. Luke was doing something to the lock, but it was impossible to make out what it was.

'Did he have a master key?' wondered Nigel. 'Or did he steal it from somewhere?'

'Nobody's mentioned it,' said Malik. 'Every one of the

biologists showed up with their own key, and they're sitting polygraphs right now to see if any of them could have helped these guys, but no luck so far. It's a six-inch bolt, and it looks destroyed. Must have been a tool of some sort.'

Nigel blinked.

'So it was planned.'

'His rooms are empty,' said Malik.

'We know,' said Nigel.

'Hers aren't. Looks spur of the moment.'

Malik looked knowledgeable.

'She left behind her Ladyshave.'

'That's a sign?'

'Women running away of their own free will with men they genuinely like,' said Malik, '*always* take their hair removal products.'

Nigel looked around the nearly empty room. It was almost six o'clock. 'Where is everyone?'

Malik raised an eyebrow at one of the few young police officers there.

'Still out with animal control, sir,' said one of the younger recruits. 'Children are ... they're not over the moon about giving the rabbits back if you want to know the truth, sir.'

Nigel put his head in his hands.

'You're telling me we have a potential major criminal on the run—' *And civilisation hanging in the balance*, he didn't add. '—and your police force are out fighting children for guinea-pigs?'

There was an embarrassed silence. Malik cleared his throat.

'Just ... tell everyone they can keep the animals they find and get back to the police station, stat.,' he said as the young officer got on the phone.

There was another pause.

'Um, except the monkeys,' said Malik. 'We need the monkeys back.'

Nigel rolled his eyes and called Annabel to say he'd be late. Annabel got out of bed, where she had been lying, wondering if she could tempt him into ravaging her with this very slutty nightie she'd been talked into buying at an ill-advised Ann Summers evening with the girls. She looked at herself in the mirror and sighed, then shoved it to the back of the wardrobe and put her old, comfy dressing-gown back on.

'Okay,' said Nigel. 'Arrest warrant. Tell Interpol. Luke Beith. For murder. Possible abduction. Possibly dangerous.'

Connie stumbled across fields under a pinkening sky. It was the oddest thing, the beautiful, shining map Luke had given her: it went as the crow flies, directly east. So once she had passed the outskirts of Ipswich, with its long streets of mattress warehouses and discount deals, she dodged under ditches and stiles, tried to follow footpaths but always went across every immaculately marked field, through the alleyways of tiny villages.

She saw almost nobody. It was a sleepy, late-spring evening in a quiet part of the country. Even as she grew closer to Queen's Fleet, near Felixstowe, where the huge ferries made their way to the Hook of Holland, and goods rumbled in on great lorries from all across the worlds – cars, toys, steel, cheese, silk – she saw only an occasional tractor in the distance; the odd lonely rep's car driving across the hillsides, taking the scenic route from Lowestoft to Carlisle or from Ipswich to Manchester.

Forcing herself onwards so she didn't miss him, she thought with fluttery panic about everything they'd done. They were on the run. It seemed so strange, so unlikely on a beautiful English evening.

It didn't happen to nice girls like her, with cycling proficiency tests. She was a member of the National Trust! Well, she wasn't. But she'd been meaning to get round to it for absolutely ages. Also once, guiltily, she had ordered something out of the Boden catalogue, even though she didn't have any of the cute, smocking-clad children required. The catalogues had followed her when she'd moved, though she hadn't told anyone her new address. Maybe that's how they'd track her down. Through Boden. Like Hogwarts letters, only more lethal.

She sighed. She couldn't think of the craziness of what she was doing; of what her parents might think if – *when*– they found out. That they would find them gone, and blame them, of course, for the death of Professor Hirati which she was sure – was absolutely, definitely almost sure – that Luke had nothing to do with.

That even without that, they had committed a crime in the biology labs for sure; criminal damage would be the absolute least of it. She was, whatever happened, in serious trouble.

She couldn't think of that now. She could only focus on one thing. And when she did, the panic didn't seem so bad any more; the fear not so strong. She focused on the smell and the feel and the touch of him; on Luke. The whisper of salt in his hair; the strength that belied his slim frame; the way he looked into her, into all of her.

It was worth it, she told herself. It was worth it, even as she stamped on, alone and weary; lost, but following the line he had drawn for her.

If they could save him. If she could help save him. Even if they couldn't save him. All she needed was to spend some time with him. To see him. That was all she could focus on now. It was all she wanted.

It was unusually hot. She had slipped her jacket off some time ago, but couldn't risk taking off the hat and letting her hair show. She had tied it back as tightly as she could manage, but red-gold fronds persisted in freeing themselves and, as her forehead got damp, sticking to her head.

She stopped in a sleepy-looking village with one pub and one shop. There wouldn't be a huge manhunt for them would there? Would it have reached that far? Would their friends have betrayed them? It wouldn't be Arnold, she was pretty sure of that: she knew how he felt about authority. Evelyn, ditto. Plus, she was her friend. Sé – could she count on him? He was so hard to read. But if he meant what he said about protecting her ... then he would. But she worried about Ranjit. It wasn't even necessarily that he would mean it; she was just concerned that they would offer him an ice cream or something and he would spill the beans by mistake.

Anyway, she had to risk it, because otherwise she was so hot and thirsty she was going to pass out and the whole thing would have been pointless anyway.

There was a young, plump girl behind the counter of the little Spar. Connie bought two sandwiches, a large bottle of water, some bananas and nuts for energy and a couple of bars of chocolate. Then, on further consideration, some more chocolate. She had planned to say something along the lines of, 'Hot out cross-country walking today,' but the girl was absolutely fixated on her phone – it crossed Connie's mind how much harder it would have been to escape something before people started being obsessed with looking at their phones every single second of the day – so instead she just passed over the money in silence, grunted and quickly left. The girl barely lifted her head. That was good, Connie thought.

Nigel was still trying to contain them through normal means, without throwing open details of the facility to all the world. The train stations, the ferry ports, the airports, the motorway service stations: they were all on full lockdown. Anyone leaving the country that night – particularly Caucasian couples – were in for a slow and tedious time of it and would complain, as they always did, that Britain was absolutely broken, and maybe they should go abroad and stay abroad when they were treated like criminals in their own country, and the security guards tried to stay calm and not rise to belligerence even as the evening wore on and people had had more opportunity to drink while waiting for their delayed flights and boats, and a general sense of unease would settle over the land, exacerbated, as it always was, by a warm night and a full moon. A&E would be busy.

Connie reached Queen's Fleet at full sundown, just after 8.30 p.m. In other circumstances it would have been the most beautiful evening.

She wondered idly what Luke's plan was. Presumably it had something to do with the big ferries she could see from here, ploughing their way between eastern England and the Netherlands. She hoped he didn't mean for them to stow away on one. It couldn't be that easy. Or worse – there were some weekend hobby boats bobbing around the little jetties at the edge of the river. Surely he wouldn't . . .

She thought of his extraordinary strength, and wondered about that. With Luke, it was difficult to know exactly what he thought was possible; whether he even knew himself. She took a long pull of water and ate another bar of chocolate. She wished she could phone somebody, but their phones had been confiscated. She still missed it. But who would believe her? Her dad?

Under the rising moon and the pink and purple sky, she waited for Luke, waited and waited, staring at the sky, carefully hidden under a huge, spreading oak tree that gave her a view of every inlet without being seen. But it was no use.

175

Sleepless night after sleepless night, and a fifteen-mile tramp across the flatlands and moors of eastern England finally overcame her and, as the last pink frond lit up the distant horizon and the lights of the ferry boats turned into enchanted fairy ships, and the oil rigs on the distant horizon lit up like Christmas trees, she fell fast asleep.

'We've had reports that they robbed someone of their wallet,' said the young constable, nervously rubbing his acne.

'Okay, good,' said Nigel, looking at what so far was a very bare incident board. There had been a possible sighting at the railway station, round about the right time, but there were about forty destinations they could possibly have got off at, if they hadn't just alighted at the next stop and walked home.

'What was the name of the vic?'

'Ah,' said the policeman, looking up from the report.

'"Ah" what?' said Nigel.

'Ah, well, anyway, the girl was talking to the man at the station then she said it would be quicker just to tell the policeman and went off to tell the policeman.'

'Good. Which policeman?'

'Ah. Well. It turns out no policeman, sir. Railway Supervisor Kenneth Turlington called it in from Ipswich, said we'd have it already but he just wanted to cross the t's and dot the i's.'

Nigel stood up.

'Really? None of our boys have anything? Nothing came in?'

PC Mbele shook his head, anxiously.

'Nothing at all, sir.'

'Well, that's brilliant,' said Nigel, marching to the map.

'Sir?' said the constable, who'd thought he was in for an almighty bollocking.

'Well, yes,' explained Nigel kindly. 'If a girl got robbed and didn't make a police report – with a bunch of policemen right there – about her wallet, when she said she was going to, any ideas as to who she might be?'

The light dawned in the PC's eyes.

'Was it her do you think?'

'Any mention of hair colour?'

The PC looked down. 'Just a hat.'

'A hat. On a twenty-six-degree day.' Nigel ran over to Ipswich and stuck a pin in the map.

'FINALLY,' he said. 'A breakthrough. Well done, that railway station man.'

He looked at it closely.

'I wonder if they've split up,' he said. 'Would make sense.'

He traced a line with his finger on the map.

'Where would you go from here, DCI?'

Malik approached it with a frown, and followed the line of Nigel's finger.

'Felixstowe,' he said. 'You change at Ipswich.' Then he laughed. 'You know we spend half our time opening those lorries coming *in*to the UK.' He shook his head. 'Will make a bit of difference doing it the other way round.'

Nigel nodded.

'Yup, up the ferry port security, both ends,' said Nigel. 'You know, if I was going to sneak out the country, that's what I'd have done.'

'Not me,' said Malik promptly.

'Oh no?'

'Nope. Big party hat on, join a stag night conga line, cut out a pretend passport from a kiddies' colouring book and samba through Stansted at 5 a.m., the big dozy buggers.'

'Interesting,' said Nigel. 'Well, we'll call them too.'

The young coppers got on the phones, then jumped into their cars to get to Felixstowe to give the local boys a hand. PC Mbele brought sixty extra evidence bags.

'What are those for?' said Nigel. 'Two pairs of handcuffs should just about cover it?'

'You won't believe the other shit we'll turn up, sir,' said Malik. 'Incidental, like.'

'No, I suppose not,' said Nigel. He'd never been a policeman, and he knew they knew it. He hoped it wouldn't hold them back.

Chapter Eighteen

Connie didn't know how long he'd been standing there, nor what exactly woke her. All she knew was that she was in the middle of the loveliest dream, where the air was soft and warm and smelled of the sea, and everyone else had gone away and there was nobody else in the world except Luke, he was there, standing in front of her, smiling that uncertain, lopsided gentle smile at her, the one that went straight to her heart, that felt that it had only ever been for her, and she knew for absolute certain that everything was going to be all right, that it was all going to be completely and absolutely fine as long as they were together, she knew it absolutely for certain.

Then she breathed in and something woke her – a honking from one of the ferries just round the landing – and her eyes blinked open and couldn't focus and for a horrible moment all she could see was a shape in front of her, dark, blotting out the stars, and then sleep fell off her like dust and she saw it was Luke and was just about to shout his name when he put his finger to his lips.

'Sssh,' he said, but his eyes were dancing with mischief.

'How long have you been standing there?' she demanded quietly, her heart beating fast, all happy and terrified all at once, adrenalin shooting through her just at the very sight of him.

'Um. Less long than would be creepy?' he volunteered, and she smiled at him and stood up, facing him.

Connie realised suddenly she had never wanted to kiss somebody more in her entire life, not even the first time she was ever kissed (age fourteen, Math Olympiad training in Bath: Chester Carson, the fifteen-year-old superstar who had won a gold medal at the IMO the year before, who was greeted like the rock star he resembled. Now he posted lots of pictures of himself on his jet ski in his Hamptons house. More pictures, Connie occasionally thought, than someone who was truly fulfilled and happy would bother to post of themselves. He had never followed up that early promise in research terms; had taken the grant cash and made it work for him. Each to their own, she supposed. She was the one on the run from the police sleeping on the beach).

But now, with Luke here, standing in front of her – now it was a stronger impulse than any she had ever felt. She swallowed hard, and blinked. NO. No. It was ridiculous. She had seen his arm with her own eyes, she knew it was wrong and he was different.

But it didn't change how she felt about him. How much she longed to be in his arms again. She took a step towards him.

'It is good to see you,' he said.

She told herself to stop it. It was ridiculous. This was ridiculous.

'Would you like some chocolate?' she said. A confused expression passed over his face.

'Um, I don't know,' he said. 'Would I?'

'It's biscuit,' said Connie, in case that was important. Oh for goodness' sake, she thought, stop being such an idiot.

Luke regarded the piece of chocolate carefully.

'You eat it,' added Connie helpfully.

He sat down cross-legged, and she moved closer towards him. He unwrapped the bar carefully, then sniffed it and snapped off a piece. Connie giggled suddenly.

'What?'

'You doing alien stuff.'

'Hey,' he said, hurt. 'I was actually doing very brilliantly until they found me! You're the civilisation that puts holes through your own skin for fun.'

'True,' said Connie.

'And have stupid bony legs that nobody likes using. Nobody likes them; it's not just me.'

Luke bit into the chocolate.

'Oh,' he said. 'Oh. Well.'

Connie laughed. 'Don't get your nose stuck in the honey pot.'

'I shall arrange my I-don't-understand-this-cultural-reference face,' said Luke gravely, which made her giggle even more.

'What do you mean people don't like using their legs?'

'Oh, the round moving things,' said Luke. He ate another square of chocolate.

'See, what's interesting about this is that it melts at thirty-eight Celsius, which is the same ambient temperature as a healthy body, which gives it a particularly luxuriant ...'

'Luke,' said Connie. 'I'm an Earth girl. I can assure you, there is very little you need to tell me in the way of chocolate. What do you mean "round moving thing"?'

Luke waved his long fingers. 'You know, car things.'

'Car things. Do you mean, "cars"?'

'Yes,' said Luke. 'Why do people move about that way?'

'Because it's quicker?'

'So what? It's bad for you and bad for the air you breathe and bad for people who fall in front of them and bad for children

181

who get stuck in them and bad for trees that get in their way and bad for countries that fuel them. Why can't you just go places a bit slower on your big stick things?'

'Because ... um. Hmm. Because we have to get overseas in a huge hurry?' She glanced at him. 'So do you ... I mean, were you thinking about ... I mean, how we're going to get to Belarus?'

Connie didn't want to admit she only roughly remembered the bare facts of Belarus from school. Now they were on the very edge of England, on the very cusp of adventure, she very much hoped he had a plan.

Luke took her hand and helped her up. Then they both turned round to stare at the sea. Luke let out a great sigh.

'Oh,' he said.

'Is it hard to look out on the water?' said Connie.

'Why do you think I moved somewhere I couldn't see any?' said Luke. 'Not a thing. Completely land-locked.'

His gaze didn't move from the waves.

'Otherwise it is too hard, you know?'

He turned to her.

'It is already too hard. Are you sure you want to come? It isn't too late to turn back.'

She shook her head.

'It is for me,' she said simply. They looked out at the waves. 'Are we going to catch a ferry?'

'A what?'

'A ferry. The boats. Down there? See?'

Luke glanced at them very briefly.

'Those are boats?'

Connie started to get seriously worried now. What if she'd run away with an alien version of Ranjit? What if he had absolutely no idea what to do? She had no idea how to get them to Belarus. She had absolutely no idea what they were

182

doing at all. In a crazed rush of infatuation she had done this, had run away with him, and now . . .

'Luke, have you any idea how we're going to get there?'

She tried to keep the note of panic out of her voice.

He turned to her, smiling.

'Of course. Of course I do.'

He gently caressed her hair again. It seemed to soothe him; the hat had fallen off while she was sleeping.

'We're going to swim.'

At first she'd just laughed, then wondered if she was in some madman's dream, that the entire thing had been some kind of an illusion, that she'd been totally taken in. Luke hadn't noticed her laughing, simply started taking off his jacket.

'Do you have a bag?' he said. 'Is it waterproof?'

She did have a plastic bag inside her rucksack, and he took it from her and started filling it.

'Look, I can . . . I mean, I can swim, but I can swim for, like ten minutes.'

Connie was babbling.

'I mean, I know it's summer, but that's the North Sea – it really does get too cold, I mean, people die in there all the time. And it's . . . I mean, it's miles to Europe, really far. It takes the boats hours. I know . . . I mean, I know you say you could do it and you're kind of a fish thing and everything but me, no. I can't do it. I thought . . . I thought we were going to sneak onto a ferry or something.'

Her voice quietened.

'Well, I didn't even really think that far.'

Luke eyes were amused.

'Do you think I won't help you?'

'I don't think it will matter,' said Connie. 'Unless you carry, like, an inflatable lifeboat underneath your skin.'

They looked at one another.

Luke stepped closer.

'It's okay,' he said. 'I'll help you. Can you trust me?'

Connie thought briefly where trusting him had led her to.

'I want to,' she said.

'Well,' said Luke happily. 'That ought to help. Come with me.'

'I don't have my cossie,' said Connie weakly.

'That's okay,' said Luke. 'I don't know what the rude bits are.'

'Well, keep your underpants on,' said Connie, watching him as he ran into the water, then turned back. Standing, slim and straight, his face smiling at her, she felt her heart leap.

'Come on! Come on! Put your clothes in the bag and come on! Come, swim with me.'

Connie's heart was beating nineteen to the dozen. She couldn't possibly. She couldn't . . . Maybe if she swam a little, near where she could see the land . . . this was madness. This was absolutely and completely crazy.

'In for a penny,' she shouted, pulling off her shirt and trousers and tearing down the beach.

Connie was out of her depth, and she knew it.

But on they swam, deeper into the dark water. The surface was still warm, but as Connie kicked her legs underneath she could feel its cold, dark pull beneath her. The lights of the Folkestone ferries were just visible to her right over her shoulder. She turned and paddled lightly on her back to watch Luke. He was clumsy in the water, moving with a kind of awkward doggy paddle, the sealed bag bundled over his shoulder.

'I thought you'd be a really good swimmer,' she said, frowning. 'I thought you being half fish and all that.'

Luke smiled. In contrast to her nerves and fear, he was completely and utterly relaxed.

'Just you watch,' he said, suddenly sounding wolfish. 'I'm coming for you.'

She giggled and squealed in the water, getting away from him, splashing her face as she laughed out loud and did a somersault in the water.

Connie had always loved to swim but it had been so long. She gasped at the cold of the water – although she was getting used to it, enjoying the large waves buffeting her; feeling, for the first time in ages, free. Even with everything that was going on and the way things were going, out here, under the stars, the lights of England behind them, just the two of them in the water ... They moved out further, and Connie felt herself become slightly nervous about how far away from land they were. But he could rescue her, couldn't he?

Treading water, she turned and looked round for Luke again feeling, as she did so, how cold the water had become under her toes. He caught sight of her, held her gaze, one second, two – then he was gone in a flash: he had dived underwater.

Connie looked for where he was, and then saw, suddenly, something else: a phosphorescent sparkle on the waves. Something was underneath her, flicking in and out underneath her legs, glittering. Something ... she realised was Luke.

Her heart started beating fast. She fought panic, realising that the sweet, mild, eccentric man she'd got to know over the last few months ... had gone; had disappeared, was nothing like the same as her and around her instead was this blur of flashing lights, shimmering and moving through the water like quicksilver. She felt her breath get shorter in her throat; looked at the land, which now seemed so far away ... What was she doing? This terrible mission, this ridiculous set of events that had led her to this awful catastrophe; that out here on a wild goose chase would be the last night of her life ... She thrashed about in the water; found herself swallowing a lungful, which made her choke and splutter as she felt panic overtake her ... She tried to push herself up and out of the water, but failed, of course, and fell back, feeling herself caught in terror's grip, and yet somehow unable to control her reactions; then she slid under the water for the second time, and thrashed about there in fear, gulping down more salt water as she did so, her throat constricting. This is absurd, she told herself, found herself thinking, I could still get back, I could still reach land. But knowing it was absurd didn't seem to be able to help her as she slipped further and further beneath the waves, the water, below its sun-warmed upper layer, now freezing, and black, and endless, and welcoming her into its huge embrace ...

She was grabbed, held on to. She couldn't feel anything – she was too numb; just conscious of a strong, warming, solid presence, and the flicker of lights invading her peripheral vision.

'Hair,' came the noise over the breath of the waves.

She choked and spluttered and, very unattractively, coughed up half the ocean. Luke laughed his familiar laugh, but it sounded deeper. She could feel him, but her eyes were tight shut.

'Is that you?' she asked stupidly when she'd stopped retching, still keeping her eyes closed.

She told herself it was because they were full of stinging sea water, and not because she was too terrified to see what Luke had become.

She was in his arms, she could feel that much, and they felt like arms, but they were much bigger and more powerful than in the physical shape she knew – damp, but warmer than her own skin. He held onto her tightly and she felt a powerful chest close by her. And she became aware now that they were moving, clipping through the waves many times faster than she could swim, or even a boat could travel.

'Are you keeping your eyes shut for a reason?'

Luke sounded so like himself, his normal, amused tones, even in a lower register – that she couldn't believe it wasn't him. She quickly opened her eyes, then slammed them shut again.

She was pressed against the chest, the strong, large, translucent chest of . . .

'Oh shit,' she said.

'I know,' said Luke. 'Trust me, I'd have really liked to have been a hairy pathological liar with bones all this time too.'

'You said you didn't have a tail,' said Connie in an accusatory manner, as they zoomed along through the waves as if . . . Well, as if being carried along by a powerful sea creature. She sighed.

'I don't,' said Luke. 'Have a look. Nobody asked me about fins.'

'You have fins.'

'I have fins.'

There was a pause. All that could be heard was the splashing of the waves.

'I might open one eye.'

'Do that,' said Luke. 'You're not the only one looking for the first time.'

'What do you mean?' said Connie.

'Oh. I can see fine under the water, when it's dark enough. No problem at all. I can see you now.'

Her heart started to beat more quickly again. She knew she should have done that swimwear diet. Too many of Evelyn's cookies. This was, she was instantly aware, a completely stupid thing to be worrying about at this juncture. What if her shape was horrible to him? What if he hadn't seen her before and now couldn't believe what she actually looked like ...? Nerves threatened to overtake her again

'Um, and?'

There was a pause. Everything suddenly seemed very quiet, under the dark of the summer moon, the shimmering stars within touching distance; the water no longer cold from the warm proximity of him.

Suddenly they stopped moving so fast, although he still held her in the crook of his arm.

'Open your eyes,' he said. Connie took a deep breath.

'I mean it. Open your eyes. Please. Look at me, Connie. At who I truly am. Everything I am.'

Connie bit her lip hard, counted to three, took a deep breath – and opened her eyes.

The lights of the shoreline had totally faded from view now; they were only in the North Sea, she knew, but it felt like they were far, far out in the middle of a totally deserted ocean instead of one of the busiest sea routes in the world. At first she couldn't properly see him: he was simply an outline of stars against a backdrop of greater stars; a movement in the sky.

Then her eyes focused and she could look at him more closely; took in his features – still there, more or less – a little larger, the eyes now less huge in the face; even the hair, although it was now completely colourless, was still thick and curled down his head. He was smiling. His strong body, through which the stars raced and the water could be seen, was the real difference: larger and slender; muscled. He was so obviously his true self, sleek and free; he looked as at home in the water as a dolphin. He held her as she looked.

'Oh, thank God,' she murmured.

'What were you expecting – eel?'

'Yes,' said Connie. 'Yes. Maybe. Bit more eel.'

'I'm not an eel,' he said, looking at her through the waves.

'You ...' She felt strange saying the words, but she didn't know how not to. 'You are beautiful.'

Luke smiled, bent his huge head so the stars popped out once again behind it, even though at the same time she could almost see through him. It was very discomfiting.

'So are you,' he said.

'No, I'm ...'

Connie looked down, but Luke hushed her.

'Ssh,' he said. 'Oh GOD, it is good to be back in the water. SO GOOD. You know, right now I don't care if they catch us in five minutes and I don't care if they shoot us out of the sky and I don't care if I get harpooned like a ...'

'Like a what?'

'I don't know. You do bad things to them. We have a version.'

'Whales?'

He nodded. 'Kind of. Except ours make excellent systems analysts.'

Connie stared at him.

'I need a run, a proper run. I have been cramped inside that body for years. For YEARS. It was like living in a tiny cell. Like a coffin. This entire world is plagued with fishermen, do you know that? I couldn't risk it, not once, not ever.'

He shivered, water flowing down his neck.

'And even if you and I have buggered up the entire world, Hair – even if we have answered a call that should have been ignored; could have been prevented – you have set me free. Thank you. Thank you for setting me free.'

189

He put his large arm around her waist.

'Want to go for a run?'

It was the most astonishing sensation Connie had ever know. Before, she had thought they were moving quickly through the water, but that was as nothing to now. He ploughed through it like they were galloping downhill. One kick of his strong legs and they shot off above the waves, although sometimes, holding her aloft like precious baggage, he would dive underneath; flicker and gallop in the depths. Once he threw her in front of him in the water then darted to catch her, which at first terrified her, then made her giggle so much he did it again and again, veering up above the water like Neptune, then darting through its churning wake. It was like being tossed around by a cloud. Connie lost track of up or down; couldn't believe the astonishing sensation of freedom, of speed, of pure liquid joy as she moved along with him in his arms; spiralling or flying as he tossed her like mistletoe across the sea; and she opened her arms and laughed hysterically, yelling as the waves and the wind caught all sound from her mouth before it could be uttered.

They were lucky, and pinged on passing radars as nothing more than a twisting shoal of fish, unremarkable in the dark, except for one lady returning on a booze cruise hen party to Felixstowe, who stared blearily at them from the top deck, where she stood all alone on a warm, windy crossing, wondering if she was going to throw up or not, who watched through doubled eyes the pair dance, and blinked, and thought gloomily that it really was time to get her life sorted out, and decided to do so. Then she went home and chucked her crap boyfriend, Gordon, who never took her swimming in the sea, and became a spirit healer and dolphin trainer, and lived a long, lucrative and happy life doing so.

When the lights of Holland came into view they finally stopped, both of them out of breath, both giggling hysterically. Connie was hot, although she knew the water must be cold. Luke was so strange, so alien; magnificent in the strangest of ways. But he was still himself.

'4.13418,' he said, frowning. 'We must be nearly there.'

'Or we could just look at the lights and, you know, go to the big lit-up place over there,' she said.

His face fell as he slowed down.

'I'll have to change back.'

She nodded.

'I know.'

'I don't . . . I don't want to.'

'Can't you swim all the way around?'

'Around that top wobbly bit?' he said. 'One, it would kill you, and two, they'd harpoon me for something. Can't get away with much round there. No. Always stick to the latitude.'

He sighed, his great chest rippling above the waves. Connie thought all he was missing was the trident.

'And now,' he said. 'Now, when we reach land I must fold myself up again, back into my coffin of skin and colour and' – his voice shook – 'bone.'

'Come here,' she said to him.

But he was already there. And suddenly, she was in his arms, and closer to him; he was encircling her entirely, and the sound of his heart beating was the only thing in her ears.

She didn't know what she wanted to do. Did she want to kiss him? Did he kiss? Did they? But she could feel him breathing. And she knew, she just knew – regardless of the fact that he was from a totally different species, from the other end of the galaxy. Connie had been unsure about a lot of things in this life, but she wasn't in the least bit unsure about this one.

He looked at her, their faces nearly touching; his heart visible, a cluster of pulsating lights.

'Can I ... ?'

She tailed off.

'Are you going to ask me a question about spawn?' he said.

'No, I ... '

There was a pause.

'Well, yes. Spawn might have crossed my mind.'

'Well, are you full of a thousand million eggs?' said Luke.

'No,' said Connie. 'But I do have one. Which, you know.'

'Ssh,' he said. 'We're completely incompatible.'

'Well, that's strange,' said Connie. 'Because, one, in *Independence Day* all the aliens had USB ports. And two ... '

She stared straight into those deep dark eyes.

'I don't feel in the ... I don't feel in the least bit incompatible with you.'

It was true. He looked different, but it was still ... it was still Luke in there. Still him, even though he did look different. Connie told herself it was as if he'd been in an accident. She wasn't ... it wasn't like she was doing anything bad. She wasn't trying to kiss a dolphin. Was she? No. She half laughed to herself.

'Is this always this embarrassing?' said Luke, stretching his long arms outwards back in the water, which rippled across his incredibly broad chest.

'Actually, yes,' said Connie suddenly. She was amazed how reassuring she found this realisation. 'Actually, yes, it is always completely embarrassing. Have you got any booze in my bag?'

'Really?'

'Always,' said Connie. 'But tonight I would say doubly so.'

Luke smiled at her, but it was a confident smile, not a nervous one.

'You're like Superman,' she said. 'You totally are. All shy

with the horn-rimmed spectacles, but get your cloak on and look at you.'

She laughed suddenly, despite herself.

'Ha. In your element.'

Luke shook his head.

'I don't understand.'

'Of course you don't.'

She thought about it.

'Oh,' she said. 'I forgot to ask. I don't know how I could forget to ask, but I forgot to ask.'

Luke – or this beautiful, glistening, sparkling creature that was also Luke – tilted his great head.

Connie swallowed.

'Are you,' she said in a small voice. 'Are you a boy or a girl?'

Luke put back his head and gave a shout of laughter.

'Humans are *obsessed* with gender,' he said. 'I don't think you even realise how weirdly obsessed you are. What are you?'

'Seriously?' said Connie. 'You're asking me this now?'

'It's not a very important question to me.'

'Oh,' said Connie. 'Well. I'm a girl.'

Luke nodded.

'And . . . ?' said Connie.

'Well, gender is more fluid where I come from,' said Luke. 'You can change it; transition.' He shrugged. 'It's not a massive deal.'

'How many are there?'

'Four.'

Connie's eyebrows shot up.

'Okay,' she said, treading water. 'And which would you say you were at the moment?'

There was a slight pause. She wondered if he would tell the truth. Then she realised that of course it would not matter; her heart was racing so fast she felt like it would burst.

'Not sure,' said Luke. 'It doesn't really translate. Is it important?'

'Oh lord,' Connie said to herself. She moved closer and put her hand on his jaw. She closed her eyes one last time, then opened them again, her heart beating more wildly.

'Do you kiss?'

He shook his head. 'The lip thing?'

'Uh yeah. The lip thing.'

'That looks weird to me.'

'Ha HA! Yes, THAT is what's weird.'

She had been trying to ignore the inevitable, but she couldn't help it and tried to look under the water.

'Oi,' he said, smiling. 'Are you looking for that bit? It is that bit, isn't it?'

Connie couldn't stop giggling.

'Generally.'

Suddenly she felt his strong arm grab her and pull her close to him, chest to chest. She looked up at him; thrilled, excited – terrified.

'Shall we try it my way?' he enquired.

'Oh,' she said. 'OH.'

He pulled her close to his chest, and carried on encircling her until there was not a single part of her exposed to the elements and he was all around, covering every inch of her skin, absorbing her: she was inside him.

And after that Connie understood only two things: colours were unimportant when you could feel the explosions of the stars running through your veins and every drop of liquid in you shone like the sun – and she understood why Luke hadn't the faintest idea where his erogenous zones were. He was nothing but.

Chapter Nineteen

'Nothing, boss.'

Nigel swore. He had been so sure. He had held up the entire night's ferry timetable; cross-checked every walk-up and every ticket purchase; had people poring over miles of dark-tinged CCTV. He had spoken to the Netherlanders, got them to double-check everyone coming in. He had asked for radar sweeps and for boatyards to check that no one had got in and stolen a boat, although the idea of two ordinary people managing to get all the way to the Netherlands in a stolen boat across 180 kilometres of incredibly rough sea was unlikely to say the least. But there was nobody marooned, no boats unaccounted for on the scans.

'Call Holland again,' he said. 'Call them. I want searchlights up. I want everyone coming through that port to have a torch-light in the fucking face. I want men patrolling the barbed wire. I want every single lorry open and every single person trying to get somewhere cursing my name because it takes so bloody long. I want the entire *Great Escape*, do you hear me?'

Young PC Mbele reflected that some people did manage to get away in *The Great Escape*, but he didn't feel this was the right time to mention it. They'd all had a very long day, and he didn't appear to be going anywhere anytime soon, which was annoying because he had a date at the cinema with Magenta, the really hot A&E nurse. But she'd laughed that low, sweet laugh she had when he called her. She knew a bit about shifts overrunning. He smiled just thinking about her voice: it was like syrup.

'Something funny?' snapped Nigel.

'No, boss,' said PC Mbele, turning back to his phone.

Nigel stood in the door looking at Evelyn. She would be, he suspected, the toughest nut to crack. Arnold was all talk, but he wouldn't like the discomfort and would likely give them up for *Amazing Fantasy* Vol. 15. Ranjit talked a lot of rubbish and was probably a terrible choice, in retrospect, for the project. Sé was all about sitting stoically with his mouth shut, but Nigel reckoned Evelyn was the toughest of the lot.

'How are you getting on?' he said, standing in the doorframe. Evelyn had her own pile of papers she was working on half-heartedly.

'Dinner was awful,' she stated. 'And late. And I want to go home.'

Nigel looked down.

'I'm sorry,' he said. 'Last time we let you go home, two of you ran away. You do understand that?'

Evelyn made a tight jerk with her head.

'I can't believe they left you like this to pick up the pieces and pay the price for their behaviour,' said Nigel, shaking his head.

'Well, you haven't met many people then,' observed Evelyn calmly, carrying on as if she were marking undergraduate essays.

Nigel shook his head.

'You are one of a handful of people in the world who knows what they are risking,' he said. 'That without their help we might never understand the message and what it means to us. To everyone on Earth.'

Evelyn stared into space stoically. She bit her lip then turned round and opened her mouth. Nigel held his breath.

'Also, could you ask them not to be late with breakfast? It's not good for my brain alertness if I'm trying to work hungry.'

Connie had a near-perfect internal clock, always had done. When she was very little, she had been fascinated by the old grandfather clock that was screwed into the walls of the communal hallway of the big Victorian house subdivided into flats she was raised in. As soon as she could talk, she had made her father, a logistics manager at a chemical factory, teach her how the day was split into hours, and had toddled about, at three or thereabouts, announcing the time to strangers and dividing things by twelve. It was the first time the MacAdair family had first noticed something different about her, but not the last.

Ever since, Connie had kept a clock in her head almost by accident; she couldn't help herself. She always knew what time it was.

She had no idea what time it was.

They had washed ashore in a tiny inlet. As soon as Luke was no longer a part of her – and he had, she realised, blinking with astonishment, he had been a part of her, part of the whole of her, encompassing her, just as she had been a full part of him – she knew on some level she was cold. She lay on her back with her hair in the wet sand, and discovered another thing: she couldn't move. Or rather, she didn't want to move. The cosmos had lifted her up, squeezed her, wrung her dry, and now she wanted to lie here, emptied, clear, and let the echo of the afterglow run through her.

Where was Luke? Where was he? Suddenly, she sat bolt upright. She stared out at the dark waves, blinking several times to clear her vision; to adjust it again to look at the ground, not sink into eternity. She focused gradually, and stared out to sea. There he was, although she could not see him properly; he was flickering, a dense, glistening shadow underneath the water.

She put her arms around her legs, which suddenly appeared to be made completely of jelly, and rested her chin on her knees. Beside her was the plastic-bagged-up rucksack, miraculously still watertight – they really were bags for life, she thought – and she shook out Luke's coat and put it around her shoulders, and watched him flicker happily. Beyond happy. She couldn't think of anything other than that: not what they had left behind, not what they were going towards – nothing but this moment. Even if it was beyond sense . . . she couldn't think about that now, she knew; she couldn't. Couldn't think about what it meant for her. She forced herself not to dwell on it; just to keep herself in the moment.

And this was the moment: watching someone she knew she would be with, wherever they went now and whatever happened, without a question of a doubt, and without a glance back, as they ran towards whichever strange, new world they now inhabited.

There was a huge whomping noise suddenly, and a hooting alarm went off. Lights – great big spotlights that reminded Connie of a war film – suddenly flicked on up and down the barbed-wire fence of the nearby ferry port. Luke must, Connie realised suddenly, have travelled in a straight line, just as the boats did. Why hadn't he come in somewhere else? Regardless, he would barely see the light and wouldn't recognise the sirens. She jumped up and waved wildly at him.

'Luke! Luke! Come in! Come in!'

There wasn't the tiniest sliver of doubt in her mind, not an ounce, that they were looking for them. Of course they were looking for them. They held the key to the biggest thing to happen to the world since the asteroid that wiped out the dinosaurs. Her heart started to beat more quickly.

'Come in! You have to come!' she shouted, waving her arms. Finally he noticed her and surfaced, his big, clear head shaking off the droplets of water.

'I don't want to,' he said. 'I don't want to come in. I don't want to get back in there.'

'I know,' said Connie, glancing behind her. The lights were getting closer. From the furthest perimeter she thought she could hear dogs barking. They couldn't be searching them with dogs. They couldn't.

'Quick, Luke. QUICK. Quick. If they see you ... if they see you and they see you like that, you know what will happen. You know.'

For just the tiniest of seconds Luke stood there, looking defiant, glancing back at the sea she now understood why he could never bear to gaze upon; looked back for one last time at his freedom and the only place he could truly be himself.

Then, he came towards her, shuffled up the beach. With every step, as the water splashed off him, his beautiful, shining skin contracted, became more and more solid, until he was once again human-shaped, and then, as she gave him his shirt and he began to return to air temperature, the pigmentation too began to show, until he was, once again, a man – a tall, rangy man with long fingers and toes, but nonetheless a man, with dark brown eyes and a shaggy mop of curly brown hair, high cheekbones and a full mouth, which at the moment was drawn back in pain.

'Does it hurt?' asked Connie anxiously. Luke nodded, not trusting himself to speak.

'Give me a second,' he said, clear beads of sweat appearing on his forehead, which he quickly wiped away with his free hand. He grabbed her, briefly, to steady himself, and let out a small 'oh'.

'We have to move,' said Connie. 'We have to go somewhere. They've got dogs.'

'I can't . . . '

Luke could barely move: his legs wouldn't support him.

'Argh,' he said. 'Sorry.'

'It's okay,' said Connie. 'Lean on me.'

He was heavy; far heavier, of course, than he looked. She half dragged him, half stumbled up towards the cliff and up the scree.

'Oh God,' she said, her heart pounding. 'Those dogs probably can't smell you. But they will sure as hell be able to smell me.'

She kept away from the perimeter, trying to watch her feet, as gradually Luke pulled himself back together, and was able, finally – although he could not yet speak – to keep up with her, both of their breathing tight in the night air. At the top of the dune he turned round, once, very briefly, and gazed out at the roughening sea. He looked at it for a long moment. Then he turned back, grabbed her hand and they stumbled on.

'Don't stop,' Connie told herself. 'Don't look back. Never look back.'

They kept moving, only just metres ahead of the lights, it seemed, that were pointing behind them, as the port and the town and the road were lit up, *bang bang bang*, the light chasing them across the darkness of the great continent that lay before them, and they ran until Connie was exhausted, Luke hurling her over walls and fences if she needed that, and offering to carry her, which she felt would only slow them down even further.

'Go!' She pushed on, muttering under her breath. 'Go, go, go.'

But the noises of the dogs and the sirens seemed to be

falling behind them. She looked up, incredibly grateful there was no helicopter. Then she tripped in a dark ditch, and fell straight into a barbed-wire fence.

'Shit,' Nigel was saying. 'Shit shit shit. It's been hours. They could be anywhere by now.'

'We're still searching the ferries,' said Malik. 'There's a million places to hide on those. We don't know if they even took one. They might still be hiding down Ipswich way. We've got the helicopters out. We've got as much manpower as we can summon.'

'It's not enough,' growled Nigel.

'This isn't an ordinary manhunt, is it, sir?' said Malik.

Nigel didn't answer.

The fence seemed unending in either direction.

'We'll have to find another way,' said Connie.

Luke shook his head. 'This is the way,' he persisted.

'Yes, but on Earth we have these things called roads,' she said.

'Incredibly impractical,' said Luke. 'Just take the latitude.'

'But it runs you into things like this.'

Luke gave a weak smile. 'Call this a wall?' he said.

Connie was still terrified from the great commotion at the ferry port, and wasn't nearly as far away from it as she'd like to be at that precise second.

'Can we go please?' she said anxiously. 'I don't care where. Just keep moving.'

Luke nodded. Behind the barbed-wire fence were lines and lines of trucks. Connie looked up and down but she couldn't see a camera.

'Through,' said Luke without hesitation. 'The best way out is always through.'

He picked her up by the waist and held her over the wire, letting her feel with her feet on the other side. She saw the lights, bright at the port beyond, and shut her eyes briefly. When she opened them again, he hadn't moved or changed: he was still holding her straight up in the air like a ballet dancer, without the least strain or effort.

Lightly she lowered herself down the other side. Luke clambered to the top of the barbed wire – the sharp points didn't seem to bother him – and jumped down lightly.

'Wow,' said Connie, following him down.

They were in a large scrubby area, dimly lit, full of lorries. It was dark and gloomy. There were, Connie assumed, people asleep in the lorries, which gave it a sinister atmosphere. Sure enough, she could see three men around a campfire at the bottom end of the field, lit ends of their cigarettes going. She stayed in close to the edge, flattening herself out of sight, breathing heavily and wondering what on earth they were going to do next.

Luke wandered closer up to the men. He stayed behind in the shadows, Connie watching him, wondering what on earth he had planned. He stayed, quiet, listening, then snuck back.

'Well?' said Connie.

'They're on their way to Poland,' he said. 'Making jokes about being stopped and searched, wondering what the hell for. They don't think there's anything to transport out of England except rain and fish and chips and fat children. Sorry, would Evelyn say that is rude?'

'You speak Polish?'

'What do you mean?' said Luke.

'You understood what they said?'

'I don't understand what you're asking me now.'

'You know there are different languages? That people speak differently?'

'Ohhh. Yes. I do know that. I just forgot. So you wouldn't understand him?'

Connie shook her head. 'Not a word, no. Of course not. Can't you tell he speaks entirely differently from me?'

'Everyone speaks differently from you,' said Luke puzzled. 'Nobody sounds the same.'

'Seriously?'

'Do you think you sound like Ranjit? You don't to me.'

'But you seriously understand everything everybody says?'

'Of course,' said Luke. 'It's just mouth shapes and noises that apply to subjective worldviews.' He looked confused. 'You know those very large brains humans haul about everywhere that weigh down the rest of you?'

'Hmm?'

'You could probably use them a bit more efficiently.'

Somewhere, from across the distant field, a faint church bell rang. The men around the campfire looked at their watches: 2 a.m. They worked to tightly controlled shifts on how long they could drive for, and a new one was just beginning. They threw their cigarette ends into the fire and started to disperse, anxious to get going.

'Luke,' said Connie. 'Can we ...? I mean, Belarus is that way, isn't it? If we go with them?'

'What do you mean?'

She rolled her eyes. 'They drive these things. What did you think they were?'

Luke regarded the lorries all around them.

'Oh. Yes.'

'Well, they move,' said Connie, 'in the direction of Belarus, unless my geography is worse than I thought, which it isn't because I got straight As in everything.'

'Oh,' said Luke.

'How on *earth* did you make it coming the other way?'

'I just walked in a straight line,' said Luke, 'until I found some maths.'

'How long did it take you?'

Luke squinted. '5.2. About three months.'

'We've got three days,' said Connie, threading her way through the trucks until she came upon one just starting off. It was huge, oppressively big, each of its enormous twelve wheels nearly the height of her. Some words she couldn't read were written on the side, along with WARSAWSKA. She nudged Luke. 'That one,' she said.

Lightly, he jumped up the back plate and, with a quick downward pull, opened the lorry's huge strong lock. The noise of the engines was incredibly loud, and the cab of the truck was on a suspension pivot. The driver did not feel the weight of their arrival: compared to the contents under the tarp, it was nothing. They slipped inside the door and rebolted it, just as the huge beast started to slowly pull away.

There was a flap of tied-down canvas at the side of the truck and Connie threw herself on the ground and peered through it. She saw a light at the gate of the lorry park. To her horror, there were men with dogs on leads patrolling it.

'Oh God,' she said. 'Oh bollocks. They're going to catch us.'

'How?' asked Luke mildly.

'They'll smell us. Well, they'll smell me.'

'The people?'

'The dogs,' said Connie. 'Bugger. We've got so far.'

Luke blinked.

'Why won't they smell me?'

'I don't know. It's hard to understand. You don't smell like person. Nothing like. You smell good, but you don't have a human smell. I don't think they could find you, I truly don't.'

Connie remembered the way the dog at the railway station

and the animals at the facility had completely ignored him. She didn't think they were fooled by his human glamour for a second.

Something occurred to her, and she looked up and him, awkward and blushing.

'Um.' She cleared her throat. 'Maybe you could do that, um. Thing again. That thing where you kind of, uh ... Completely surround me? I mean, uh, I think I ended up slightly unconscious before. That last time you ... we ... ha, ha ... did it. But ...'

Luke shook his head.

'It's too warm in here.'

Connie went brick-red.

'Uh, yes, it is,' she said. 'Um ...'

She plucked at her collar, and sighed. The cab had slowed to nearly a standstill now at the gate.

Luke whirled around wildly to look at the contents of the truck.

'What's in here? It's all stuff.'

Her eyes had gradually adjusted to the dim light.

'I don't know,' she said. There weren't, as she'd been expecting, boxes of goods; instead, the huge truck was piled high with bales. At first she thought it was rolled-up carpet, but instead, as she grew closer, she saw it was cloth: tweed, when she bent down to see it. Harris tweed.

'Quick,' he said. 'In here. If we bundle you and bundle you, maybe? Under lots of layers of other stuff?' He frowned. 'Will that work? Don't suffocate.'

'No!' said Connie desperately. 'Dogs are ... I mean, they can smell absolutely anything. All they'll do is sniff and think, "Ah, that's a load of Harris tweed next to Connie."'

'Finally,' murmured Luke. 'A species that can do cool stuff.'

Connie looked at him as he pulled off his coat, trousers and shirt and made her put them on.

'What are you doing?'

'Here,' he said. 'If I really don't give off a scent, if I really do turn dogs away, then these might help mask it.'

Connie couldn't think of a better idea. And now the lorry had come to a full halt.

She covered every inch of herself with Luke's clothes and knelt, feeling horribly exposed in the middle of the bales, unable to see. Luke knelt over her. He could not be the all-encompassing force he had been in the water, but he was still a big man, and he enveloped as much of her as he could, clasping round her ankles. The very fact of him being there was comforting, protecting and safe.

There was chatter outside from the two men, who clearly knew each other.

'Have they not found fuckers of sheep yet?'

'Don't think he go to ex-communist shit bloc to where you drive.'

'All right, orange son of bitch. Hey, does dog want sausage, I have?'

'Oh, that's why he's fuss. No, hein, he's busy looking for people that don't smell of the sausage. That smell of bad beer and are probably drunk, *hé*?'

There was a laugh from the Polish driver, who then said something Connie didn't understand.

Then there came a pause and a rustle of documents. Connie held her breath, as if terrified of releasing even a few molecules of herself into the air. She waited for the barking to begin, the tearing, growling noise of the dog, primed to get at her, to rip and hold any humans it came across. She shut her eyes tight and wondered if the dogs would bite her or whether they'd call them off when they hauled them in. She wondered if it would hurt.

Her hands started to shake and tremble, her throat choking so she could hardly breathe. Luke, his head resting on her head, attempted to gently stroke her quivering back, to calm her down, but she couldn't feel him, was lost entirely in her own fear until, with enormous slowness, a light passed over the cloth side of the truck, passed slowly along the sides, and she squeezed her eyes closer than ever and waited for the light to stop …

… but it did not, and the great vehicle itself slowly creaked into gear and lumbered forward … and forward, picking up speed, and now the lights were flashing overhead faster now: the great motorway lights high above the road, flickering past from the terminal buildings and the great junctions to Europe – south to fragrant France and warm Italy; north to the cold Scandinavian countries.

But as the lorry confidently took the road, and the flickering lights on the tarpaulin ceased and became only the occasional glare of passing headlights at this, the quietest hour of the day, Connie knew deep inside that they were going east, ever east. And even when they were moving quickly, they stayed in the same position, curled up on the dusty floor, holding each other fast, for a long, long time, until Connie had finally stopped shaking, and even beyond then, as her breathing slowed and, entirely wrung out, she gently fell asleep in his arms.

She awoke just before dawn and they looked at one another in the dim light. Connie smiled at Luke, as he handed her the bottle of water she had bought what seemed like so long ago and she took a long pull from it. Her fear had receded now they were on the road; now she was worrying what was happening to the others back in England. But there was something about the physical act of moving that made it impossible not to be at least a little bit excited. They were moving; she could feel the kilometres pass under their feet, and that, she knew, was absolutely the best she could hope for. And she didn't want to think about home, or Arnold and everyone; she wanted to move, keep moving forward, never looking behind her. She turned to the man sitting on a huge pile of brown papered pillows, lost in thought.

'Hey,' she said, smiling at him. He smiled back.

'Hey,' he said, pulling her to him. 'How are you?'

'Better thanks. How are *you* feeling?' she said. 'Are you still sore?'

He nodded. 'It's okay. It ... it doesn't pass, but I do get used to it. More used to it.'

Connie blinked and sat down next to him. She was still wearing his shirt.

'I wonder,' she said. 'I mean, you basically work like a person ... a human person, don't you?'

Luke nodded. 'Yes,' he said glumly.

Connie nodded, a smile starting to play around her mouth. She took a long drink of water, then pulled out the band she had in her hair, letting it tumble down around her ears. She knew he couldn't fail to look at it, and he did.

'You know that ... that lip thing?' she asked shyly, now she had his full attention.

Luke gazed at her.

'Mmm?'

'Have you tried it?'

'No,' he said. 'It looks weird.'

Connie laughed and widened her eyes.

'You said it. Captain Weird.'

'I am actually not at all weird,' said Luke. 'I am the most normal individual you could possibly meet.'

Connie looked at him.

'I am,' said Luke. 'I never did an interesting thing in my entire life before the wall. I grew, I studied, I swam, I ... hmm ... did a sport you don't have a word for. I did everything the Extraction wanted me to do. Then one day ...'

He waved his arms.

'Et cetera.'

'Seriously?' smiled Connie. 'Genuinely, you're dull?'

'Very dull,' said Luke. 'I like being in the water, and music, and four-dimensional regular polytopes and building structure and raisin cookies and beyond that I am not in the least bit interesting.'

Connie laughed.

'Well, you are incredibly interesting to me.'

'You say that *now*.'

She moved closer.

'Well, would you like to try something completely different?'

The fresh, clean salt smell of his skin was near her again. It was irresistible.

He smiled slightly nervously.

'What do I do?'

'Just follow me,' said Connie. 'And your instincts. They're in that shape somewhere. If you can eat a cookie and climb a fence, I reckon you might as well give this a shot.'

And as the lorry thundered through the dawn onwards, ever east, along a long, straight, flat road, past the Netherlands, past Belgium and on through northern Germany, she began, slowly and tentatively, to kiss him. And equally slowly and tentatively – at first – Luke kissed her back, then, gradually, engrossed, he became more forceful and raised his hands to weave themselves in and out of her hair, both of them breathing faster and faster.

Connie shifted, moved herself onto his knees then, modesty forgotten, simply sat astride his long legs as they kissed deeply and fiercely while the slight wailing of a Russian music CD came wobbling slightly through into the back of the truck, and the man in the cab upfront drove on at a perfectly even ninety kilometres per hour, completely oblivious to their presence.

She moved his hands up underneath her shirt.

'What are these for?' said Luke huskily, exploring.

'Doesn't matter,' she muttered. 'Just keep doing it exactly like that.'

'Oh,' he said. 'This ... this really does help.'

'Good,' she said, smiling, her breath coming short in her throat. 'Now, those zone things we were talking about ...'

Luke's face changed suddenly.

'I can feel it,' he groaned.

'So can I,' said Connie.

'I think ... I'm not sure about this. It feels like it's going to burst.'

Connie let out a short laugh, which changed to curiosity and excitement as she felt through his trousers.

'That's how it's meant to feel,' she said, breathlessly unbuttoning his shirt, and feeling downwards with her hand. 'Oh, Luke, you've made it too thick.'

Luke glanced down. 'Sorry. Oh. I can ... next time I change I can do it differently.'

'Uh, no, you know what, that's okay.'

His human shape was so smooth: hairless, and warm against hers. She took her own clothes off quickly, astonished, suddenly, at her boldness. She had never been in the least bit like this; not at all forward – quite the opposite.

But then she couldn't remember ever feeling so compelled before. Had never wanted anyone or anything so much. The memories of what had already passed between them only spurred her on. She pressed herself up against him, and they both shivered in the musty air, although it was not in the slightest bit cold.

'Now it's my turn to ask you if *you're* sure,' she whispered, smiling.

Luke nodded fiercely.

'Good,' whispered Connie 'Keep following your instincts. Trust them.'

'All my instincts are you,' he said, pressing her closer, then painfully closer still, then finally, agonisingly slowly and carefully, they were together. Sweat burst out on both of their foreheads, and Connie's hair tumbled down her back. 'Oh God. Oh God.'

And now it was Luke's turn to close his eyes as the truck rumbled on through the early dawn, and the birds started from the trees as the heavy wheels thundered past.

Chapter Twenty

'Day two.'

Evelyn had managed to hiss it out of the corner of her mouth to Arnold, as she had been marched past his room to wash and Arnold was being brought out. Arnold looked up startled.

'It's day one today!' he whispered. 'Yesterday doesn't count as a full day.'

Evelyn raised an eyebrow.

'It does to me,' she said urgently.

Arnold shook his head.

'What are you two whispering about?' said the guard unpleasantly. He disliked smart alecs.

'Where's breakfast?' said Evelyn. 'Also, we need a lawyer. Or to be charged with something.'

'Wouldn't know anything about that,' said the guard.

Breakfast was porridge. They weren't allowed to eat together. Nigel had ordered that they be kept apart to stop them conspiring about whatever it was they were up to. If they had to ask each other work-related questions, they could send each other notes. Evelyn had, of course, already mocked up some modular arithmetic steganography she expected the boys to recognise immediately but which would be inserted as a formula on each page without arousing suspicion in anyone below doctoral level. She awaited the results with interest.

Ranjit was just falling off to sleep. Nigel had sat with him for two hours. Did he never get tired?

'The thing is,' Nigel was saying, and it sounded so persuasive when he said it. 'It seems something has happened. Something that has made two of your colleagues run away. Can you understand why we are so worried by what's in that message?'

'Yes,' eeped Ranjit. He was terrified of authority. Nigel sensed he was the weak spot and pushed harder.

'Ranjit, if you know something about this signal . . . or what happened with Luke and Connie and the professor . . . if you know anything about this signal which could mean something for everyone in the world; that could influence history . . .'

He was laying it on thick, but he didn't care.

'You owe it to the world to tell us,' said Nigel. 'You owe it to use. Stop protecting your friends and tell us.'

Ranjit finally burst into huge racking uncontrollable sobs. Nigel waited for him to stop, but they only seemed to get more and more hysterical as time went on.

'What is it, Ranjit?' said Nigel. 'What do you know?'

But Ranjit only shook his head.

'No,' he said through choking sobs. 'That's not it.'

Nigel damped down his impatience.

'Well, what is it?'

Ranjit burst out into a fresh bout of tears.

'They're the only friends I've ever haaaaaad,' he wailed.

Frantic messages were passed between Evelyn and Arnold's cells all morning, and very little actual work, which didn't matter on balance. Regardless, their coding degenerated into solid insults faster than expected. Arnold wanted this to count as the first day. Evelyn wanted to give Nigel the information protocol and get it over with, get it done. They had no idea what Luke and Connie were doing nor where they were, and in the hard, cold light of day Evelyn thought it was time to give up. Neither could agree. 'They're probably lying about somewhere bonking,' said Arnold savagely at lunch when they were allowed to pass each other at the fridge.

'Don't be ridiculous,' said Evelyn stoutly. 'They're trying to save Luke is what they're doing. I'm not doubting them. But . . . '

Arnold glanced at the guards.

'Well, I fucking wish they'd hurry up with it. Did you see Ranjit's face?'

Evelyn nodded.

'I know. And I don't know how much longer we can hold them off.'

In Sé's cell, he sat alone, pretending to focus, stimming, and occasionally kicking hard at the wall without the slightest idea that he had done so. He was horrified that he had sent Connie out into the world with an alien. Horrified he had been so blind. What if Luke had done exactly the same to her as Sé still thought he might have done to the professor? What if she was lying, right now, in a copse somewhere, drained of all colour as Luke searched for his next victim, blending into the background, maybe even changing the way he looked. Maybe they'd never ever find him. And it would be his fault.

But he had made a promise.

'What the hell is going on?'

Nigel sighed. When Anyali was fierce, she didn't mess about.

'I mean, I thought you guys were trained in interrogation!

Knew how to get information out of suspects. That's what we pay you for, right?'

Nigel sighed again.

'Yes.'

'Well?'

'Well, normally we do it by separating them from their family and friends . . . putting them in a room with nothing to do, refusing them phone calls or contact with the outside world, cutting them off completely . . . I mean, that breaks most people down into a total panic with a few hours. And that's hardened crims, never mind total newbies.'

'So?'

'So I have a horrible feeling this lot don't really mind it. I'm not sure they're not having quite a relaxing time just doing sums all day in peace and quiet. One of them asked for a phone call to renew his Netflix subscription.'

Anyali let out a low hum of frustration.

'And the astronomers, they're still getting this stuff in?'

'Yes. I tried to put them together, get them to tell the other guys how to work it out, but they came out reeling.'

This had been entirely Arnold's doing. He had just cut out any filters in dealing with non-mathematicians and had told them in detail exactly what he was doing, thus completely stymieing any hope of progress.

'The PM isn't pleased.'

'Look,' said Nigel, lowering his voice. 'I think if an alien civilisation has reached us, and hasn't blown us up just yet after having heard some Miley Cyrus singles, you never know, they might be friendly. Or, they might have enough goddamn intelligence to know that this kind of stuff doesn't solve itself overnight.'

'But what did the other two read, Nigel? What do they know? What have they done?'

Nigel brought his fist down on the desk in frustration, and turned back to the cells.

The fine glittering line that outstretched from Luke's palm shimmered in the heat.

'What *is* that?' said Connie wonderingly. They were both raw, exhausted, lying companionably on a pile of Harris tweed. It was afternoon, and the lorry was jolting along. The novelty of movement had slightly worn off, but everything else to Connie was fresh and vividly alive.

Luke squinted. 'Just a bit of extra electrical energy my body doesn't need, which I can use,' he said. 'It's not very complicated. And I can see it, which is a lot better than all the screens you have around you.'

'I can't believe you have any extra energy left,' smiled Connie, but Luke was already leaping up.

'21 0,' he said. 'We're nearly here, Hair. And I think we need to go before he stops.'

Connie scrambled up, her temporary calm gone in an instant, the adrenalin shooting through her once more.

'Yup,' she said. She pulled her own clothes back on.

'Look out of the covering thing,' Luke said. 'Are we somewhere safe to go? I can't tell. But we're in Warsaw.'

Connie crawled over to the side of the trailer and lifted a flap.

'Wow,' she said.

'What?'

'Oh, nothing,' said Connie. 'It's just bigger and fancier than I'd expected.'

She blinked in the sunlight. Outside it was sunny, but distinctly chillier than the Netherlands had been. The Warsaw skyscrapers and huge, old buildings shimmered in the light; they were thundering up a wide boulevard crammed with cars.

Closer at hand, the buildings were painted bright pinks and orange. The overall effect was extremely pretty. The pavements were full of the usual ragtag found in contemporary cities: businessmen, hawkers, beautiful women with little dogs, anxious backpackers.

'Hmm,' she said. 'Probably not *right* now.'

The huge lorry steamed and jerked its way through the traffic while Connie searched in vain for a place they could make a subtle escape. Finally, the truck started nosing its way downwards into a huge underpass, absolutely crammed full with rush-hour traffic.

'I think this might be us,' whispered Connie. 'Everyone is driving in here with their sunglasses on. They'll all be as blind ... well, as you,' she said, smiling and taking his hand. 'I think this is our moment.'

They looked at each other for a second.

'I do too,' said Luke. 'We have to go.'

Connie nodded. 'Okay,' she said. 'When I say.'

The traffic entering the tunnel was coming to a complete standstill; either there were lights up ahead or just a massive jam. The light passing through the gaps in tarpaulin changed from brightness to plunging darkness, and the truck came to a halt again.

'Okay,' said Luke. 'Let's do this.'

He pulled the great clanging door down, but among the traffic noise in the enclosed space of the tunnel, nothing could be heard in the general din. Connie espied a small side pavement that led back to the surface – it was easier to see out of the tunnel than in – and indicated to Luke that they would head for that.

'Take my hand,' he said worriedly. 'It's just white and black to me.'

'I know. One, two, three ... '

Of the four cars that saw them jump, one saw only a blur, one was texting furiously on his phone and didn't notice a thing, one was a very old lady whose father had escaped from a forced labour camp, who crossed her fingers for them and wished them well, and one was a harassed mum who thought to call the police then realised she couldn't have described them anyway, it was so dark in there, and there would be more traffic holdups, and she had to pick up the children and was running late as it was, never mind dinner, so she was just going to casually turn her head to the side and hope that they hadn't left two kilograms of plastic explosive in there, although the way she was feeling at the moment, sudden obliteration was oddly appealing if it meant she didn't have to make another bloody dinner.

Connie, hat back tightly on, held Luke by the hand, swallowed and tried to look as normal as possible walking up the pavement to the tunnel as if they had simply got lost on a stroll. At any moment she expected someone to shout and ask them what they were doing there, but nobody did; everyone was huddled in their cars, wrapped up in their little tin boxes, concentrating on their own lives, their own problems.

Just before they turned to cross the four-lane road at the top of the tunnel, Connie cast a glance back at the truck. She wondered who the driver was, what he looked like, how he would never know what he had done for them. She hoped his life would be kind.

Then they ran.

Warszawa Centralna railway station was an ugly place, a big seventies blocky building with damp stains seeping down its concrete walls and numerous confusing signs everywhere. But on the upside, it was absolutely teeming with people. Absolutely hordes of humanity was here, from old ladies in headscarves carrying animals and workers, plainly dressed and well built, heading to the homes and cafés of London, Copenhagen, Dubai; to the sleek-suited, new eastern, wannabe-oligarchs with their expensive phones and watches and briefcases attached to wrists with handcuffs.

Connie changed some money quickly in an automatic machine to avoid getting into another debate with Luke about universal currency, while he, in rapid and fluent Polish, bought their train trickets: an overnight stopping train through Kalinkovichi would take them to Mozyr, Belarus early in the morning.

'We'll be two hours ahead,' said Connie. 'Will that give us time . . . ?'

She looked at him.

'Do you know where your ship is?'

Luke nodded.

'Of course.'

'And you can fix it?'

'Of course.' He sounded insulted. 'The only reason I didn't was that I knew I didn't want to go home again. I don't want to go home again.'

Connie wandered off to buy slightly odd-looking sandwiches, fruit, water and, on impulse, a bottle of the local vodka that appeared to be everywhere. She glanced briefly though the British newspapers in the newsagent, but there was no mention of her and Luke anywhere, or anything about the signal. She gave a sigh of relief. She toyed with the idea of going to a nearby internet cafe and emailing Arnold, but quickly told herself not to. They had ways of figuring this stuff out nowadays, she knew; she could probably trace the IP herself. It would be suicide.

She browsed the shops a little longer, buying a grey T-shirt to change into. Luke simply didn't seem to need fresh clothes.

He didn't do everything like a human, then. A smile played on her lips as she turned around ...

'CONSTANCE MACADAIR! Well, bless my whiskers!'

She froze. A large man with a bushy beard and a ridiculous, deliberately OTT moustache stood right in front of her in a shirt which appeared to have food on it, and holding a large bundle of messy papers. Behind him was a long line of anxious-looking students, all boys. Connie clapped her hand to her mouth.

'Professor Knighting.'

'The very same, Dr MacAdair! Well, isn't this a coincidence!'

Professor Knighting had been her PhD supervisor. She hadn't seen him for five and a half years.

'Extraordinary luck! Now, students, this is one of my finest candidates ever. Knocked her viva out the park ... by the end of it she'd expressed a few notes and asides on re-normalising probability algebras with particular complex measures – she thought they seemed trivial – which, I don't mind telling you, really confirmed some results I was finding in my own research. Yes, ladies and gentlemen ... ahem, gentlemen. Yes, indeed. Now, Constance, where's that glorious hair of yours? I do love a natural redhead.'

His voice boomed around the terminal. Connie held on to her hat.

'Ha, well, you know ... lovely to see you.'

'Yes, are you here on this British Council trip too? There's the most fabulous conference on at the university on some results that have recently come out in local invariant in probabilistically defined elliptic curves. It's going to be a wonderful fun; are you attending? What about that nice young man of yours, Dr Weerasinghe, was it?'

Connie felt like she was in a nightmare. Where was Luke? They had to get away. She looked around desperately.

'Haven't got a pass, eh? I'm sure the consul can help you out ... well, cultural attaché, you know, but I say consul to be polite ... Bridford!'

Very slowly, an immaculately dressed man with a thin face and very, very pale blue eyes turned round and looked at Connie. And the instant he did, he frowned.

Connie stared at the floor, her face flaming. At that precise moment, Luke blundered his way over to her.

'Oh, there you are. I can't see a damn thing. You are impossible to find ...'

He was right in the middle of the group.

'Ssh,' said Connie desperately, as the consul took in, slowly, both of them together, with a nervous look. Then, unhurriedly, keeping his eyes trained on them, he drew his phone like he was drawing a gun.

'We have to go,' said Connie loudly, sounding alarmingly fake to her own ears. 'Late for our train ... TO PARIS!'

Ignoring the confused look on her old, well-meaning professor's face, she grabbed Luke by the arm and tore him away, half jogging, half marching him across the terminal. Glancing back, she saw the consul still staring at her, still holding his phone like the weapon it was. They dashed down the nearest flight of stairs, vanishing into the crowd, thankful for the first time that the railway station was confusing and crammed and vast.

They went outside the station, Connie trying not to panic. Luke calmed her down, reassured her there was nothing she could have done, bringing up a map of the station on his hand. He inspected it carefully, all its 3-D passages and platforms, and finally identified a service door that would get them onto the platform without going through the ticket barriers. They picked their way carefully across the tracks on a back-staff access bridge, empty at this time of night, hurrying them down to get on at the wrong end of the train, away from the checks and controls.

Once their cabin door was firmly shut behind them, Connie took a deep breath and closed her eyes. Please. Please let them stay ahead of Interpol, or whoever it was. Please just get moving. Please let the consul have had trouble calling in his discovery (he did, of course – Dahlia was tied up on the phone, as since the description had gone out on the wires, every bored bureaucrat from Calais to Hyderabad had been calling in redheads and it was driving her nuts; she was meant to be in Dorset this weekend, and at this rate she hadn't a hope in hell of getting there – and it took for ever for the local police station to pass him up to Malik).

At last there was a jolt, a screech of engine brakes, a slow huff and the train began to move. Connie leapt in the air. At home, the cultural attaché, who never got cross, hence his general usefulness to MI6, swore and poured himself a glass of whisky over his ridiculous evening wrangling with the telephone. He wondered what would happen if there was ever a matter of real national security, rather than some runaway with a boyfriend.

'Oh, thank God! Thank God!'

The huge train was not busy – there was a quicker, express service – and their first-class cabin had two freshly made up bunks with tight white sheets. Connie looked at them longingly. At the moment, she was absolutely desperate for a shower, but a clean bed was a good start.

Luke lay back on his bunk.

'Do you sleep?' asked Connie. 'I've never seen you do it.'

'Sleep is to repair brain cells,' said Luke. 'My job is to get rid of a few, before they start leaking out of my ears.'

Connie laughed.

'Seriously?'

He smiled his lazy smile at her.

'No. But I can rest and process things.'

His gaze fell on her. She had changed into the grey T-shirt, her hair loose, and was sitting in a tiny chair by the window, looking out at the landscape as the train picked up speed.

'Are you coming to bed, Hair?'

Connie turned round.

'Do you have to call me, Hair?'

'What should I call you?'

She thought about it for a moment and smiled shyly.

'Well, you *could* call me "my love".'

'My love.' He tried it out on his tongue. 'My love.'

She looked down, blushing.

'Well, you know, if you like.'

Their eyes met.

'I do like,' he said. 'Come to bed, my love.'

'Soon,' she promised. She wasn't the least bit sleepy. And she refused to miss a second with him. She wanted to soak it up, everything she could see, everything they experienced, every single minute they spent together, even if it was simply sitting in companionable silence.

There was so much she wanted to ask him. So much about him she wanted to know, and so much she wanted to tell him, even though sometimes she felt that he already knew her inside out, had turned her inside out, that there was nothing she could ever say to him that would be a surprise.

And she would not ask him right now. She gazed out of the window again, at Europe rolling past under a heavy dusk. She wanted to believe – had to believe – that they had time ahead, so much time stretching out in front of them, where they could lie together, and chat and share everything about their strange, strange lives in a conversation that would never end.

She found the last piece of chocolate in her pocket, and threw it over her shoulder at him. He caught it without even glancing at it and, without turning round, she knew he was smiling at her, and in her reflection in the window glass she smiled back.

She refocused her eyes and stared out of the window at the shadowy passing landscape. What were the odds, she thought. What were the chances of this happening? It was so mad and strange.

On the other hand, she thought, so was love. She had thought she had been in love before; had known bright crushes that would not let her sleep; been treated badly by men she had desperately wanted, and well by men she didn't; and had occasionally prolonged relationships that were comfortable and pleasant, but were nothing, she realised. Nothing compared to this, all-consuming, all-blinding sensation; this extraordinary excitement.

She glanced at Luke, his long form stretched out on the tidily-made bunk with its scuffed aluminium sides and small, neatly situated reading light. He had found a copy of what looked like *Practical Mechanic* in Russian, and was flipping through it, a smile playing about his lips. She wished beyond anything that she had her phone for no other reason than to take a photograph. She was conscious, suddenly, that she didn't have a photograph. She wanted one desperately, even though she told herself not to be silly. She would always be able to see him.

They had left the big city now, with its huge, ranging housing estates on the edge, its ragged factories stretching out into the countryside. It was late – 10 p.m. – but the sky was still full of light. At this latitude, she thought to herself, smiling, it wouldn't really get that dark, or at least not for long at this time of year. She stared at the cosy little farms and villages that passed by the window of the noisy, old-fashioned train, its rickety movement soothing. The view became gradually emptier and emptier, until the moon rose and they were making their way through a deepening green landscape, endless, fertile farmlands, cornfields, hops and ploughed fields and long meadows.

Suddenly, they came upon a large lake. The dipping sun was reflected on it, making it smooth and glassy as if it were frozen solid. There was a single hut on the side of the lake and, outside it, a single figure sitting, quietly and contentedly fishing. He glanced up momentarily at the train passing – perhaps disturbing his fish – then bent his head again, crouched on the edge of the little pontoon that led out from his home.

In a flash Connie saw it. She saw both of them. Somewhere far, far north, where it was always cold – Archangel? Higher? Did people even live higher? Somewhere way, way up in the Arctic circle, where nobody lived, and the people who did minded their own business. A little hut somewhere, brightly painted in red and white, with a little pontoon. And she would live in the house and Luke could live in the house if he wanted, but also live totally free, out in the water. And she could join him there – she smiled happily at the thought – and he could join her indoors. And they would live out their lives like that, in one element or another, perfectly happy with each other, and Arnold could send them maths work he was too lazy to do, and they wouldn't need so much to get by after all – some fish, some gardening, maybe. She could learn to sew. A little fuel. They'd deal with the spawn issue as and when.

Excitement shot through her; the vision was so strong she could practically see it.

'Luke,' she said softly from the depths of her reverie as the beautiful lake flickered past. 'If you can talk your people into letting you stay – and you can, I know you can, I know you can. I know you can make them see.'

Luke didn't answer that.

'Well, if ... WHEN you do ... '

She paused.

'Is there an Earth prison that could hold you?'

He shook his head.

'Wouldn't have thought so,' came the low voice. 'I don't think anyone realises how strong I am here. They won't: I had no idea. I'm not, back home.'

'Thought not,' she said. 'And if I had to go to prison, would you wait for me?'

'No,' said Luke.

She turned towards him with an enquiring look on her face.

'I'd come and get you,' he said.

She smiled.

Two seconds later, they blew up the moon.

Chapter Twenty-one

There was no noise, of course: nothing that could travel across the vacuum of space. But the effects were immediately obvious: a huge, fiery meteor storm visible from everywhere on the night side.

All across the hemisphere, people ran out of their houses, those who grew up in the seventies noticeable by their sunglasses.

Above the SPIC, the astronomers groaned and threw their headphones across the room, half deafened by the static hiss which had become the noise of a thousand snakes filling their heads. But in the next second, they too were running to the window.

'What the fuck is that?' said Nigel, leaping up from the desk. He marched outside. 'Christ,' he said. One of the astronomers sidled up to him.

'What's our status report?'

'Um,' said the young man, whose name was Damon but liked to be called D'amon. 'It's ... and Hawaii and VLA are confirming this ... it looks like a chunk of the moon has simply exploded.'

'Fuck. How much? How big?'

D'amon shook his head. 'Not very big. Doesn't need to be.'

'It doesn't,' said Nigel. 'If this is a warning. It's a warning.' He felt his insides turn to ice water. First the moon, then what? What did they want from them? What did they need to know?

'The special frequency is going bananas,' mumbled D'amon.

Nigel looked at him.

'Right. Thanks,' he said.

There was something they wanted. There was something they needed from them. And the only people who could tell them what it was were God knows ...

Malik came through the door.

'Sir?'

He looked as solid and untiring as ever. Nigel was desperate to get home and take a shower and change, and he looked at the DCI with some resentment.

Malik held up a paper message.

'There's been a sighting. Warsaw.'

'Good,' said Nigel wearily. 'Wake up Interpol and shout their fucking heads off. Bring these buggers back and do it now, and spend the GDP of a small country to do it if you have to. I have a call I have to make.'

The sky was filled with the beautiful falling meteor storm twinkling through the sky, most to burn out harmlessly in the ocean. Children watched through bedroom windows; drunks thought they'd imagined it; couples got engaged and conceived children to it.

The news media was going absolutely ballistic, and the internet was close to meltdown. Nigel picked up the phone.

'It's them?' came down the line.

'It is.'

Anyali sighed.

'Tell NASA to accept responsibility,' said Nigel. 'Promise them we'll talk to them tomorrow. But you get the PM to call the president, tell them we've got this all under control, we know what we're doing, and please, please, please get NASA to say they blew up a fucking Mars Rover or a piece fell off a satellite or something.'

'You have to give me more than that,' said Anyali, her voice sharp. 'You have to.'

'Send me two guys,' said Nigel grimly. 'It'll be done. Sooner rather than later. G-trained.'

'Seriously? Mr Principles?'

'They just blew up half the fucking moon,' said Nigel. 'What's next – Tokyo?'

'The Americans aren't going to be happy,' said Anyali.

'Nobody,' said Nigel, 'nobody is fucking happy.'

'Can't we just say it was a meteor shower?'

'You can, till someone notices there's a chunk missing from the fucking moon.'

Anyali sighed. 'The conspiracy theorists are going to go nuts.'

'What could they possibly theorise,' said Nigel, 'that's worse than what's actually happening?'

Luke and Connie watched the meteors fall from the sky as they crossed the border into Belarus.

'Oh my God,' said Connie. 'Was that them?'

Luke nodded. 'Of course,' he said. 'Oh GOD, this thing needs to get there. Everything on Earth is so *slow*.'

'We could have flown,' said Connie. 'But I think they'd have caught us.'

'I should have spoken to them from the beginning,' said Luke, balling his fists. 'I should have gone straight to the white place and done it right away.'

'They'd never have let you,' said Connie. 'Be serious. They

229

wouldn't have believed you. Then when you'd proved it, they'd have put you in some stupid lab and cut bits off you. They would have given you up in ten seconds. You'd have been halfway across the galaxy by now.'

They watched the lights arc across the sky.

'Even so,' said Luke. Up and down the train, they could hear the *ooh*s.

'I wonder where he is,' he said. 'The one who's already here.'

'Can they pick you out?' said Connie.

'Did you?'

'Yes,' said Connie. 'But not for that reason.'

He nodded and glanced out of the window.

'Oh God, hurry up. Hurry up.'

As long as they don't stop the train, Connie thought. As long as they don't stop all the trains and planes and buses and tear the earth apart looking for him.

But the train did not stop; it rocked on through steppes and ever more mountainous terrain, towards the east, and it grew darker, and the lights seemed to burn in the sky for ever, searing themselves onto their retinas so that Connie could still see them go after she closed her eyes.

They were so close. So near. Mazyr was a small town, on the opposite side of the river, so close they could almost touch it when the train came to a deliberate stop in the middle of the fine, high, metal bridge. It was night but not pitch-dark; the moon was bright. Connie looked at the distant town in anguish.

And up the corridor of the train she could hear, suddenly, knocking at all the small cabin doors. Polite enquiries. 'Passport, please? Passports. *Reisepässe. Paszport.*'

Nigel stole a look at his Breitling. 11 p.m. That made it 1 a.m. in Poland. They were sending men up from London. He had time to go home and change quickly before the next phase. He wasn't looking forward to the next phase. He didn't think they were bad people. But they knew something, goddammit. They knew *something*.

The roads were empty driving home; everyone was out watching the lights fall and burn up sparkling in mid-air – it was beautiful – or was uploading pictures of it from their phones, or writing long blog posts with black backgrounds, white type and lots and lots of capital letters.

Nigel sighed in frustration as he turned into Meadow Oasis Dwellings. Normally he was careful and quiet when he got home, but not tonight. Ignoring his phone which was full of missed calls and voice mails which would lead to more conversations with Anyali that he wasn't looking forward to in the slightest, he slammed the front door until the house's flimsy foundations shook. Upstairs Annabel, who had drifted off in front of *One Born Every Minute*, then woken up at the lights outside her window, had moved to the 'feature window' in the back, spare room and was sitting there on an expensive, pink corner-seat feature they never used, hypnotised by the sight.

'Darling?'

She moved through to their bedroom, and started re-piling cushions on the bed – there were a lot of them – nervously.

'It's just me,' said Nigel in a low tone, mounting the stairs two at a time. He was already pulling off his tie and instead of hanging it up like he normally did, he balled it up and hurled it into the corner of the room with some force. 'I'm just back to change.'

'What's going on out there, do you know?'

'How the hell should I know?' said Nigel tersely. Normally Annabel knew better than to ask him about work and she looked down guiltily.

'The radio says NASA blew something up by mistake,' said Annabel.

'Did it now,' said Nigel.

Annabel blinked.

'Tough day?' she asked gently.

'You have NO fucking idea,' snarled Nigel, then turned to her, crestfallen. He really couldn't bear the idea of shouting at her.

'Sorry,' he said. 'I'm so sorry. I've had an absolute . . . Well. I can't tell you. But I shouldn't have taken it out on you.'

Annabel looked up at the beautiful light show still streaking across the sky. She moved over suddenly to the bed and pulled off her demure nightie. She looked straight at him.

'Take it out on me,' she said in a tone of voice Nigel had never heard before.

'What? Sorry, love . . . '

'Take it out on me,' she said again, and if she hadn't been so deadly serious, it might have been funny.

Nigel glanced at his watch.

'I have to . . . '

She shook her head and moved towards him putting her fingers over his mouth, while it looked like the stars themselves were falling behind them.

'This won't take long,' she said. And she raked her perfect nails down his perfectly creased shirt, and tore off the buttons, one by one.

Afterwards, Nigel showered quickly and changed. Annabel lay there, happy, pink, watching him.

'So are these little green men?' she said. 'Is that what this is? Have they come to Earth to blow up the moon? Are they everywhere?'

Nigel shook his head.

'No, of course not,' he said.

Then he turned sharply and looked at her, blinking rapidly.

'If they were everywhere ... if they were here ... if there was a reason for the six to be so obstructive ...'

He swore and pounded his fist on the windowsill.

'Jesus,' he said. 'Jesus. I think you might have it. I think we've been looking for a murderer. They wouldn't protect a murderer. But they might protect ...

'I have to go.'

Connie ran to the train window and looked down. It was a spare, skeletal, steel bridge with high square arches up above them, and a huge, nine-storey drop to the water below. It wasn't so much the drop though, but the look of the river; there were mountains up ahead, and the water churned and bounced its way at a frightening speed, licking white, along lines of treacherous rocks on either side. She glanced at Luke.

'It's suicide,' she murmured.

He looked at it, and shrugged. 'What do you think?'

'Couldn't we ... I don't know – knock out the guard?' said Connie.

'Hit him?'

'Um, yeah?'

He looked at her.

'What?' said Connie.

'You would just hit another human being to stop them getting in your way?'

'If it would save us I would,' said Connie, shaking. The knocking was getting closer; people she could hear were grumbling about being woken up. They didn't have much time.

'But an attack against the person,' said Luke. 'Does it help us move on from where we began?'

'Aargh,' said Connie. 'I don't know. They do it all the time in films.'

'I haven't seen a lot of films.'

'Have you seen any?'

He brightened briefly.

'I've seen *Mary Poppins*. I liked it a lot.'

'Okay, well, you summon some dancing penguins,' said Connie, starting to fret. 'Next time you decide to see one human film, can you make it *Die Hard*?'

'*Die Hard*?' mused Luke. 'What does that even mean ...?'

The knocking was next door now.

'Not the time for our first row,' said Connie in a warning tone.

Luke moved over to the window, and squinted so he could see down.

'We could do this,' he said.

'You could,' said Connie. 'I'd crack my head on the rails and plummet to a tumbling death like ... someone in a film about a big boat you haven't seen.'

He shook his head.

'No, we could.'

'I can't swim in that.'

'You can if I hold you,' he said.

'I don't think this is the time for ...'

'No. I can ... I can absorb you without it being that ... I think it's like ...'

His brow furrowed.

'I think it's like what Arnold says.'

'What does Arnold say?' said Connie, unable to help herself.

'He said girls say, "Oh, let's just cuddle."'

Connie looked at him for a long moment and suddenly burst out laughing.

'Oh my,' she said. 'Oh lord. Okay. Okay. Every time I've trusted you so far, it's gone ... Well, it's happened.'

There was a knock at the door.

'Passports! *Reisepässe! Paszport!*'

As if he were casually pressing a button, Luke pushed the large train window straight out of its mouldings. A fierce wind tore into the carriage as the window immediately caught on the rails beneath their feet and shattered into a million pieces.

There was no help for it. Nigel couldn't get Annabel's idea out of his head, but he couldn't get through to the group in any way.

Nigel pushed back his hair, still wet from the shower, and stood outside the SKIF facility in the dark, hating himself. A large, expensive and slightly sinister-looking black car slid into the courtyard. He rolled his eyes. He supposed this was all part of their culture of intimidation and entitlement. When two white men got out, both shaven-headed and thick-necked, and gave him the old up and down he felt like rolling his eyes again, but he didn't want to get more into it.

'Ah, the Kiefers are here,' he said, aware as he did so that they would think he was yet another fey Englishman. 'Follow me.'

He glanced at his watch. It was 11.30 p.m.

After the corridors with the locked doors was a room at the end with a sluice. It was deep underground, with no windows and natural soundproofing. Nigel had to believe that when they had extended the facility, they had had absolutely no idea what it could possibly be used for. He wished he was in his pretty office at the very top, having Dahlia be rude to him.

He looked down the list of names. Regardless of political correctness, he couldn't bear the thought of bringing a woman in here. Couldn't bear it. Couldn't bear that he was even having to make these decisions. Kiefer 1 and Kiefer 2 moved into the room, pacing around it like panthers, starting to set up by the large sink. Nigel didn't look at them but instead concentrated on what was more important: the world. The world. Someone was coming for the world and he needed to find out who, and why.

It didn't help. The world at this point seemed all too real and cruel, right in front of him.

He looked at the list again, and mentally crossed off Ranjit. He was a child. He couldn't have that babbling baby on his conscience, and he was highly suspicious of his ability to formulate anything like the truth in his mass panic.

The Kiefers were testing a syringe. They worked in silence. Nigel wondered how long it would take to learn how to do this happily in silence, then tried to stop thinking about that too.

Two names left. Arnold annoyed the shit out of him. That would rationally be a good reason to get him in here first, but to Nigel he felt less of a ... Bad Guy ... he realised to himself.

His knock on the door was gentle. Sé was not asleep.

There was swearing from the other side of the door as the guard heard and felt the roar of the wind and tried the handle, finding it locked. The noise was unbelievable, the torrid air and the roar of the river filling Connie's ears. What had looked rather high from inside the carriage, as she joined hands with Luke and peered over the ledge, was now absurdly dangerous: a long ledge to clear, then a huge drop to a river they hadn't the faintest idea – now, in early summer – how deep it was. There was nothing to say that they wouldn't simply hit their heads on the bottom. Connie hoped fervently, looking down, that at least it would be quick.

There came a kick on the door. It shook inwards. It

wouldn't hold for long. Luke clambered up onto the empty window frame, holding onto the corner with one hand, and reached his hand back to her behind him. Connie suddenly felt paralysed with fear. Up until now she had been worried, adrenalised; but she had never, truly, been in fear of her life. Not with Luke beside her, not wrapped in a carpet, or in a rattling train, or even running through a station filled with policemen.

The door clicked again. The lock was giving. She glanced behind her, then ahead of her, both options equally terrifying. Luke was watching her, seemingly perfectly calm, hanging halfway out of a railway carriage ninety feet up in the air.

'I can't,' she said, her mouth drying up suddenly. 'I can't jump out there.'

Luke's dark eyes stayed fixed to her patiently, as if they had all the time in the world.

'Not alone you couldn't,' he said. 'Alone, you'd die for sure. Or be terribly wounded.'

Connie breathed heavily through her nose.

'Thanks.'

He beamed at her.

'But fortunately,' he said, 'you'll be with me. Do you see? So.'

He held out his hand. She looked at it and once again glanced desperately behind her, just in time to see the door burst open and a short, chunky train guard panting hard and very red in the face.

'HEH!' he said, just as, with one swoop, Connie, without thinking about it, ran and jumped, fleet-footed, straight up to the windowledge, and without missing a beat Luke caught her hand and, propelling himself from the window frame, pushed her bodily out of the window and clear of the train and the railway line and down, down, down, the meteors winking out

237

over their heads, flashing across the sky as they fell; the guard, his mouth wide open, gasping at the window, saw them: frozen for an instant, caught in mid-air, Connie's hair streaming behind her like a flag, her hands thrown out over her head; Luke's arms already stretching out in the rushing air to take hold of her.

Chapter Twenty-two

Sé sat at the desk in the windowless room. He looked at the clock on the wall. It was large, standard academic issue; you could see the second hand tick round with heavy thuds, the hands dunk from minute to minute. It was 11.36 p.m GMT. Come on, Connie, he thought. He assumed they didn't have her already, which gave him some relief: he would hate to think of her in this room, with these men behind him making a show of preparing things.

Unless of course she was dead. His face twisted. Where could they be? If they hadn't found them, what had they done? Anything could have happened. They could have tried to steal a car, been shot. They could be languishing in some foreign jail, or could have fallen off the back of a ferry. Anything could have happened. Perhaps the alien had killed her. Sé swallowed hard, but he would not cry. He didn't understand it. He would never understand it. A man was killed in an alien way. And there was an alien in the building. He was mad to have let her go. Absolutely mad. And if they still had not found her ... What was more likely – that a young girl and a strange alien with bad eyesight had managed to avoid all of Europe's most elite security forces? Or that she was dead and he was gone?

His ankle was handcuffed to a chair that was bolted to the floor. He thought this was probably unnecessary. He was a grown man, but pain didn't make people jump up and fight like they did in films. His father had shown him that. It turned them into children, rolled up in a ball: weeping, terrified babies who wanted their mothers.

Perhaps Connie had got there after all. Perhaps it had been a success. He looked at the clock again. But they knew. They knew about the three days. And they must have noticed the moon, what had happened. They must have known how much that escalated the stakes for them all. And they had not got in touch, and here he was.

He deliberately rubbed his ear with his right hand in the hopes that they would think that that was the hand he used, and take the finger from there. He looked at his long fingers splayed out in front of him. Perhaps it would not be a whole finger. Perhaps a fingernail would do. His fingers shook a little. He stared at them until they stopped. Then he looked at the clock again. 11.37 p.m.

'It'll take as long as it takes,' said one of the men, sniggering. He had an American accent. Taking their time was all part of their job.

Nigel stood in the room. He could have left for this bit, he knew. Could have left a list of questions, come back when all the nastiest work was over, when the results were on an audio file only he would ever know the passcode to.

He would not do that. He had approved it. He would endure it.

He stood subtly by the door, back straight, staring ahead. He and Sé did not look at one another. Sé thought he was an evil monster. That was fine. He was, and this was what he deserved. He forced his voice to remain calm.

'There's still time, Sé. Tell us what the explosion was. Tell

240

us what was in the message. Tell us what happened to Luke and Connie. We know you know.'

He leaned closer.

'We know you and Connie had ... a thing. Surely you want to make sure she's okay?'

'She means nothing to me,' said Sé, staring ahead, eyes still fixed on the clock.

'Does anybody mean anything to you, Sé?' said Nigel. 'Anybody in the world? Anything at all?'

11.38 p.m. The two men came towards him from the back of the room, carrying towels and a black binbag. They were unhurried.

Chapter Twenty-three

Attention all shipping, especially in sea areas Dogger, Bight and Humber. The Met Office issued the following gale warning to shipping at 22.45 today. German Bight: west or northwest gale 8 to storm 10, expected imminent. Fastnet Cromarty Wight Forties: west gale force 8, storm warnings force 7 all levels, unusual tidal activity.

That completes the gale warning.

The shock of the cold water entered at speed burst Luke out of his human shape in an instant: he practically exploded like an airbag, grabbing Connie and pulling her to him – *into* him – protecting her from the cold which to him was a balm but to her was like falling onto a knife.

Tumultuously, against the current, he swam upstream to the town in the mountains as Connie's world turned into a burst of ice and lights and confusion, and she twisted round and round, under and inside him, plunging freely through the waves.

Finally she spluttered free as Luke made for a bank. It wasn't until they were hauling themselves out of the water that Connie realised there were people sitting on the top of the waterside on a gorse-covered outpost beside some rocks.

It was a group of young men, mostly red-eyed. There were cigarette ends and empty vodka bottles scattered all around their feet. Evidently, they were watching the light display from the moon above. But now, they were watching them, with mounting horror.

'*Co do cholery?*' said one. Connie glanced at Luke, who once again was struggling to regain his human form, bent over at the waist in pain as his body solidified.

'Um, it's okay?' said Connie, but they weren't looking at her; they weren't paying her the least bit of attention at all. All their eyes were fixed on Luke, who glanced upwards, his head gradually seeping in with colour. A few were scrambling backwards: one was clinging to his vodka bottle as if that would help; another was glancing at the light show in the sky then back to Luke, as if putting two and two together.

In his deep voice, Luke said, '*Szklana pułapka*,' and after that, they really started to move. In fact, the young men jumped up and ran down the road as fast as they could manage.

Connie, out of breath, rested her hands on her knees and turned to him.

'What did you say?' she said. Luke's face was pained, but he was back, weak and fragile-looking. He was wearing a puzzled expression.

'Oh,' he said. 'I asked them if they wanted to "die hard".'

Connie looked back at the bridge, up the valley. The train hadn't moved, all its lights were on and there were distant shouts and torches showing as the guards searched for them downstream. She dried herself off as well as she could, which wasn't very, and they scrambled up the little cove on to the road, although they stayed in the ditch by the side of it, out of sight.

Connie knew the time, but she checked her wristwatch anyway.

'Do you have another appointment?' enquired Luke. 'Are you missing something on the square picture box?'

'It's 3.45 a.m. here' said Connie. 'That means it's 11.45 p.m. in the UK.'

He looked puzzled.

'It's the end of day two,' she explained. 'At one minute past midnight, that will be day three. That's our time up. Then Arnold can give the frequency codes to that guy and they can get in touch.'

'I thought yesterday was day one.'

'You'd think for a bunch of people who work with numbers we could have figured *that* one out a bit better,' said Connie. 'But, Luke, you know, with the moon thing, everyone will be going crazy. Oh God, I hope they haven't called them in again. That prick Nigel, you don't think ... Oh God, Luke, I'm so worried about them. So worried. And I think come midnight ... I don't think we could ask any more of them.'

'Yes,' said Luke, staring straight ahead. 'It's due east: not far from here, but I don't know if we could get there by midnight ...'

Then they both saw it in the middle of the road: a very tattered, old Trabant car with its doors open and bottles scattered about its interior.

'I think this might be those guys' car,' said Connie. 'They've abandoned it for some reason.'

She looked inside. The key was still in it. She experimentally turned it.

'Nothing,' she said. 'They must have panicked.'

Luke peered at the engine.

'So, what, the key ignites a spark that sets the engine working?'

'Um, I think so' said Connie. 'Or magic pixies, I'm a bit hazy on the whole thing.'

Luke opened his hand and let a spark of blue electricity

leap from his fingers to the motor. Instantly, the engine sounded up.

'That is WITCHCRAFT,' said Connie, staring. Luke was confused. 'But humans have electrical impulses and you use those things that need electricity all the time, for shouting and taking pictures of sandwiches.'

Connie gave it a second.

'Oh, phones?'

Luke nodded. 'It's a pretty logical next progression. Don't worry about it.'

Connie sat in the passenger seat.

'We shall borrow it and bring it back,' she decided. 'We haven't got the time.'

Luke sat in the driver's seat. Neither moved.

'Come on!' said Connie. 'Let's go!'

There was a pause

'Oh LORD, I forgot.' Connie shook her head. 'You can magic electricity out of your fingers but you can't drive a suddenly VERY USEFUL car.'

Luke didn't say anything.

'Fine, budge up.'

Luke pointed out roads as she drove at full pelt in the unfamiliar left-hand drive – the Trabant made an awful noise – and they headed out at speed. The roads were empty, but Connie no longer cared who saw or heard them. She imagined the drunk young men would have a story to tell in the morning anyway – assuming they remembered it – but for now, all she could think about was the panic of the meteor storm, and what would be happening to her friends.

At six minutes to three, Luke raised his hand.

'It's here.'

*

Sé had heard that drowning was a pleasant way to go; that it was not the worst by a long shot. But this did not feel like that. As his nose was stopped with a towel and water sluiced down him, as he was tied to a large piece of wood and his whole world turned into an agonising attempt not to breathe, and then, when it could no longer be avoided, taking the breath that filled his lungs with water, struggling, feeling his eyes roll up in his head, and the terrible, terrible burning inside, the tightness and strain of his lungs, battling to keep him alive, the red flashes in front of his eyes as he felt the blood vessels pop one by one, every nerve, every sinew straining, but no scream could come as he was filled, again and again ... and just, finally, just when blissful unconsciousness was arriving, the black at the very edges of his vision – a memory of his father, making pol roti, throwing the coconut dough up in the air effortlessly with his four fingers – then he was brutally vomiting again and again, throwing water up all over the floor as the two men stood by and watched, taking big tearing breaths of oxygen, crying and heaving, his body trembling against the board.

Nigel's touch on his shoulder was gentle and the tone of his voice was kind which made matters altogether worse for everybody.

'Please, Sé,' he said sorrowfully. 'Please. We hate doing this. I don't want to do this. Nobody wants to do this. Please just tell us. Please, then we can go home and stop all this. Please. We need to work on this together.'

Sé looked up at him, still choking and retching, his eyes red.

'What ... time ... is ... it?'

The meteors were still falling overhead but the world was almost entirely silent as Connie and Luke got out of the car. They were standing in a field, with trees at one end, in the shadow of a rocky hill and, further behind that, the great plains of Palyessye. Two fields over, some cows dozed by a water trough. An owl hooted in the trees. There wasn't a building to be seen, apart from a distant barn. It was astonishingly peaceful.

Luke glanced around.

'Can you see it?' said Connie anxiously.

'Thankfully, I don't need to,' said Luke. He moved confidently towards the undergrowth.

'There's nothing there!' said Connie.

Luke held up his hand, pressed it lightly on the side of something – and then she saw it too.

'Oh,' she said.

The vast object hummed under his hands.

'Come on, girl,' said Luke. 'You can do it.'

The object, faintly traced in glowing lights was completely clear and spherical. In fact, Connie thought, it looked like a gigantic soap bubble, nearly as tall as the trees, but completely invisible until Luke had brought it to life. She touched it: it felt like tough jelly. It moved a little, and the lights flickered up and down even more.

'It's beautiful,' she said in wonder. Luke beamed.

'Isn't she?' he said proudly.

'Can I go inside?'

He frowned.

'Well, you could, but it's full of ... '

There was a long pause.

'What?' said Connie.

'I don't know. Closest I can get is ... nutri-jelly?'

'Urgh,' said Connie.

'Oh no, it's ... ' he saw her face. 'No time.'

It was the oddest thing: he disappeared into the huge, clear bubble, seeming to pass through its walls – Connie pushed;

she could not penetrate them – but once inside she could not see him. She stood back from the bubble, and as soon as she was a couple of feet away she realised she couldn't see it at all. It was incredibly strange. And strange also in that, weirdly, it brought the very alienness of Luke much closer, that he was something so peculiar. She pulled her damp shirt closer round her shoulders: the night was clear and chill. She missed him while he was gone.

Connie didn't know what she'd been expecting Luke to remove from the vessel: some kind of space telephone? Regardless, he came out with a small, smooth, round chunk of what seemed like – but couldn't be, surely – glass.

They sat down cross-legged next to the ship on the ground.

It was Evelyn who started it. She took her enamel mug (she'd managed to bribe a constant supply of tea off one of the guards by helping him with, of all things some tricky integrals that he'd clearly known how to do way back in the halcyon days of his undergraduate years, but hadn't needed since. He was a PhD student, working as a guard to supplement his meagre grants. Except he was slightly worse than the professional guards, because in between going over old ground, he'd repeatedly apologise and tell her she wouldn't believe the things you had to do for tenure these days to which Evelyn could only grunt).

The churches of the city – Great St Mary's, St Bene't's, St Andrew's – chimed their bells, ding-donging the new day.

Evelyn stood up with her cup and banged on the heavy, locked door as hard as she could. And then when he heard, Arnold too started banging and shouting. Ranjit woke up, slightly confused, but when he remembered where he was, he jumped up too and hollered along, even slightly daringly trying some swear words in Hindi. And they all yelled their heads off.

Francis the PhD guard was first on the scene.

'What is it?'

'We're ready,' said Arnold. 'We're ready. Get us out of here. Where's Sé?'

Francis took the good news to Nigel, who tried not to betray his delight and keep his cool head. He nodded to the American soldiers to untie Sé immediately. Sé continued to vomit and vomit on the floor and could not stand up without help. Nigel waited patiently for him, then indicated to one of the soldiers to carry him down to the conference room, and for the others to join him there.

Arnold couldn't believe it when he saw what they had done to Sé. Evelyn could. All three rushed towards him as he was brought in. Arnold had to try very hard not to cry. Evelyn took Sé in her arms, sat him down and rocked him back and forth like a child.

'What did they do to you?' Ranjit kept saying. 'You were amazing, man. I bet you didn't tell them anything! I bet you were, like, as tough as it is possible to be. You're, like, the best. I would also have been totally okay.'

'Ahem,' said Nigel quietly. 'Can we begin?'

Luke splayed his fingers over the surface of the device. Connie was reminded how as a child she would run her fingers around the top of a glass to make it sing. It hummed into life, then suddenly crackled. It was not especially loud, but it had the noise of a hundred – a thousand, more – frequencies on it, as if every broadcaster on Earth was suddenly coming through on the same time. This was exactly what was happening. 'Ow,' said Connie. 'Tune it out, tune it out.'

249

He looked at her bemused 'Oh, I think it sounds nice ... '

'TUNE IT OUT.'

'Earth frequencies are alarmingly close together,' he grumbled. 'And you all talk SO MUCH. And I can't work it with these stupid sausage things.'

'Stop complaining about fingers,' said Connie. 'Fingers are great.'

She was bouncing up and down with nerves and anticipation now, staring at the faintly glowing pebble he had in his hands. Luke moved it on through crackle and hiss, glancing up from time to time, searching out areas in the sky. Finally, there came a sharp crunching noise that sounded like a car crash, a loud thump. Then another. It was ominous and jangled, like a horrible alarm.

Arnold wrote out the details he'd memorised on a piece of paper and handed them over.

'This is how to contact them,' he said gruffly.

Nigel stared at them in disbelief.

'You've had this for *three days?*'

They hesitated, then nodded.

'This is treason,' said Nigel.

'Yeah, we know,' said Arnold. 'Can I linger and die in Britain, please? US prisons are really, really, really nasty places.'

'But why, WHY? Why didn't you just tell us? Why are the other two on the run?'

'There is a message,' said Evelyn. 'You might want to sit down.'

Nigel did so, trying not to let his hands shake. He glanced at Sé, who had his head now in Evelyn's lap, and whose alarmingly bloodshot eyes were focusing on nothing at all.

'The aliens are looking for an escapee from their planet, who is hiding here.'

'She was right,' said Nigel wonderingly, shaking his head. He leaned back.

'It's not Godzilla, is it?' he said in a low voice.

'Ooh,' said Ranjit.

'No,' said Evelyn. 'It's Luke.'

There was a long silence, as Nigel tried to take this in. To finally hear it said out loud.

'All this time,' he said finally. 'That nerdy guy in the spectacles . . .'

He paused.

'Of course. Of course it is. And he killed the professor when he found out. Who else could possibly do that? And then he went on the run. Christ.'

'He says he didn't do it,' said Evelyn.

'Did he . . . ? I mean, did he just *say* he was the alien?'

They shook their heads.

'We saw it! He's all jellyfish,' said Ranjit. 'Like a shiny jellyfish!'

Nigel shook his head. Then he banged his fist on the table.

'And you let him escape and didn't tell us?! What on EARTH where you thinking?'

'You're right,' said Evelyn. 'We should have trusted him to you, and how you treat people.'

She stroked Sé's head possessively.

'What's with the girl? Is he holding her? That's it, isn't it? She's his hostage. But still, you come to us; we have ways of dealing with these situations.'

The three looked at one another.

'Uh,' said Arnold. 'Not exactly.'

'That's a bit personal,' said Evelyn.

'She knew and she still chose to go with a murderous alien? Oh God. Oh God. Where the HELL are they?'

'They were heading for Belarus,' said Evelyn, feeling the

weight of betrayal as she did so, and speaking quietly and quickly. 'We don't know if they got there. We haven't heard from them. They promised to contact us if they got there and we promised that after three days we were going to turn everything over to you.'

Something clicked over in Nigel's mind. Malik's sighting. Warsaw. He glanced down at the new messages on his phone. Mazyr. Mazyr? Something about a train. Where the hell was that?

He blinked grimly.

'I believe they did.'

'YAY!' said Ranjit.

'Why?'

'Luke's ship is there,' said Arnold. 'His spaceship. He has a spaceship. My buddy Luke, right. He has his own spaceship. Wow. I liked saying that.'

'So he's going to escape again?' said Nigel. 'Thanks to you. When an alien civilisation is looking for him. And you put the entire Earth at risk to do so?'

He looked at them all and shook his head. Ranjit's ears flamed bright pink.

'Give me the details. Give them to me now.'

He picked up his phone.

'Dahlia?' He listened for a moment. 'No, listen, I don't care about your annual leave plans right now. No. Not now, no. Listen. Just get me Vauxhall and Number 10 please. It's Code N. Double N. Fuck it, triple N. All the fucking Ns.'

Evelyn had never been in the telescope control room before. It was impressive. Even after midnight it was buzzing with serious-looking staff looking harassed – as well they might be, given the amount of data they were dealing with and their inability to understand any of it, not to mention a switchboard entirely jammed up with people wanting to ask them what had just happened on the moon.

Everyone looked nervous but excited at the same time. She had wanted to take Sé back to his rooms, but there was no question of that. They were all to stay together where people could see them. Someone found him a seat at the back of the room and he slumped in it, oblivious.

'Who works the audio comms?' demanded Nigel. 'Communications manager?'

An incredibly thin, young-looking man wearing a bow-tie stepped forwards.

'Can you ask your dad to come and assist us please?' snapped Nigel as the boy fumbled with his white coat and nervously cleared his throat.

'I think you'll find I can assist you.'

Nigel turned to Arnold. 'Now what the hell do we have to do?'

Arnold took a piece of paper and wrote down the galactic coordinates derived from the frequency sequence he'd memorised and, glancing at the others, who nodded, passed it over. Nigel glanced at it, but it was gobbledegook to him.

The young man, whose name was Pol, looked at it.

'This can't work,' he said crossly. 'This is dust clouds and space between stars. It's nothing. There's nothing in that quadrant.'

'Well, can your instruments detect where it's meant to be?' said Arnold. 'Or are they just for trying to look up girls' skirts five miles away?'

Pol bristled.

'Of course we can't detect it,' he said. 'We could if there was anything there. I'm just telling you: we scan it every day. There's nothing there. There's no way it could reach out across space. It's physically impossible.'

Arnold folded his arms and stood in a line with Evelyn and Ranjit.

'Well, we're mathematicians,' he said. 'So physically impossible to us just sounds like this: "yah yah yah boo hoo".'

Pol scowled.

'Please, can we just get this fixed up and see?' said Nigel, struggling to keep his temper. 'Let's just pretend for a moment that there's more at stake than a little bit of territorial arseholeness.'

Pol took it from him and moved a young woman off a huge computer bank with three screens.

'THAT'S your amazing advanced space-scanning equipment?' said Arnold, who had found three days locked in a cell being quiet extraordinarily difficult. 'I've got better kit for *World of Warcraft*. AND a panini maker.'

The others looked at him as Pol fired up the machine. The three screens sprung into life, showing graphs of peaks and troughs on one, and a scanning star system on another.

'What? You get hungry.'

Pol put on his headphones in a very deliberate fashion, looking at Arnold all the while. He moved a mike in near his mouth.

'Oh look, it's Madonna,' said Arnold.

'Ssh,' said Evelyn.

'I won't *shoosh*,' said Arnold. 'I'm holding the secrets of the universe in my hand and Prince George here wants to pull fucking rank.'

Pol ignored him, saying into the computer's mike in a low voice, 'Fifty-five phased array one hundred and fifty-five giga-hertz.'

There was a perceptible creaking and Evelyn looked out of the window. Against the dark of night, the great satellite dishes gradually started to turn on their hydraulics. All of them moving together was faintly sinister: they resembled large heads which had been resting, all suddenly turning, as if cocking an ear towards something they had heard, then gazing at it implacably.

She shivered and looked back at Sé. He was slumped in his seat staring at nothing. She wanted to move, but Nigel glanced at her and made it clear with a quick shake of his head that she must not. She tutted sharply.

Pol was listening intently to his headphones until Nigel ordered a speaker to be switched on. There was nothing but rustling and hiss; interference and static from deep within the galaxy, and Pol's face took on a satisfied look. Arnold and Evelyn swapped glances. There was a long pause. Nigel thought – hoped, for the very last time – that this all might be some ridiculous misunderstanding; that they were wrong; that there was an easier, simpler explanation involving goodies and baddies, with the baddies ending up in jail.

Then quickly, a split-second before they heard the noise, the graph on the screen peaked; peaked and peaked again.

And then they all heard it. A crunching noise. Then another. Then another. And a bright light beamed in from outside the laboratory windows.

Chapter Twenty-four

Luke rubbed his throat anxiously. Connie was thinking practically.

'If you want to talk to them properly, talk to them in your language ... I mean, if you go back inside your ship, isn't it ...?'

Luke shook his head.

'I don't want to,' he said. 'I don't want to speak to them as one of them. I want to speak as one of you. As us.'

He paused.

'Is that all right?'

Connie nodded, and put her hand in his. Luke leaned forwards and very quietly spoke into the glass.

'Hello.'

The noise was louder than what was coming through the speakers. It was more of a *wop wop wop*. And the light ...

The room froze.

'That sounds exactly like a helicopter,' observed Evelyn as the room stood, paralysed with fright.

Sure enough, when the light went off outside, it became obvious that a helicopter had landed in the grounds of the facility. Every head turned: from out of the helicopter came, carefully, a strong-looking woman with very curly hair, two security men wearing headsets, another tallish person and, behind them, the shambolic, besuited, instantly recognisable figure of the Prime Minister.

'I thought this circus didn't have enough rings,' remarked Evelyn quietly.

The Prime Minister looked excited and was beaming as Anyali brought him into the lab, shooting a filthy look at Nigel as she did so. People naturally stood up a little straighter, put their hands together.

'COBRA decided this was best,' said Anyali. 'The Chiefs are right behind us.'

'Who's the CSC?' said Arnold.

'Combined Services Chiefs,' said Ranjit instantly. 'What? I wanted to join the Territorial Army. *What?* It's not my fault I'm allergic to ferns.'

'That's all we need,' said Nigel. 'The cavalry in here. Can we possibly keep them out?'

Anyali shook her head.

'You may or may not have noticed, but we're under attack?'

'You may or may not have noticed, but we're not?'

'The moon is sovereign to the Earth.'

Arnold watched this exchange.

'Huh, so you'll happily let the Maldives drown and the Middle East go to hell in a handbasket but someone blows up five rocks and you're all over it?'

'Shut up,' said Nigel and Anyali simultaneously without looking at him.

'Okay, good evening,' said the Prime Minister, who had been going round the room shaking hands. 'Now, I have here a prepared speech for our new galactic intimates. It has some Latin but not much ... have we got a translator?'

Nigel looked at the mathematicians.

'Luke spoke English perfectly,' said Evelyn. 'I don't know if that'll work, but they're certainly capable of understanding other languages.'

'That's all we know,' said Nigel.

'Fine, fine,' said the Prime Minister.

'Has he been fully briefed?' said Nigel. Anyali nodded.

'Give me two minutes.'

Nigel dragged Anyali to the side.

'What's our play?'

'Boss isn't sure.'

'What the hell do you mean, he isn't sure?'

'Well, extradition treaties and all that.'

'This isn't a person we're talking about! This isn't a case for Amnesty freaking International!'

Anyali shrugged.

'I know. Tell *him* that.'

'But Christ, it's obvious. He's a fugitive from whatever the hell it is aliens do in alien places. We offer to give him up and ask them to leave us alone. Why isn't that straightforward?'

'Have you even got him yet?'

'We're getting closer.'

'Belarus is huge.'

'Yes, and their army is also huge.'

Anyali shook her head. 'You know the boss doesn't want any ... anything getting out, particularly involving our political theoretical allies in the east?'

Nigel nodded. Malik's message from Interpol had been short and to the point: they had been seen escaping from a train near Mazyr. They couldn't have gone far. They were borrowing some special forces operatives, but had been very cagey about the reasons.

'It's really just a case of stalling them until we have him pinned down.'

'Well, there you go,' said Anyali. 'Start the PM yacking their ears off and you'll have all the time you need. If they have ears.'

She looked at Pol's station.

'Do we seriously have contact?'

Nigel nodded, his mouth dry.

'We think so.'

They looked at each other.

'Well, well,' said Anyali, shaking her head. 'Contact.'

Nigel nodded again.

'Good luck, Field Agent Cardon,' said Anyali.

'And you,' said Nigel. It was the first time they had ever met in person. Formally, they shook hands.

'Put the speaker back on,' said Nigel as the Prime Minister stood, looking grave but unable to stop his lips twitching entirely.

The computer once again started peaking, and the great cacophony of noise poured through the speakers. Pol concentrated hard. A microphone was set up in front of the Prime Minister, who thanked them quietly.

Pol typed something furiously into the computer with three screens, then held up his finger for silence. He brought it down again slowly, and made a 3-2-1 motion with his hand.

The Prime Minister moved forwards and cleared his throat.

'Hello?' said Luke again. He frowned and rubbed it.

'Technology,' said Connie sympathetically. Please let it be someone they could talk to. Somebody who would understand. Somebody they could communicate with.

*

'Good evening, friends from across the stars,' began the Prime Minister. Nigel shifted from foot to foot uncomfortably. One of the technicians was surreptitiously recording on his mobile telephone. The Prime Minister's security gently took the phone off him without disturbing the rest of the room, and crushed it underfoot.

The car-crashing, squealing, metal noise they could hear moved up and down the dials again. And now something else: there was an odd, metallic feeling in the air; a heavy pressure, like before a static storm. People rubbed their ears.

'This is Great Britain calling,' said the Prime Minister. Had Connie been there, it would have reminded her of the Eurovision Song Contest.

'We wish … to extend to you … a hand of greeting and peace … '

The great crashing noise started to thin. It was still a massive cacophony, but it no longer sounded like a symphony of cars in a tornado. On the audio files, one could clearly see one layer after another being stripped away, like a rock band stripping down to acoustics.

'… and welcome you to our solar system, if indeed you have not sampled its delights before … please do ask before taking moon souvenirs.'

'No jokes!' hissed Anyali. 'I said no bloody jokes! I swear, if the French can't get them, God knows how an alien civilisation is going to react!'

The noise thinned out again and again, until finally something made a single noise: a tone. Then another. Then another.

'Sixths,' said Evelyn and Arnold simultaneously.

'No,' said Arnold. 'Sixths and a half'

'What?' said Nigel.

'It's a mathematical measuring of tone. Universally consistent. But in a horrible key.'

'Like Luke de-tempering the piano,' said Evelyn. 'That's what he was trying to do.'

'They must speak a tonal language,' said Arnold. 'That's why Luke thinks garbage pickup is singing. Hang on, scale the sound frequencies. They don't use rational harmonics: scale it by the square root of three.'

Pol nodded quickly and typed rapidly.

The tones took on a vocalisation of sorts: an *ahh*, and a *ddd*.

'Very good!' said the PM encouragingly. Anyali's face was stern.

Finally, as Pol fiddled to strip out the background hissing still raining down on them from the moon meteors, they caught it. A deep, ominous noise but a recognisable sound.

'O n e.'

The room held its breath.

'One; one, two!' said the PM. 'Very good very good! Testing! One, two, three! You're on! We can hear you!'

'O n e,' said the voice again. It sounded neither human nor robotic; neither male nor female: simply a sound making English noises. Evelyn couldn't think what it reminded her of. Then she did: it spoke at the same low, dissociative timbre as the shipping forecast. And Luke, of course. Gently, as if he could never ever dream of causing harm.

And look at the harm he had caused: harm just as clear as the forecast that announced the terrible storms; the moon explosion; the peril. The voices were not responsible, but they bore witness.

'Y o u   h a v e . . . o n e   o f   u s,' came the voice. There was a small delay.

The Prime Minister nodded.

'It can't see you,' said Pol.

261

'How on earth would you know, young man?' shot back the Prime Minister off-mike.

'Yes,' he said back into the microphone. 'We understand, and we wish to extend you our full resources.'

That was too much for Arnold. Francis the PhD guard was distracted watching the Prime Minister, whom he had voted for, hoping he would back up his belief in education by funding increases. This had not happened.

Arnold in any case had forgotten he was being guarded at all. Instead, he simply lurched forward and threw himself at the mike

'YIPPIEKAYAYMOTHERFUCKER!' he screamed 'I DRINK YOUR MILKSHAKE! AND I WILL HAVE MY VENGEANCE IN THIS LIFE OR THE NEXT! LUKE!'

Luke held it up, beaming, as it glowed a little and the cacophony from Cambridge broke out.

'Arnold?' he said in delight. 'Arnold, is that you?'

'LUKE!' screamed Evelyn, even as Arnold was wrestled to the ground by the two security men. The man who'd had his phone ground down used the opportunity to tread on the security man's hand and pretend it was an accident.

Sé suddenly sat up.

'Where's Connie?' he said. 'Where's Connie? Is she there?'

Immediately the feed burst into a howl of feedback, an enormous mélange of noise.

Luke, patched through, sitting in the field in Myozr, held steady.

'No,' he said calmly to the noise. 'I have a new language now.'

The noise continued to rage, and Luke waited patiently for it to stop, which it did gradually, stripping away layers and layers of aggravated dissonance, until it was one voice.

'O n e o f u s,' came the voice.

The Prime Minister looked around the room in consternation.

'Is this our vagabond?'

Anyali looked at Nigel, who glanced at Evelyn, who nodded.

'Well, EXCELLENT news,' said the PM. 'Where are you?'

'Don't tell him!' shouted Arnold, inviting another kick in the ribs, which he got. It didn't matter. Pol was already working on a third computer screen, which was tracing the signal in double-quick time.

'A n d y o u g i v e y o u r s e l f u p?' came the voice.

SCIF control held its breath.

'Can you tell me what happened?' said Luke, still in that gentle voice. 'After I did what I did?'

'Is CONNIE there?' shouted Sé desperately.

'Yes,' came Connie's quiet voice. 'I am here.'

'Are you all right?'

'Shut up, Sé, we're trying to do a thing, right?'

'She hasn't changed,' commented Evelyn.

'W h a t h a p p e n e d?' repeated the alien voice slowly, as if it had misunderstood.

'After the wall came down,' said Luke, 'what happened? Tell me. Did you just build another one?'

There was a long pause. Then the voice spoke, less hesitant now, as if it was getting the hang of the language.

'No,' said the voice. 'We did not build another one.'

'Why not?'

'Because ... at first. At first it was hard. With what you did. With everyone mixing up and mixing together. It is not natural to us. Just because you are a ...'

It looked for the word.

'Mutt,' said Luke. 'Apparently the word is "mutt".'

'Y e s,' said the voice, sounding unconvinced.

'Then what happened?' said Connie, genuinely interested.

'The mingling could not be avoided and, over time – it took time. But, over time . . . there was . . . there was mixing, and slowly people stopped being quite so fearful. And it was . . . it became good.'

In the SCIF room, Arnold punched the air. The security man kicked his hand. In the dark field, Luke's face broke into a wide grin. Connie jumped on his back, kissing the back of his neck.

'Yes!' she whispered in his ear. 'Yes yes yes!'

'So there is more conflict since the wall came down? Or less?' said Luke.

'We are not in the way of conversing with criminals,' said the voice.

'Please tell us,' said Connie, hollering into the pebble, although this was patently unnecessary and nearly deafened Pol. Which pleased Arnold. Connie went on, 'Please. You've found us. We're here. Please tell us.'

There was another pause. The voice didn't change timbre, but Connie believed she heard a weary note in it.

'They . . . there are some who have built memorials in your name and would call you a saviour.'

There was a pause after this as everybody took it in.

'Why, this is WONDERFUL news!' said the PM in the SCIF. 'Shall we have a diplomatic summit? I do love those. We all take photographs, you see . . . you would be the guest of honour. The food is generally very good.' He paused. 'Out of interest, how big are you?'

'So you don't need him,' said Connie urgently. 'You don't need him to go back with you.'

'He is a criminal,' said the voice. 'We have orders to return him.'

'What if you say you couldn't find him?'

'We find him.'

'But you can't take him away! What will you do to him if you take him?'

'Justice.'

'Thank God,' said Connie, but Luke was shaking his head.

'People of Earth. We shall not forget the service you have done for us. Then we shall go and not return, as is the mandate of all peoples of the universe: you are not discovered, you discover. When you are ready, you come to us. We do not invade and we do not contact. Except in very exceptional circumstances.'

'Hang ON,' said Connie. 'These are good exceptional circumstances. You just said, like, he brought massive peace to your world.'

'He did.'

'And you're going to take him away and kill him?'

'As leader of . . . this world,' interjected the PM. 'No, hang on, I got that wrong didn't I? Let me see. As leader of . . . a part of this world. Quite a small part, but we like it. ANYWAY. I think, if you're amenable, we'd rather like to keep this chap. Have a look at him. You know. See if we can learn anything . . . um, from each other, you know. We could make sure he's kept out of trouble, mind you. No problem at all.'

'YES!' said Connie excitedly. 'Yes! Do that one! The locking up and experiments one!'

'Shut up, Connie,' said Evelyn. 'Just shut up.'

The voice came again. There was still the faint, two second delay on the broadcast.

'It is our job to find the criminal and bring him back.'

'Yes,' said the PM patiently. 'But you have also said he has done your world a service. Therefore can he not choose his residency? After some mutually beneficial work for both our

265

societies, perhaps? He shall be treated as a criminal here, I assure you.'

There was a long silence.

'We shall consider this.'

Luke gently unpeeled Connie from his back, and set her down in the field. She couldn't sit still though, and hopped up again, bouncing from foot to foot. He held up the glass once more.

'I must tell you,' he said. 'I must tell you. Please pass on to the –' And here he said something Connie did not catch. '– that I meant no harm to anyone. I sabotaged a construction I thought was terribly, terribly wrong. I didn't mean anything bad to happen. I meant . . . I meant for the walls to come down, for people to realise they could live together. That is all I meant. I was young then, and foolish, but . . .'

'Would you do it again?' came the voice, implacable.

'Yes.'

'And if you find walls on this world, will you bring them down?'

Luke hesitated.

'I do not understand these people.'

'How can you expect to live among them?'

Connie squeezed his hand. There was a long pause.

'The best I can,' said Luke quietly.

There was another silence.

'And you,' said the voice. 'Ruler of this world.'

'Um, yes?' came the PM's voice.

'You are agreeable to this person staying within the bounds of your environment? Knowing what he has done and what he is capable of doing?'

'Totes,' said the Prime Minister, delighted. 'I mean, yes. Yes, we are. On behalf of Her Majesty the Queen, I believe I have permission to invite this personage to become – under

266

suitable conditions of course, for his own safety – part of our world empire, to pass on his wisdom and knowledge beyond the stars and help us all become better citizens in a new inter-stellar democracy.'

The PM beamed around the room. Arnold, still in a choke-hold on the ground, held his breath, as did Evelyn. Sé watched intently. Ranjit bobbed up and down.

There was a long pause.

'We shall debate this with our seniority,' came the voice. Then the terrible cacophony came back over the speaker and Pol whipped off his headphones, and then it went quiet and people's ears popped, and the odd static feeling was gone.

In the room, there was a terrible rabble.

Pol had plotted two things now on his computer screen: the position of Connie and Luke's signal ... and the position of where the alien signal was coming from. It was just, as far as they could see, at the very edge of the solar system.

'Why did nobody notice this?' barked someone at the edge of the screen. 'They're basically around the corner.'

Pol was shaking his head. 'We monitor it all the time. All the time.'

'Scanning now, sir,' said somebody else.

In the commotion, nobody heard the doors open. In marched several distinguished, heavily medalled, middle-aged men.

'Ah, good, I knew you were right behind us,' said the Prime Minister, rather weakly. 'Um, we couldn't quite wait for you, but Anyali will debrief you immediately.'

'You've *communicated* with the enemy?' said a rear admiral, going rather pink in the face. 'You didn't wait for us?'

The Prime Minister did his patented head tilt which was meant to look boyish and adorable. It didn't cut much ice with a rear admiral.

'I had absolutely no choice,' he said. 'They started to speak, and, well, here we were. Let's not have a coup d'état about it, old chaps.'

'Let me talk to them now,' said the army general, marching forwards. 'We'll tell them what's what about blowing up our moon.'

'Um, yes,' said the Prime Minister, who didn't mind being taken for a foolish man, but was not one. 'Actually we're rather in the matter of settling matters peacefully. And we're also getting to keep an alien. So actually, so far it's going rather well. I think we can manage the rest without you.'

The CSCs, who normally despised one another, swapped furious glances.

'How do you know they aren't saying that, then they're going to blow up the world?' said the general. 'After all, they blew up the moon.'

'Oh, we could blow up the moon any time we bally well liked,' said the PM. 'Doesn't prove a thing. Why would you, anyway?'

The general looked at him.

'I thought you were the classical scholar, sir. Why wouldn't you? Planet full of minerals and cheap labour. I know what I'd do.'

The glass in Luke's hand went opaque and he looked at it for a long moment, then looked at Connie.

'I have never heard a justice person say that before,' he said wonderingly.

'He's going to think about it!' said Connie, throwing her arms around his neck. 'He's going to think about it! That always means yes! It's what your dad says when you ask him to buy you an ice cream.'

Luke frowned.'Or what you say when you want to pass the decision to somebody else.'

'Exactly!' said Connie. '"Can I have a discount on this car please?"; "I'll think about it . . . Oh, okay then – I just wanted you to think I was tough".'

She flung herself around him and he held her, burying his face in her hair.

'It makes me . . . it makes me very happy that you have so much belief in me,' he said.

'Are you kidding?' said Connie. 'Did you hear what he said? You basically saved their entire planet. There are statues of you! You're famous.'

Luke made a face.

'What?'

'"Famous" is a strange concept to me. You emotionally torture physically symmetrical individuals. I don't really understand it.'

'No,' said Connie, vowing to stop reading internet newspapers with pictures of women in bikinis drinking coffee. It was odd, but the weird purity of Luke, his lack of cultural context . . . it made her feel like a blank canvas too. It made her want to fill her brain and her heart only with the beautiful things and beautiful places of the world, and share them with him for the first time too.

Suddenly, Luke stiffened. She felt it, then moved backwards out of his arms to attempt to see what he was gazing at. She turned around and gasped. A thin, bald figure, ghostly white in the moonlight, was moving towards them from the other end of the field.

Chapter Twenty-five

'Can I get up now?' said Arnold. 'Only this floor has physicist cooties all over it.'

Everyone ignored him. There was an absolutely massive barney going on with everybody shouting at once in stern voices, threatening to go to the papers or speak directly to the US or Russian presidents which, it was pointed out, would trigger a massive international panic and ruin the world just as surely as the aliens could manage blowing it up. The security guard was glancing around the room to make sure nobody left or took out their phones, but hadn't had the order to take his foot off Arnold's neck, so he didn't bother. Ranjit was looking at the other security guard next to him.

'Can I touch your gun?'

'No.'

The noise levels rose, with even the Prime Minister unable to do much in the way of restoring order, and Anyali managed to thread her way across to Nigel.

'What the hell do you think we should do?' she said.

Nigel shrugged. 'I've done my bit,' he said, hanging up his phone. 'Belarussian forces are on their way.' He answered her enquiring glance. 'No, they just think he's a suspected terrorist. But they're under strict instructions not to shoot him.'

'Oh, well, if you've told them off in a stern voice,' said Anyali. 'I'm sure that helps scared, trigger-happy young soldiers in the dark.'

Nigel rolled his eyes. 'Special forces,' he said. 'They're not sending down the Boy Scouts. They know he's molten gold to us.'

'What if we don't get him?' said Anyali. 'What if he does some alien thing to them and kills them all?'

Nigel had considered this too and didn't want to think about it.

'Not sure,' he said. 'Have we still got all those nuclear shelters?'

Pol was holding up a sheet of paper.

'Well, this is ridiculous,' he said loudly, and everyone went quiet to listen to him.

'What?' said Anyali impatiently. Pol was rather milking his moment.

'We've found the sector it's in, we've focused the telescopes – but there's still nothing there: nothing to see at all. It's like they're completely invisible.'

The night was growing less dark, and Luke straightened up slowly as the figure came towards them, slowly at first, then faster and faster. When it got close enough for Luke to see it properly, he let out a cry and opened his arms, and the figure ran full pelt towards him.

'Galina!'

'Luke!'

The thin figure threw herself into Luke's arms, and he pulled her close. Connie felt a flash of totally uncharacteristic jealousy. Who was this?

The woman – it was a woman – had been wearing a headscarf, which had fallen off, but which she now wound expertly again around her head. She let out a long stream in a foreign language, as Connie looked on, baffled, and then she pulled herself back from Luke's embrace and started to touch his face all over, remarking as she did so.

'Um, hello?' said Connie. Luke turned around.

'Sorry,' said Luke. 'Sorry, how could I . . . Galina, this is . . .'

If you forget my name right now, thought Connie, I shall kill you, spaceman under pressure or not.

'. . . um, Connie. This is Galina.'

Galina started talking again.

'I can't understand what she's saying,' pointed out Connie.

'Oh yes! You speak different things. Sorry. Do you speak her language?'

'No.'

Luke smiled.

'Wow, there's a lot of languages you don't speak.'

'Uh, yeah, let me see you do up some buttons?'

He smiled at her and turned back to Galina. '*Ci možacie vy havary pa-anhie sku?*'

Galina nodded. '*Dy.* Yes. Yes. Hello, how are you?'

Connie shook hands.

'Nice to meet you.'

'I say to him, I see blowing up of moon and I think, that will be him! I have not seen this boy in years and years . . . how handsome he is, no? He look same as my Artem. Just same! He is exactly what my boy would be if he had . . .'

Her voice trailed off.

Connie glanced at the glass pebble in Luke's hands. It was completely immobile, without its usual glow. Whatever was being discussed, there was nothing they could do about it now, and she had absolutely no idea how long it might take.

'Why don't you tell us all about it?' she said.

*

In the end, they sat down close to the trees. Galina expertly made a little fire out of bracken and twigs, which flickered merrily in the pre-dawn chill, and Connie remembered the bottle of Polish vodka in their bag which had miraculously survived the fall, and which she and Galina each had a swig of.

'I was born,' Galina began, her English improved by the vodka and, she said later, the days she spent watching American films when she felt too weak to move.

'I was born in the autumn of 1986.'

Connie was shocked: there was hardly any difference in their ages, but Galina looked old enough to be her mother.

'I know, I know. I am not doing the age well,' Galina said dryly, leaning her hand out to caress Luke's hair again. 'You have *girlfriend*?' she asked, smiling. 'Does she know about you?'

Luke nodded.

'Yes.'

Galina had no eyebrows, but if she did she'd have raised them. She looked at Connie.

'You love Fish Man Thing?'

Connie flushed to the roots of her hair. She couldn't look at him.

'Um,' she said. 'Yes. Yes I think so.'

Luke turned to her – for once, the wry smile was not playing on his lips. Instead, he looked solemn. He reached out and took her hand. Galina chuckled. 'Well, everybody need somebody love, yes? You have Fish Man Thing, I had my Artem, and so the world goes.'

She took another slug of the vodka.

'I was in mother's belly when explosion happened. You have heard? Chernobyl?'

Connie gasped in surprise. She had had absolutely no idea where they were.

273

'One hundred kilometres from here. You could hear it, mother said. You could see it. And authorities they said, don't worry, it is fine, is mighty Soviet engineering, and then authorities say no actually thank you very much you should move but we were poor and we could not move. And what Chernobyl did we do not see: it put something deep inside me, you understand? In the insides of bones, and I can never be well.'

Luke's other hand went out to pat Galina on the arm, but she grabbed it and held on to it.

'But one time, I am young, I am "in remission" is called, and I want go out with friends and be like other girls, and I go dancing and I drink too much vodka, and I meet a handsome boy.'

She stared unabashedly at Luke.

'He look very like you.'

Luke nodded.

'And so. And boy, he left joined the army, but he left something. And I was happy because I was sick and I wanted something, something good to happen, for once in life, one good thing. And my mother happy because she had sick child and she want healthy child. And when Artem was born, he most beautiful, wonderful boy in all of world.'

She sighed deeply, and buried her head in her hands. Connie moved round to the other side of her and put her arm around her.

'But he was sick too. Everyone here sick. The government said, do not worry, no sick. We are all sick. Not straightaway, you know, not fast. No. But it is inside, deep inside and it was inside boy. My boy.

'And he often could not go to school, and treatment burns him. But so clever! He worked and he worked and he had best computer we bought for him and he was best quick what he could do. He was brilliant genius.'

Luke nodded. 'He really was.'

'And one day he wants to go out, get out of bed in the night ... he has discovered something, he says, something that is strange and giving out things that are strange ...'

Luke nodded at the memory.

'It was my fault,' he said. 'I'd just landed, and I took the communicator device outside, which means it gives out a signal.'

His head drooped.

'It was a mistake. Beyond any mistake I ever made.'

Galina rubbed his head.

'Ah, *chlop yk*, it was not your fault. You did not mean it. And to us you were never mistake. You were best thing that ever happened.'

'And to me,' said Connie. There was a pause.

'Please go on,' she said to Galina.

The SCIF team gathered round the monitor. The display from the telescopes was utterly, utterly beautiful: the edge of the solar system, the termination shock visible, hot orange colours dancing and swirling as the solar winds and interstellar gas started to mix. Suddenly, something flashed, and they all saw it.

'Was that ... ?'

'It has to be the bow shock,' said someone. 'Look at the bubble shape.'

Everyone leaned closer. There was barely any light, nothing could reflect and they were too far away from the sun. But there was the definite sensation that something was hanging there ... something that looked like a massive soap bubble.

'We'll just have to wait,' said the PM. 'No calls, no plans, no nothing until they talk to us again.'

He turned to Nigel, his voice stern.

'And GET YOUR CHAP IN HERE, do you understand me?'

'Yes, sir,' said Nigel.

'Can we order pizza?' said Arnold from the floor.

'They met. By river,' said Galina. 'Artem, he never wanted to be outside. Before. Being with computer, that was all he wanted. No trees, no grass, no anything. And then, he meet fishman and he make friend.'

'Seriously,' said Connie.

'He was scared at first,' said Luke. 'I was scared at first.'

'Then he go every day – in cold – and I say why and he say I make friend and I think bad man, bad man in wood want my boy and I scared too. Everybody scared!'

'What did you do?' she said to Luke. Luke shrugged. 'He liked maths.'

'You talked to him about *maths*?'

'He was such clever boy,' said Galina. 'Clever, clever boy. And I go and they do every day the equations and the talking I do not even understand it! And they draw in the sand! And he is nine years old! Brilliant.'

'You just did maths?' said Connie again. 'You didn't ask him about the world, learn lots of stuff?'

Luke shrugged.

'A little bit. But he wasn't really interested in the world, and I didn't understand it, and maths was the same for both of us, so . . .'

'Boys,' said Connie.

'I know he loved his mother,' said Luke.

But Galina was not to be side-tracked now.

'And then,' she said. 'And then summer come.'

'The river,' explained Luke. 'It is cold enough where we

jumped . . . but here, hidden, it gets warmer and . . . and I start to . . . '

'I know,' said Connie.

Luke nodded. 'We discussed the problem. I could form my body; I could make it the shape of a human, more or less. But without any colour.'

'Mmm,' said Connie.

'And my Artem, he very sick. Sicker every day,' said Galina. 'There was nothing that could fix him. All he wanted to do was see his Luke, his *Luca*. It was a joke, you see. Stupid English joke they had. Because he could not see things. Look, Luke! Artem learned English from television you know. So clever. So clever.'

'You couldn't fix him?' said Connie. Luke shook his head. 'Sorry. I had no idea what it was. It's not . . . I don't think it's something we get. And I am not a doctor.'

'But he helped him!' said Galina, indignant Connie might think Luke had done something wrong.

'He took him swims before it got too warm. He was so happy swimming,' she went on. 'So happy. It was best times of his life. Because his life was not good and my life was not good. But you know, you should see how Fish Man swims.'

Connie smiled a little, and nodded.

'He can swim, Fish Man Thing, and Artem, he loved that more than anything; he would laugh and laugh. Until that summer. And he too sick then, he was worse and worse.

'And then when he was close, they thought . . . they thought . . . '

'He gave me his colour,' said Luke. 'He gave it to me. I didn't take it, Connie, I promise. I didn't even know I could take it. It was his idea.'

'There was nothing to be done,' said Galina.

'I have always believed you,' said Connie. 'But, how?'

277

'Before he died, Artem told me what he wanted to do, and we tried it a little.'

'Ach, his hand!' said Artem's mother. 'That was, you know. That was the last thing he ever thought was funny: the see-through hand.'

'And it did not hurt. But it made him very sleepy. And to do more . . .'

Galina took another swig of the vodka and turned to face Connie, cross suddenly.

'You are not mother.'

'No,' said Connie, although it was not a question.

'You have never had child built to suffer. I will tell you, English girl, it is a pain worse than anything in world. It is worse than anything universe could devise or visit on you. I begged him.'

She spat into the fire. 'I begged him to take Artem's pain away. Pointless, endless, meaningless pain.'

Luke's eyes were watering and he rubbed them fiercely.

'Artem never cried.'

'You did not see him always last weeks,' said Galina. 'For you, smiles. Every second else, he was crying, or screaming, or begging, because cancer eats you; it eats you and it eats you from inside out, and it will not let you die and now it is doing the same to me.'

The anger left her voice.

'But for me, I do not care,' she said. 'I should kill myself. But I always hope; I always wish I see Artem again.'

Dreamily, she played with Luke's hair and hummed a little.

> *Jurja! stavaj rana,*
> *Jurja! myjsia biela,*
> *Jurja! Va mi kliu y,*
> *Jurja! Vyjdzi polie . . .*

'What happened?' said Connie.

'I held him,' said Luke. 'He gave it to me. I took it. It was not painful for him. He was not unhappy. He slept.'

There was a long silence. In the distance, an owl hooted.

Luke lowered his head.

'Then I had to leave, of course. Because of the questions.'

'There were no questions!' said Galina, banging down the now half-empty vodka bottle for emphasis. 'They did not even ask questions! They do not ask questions around Chernobyl because they are cowards, they are scared, they took my boy away in a closed coffin and they say NOTHING in case they lose their jobs, even though he lies there beautiful as if he made of ice. But I knew he was not really dead. Because there is some of him in you.'

'And I am privileged,' said Luke. 'Beyond privileged.'

'Here's the thing I want to know,' said Connie. 'Artem must have told you about the frozen north. Why didn't you just go north, live up there, be cold all the time, live out your days naturally? Why did you go to the UK?'

Luke gazed at her for a very long time.

'Because I was lonely,' he said simply.

Connie held his gaze as, unnoticed by both of them, the little pebble on his lap began to pulse-pulse-pulse even as, close by, there came the flip-flip-flip of a helicopter.

Chapter Twenty-six

The great crackling filled the room again as the air turned heavy and static, and everyone stopped bickering as if someone had flicked a switch. There was a cacophonous noise, which Pol turned down. Everyone glanced around the room, and Nigel wondered if they were all thinking the same thing: does the fate of the world really rest on this bunch?

'I can't believe the fate of the world rests on you bunch,' said Arnold.

'Can't we get him out?' said Anyali.

'Yes, I'll totally just walk out,' said Arnold. 'Will you shoot me in the back or just a quick head shot?'

'SHUT UP!' said Pol.

Again, the filtering process worked on the translation and many, many noises became just a few.

'E a r t h,' came the oddly gentle voice.

Connie jumped up. 'It's glowing!'

Luke hurriedly got to his feet and held it in his hand. They all listened in.

'E a r t h.'

*

Connie moved over to Luke and squeezed his hand.

'Yay,' she whispered. 'They're coming to take us back to England. Then you just Hulk-smash your way out of whatever horrible facility they put you in and we'll be free! You and me! For ever. Or however long you live for. If it's thousands of years, then probably not.'

Luke squeezed her back and gently kissed the top of her head.

The voice became clear.

'We have discussed the status of the escapee. It was an act of heroism and good for our world.'

Connie was nearly punching the air.

'But we cannot encourage sabotage on behalf of all those who have a grudge of some kind. We shall keep to what we have promised you, and leave your world alone. But you must fulfil what you have promised us. You will give him up to us. Where you are. We will come for him when it grows dark again where you are.'

There was a pause.

In England, the PM leaned over, clearing his throat to buy time, and coughed.

'Well now, are you absolutely sure that's quite reasonable? I mean, I think there's quite a lot we could discuss on extradition treaties and everything we could manage, but we are, on the whole, very much ... I mean, it appears you're going to kill him from everything we know down here, and ... I mean, if we were America we wouldn't have a problem but ... '

There was no response.

He leaned forward again.

'I suppose what I'm asking is ... what happens if we won't give him up?'

*

281

Nobody spoke for what seemed like a long time. The room held its breath. Then the speaker crackled back to life.

'F u r t h u r ... c o n s e q u e n c e s,' came the gentle voice. There was a hiss from the speakers, then the jumble of noise started again, rose, became an unbearable jumble of terrible industrial screaming and noise. Then it cut out.

Silence: complete and utter silence. The aliens had gone. And it didn't matter how much Pol or the Prime Minister or anyone shouted down the microphone, or how they communicated on the frequency. It was as if nobody had ever been there.

Ranjit burst into tears. Even Nigel shook his head in disbelief. Then Arnold did something his cardiologist would have been very, very surprised to see him do: in a moment of extraordinary strength and agility, he jumped up off the floor, pushing the huge security man over, who fell like a stack of rocks, jumped over to the microphone, pushed over the Prime Minister and screamed into the mike

'LUKE! KEEP RUNNING! THEY'RE COMING FOR YOU! KEEP RUNNING! NEVER STOP! *GO!*'

It took them longer to subdue him this time.

Galina was still staring into the fire, sipping the vodka bottle. But Connie and Luke were up, staring at each other.

'No way!' Connie was saying. 'No way! Patch in. Tell them they're wrong!'

Luke shook his head.

'It was always going to go this way,' he said. 'It was, I think, a diplomatic nicety to pretend to think about it. Gives them the aura of mercy. Without the mercy.'

'You thought that and you sat here?'

'With you by my side I would sit anywhere.'

Connie turned back to his ship. It was hard to spot, even as dawn was coming up over the fields.

'You said you can fix it,' she said. 'Fix it. FIX IT. We'll just go and find the next planet. Run away again. It'll be fine. We've run away once, we can do it again.'

Luke shook his head. 'Oh, my love.'

'Forget about it. I'm sick of Earth anyway. Come on. Let's go explore the universe! It'll be great!'

She ran up to the huge sphere, then turned back to see Luke's stricken face.

'My love,' he said. 'It can't . . . it can't take you.'

She froze. She knew this on some level. She knew they were not the same. They advanced towards each other.

'Because I don't have those bloody gills,' she said, hiccupping with tears she couldn't hold back.

Luke nodded.

'Stupid bloody gills.'

Connie turned and put her hands on the sphere. She felt it for a long time. The helicopter noise was getting louder. They must be searching the area. It wasn't going to take them long: they hadn't even put the fire out. She bit her lip, then turned back.

'You go,' she said. 'You can get away. Just you. You take this, and you get away now. Do it. Now.'

Luke stared at her.

'And leave you here to suffer the wrath of my people? Are you completely insane?'

Connie looked at him.

'We'll figure something out. Say you got lost. Kill a scarecrow or something and dress it up as you. Who would know? We'll just have it do some equations and complain about animal rights.'

Her voice was choked.

'No, *darahi*.'

He tilted her chin up to hers.

283

'As if I would ever go anywhere without you. It's both of us or nothing.'

They had to shout now. The helicopter – a huge Chinook, with two sets of rotating blades – was hovering over their heads.

'DO IT!' said Connie. 'I'D RATHER YOU WERE AWAY AND ALIVE THAN HERE WITH ME AND BEING KILLED.'

'WOULD YOU?'

'NO!'

Their hair was blown up in the downdraft of the huge craft as it came in to land.

'Down! Down! Down! Hands behind your head!' was being shouted from above. Galina glanced up at the huge craft, barely interested, still gazing into the fire, lost in her memories.

'USE YOUR GIANT BRAIN TO THINK OF A PLAN!' screamed Connie. 'DO IT! DO IT NOW!'

But just as the helicopter touched down, with half a dozen fully black-clad men with guns trained on them both, Luke suddenly made a bolt for Galina. He took her hands in his and held them to his mouth. She gazed up at him, her hollow eyes huge in her thin face, and came back to life.

'*Ci ba u ciabie zno?*'

Luke buried his face in her shoulder. '*Ja nie viedaju.*'

'DOWN! DOWN! HANDS BEHIND YOUR HEAD!'

Galina's shaking hands reached out to caress him one more time.

'*Bratka,*' she husked.

'*Za siody,*' Luke bowed his head as they shot him in the back of the neck, and Connie screamed the length of the field and beyond.

Chapter Twenty-seven

All the boyishness had drained from the Prime Minister's face. There seemed no point in going back to COBRA in London when all the main players were there, and they were only waiting to hear from the Belarusian forces telling them that they'd entered UK air space. Tea was made and brought in, and the staff was left behind manning the comms with strict instructions to contact the commanding force if anything at all came up.

Arnold was unconscious, and Sé not actually that much better, so the two of them were being hauled back to their rooms by security.

'Put them in the main room and leave me with them,' said Evelyn. 'Someone needs to keep an eye on them. You may think you can behave with impunity wherever the hell you want, but there'll be consequences if anything happens.'

'You can write me a letter of complaint from Holloway,' said Nigel. 'Or do you want to go back to DRC? I hear in their prisons, if you pay enough to the warder, you can buy a space to lie down in.'

Evelyn eyed him levelly.

'I want you not to kill my colleagues through a duty of care issue,' she said stiffly. 'Up to you, obviously. You never know, we might end up in the neighbouring cells.'

Nigel heaved a sigh.

'We don't need you any more,' he said.

'So we're all going to die in mystery car accidents?'

'What?' Nigel was very tired. 'No. No. No, all I meant was, I don't think it matters if you share a room any more. So. Fine. Fine. Whatever.'

He waved his hand at them to go away. 'Just go ... And keep that fat one out of my way, *please*.'

'What about the one you tortured?' said Evelyn. 'You want him swept under the carpet too?'

Nigel looked at her.

'We had NO idea what was up there. NONE. So they want to kill one guy. They could kill a thousand guys. A million guys! They still might!'

'We wanted to give Luke a chance,' said Evelyn.

'Yeah, you protected your friend and you risked absolutely everybody else's friends,' said Nigel, his face red with anger. 'And for what? For nothing. We have him now, and we're bringing him in and we are going to do what the big aliens with the moon-blowing-up gun want us to do, and if you think I feel the least bit good about that you are fucking wrong, and if you think my job is to protect as many people as I possibly can from getting blown to fucking bits, then that would be more like it, no thanks to people like you who think because you can do some fucking sums you are somehow better than the rest of us.'

He calmed down.

'But yes, you may share a room. And you may also say thank you.'

Evelyn looked at him.

'I don't consider myself better than non-mathematicians,' she said. 'But I consider myself better than you.'

She took Sé from the guard, and motioned the other guards,

who heaved the large bulk of Arnold into the room and draped him ungracefully across three chairs. She supported Sé, who could walk but still a little unsteadily.

'Do I have to come?' said Ranjit. 'Because actually I'd really like to go home and just watch the rest of this on television.'

'This isn't television, Ranj,' said Evelyn wearily.

'No,' said Ranjit, following her, shoulders drooping. 'I wish it were television. Although I would probably change channels to *Strictly Come Dancing*.' He perked up. 'Hey, do you think when this is all over they might want me on *Strictly Come Dancing*?'

'That,' said Evelyn heavily, 'is a world I don't even want to think about.'

Luke jerked awake, immediately alert two to three hours before he ought to have done given the dosage, to find himself strapped to the wall in the belly of a large helicopter with space for twenty to thirty people. The racketing noise level was unbelievable: he found it soothing. At first he couldn't focus on anything, but looking around, more and more in a panic, he finally recognised Connie sitting opposite him, strapped in too and staring at him intensely.

'Thank God,' she said. She reached out for him, but she couldn't get past the straps holding her in. They were both in handcuffs.

Luke glanced around.

'2.3508.' He frowned.

Immediately a soldier trained his gun on them.

'No talking,' he said.

Luke glanced down at his handcuffs, then pulled at them experimentally.

'DON'T,' hissed Connie. 'Leave them on. Or I don't know what they'll do.'

'NO TALKING.'

'Find a way,' said Connie. 'Work it out. You know you can.'

'Well . . .' said Luke. He pulled again at the restraints, and one loosened from the wall.

'What are you doing?' said the soldier, but before he could respond, someone else shot Luke again.

Back in a room off SCIF control, as the technicians desperately tried to re-establish the connection, a solemn meeting was taking place.

'What does he look like?' said the rear admiral.

'He's just a bloke,' said Nigel. 'That's what's been diverting us all along. Just a tall, skinny bloke.'

'How did he get so far then?' said the general.

'Because he just looks like a bloke,' said Nigel. 'I think if he'd had the giant tentacles we'd have probably nabbed him a little faster.'

'Well, all of that doesn't matter now,' said the Prime Minister. 'All that matters is what we do.'

The room fell silent.

'If we have hard decisions to make, we must make them,' he went on.

He looked up.

'Is anyone seriously opposed to doing what we are asked and handing him over?'

'How do we know they won't just blow us up anyway, regardless of what we do?' said the general.

'We don't,' said Nigel. 'We have no idea if they are lying to us. Or even if they know what lying is. All we have to go on is what they've said. And . . .'

He sounded reluctant.

'What?' said Anyali.

Nigel sighed.

'I don't know,' he said. 'But it seems that those who have met and worked with the alien ... God knows why, but they appear to find him trustworthy.'

'Quite right,' said the PM. 'I think we have to take it at face value. That said, are we prepared? Are we prepared to lose the first living alien creature ever to reach our planet and, moreover, almost certainly to send it to its death?'

Nobody spoke for quite a long time.

Anyali leaned over, staring at her phone.

'Another ferry grounded in Indonesia, sir.'

'Oh God,' said the PM. 'Casualties?'

'None as yet,' said Anyali. 'But that's the fourth ... surely it's only a matter of time ...'

'Is that definitely from the moon thing?' said the admiral. 'Accidents happen at sea.'

'I think that was the problem,' said Anyali quietly. 'I don't think the sea was where it was supposed to be. The ship ran aground off an atoll in Riau.'

The general was shaking his head, saying, 'We need to take this to the UN. We can't this decision on our own when it has consequences for the entire world.'

A tall woman had been standing quietly at the back – she had arrived on the military helicopter. Nobody had questioned her credentials. Nigel was reasonably sure she was his boss, but not a hundred per cent certain. Personal meetings were not encouraged in his line of work.

Now she stepped forward and put her hands lightly on the table.

'What do you think, Kathy?' The PM had aged overnight. His crumpled suit looked fit for the bin, and bags hung under his eyes. 'The most amazing thing that's ever happened to Earth and they want us to give it up.'

Kathy had flat, grey eyes and very dark hair.

289

'It is a calculated risk,' she said in a low voice. She looked at Anyali.

'We have moved into damage limitation now,' she said. 'We don't know the facts of what this man – or creature – has done. I think we can be reasonably sure he killed one of our agents.'

There was nodding around the table.

'If we do nothing, the moon will be destroyed, or worse. If we protect him, the same. If we do what they ask and deliver, they say they will leave us alone. They may or may not. I simply do not understand what other choice we have.'

The room was silent. The military men were nodding. The PM let out a heavy sigh. Nigel did too, but for different reasons: he wanted this to be over. He wanted to go home, to sink into Annabel's arms and not think about any of them again.

Luke awoke again after they had refuelled and were crossing the Channel. The light was early-morning cold and grey. There was a door open in the side of the craft even though it was freezing, and Connie was peering through to the sea below. The waves were like nothing she'd ever seen before: a huge storm, crashing both coastlines. There wasn't a ship to be seen out in the deadly night; vast, crested waves looked to be thirty or forty metres high – great, big mountains and furrowing troughs. Connie looked down, slightly fearful, but also fascinated by their motion.

'I've never seen a storm like this,' she murmured, then realised like an idiot she was talking to the soldiers who (a) didn't speak English and (b) were trained to kill her.

Then Luke's gentle voice came and she realised he was awake.

'The moon's disrupted the tidal systems.'

'Please don't make them knock you out again just to tell me about tidal systems,' she whispered.

But the men were hypnotised by the storm too. The Chinook was being tossed about in the wind like a toy being manhandled by a toddler. Battle-hardened marines were looking profoundly uncomfortable. One was being quietly sick in a bag. Connie didn't mind their discomfort. If she was with Luke, nothing of the sea could harm her. Suddenly, she wished the helicopter would crash, then felt awful for thinking such a thing.

'What will happen with the weather?' she whispered to Luke. 'With the tides?'

'It's bad,' said Luke. 'Tides will fall. The ocean level will drop, maybe by two centimetres, because there's less mass and less erosion ...'

Connie looked at him open-mouthed.

'You're not serious'

'I'm afraid so.'

'That's ...'

'What my people have done to yours is unconscionable,' said Luke.

Connie was momentarily side-tracked.

'How come you know the word "unconscionable" and not the word for car?' she said.

'I like Jane Austen,' said Luke.

'Oh. Okay, but no, no, what I mean is, the sea level in the world is too high! Far too high! If this brings it down – even a tiny bit ...' Connie's eyes were round. 'Oh my goodness. No, but no, I mean, this could be a good thing. If this storm ever blows itself out.'

'It will,' said Luke. His face was confused. 'Why did your planet let the tides rise so high? Don't you know you have to look after the water?'

'It's ...'

'... complicated?'

The helicopter lurched from one side to another. Luke was thrown halfway across the space, and briefly, briefly, they managed to touch hands. A soldier growled at them and they pulled apart. When Connie glanced down at her palm, she saw there was something written on it in the faintest of sparkling lines.

$$e^{i\pi} + 1 = 0$$

'That' said Luke. 'That is what you are to me.'
She beamed at him.

Anyali was grimacing at her phone again. 'They're reporting terrible weather conditions,' she said. 'But they're coming in. The bird is coming in.'
The room straightened up nervously.
Nigel nodded and glanced around.
'Have you a squad going to meet them?'
Nigel nodded.
'Yes. The local boys have worked hard for this.'

The Chinook staggered to a halt at a landing field just outside the town. They had beaten the dawn, but only just.
Stiff, nervous, Luke and Connie were unbuckled at gunpoint by a slightly green-looking special forces soldier, and they staggered forwards on stiff legs, letting themselves down from the side. In the chill of the early dawn, the spires of the beautiful distant city rose out of the mist. Connie felt so strange to be back again, looking at the timeless golden brick, the flat lands, the damp, smoky green. Luke tried to take her hand, but the butt of a rifle held them apart. All she wanted, she thought crossly, all she wanted was time. To sit, to talk, to get to know one another more. A little time. She looked at him.
He must be planning something. He must be. He acted

mild, but inside he was as strong as steel. Stronger. Connie racked her own brains to think if there was something she could do, but all she could come up with was Luke pulling off his handcuffs – which she knew he could do without breaking a sweat – grabbing her, and carrying her away again. And what good would that do? What would they do next? Blow up Australia? Thailand? What on earth was the point in them continuing to run when running in the end would do no good; would bring them no peace or contentment? There was nowhere left to run.

There must be another way.

DCI Malik strode out of his Black Maria towards the special forces men.

'Morning.

'I can handle it from here.'

The commander looked at him. 'Who are they?' he asked.

Malik tapped the side of his nose.

'Big suspects,' he said. 'Murder case. Thanks for picking them up.'

Paviel, the Chinook commander, was puzzled. Picking up murder suspects was not generally special forces business. But on the other hand, asking questions was not really special forces business either. He nodded at his men, who escorted them roughly to the back of the police van.

'Come on, in you get,' said the DCI curtly, indicating where with a nod. 'You two have caused us quite enough trouble already.'

They sat bowed in the back, holding hands tightly.

Malik glanced in the rear-view mirror.

'Are you hungry?'

'No,' said Luke.

Connie shook her head. Sitting in the back of a police van back in England, back where they started, shivering in the chill, looking out of the barred windows and coming to terms with the consequences of what they had done – everything they had done, and what they were going to do, what they were proposing to do – had sunk her spirits, even as she tried to get as close as she could to Luke, to huddle in his warmth, to take in every bit of him.

Ignoring them, Malik pulled into a service station, parked in an isolated bay amid a copse of trees, locked up the van – Luke could have punched out of it in a second, but of course he did not – and returned five minutes later with three mugs of steaming coffee, a bacon sandwich and two salads.

Luke stared at him, confused, through the grille, as he unlocked the van door. Then he stood up and handed the salad to Luke.

As he did so, his hand touched Luke's hand.

And, astonishingly to Connie as she watched, his hand passed *into* Luke's hands, right through it, so the two of them were suddenly connected completely, like plasticine rolled into one another.

Luke dropped the salad and glanced up, astounded. Malik made a face at him to keep quiet.

'I cannot find a word in this tongue,' he said in a low voice. 'But I think I shall call you "Brother-Sister".'

Connie leapt up.

'No way! You're another one!'

The two men were staring at each other, their hands so intermeshed it was impossible to see where one ended and the other began.

'Are you here to kill me?' said Luke in a low voice. Malik shook his head. 'No, brother. You don't recognise me?'

Luke shook his head. 'I can't recognise anyone.'

'No,' said Malik. 'I can't believe they brought you in and I didn't see it.'

'When I broke the DNA machine.'

'You didn't *break* the DNA machine,' said Malik. 'The analyst didn't understand the results. I told her we'd send it to someone else and it was all fine. For goodness' sake I've been covering your arse for weeks. I was on my way to the college to get you out when you made a run for it. That was a pain in the bum, I can tell you. I sat on that Warsaw railway station thing for a solid ninety minutes. Myozr too.'

'You came all the way to find me?'

'Yes.'

'Why?'

'To warn you they were coming too.'

'But did it take you as long as me?'

Malik shook his head. 'Oh no, things have improved a lot since your day. Cross-topographic border-working really brought the technology on a lot.'

Connie squeezed Luke. 'Because you're so amazing.'

'When I heard they had tracked a signal down ...'

'Belarus,' said Luke. 'I was so, so careless. It was just after I'd landed.'

'We knew they were coming,' said Malik. 'So I came too. A little quicker. I guessed you'd be where they would pick the signal up.'

He beamed proudly.

Luke removed his hand from Malik's intermingling and looked at him.

Connie realised what he was about to say a split-second before he did so.

'You killed the professor.'

Malik tilted his head to one side.

'Of course.'

'You *killed* someone.'

'Someone who was going to have you chopped, stuffed and displayed,' said Malik. 'I needed the pigmentation to pass. I couldn't tell which one you were, but I guessed you'd be where the signals were coming in. I kept you under surveillance – and as soon as I was sure . . . well, you needed me. You needed me. The prof would have shown you far less mercy than I showed him, let me tell you.'

Connie put her hand to her mouth. She was shocked.

'He felt no pain.'

'You can't . . .'

It was strange to see Luke angry. He kicked the side of the van. The seat unhinged.

'You can't kill to stop killing! That's the stupidest thing I've ever heard.'

'My orders right now are to drive you straight back to the SCIF. And what do you think they're going to do to you there? Bake you some scones?'

Luke shook his head.

'No,' he said.

'And if you try to get away . . . you know bullets can kill you,' said Malik. 'Those little black things? That come out of guns? That you probably think wouldn't bother you too much? Well, I can tell you, you're wrong. They can and they will, and they are coming for you: our people and their people are both as bad as each other, all desperate to wipe you out after everything you did, because you upset the people in charge. Species are all the same. And I don't even know how YOU got mixed up in this. You shouldn't even be here.'

This was to Connie. She glared back at him.

'Know a lot about Earth girls?'

'I'm guessing not as much as him.'

Connie shot him a filthy look, even as she wondered if this man was their only hope of rescue.

'What can we do?' she said finally.

'Our Extraction,' said Malik. 'The people don't know that they're still going to kill you. If we show them, if we tell them you're here, and that the government still plans to kill you . . . there may be pressure. They may be able to exert pressure on the seniority.'

'What's an Extraction?' said Connie.

Luke thought really hard.

'Um. Family? Kind of. But bigger. Quite a lot bigger. Maybe a million or so bigger.'

'Christmas must be tricky.'

'They could do that?' asked Luke. 'The Extraction could challenge the seniority?'

'You've missed sixty-eight years of politics. That's forty Earth years,' said Malik. 'Quite a lot has changed you know.' His voice softened. 'But they still remember you.'

'But without me,' said Luke unhappily, 'the professor would still be alive.'

'Well, are you going to make something good come out of his death?' said Malik impatiently. 'Or shall we just have more pointless suffering? Most of it, if you recall, yours.'

Malik opened up his hand and the fluorescent information ran across his palm. Connie could only pick up little bits of it here and there, but Luke read it all and gasped.

'I have done it,' said Malik. 'I have told them. I have told them everything.'

Luke nodded.

'I have sent every piece of information I could get, every-thing in the SCIF, everything they are doing, every single word. Our people are motivated, Luke. Every mixed child, every Extraction working across borders, cooperating. They are very angry that they would do this to you. When they bring you back, there will be trouble. They will know you are there.'

Luke frowned.

'I don't want anybody to be angry.'

'They don't want you to be killed. They are making themselves known.'

'Seniority won't like that.'

'The object is that seniority will have no choice when you are home but to set you free.'

Luke glanced up at Malik.

'What do you mean?'

'They will have to keep the Extractions happy.'

'That's never bothered them before,'

'Things have changed,' repeated Malik. 'You have to believe that. And they changed quite a lot because you changed them. And they want you back – back and free.'

Connie breathed in.

'But I don't want to go back,' said Luke.

Malik looked at him.

'Don't be ridiculous. You will go back and you'll be safe.'

Luke shrugged.

'Maybe, maybe not. But I don't want to go.'

'Seriously? SERIOUSLY? You like being trapped in this thing? It's AWFUL.'

He waved his arms around.

Luke shrugged.

'You get used to it.'

'And the GRAVITY. Doesn't it drive you crazy?'

'Uh, well—'

'Don't you want to see the world again? Go see the great jumping ... argh, that doesn't translate.'

'It doesn't,' said Luke. 'But I know what you mean.'

They were both lost in thought for a moment. Then Malik shook his head.

'Don't you just want to go home?'

Luke didn't reply. Connie couldn't breathe. Inside, her heart was almost breaking. Of course she had been kidding herself. Of course he wanted to go home, if he wasn't in danger there. Of course he couldn't stay here; it was ridiculous.

'You have your ship here?' she asked. Malik, who paid her barely any attention, waved her away.

'He can't come in my ship,' he explained as if talking to a child. 'He needs to be taken back in state and show himself to the Extractions and the seniority. Keep up.'

Connie narrowed her eyes at him and gave him the Vs in the full knowledge that he probably wouldn't be able to make out what she was doing, and that even if he did he wouldn't know what they meant.

'We need to get a message back,' he said to Luke. 'A proper genuine message from you. That's why I drove you here. It's the noisiest quiet place I could think of.'

Sure enough, there was the thundering roar of the motor-way, but nobody who could actually look at them.

'Hang on,' said Connie. 'How come you can drive?'

Malik looked at her.

'It's not difficult.'

'No,' said Connie. 'And how do you know all the police stuff?'

'Again, not difficult,' said Malik. 'You're not as complicated a species as you appear to think.'

'He has trouble.'

'Yes, but he's a weird maths geek, isn't he?'

Connie smiled and her hand went to her mouth.

'Oh yes,' she said. 'Yes, he is.'

Malik turned his attention back to Luke.

'We don't have much time,' he said. 'Can you do it?'

'It's ... these vocal chords.'

'I know,' said Malik. 'How on earth do they manage? God, I cannot wait to leave, I really can't.'

He patted him on the shoulder.

'Do your best.'

'But what ... ?'

'Just say what you think about what you did. Beg forgiveness. Talk about how much you long to see your beautiful homeland again.'

'Won't they detect the communicator?'

'They certainly will,' said Malik. 'Which is why I will then drop you back at the SCIF and you will deny you ever knew I was anything other than a policeman and I will, with the delightful fricatives of my constricted throat, run like fuck.

'Just stall,' he went on. 'Tell them they're going to change their minds. Wait for the pressure to build.'

'They have *petitions* on alien planets?' said Connie. 'Amazing.'

'The Extractions will get behind you,' said Malik. 'They will. And seniority will rescind.'

'You seem very sure,' said Connie.

'I have faith in my brother,' said Malik simply. 'I have seen what he has done. Don't you understand?'

Connie scowled as the two figures bent their heads over the tiny, glass-looking bead Malik took out of his pocket, which glowed and flickered intermittently.

'But I ... ' Luke felt his throat experimentally.

'Do it,' said Malik in a voice that brooked no argument.

*

The noise dug into Connie's head; felt like it was burying itself inside her ears as if something would bleed. She pressed herself as far as she could against the back of the van, but it acted as an echo chamber and the resounding feedback roar made everything worse. The noise was impossible to bear even – as Luke had claimed it to be – at this muted level. Whatever was inside it was making this; there was nothing human about it at all. It was most like a twisted screech of crashing metal; a million robots falling down a million stairwells. The air crackled and smelled of burning wire.

Unnoticed, she unbolted the back door of the van and tumbled out onto the motorway slip road, closed it behind her and ran back up the verge onto a neighbouring field, desperate to get away from it as passing motorists looked puzzled and fiddled with their radios.

Up on the grass verge, looking down on six lanes of frighteningly heavy traffic thundering past – and still not quite managing to block out the incredible noise – she sat down with her hands over her knees, and tried not to cry.

Malik ... Was he the answer? Could this really save them? She thought of a huge, teeming planet, filled with billions of life-forms, billions of miles away, the other side of the universe – and all of them thinking of Luke, of campaigning for him, celebrating him.

Whether it was successful, it seemed to her, or whether it was not, she simply couldn't see a way in which she could keep him.

So Connie simply sat there in the morning chill, her head on her knees, arms clasped around them, trying to block her ears to the discordant noise of Luke speaking in his own way to his own people; blocking the way it made her feel.

And what if they did let him choose? Would he be miserable

if he stayed for her? Could she be enough for everything he would have to give up if he never went home again? To live in a painful body he had to fight every step of the way? Could anyone?

Or would they make him go back? Would that be their price for not killing him? And could she survive it? And what about her friends: what price had they already paid?

The noise stopped suddenly, like pressure being relieved in her head. She blinked and looked around.

Luke was moving speedily up the hill to find her. He held out his hand.

'Have you done it?' she said. 'Will it work? Have you told them to treat you as a hero, save you, parade you through the streets?'

He shook his head.

'I don't know. I sent the message.'

She nodded.

'They will want you back.'

Luke was pained.

'Don't you want me?'

Numbly she nodded.

'More than anything,' she mumbled. 'But I don't know if I can take you away from ... from your entire life.'

Luke then lay down on the wet grass and put his head on her lap. The passing cars didn't seem to bother him in the slightest, nor the pressing time, nor the work ahead of them. He seemed as if he didn't have a care in the world. He lay down, then he reached up and caressed her hair.

'This,' he said. 'This is the only place I ever want to be. This is my entire life now. This is all there ever is to me.'

A tear dripped off Connie's chin and landed on his cheek, and he gently wiped it away.

'You're crying,' he said. 'See, look how human I am!'

She smiled at him.

'Except when you sound like hell's cement mixer,' she said.

'Evelyn always told me humans had views on making personal remarks,' he said, as she reached up to kiss him.

Malik was staggering up the verge towards them.

'What are you doing, you bloody nutters?! You're not on holiday! Get in the bloody van before they blow up New College!'

Chapter Twenty-eight

Malik dropped them at the gate of the SCIF with the security guards there. They had to put their handcuffs back on, which was painful, to Connie at least. Then he had pressed his hand deeply into Luke's shoulder and the two had pressed their foreheads together.

'Go well,' he said gruffly.

'And you,' said Luke. They straightened up.

'Thank you,' said Connie shyly.

Malik turned on her quickly and fiercely.

'Don't you dare get him killed,' he said. 'Don't you dare put pressure on him that does bad things to my world, do you understand? Do not put him in jeopardy. Don't do *anything*.'

Connie looked back at him. She knew what he was asking. She didn't know, however, if she was up to doing it.

'Mmmhmm,' she said. Malik gave her a frosty look.

'Give him up.'

She blinked and could not respond.

'If you love him, give him up.'

'It won't come to that,' said Luke.

'Look at your hair,' said Malik finally. 'You are a colour.'

'I know,' said Connie. 'But that is not all that I am.'

*

Malik let them out of the van.

Then he took his communications device and hurled it far, far in the air, where it fell into the River Cam, briefly disturbing some early-morning punters. He looked after it for a moment. Then he got back into the van and drove off at top speed, all sirens blazing, without a backwards glance.

The guards surrounded Luke and Connie and marched them in through the ultra-white interior of the SCIF again. Nigel tore down the corridors and took the fire escape stairs, swearing once again as the fingerprint recognition didn't work terribly well.

He charged up to the front door, then slowed himself down, smoothing his shirt and straightening his tie, attempting to appear calm and collected. Then he walked slowly forwards.

The girl looked wild, her hair a bright copper halo around her head, her eyes slightly over-bright and excited, her cheeks very red and wearing a grey T-shirt, stained and torn in places, with '*Kocham Warszaw*' written on it. Luke appeared exactly the same as he always did.

'Where's DSI Malik?' he said to the guards.

'Got blues and twosed,' said Francis. 'Set off like a jack rabbit.'

Nigel nodded. 'Fine.'

He turned to the two of them, shaking his head.

'Have you ANY IDEA how much trouble you've caused? And for what?'

'We just wanted a little time,' said Luke.

'Well, congratulations on risking the lives of everyone on Earth for precisely nothing,' said Nigel. 'Now, there are some people here who want to meet you.'

Connie shook her head stubbornly.

'We'll talk to anyone you like, and do anything you like,' she said. 'But first, we want to see our friends.'

'You want to keep the Prime Minister waiting?'

'He's waited three days; he can wait a bit longer. Also he's a nobber. Also, yes. Because we can be cooperative and talkative when we're in there, or we can stare at the floor. Don't mind really.'

'Um, what she said,' said Luke.

Nigel sighed and glanced at his watch. It was Luke's last day on Earth. By sundown, please God, all of this would be somebody else's problem.

'Five minutes,' he growled.

They entered the room where the others were gathered. At first there was total silence. Then Ranjit jumped up hollering, 'YOU'RE BACK!'

His glee was so genuine and unfeigned that the terrible fear Connie had had that awful things had happened to them relaxed slightly and she returned his exuberant hug gladly.

'Oh God, are you all right? Were you okay? Arnold, what the hell did they do to you?'

Arnold had woken up with a huge boot mark on his neck and a black eye. He grinned vividly at them.

'Standing up to the man,' he said cockily. 'Always knew I could. I just need to keep the print marks till I can get to a camera. Stick it on the web. Become a bit of a folk hero, you know. Move into an embassy for a couple of years.'

Connie ran up to him as Ranjit came close to Luke, then bounced away nervously again, then moved forwards again until Luke took matters into his own hands and gave him a quick, close hug.

Connie cuddled Arnold. He beamed.

'Are you sure I don't smell?' he said.

'You do,' admitted Connie. 'You smell awful. But I don't mind.'

'It's the pong of the righteous' said Arnold. 'You smell all right.'

'That's because I keep getting soaking wet,' said Connie. 'Don't ask. Oh man, I am so thrilled you are all okay. I was terrified they would do ... do something awful to you. Thank you. Thank you so, so much for holding them off. Thank you. It gave us time ... it gave us a chance ... I think we might have fixed it ... '

She was looking up and caught sight of Evelyn's grim face next to Sé.

'What? What is it? What happened?'

Evelyn indicated Sé, who still had an a-thousand-yard stare and had not got up to greet them. Connie moved towards him very carefully and stood in front of him, looking up into his fine-featured face. Her hands trembled.

'What did they do to you?' she said in shock, her entire body feeling like it was crumbling.

'Did they do something to you?'

Sé swallowed painfully; his throat was still swollen and inflamed from choking.

'It ... doesn't ... matter,' he said with difficulty. Connie breathed in sharply.

'Oh my God,' she said. 'What have we done to you?'

He shook his head, just once, stiffly, and Connie burst into tears.

'I'm so sorry,' she said. 'I am so, so sorry'

He leaned his head on her shoulder.

'It's okay,' he muttered. Then he started to cry too. 'I am very glad to see you,' he said.

'So, dudes,' said Arnold. 'Don't want to spoil the happy reunion, but what the fuck happened to the moon?'

Connie repeated Luke's theory of the effect of a smaller

307

moon on tidal patterns, and they had been both worried and impressed. Then they told them about Malik.

'The policeman!' Ranjit squeaked in excitement. 'The policeman that got here after you left! He was the alien! I talked to an alien!'

'You're talking to an alien right now,' pointed out Arnold.

'Yes, but that's *Luke*,' said Ranjit. 'That's different.'

'Yes, some of my best friends are aliens,' said Arnold dryly.

'So what's happening now?' said Evelyn. 'Because from here, I have to say, it's not really looking good.'

'I know. We heard. It's going to be fine,' said Connie. 'It's going to be fine. Luke sent a message back to everyone on Kepler-186f.'

'What was it?'

'It went kind of BLEARGHGLAWARDCLURGHGR-RHULKSMASH.'

Luke and Connie smiled at each other. Arnold rolled his eyes.

'No,' said Connie. 'But ... Malik and Luke have got it, I think. It'll be fine. They've spoken to the people on the planet and, well, it's going to be all right. He's a hero to them. They're going to let him go free.'

Luke didn't say anything, just smiled again.

But Connie was wrong. She thought she knew what was in the message – a plea for clemency and togetherness.

She was wrong.

Nigel closed the door behind him carefully in the bustling room and waited for people's attention. Gradually, everyone stopped. The PM looked expectant; the military men, as usual, were completely stony-faced.

'They're here,' he announced.

Someone made a fast intake of breath.

Anyali stepped forward. She glanced at the PM. 'We'd like to meet him first. In private.'

The chief scientific advisor stepped forwards.

'We'd also like to spend some time with him. Tissue sampling, etc. How long before we hear?'

The general harrumphed.

'Sundown.'

They looked at him, the PM shaking his head.

'Have we had no new contact?' he said, looking over at where Pol was still tapping away furiously, surrounded by his three screens.

'Nothing yet. We'll keep trying.'

'How are they going to take him?' said the general.

'I think we'll probably know it when we see it,' said Kathy.

'Have we got a cover story?'

Kathy nodded.

'New Danny Boyle project,' she said. 'In case the Olympics come back.'

Anyali looked up from her phone again.

'Another tanker washed up in Ecuador,' she said thoughtfully. 'Something's gone very wrong with the tides. The ABS and the EBS are stopping all shipping. And the Belarusian government isn't very happy with you. Not at all. They have a lot of questions.'

'One global crisis at a time,' said the Prime Minister. 'How are our dear colonial friends hanging in?'

'Going nuts,' said Anyali. 'Don't think there are a lot of people out there not discussing space invasions. Except for Fox News, which has declared it God's revenge for gay marriage.'

'I really, really would rather not deal with the Americans right now,' said the PM, waving his hands.

He turned to Nigel.

'Take me to him, please.'

'Then us,' said the chief scientist with an eager look in his eye Nigel didn't like a bit. 'You need to let us have an MRI, at the very least.'

In the end, Nigel decided to hold the meeting in his beautiful tower office. It was pretty up there; Dahlia, like all other non-essential personnel had been told not to work that day; and it was nice and quiet. They only wanted Luke but he had held his ground stubbornly and announced he wouldn't come without Connie, so she was there too. Nigel took a couple of pictures – nobody seemed to mind – of the Prime Minister and Luke shaking hands.

'Welcome,' said the PM. 'Welcome to Earth.'

'Uh, thank you,' said Luke shyly. 'It's nice.'

The PM leaned forwards.

'Sorry to meet under such ... um, awkward circumstances.'

Luke nodded.

'You must know, we have done and are doing everything in our power to ... to gain a stay of execution. And we will not give up until the very last moment.'

'Thank you.'

'Our scientist chappies downstairs ... they want to, you know. Have a look at you.'

Connie burst forward. 'No way!' she said. 'No way. No way are you chopping bits off him.'

'I think they were thinking more of an MRI ...'

'No!' said Connie, then remembered who she was speaking to. 'Sorry. I mean, no, sir. But, sir, it's perfectly clear. We can become part of the galaxy when we find it. When we discover it. Not by cutting someone else's hair.'

'Mm,' said the PM. He seemed, for once, rather lost for words. 'Are the prisons, um, comfortable where you come from?'

Luke shook his head.

'They have no prisons.'

'Oh,' said the PM. Then, '*Oh*.'

Connie drew closer to Luke.

'It's going to be all right,' she said defiantly. 'Luke's spoken to them. The people are going to save him, because he saved them. It's going to be okay.'

The noise could be heard coming up the ancient wooden staircase; a pounding of feet. Everyone turned around, and the security men leapt forward to the door.

Connie smiled.

'It's them. It's definitely them.'

The security guards opened the door to Pol standing there, out of breath, shaking.

'They're back,' he said. 'They're back online. They have something to say.'

Chapter Twenty-nine

SCIF control was bristling in anticipation, the air felt static.

As soon as Luke stepped into the room, silence fell, and everyone stopped.

The PM smiled encouragingly, although for once nobody was looking at him.

'I do hope this works out for us all.'

'So they can chop you up in a lab,' whispered Connie to Luke. 'Not bloody likely. But don't tell him that.'

The scientists couldn't help themselves. Their mouths had dropped open.

They all left their screens and their monitoring stations and crowded around. Everywhere Connie could hear, 'Well, he *looks* human' and 'Do you think he assimilates?' and 'Has he got two hearts?' and she could see a couple of nervous hands reaching out to touch him, and a wall of eyes staring, all monitors and readouts forgotten. Luke had a profoundly uncomfortable expression on his face as the whispering reached a fever-pitch.

Nigel stepped forward.

'Keep your hands off and step back,' he ordered, and for once Connie was entirely grateful for his brusque manner and tone of voice as the astronomers and astrophysicists backed up a little – even though many of them had only dreamed of getting into this game as children for the possibility – for the very reason of the thing standing in front of them.

One or two were dabbing their eyes.

'You're from another galaxy?' said D'mon, sounding hoarse. 'Really?'

'No,' said Luke. 'Same galaxy, different solar system. We're practically neighbours.'

'Is that why we look the same?'

'No.'

More people got bolder, the voices moved to a clamour and the hands started to stretch out again, but over it all Pol turned up the noise of the speaker so they could hear the now-familiar crumping noise again, feel the heavy weight of pressure in the air.

'O n e,' came the voice.

'Sssh, everyone,' said Anyali. 'Be quiet.'

The room stiffened. Connie shut her eyes.

'One has received his message. It has been discussed with the seniority.'

There was a long delay.

'To have him back on our planet would be de-stabilising.'

Connie squeezed Luke's hand fiercely.

'We do not wish to bring him home.'

The room erupted in cheers and applause. Connie threw her arms around Luke. The Prime Minister was beaming and shaking hands. Everyone came rushing over now to Luke to say hello, or introduce themselves, or to talk about their personal field of study and why he should come and work with them first. The noise levels were tremendous.

'No chopping him up!' Connie was saying exuberantly, and

Luke was smiling gently, and trying to deal with the fuss as he was positively engulfed in chatter and good wishes.

Pol was trying to get everyone's attention amid the happy hubbub.

'Hey,' he said. 'Hey!'

Nobody was listening to him.

'Hey!' he said again. 'HEY!'

Anyali was the first to turn round. Nigel saw her doing so, her face turning solemn, her hand going up.

And as if in slow motion Connie herself turned, lost in the throng of Luke's well-wishers and curious scientists; she had dropped his hand as he was mobbed and now, as everyone babbled and cheered, she caught, gradually, Anyali's and then Nigel's face, as happy relief turned grave, and she followed their line of sight until she saw Pol's face, and the fact that he was frantically mouthing something and waving his arms to try and get everyone to settle down, but it was incredibly difficult to hear and she felt once more as if she was underwater with everything coming up round her ears, even as she felt backwards for Luke, who was not there when she reached for him, and forwards, where Nigel and Anyali were converging on Pol's screens which had not stopped, which she could see, still peak peak peaked and, penetrating her slowed down senses, the *crump crump crump* of the background noise still went on … and finally, she surfaced, and could hear again, and now all she could hear was Pol, and he was shouting as loudly as he could, 'IT ISN'T FINISHED! PEOPLE, THEY HAVEN'T FINISHED! SHUT UP!' and gradually the people turned, one after another, and their mouths started to close and the noise levels came down, until all that could be heard was Pol's breathing, harsh and puffing, and the crackling air, and the hiss of the speakers as they came back to life.

'We do not wish to bring him back,' said the voice; once again gentle, unthreatening, neutral.

'He is too dangerous. You must kill him on your planet. You will kill him at nightfall. We do not suggest drowning as a suitable method. You will kill him outside where we can observe. Then we shall leave without further harm. And this will be over.'

Chapter Thirty

The heavy afternoon light shone through the windows of the little tower office, illuminating the motes of dust on the air, where a small group had gathered, heads bowed, intense and serious.

The general cleared his throat and spoke first, with some restraint.

'Should he be hung? Isn't that the penalty for high treason? Was in my day.'

'Who's going to do that?' said the admiral. 'We have good soldiers but they are still soldiers. Hanging is what the bad guys do. We don't loop ropes over scaffolds.'

'Complicated too,' said Kathy. 'It involves equipment and who knows what? And it's barbarism.'

'Oh, this is *barbarism*,' said the Prime Minister, and people shuffled respectfully.

Eventually the rear-admiral found his voice.

'I think we need to consider that we are not killing a person here,' he said. 'This isn't a person. It's a thing. A very different thing. Like a cockroach, or a seal.'

'That's another point against hanging,' said someone else. 'What if he can't be hung?'

Silence fell.

'No drowning,' mused the PM. 'What do you think they meant by that?'

People shook their head.

'Your weirdo squad doesn't know, do they?' said Anyali to Nigel.

Nigel shrugged. 'I'm not sure we're past the stage of getting anything sensible out of them.'

'What if bullets pass right through him?'

'I think he's definitely *matter*,' said Nigel.

'Well,' said the general finally. 'I'd like to see it dodge a nine-millimetre, jacketed hollow-point. And we have plenty of them. Better for the men too.'

'I can't believe we're actually going to do this,' said the PM, shaking his head.

Kathy spoke up.

'We are and we will,' she said. 'And you will be saving your people – you will be saving the world, and they will never even realise.'

The PM shook his head. 'And they'll go back to slagging me off for all those other things I did.'

'Yes, well, you did do them,' thought Nigel, but he didn't say it out loud.

Connie was half walking, half being dragged down the corridor in a fit of exceptional rage.

They were being separated. Luke was being marched in the direction of the sluice room. Connie was being sent back to the common room with the others. She was still shouting.

'WHAT THE HELL DID YOU SAY?'

Luke had a puzzled expression on his face.

'WHAT THE HELL DID YOU SAY TO THEM TO

MAKE THEM CHANGE THEIR MINDS? WHAT ON EARTH DID YOU DO?'

'I told them what I thought.'

'You should have told them what Malik told you to tell them. How much you respected their work and how you begged for leniency and how you made everything all right and you asked for your freedom so you could stay! THAT'S WHAT YOU WERE MEANT TO DO!'

'But how could I beg?' said Luke. "How could I make a special case for me, when so many live in oppression?'

Connie kicked the wall as she passed. It hurt.

'I KNOW what you said,' she hollered. 'I know EXACTLY what you said. You said, "Hey everyone, if things aren't fair, everyone leave their homes and tear down those walls. Make things right." I know you. That's what you believe, isn't it? That's what you did! Of COURSE they bloody want you dead!'

Luke lowered his head.

'You get one chance – ONE LAST CHANCE – and you throw it away on letting them think you're starting some kind of a fricking revolution!

'You can't kick people in the teeth and beg a favour! Who the hell – who the *hell* do you think you are? I'm not going out with fricking Mahatma Gandhi. How could you do this to me? To yourself? To all of us?'

Luke gazed at her, his eyes gentle.

'I did what I thought was right, Hair. I think it was right. And I thought they would understand that.'

'It was NOT RIGHT.'

'Please,' he said. So far his calm had been unnerving. For the first time he voice took on a shakier timbre. 'Please come here. Please come and be with me.'

'For some STUPID, stupid, stupid-bloody-stupid, shitty,

318

STUPID bloody thing you did! After everything we did! After everything we risked!'

'Oi!'

They had reached the fork in the corridor outside the lift. Nigel's sidekick Brian was trying to pull Connie away.

'I can't have you two screaming like you're on Jeremy Kyle, awright? Give it up. It's time to go.'

'Fine,' said Connie in high fire, not even looking at him. 'I don't want to be where he is.'

'Good,' said Brian. 'You go back to the rest. You,' he said, indicating Luke. 'That way with him. Don't try anything funny.'

'He won't try anything at all,' said Connie bitterly, and she turned and walked to the left after Brian, and did not look behind her.

'I will come for you,' said Luke.

'It'll be too late,' she hissed.

Chapter Thirty-one

Nigel walked out on the immaculately tended cloisters which belonged to the college where the mathematicians had been billeted.

The college had been shut, everyone sent away. It had been deemed private and hidden enough that they were unlikely to be seen by a distant tractor – the problem with the open fields – or one hundred astrophysicists (Mullard). They also could not block what the Keplerians could see, even though they weren't sure how much that was. At any rate, they ruled out anything with tree cover.

They weren't sure of course, but it made sense – considering the risks of getting it wrong – to make it as straightforward as possible.

He walked on the grass. This was strictly forbidden, but he didn't feel it mattered much any more. He had sent Robinson the porter home. Everywhere the sun reflected off the high windows, the lengthening shadows on the bright rich lawn, the soft stone, the distant traffic noise sounding far away, and even that wouldn't matter when they closed the road. A college: high-walled, barred, private. Something so ancient that it had seen civil wars, religious persecution, bloody kings come and go, and it had stood as a beacon for humanity and civilisation everywhere, a haven where people could come from all around the world and pursue the broadening of human knowledge, of human experience. Nearby, an apple had fallen on Newton's head. Today – well, that was quite different. Not exactly a step forward.

His phone rang.

'Sorry to ask, darling,' said Annabel, 'but do you know if you'll be home tonight? Only, it's my turn to host book group ...'

'*Book group?*' said Nigel, rubbing his eyes.

'Oh, yes! And I think almost everyone finished the book this month. Well, someone is bound to ...'

Her voice trailed off.

'So I just wondered if you'd be home ...'

Nigel closed his eyes.

'Yes,' he said. 'Yes, I'll be home. Later. After dark.'

'Oh good,' said Annabel. 'You can come and say hello to everyone. They do like seeing you. I'll get some extra nibbles. Then maybe when they've gone ...'

Her voice turned low.

Nigel nodded. Nibbles. Book group. Home. Suddenly, nothing had ever sounded so good.

'Yes,' he said, and hung up the phone.

He stopped next to a repaired piece of cloister wall, already marked and scruffy, the brickwork coming loose.

It would have to do.

Connie was sobbing passionately on Evelyn's lap, soaking her black jeans. Evelyn stroked her head thoughtfully and didn't offer platitudes, for which Connie was profoundly grateful.

'How could he do this to us?' she howled. 'He could have fixed it, I know he could have. He could have done it.'

'You can never tell what's going on in anyone else's head,' said Evelyn.

'Because he's an alien.'

'Everyone is an alien,' said Evelyn. 'Everyone. When Pansy left me she kept her façade up for months. Came home every night. We ate together. Planned holidays together. Lived our lives. And all the time behind that face was an alien: a robot. Someone who was madly in love with an undergraduate called Electra. Who thought of, she told me later, nobody else. Who filled her brain and her hopes and her dreams and her every waking moment, apparently, even as she was shelling peas with me.

'Everyone is an alien. And even when you are in love with someone, even when you think you know them better than you know yourself; even when you think you know everything about them and they you, and you live in each other's souls.

'Even then you know nothing about them at all.'

This was the longest speech Connie had ever heard Evelyn make. Her tears began to slow.

'And now,' said Evelyn. 'It is nearly dinner time. Do you think they'll remember to feed us? Maybe starvation is their way of dealing with us.'

Connie sat up.

'But if everyone is strange and unknowable and alien and totally weird . . . '

'Yes.'

'TOTALLY,' said Arnold. 'What?' he said as they looked at him. 'I know stuff.'

Connie managed a weak half-smile.

'Then what's the point? What's the point of falling in love? What's the point of love at all? Why is it all so complicated?'

Evelyn shrugged.

'I think love might be like mathematics in the end,' she said. 'It is not simple or complicated in itself. It simply is.'

*

'You're banging again.'

Brian was exasperated.

Connie had washed her face but she still looked pretty wiped out.

'I need to go back in with Luke.'

Brian shook his head.

'Sorry. I've been told now. He sees nobody and talks to nobody. In case he tries to bust out, or take a hostage, or do something.'

'It's his last day,' said Connie. 'Surely he needs someone by him?'

'They're talking about sending a priest.'

'A *priest*?' said Connie. 'Get me Nigel, for heaven's sake.'

'He's busy.'

'Get me Nigel. NIGEL!' Connie screamed down the corridor. 'NIGEL!'

'Cor, you really are a redhead, aren't you?'

'SHUT UP! NIGEL! *NIGEL!*'

The others took up the chant. 'NIGEL! NIGEL NIGEL!'

Brian heaved a sigh and turned on his walkie-talkie.

Eventually Nigel came down before Connie went absolutely hoarse. His chin was covered in thick, dark stubble and his eyes were tired. He looked, Connie realised, just like a person, not the awful enemy they had built him up to be.

'Oi,' she said. 'Baddie.'

'We're not the ...' Nigel gestured with his hands. 'Forget it. Never mind.'

'I need to see him.'

'You can't. Nobody can.'

'I need to see him, Nigel.'

'It's orders directly from the top. And if anyone *was* allowed to see him, it certainly wouldn't be you. Because if you remember the last time you two were together in this facility, you ended up fifteen hundred kilometres and several thousand pounds worth of helicopter call-out charges away.'

Connie nodded.

'But I promise. I promise I won't do anything. We won't do anything. I only ... I have to see him. I have to.'

'Brian said you were screaming at him like a banshee.'

'That's why I have to see him,' said Connie.

'I'm sorry,' said Nigel. 'I can't. I can't risk it. I can't do it. I'd lose my job for starters. But it's not just about me. It's about everyone. I can't risk him doing something to you.'

'He would never do anything to me.'

'And I can't risk you trying to free him or attempting something tricky.'

Connie shook her head and swallowed hard.

'I won't, I promise. I won't. I've accepted it.'

'You don't look like you've accepted it in the slightest.'

'I will never accept it,' said Connie. 'But I won't try to change it.'

'No,' said Nigel.

Connie sighed.

'How do you think we got to Belarus?'

'An astonishing amount of luck,' said Nigel, who'd wondered exactly the same thing himself, almost ceaselessly, over the last twelve hours.

'Seriously? You think that's all it was?'

Nigel looked at her.

'Keep talking.'

'He's freakishly strong, Nigel. We've kept it a secret but ... he's much, much stronger than anyone on Earth. He could punch through a wall. He could tear off his handcuffs and tear down the doors in a second.'

'Why doesn't he?'

'Because ... ' She swallowed. 'Because he's an absolute

fricking idiot. But also because he is trying to do the right thing. Trying not to make anything worse happen.'

Nigel blinked.

'That's noble of him.'

'That's ridiculous of him,' spat Connie. Then she pulled herself together again.

'But, Nigel,' she said, looking up at him, searching his face. 'If he doesn't get to see me ... if he doesn't get to see me at least once before ... before. I think he might try by himself. I think he might knock down the walls – which would take him one minute – and fight his way through. I think he might mess up your plans beyond belief.'

'You're kidding.'

Connie shook her head.

'That was our plan. That they would let him stay on Earth and we would burst out of the facility. And this time you would never find us.'

'We did before.'

'Oh, we let you.'

Nigel heaved a great sigh and looked round. The corridors of the SCIF were deserted; everyone was still in the control room being psychologically debriefed into silence by the scariest sons of bitches the army and MI5 could scare up combined.

Nigel leaned over. He was a head taller than her.

'Are you sure you haven't just been brainwashed?'

'Love, brainwashing,' said Connie. 'I don't know the difference any more.'

'I'll lose my job over this,' said Nigel, frowning. Then he thought about it again.

'Fuck it,' he said. 'Good.'

And he opened the door.

Chapter Thirty-two

Luke was chained to a pipe in the corner of the sluice room, head bent low. Connie thought she had never seen anyone look more alone. Nigel glanced around.

'You have fifteen minutes,' he hissed. 'No freaking funny business.'

'Thank you,' said Connie. She grasped his hand. 'Thank you.'

She took a step into the room.

'My love,' she said quietly.

Luke turned around. His eyes couldn't quite focus. He didn't say anything.

'I am so sorry,' Connie went on. She trod softly on the stone floor. 'I am so sorry.'

For a long moment, they just stared at one another. Then instantly she was in his arms, sobbing on his shoulder.

'Ssh,' he said, comforting her rather than the other way around. 'Sssh.'

The light salt wind smell of him comforted her; as long as he was here, there was a chance, there was always a chance.

'There must be something,' she murmured.

'I don't want to talk about it any more,' said Luke. 'No more.'

He stroked her hair.

'Tell me more about you,' he said. 'Tell me more. I want to know everything.'

'And I want to know everything about you,' said Connie. 'So we can be equal.'

'Well, you can be one,' said Luke, smiling a little. 'And I will be 0.9999 recurring.'

She smiled back at him

'We have no time, my love.'

'It got late so soon,' said Luke, nodding. He held her closer as the sun moved inexorably over the windowless depths of the building, over the astronomy unit, the array, the fields, the town.

'Just sit with me,' he said. 'Tell me about that time when you were little and saw the UFO.'

Connie nestled into him.

'I didn't *really* see a UFO.'

'I know,' said Luke. 'But tell me about it anyway.'

'Well, it was like a saucer,' said Connie.

'A saucer, what is that?'

'A great big flat disc.'

'Well, how would that work?'

'Well, if you took, say, a wormhole, it would pivot-spin.'

'Pivot-spin!' said Luke. 'Interesting concept.'

'And it has lights you know.'

'Lights!'

'Aliens need lights,' said Connie. 'White at the front, red at the back.'

'So they can properly change space lanes and obey space traffic signals.'

'Yes,' said Connie. 'That is exactly why.'

'And if a spaceman had landed and said, "Come with me, Small Hair Person," what would you have said?'

327

'I would have said yes, of course,' said Connie. 'I would have said yes without hesitation. Always.'

'Any old spaceman?'

'Any old spaceman would have done, yes.'

'Well, I guess I was lucky I was first.'

'Well, I guess you were.'

Nigel knocked at the door urgently. He had left it as long as he could.

'It's nearly time. You have to go.'

Connie turned round in a panic.

'You can't. We can't.'

'I'm sorry, but they're coming.'

'NO! It's too soon ... it's too soon.'

'Hair,' said Luke, drawing her to him. 'Hush now. Mathematics has no time. We are out of time, my love. It does not matter.'

'Don't you dare say that.'

'Connie, please.'

Nigel's face was pained.

'They're coming. I don't want ... I don't want them to have to restrain you.'

Connie was white and shaking. She came up to Nigel and looked straight at him.

'Will you be there?'

Nigel looked away.

'If I must.'

'You have to be there,' she said. 'You have to. Someone has to be there for him.'

Nigel looked down ashamed.

'I have done nothing for him.'

The feet grew steadily louder in the passageway. A group of men, one of whom was Brian, wearing full riot gear – which was laughable as nobody had bothered to so far – appeared in the doorway. Connie stared at them in disbelief.

'Seriously?'

'We saw what he did to the professor,' said Brian. 'We're taking no chances.'

Connie backed away.

'You have to leave now,' Brian went on.

Luke stood up then, forgetting completely he was hand-cuffed by the leg to a pipe. He nearly tripped then accidentally pulled the pipe off and ripped the handcuffs in two. Then men gasped and stood back, several taking out large, nasty-looking guns.

'Stop! Stop! It's okay,' shouted Connie.

'I'm coming,' said Luke, raising his hands. 'It's okay. I'm coming, I'm all right. Don't shoot.'

'WAIT!' screamed Connie suddenly. The masked men turned towards her.

'Last request!' she shouted, flushed. 'Last request! Every condemned man gets a last request! I just remembered!'

'I don't think there's any smoking on college property,' said Brian.

'Last request!' yelled Connie again. Brian looked at Nigel, who shrugged.

'I suppose that's true,' he said. 'As long as it's not, you know ... an escape helicopter or a piano.'

Chapter Thirty-three

The shadows had lengthened on the college lawn, and the sky was streaked with pink. The odd metallic hum was back in the air, as if a storm was coming. Except, of course, the storm was here; the storm had been here for some time, waiting for them.

The PM paced up and down the grass as his press officers in London went spare trying to explain his absence in the light of the gigantic meteor storm. Anyali kept checking her phone but was unable to read anything written there. Kathy leaned against the wall, idly trading forces gossip with the CSCs, betraying no nerves whatsoever. The rear-admiral on the other hand constantly glanced at his watch.

Nobody looked at the small cloister wall at the other end, where a short black post had been erected.

The bells of Cambridge tolled on: seven, seven-thirty, eight. The sky grew darker and the light was fading away. Suddenly an old wooden door at the other end of the lawn creaked open. Everyone started. The PM swallowed. Anyali leapt forward.

It was Nigel, looking apologetic. He came forward and explained the last request concept to the others, who sighed but eventually nodded.

'As long as they understand,' said the general, 'that if they try any remotely funny business – and that includes the fat one attempting to shout inflammatory slogans – they run the very real risk of being shot themselves.'

'I'll make that clear, sir.'

Which was how, when Luke finally emerged half an hour later – they had offered him a blindfold which he had politely declined, explaining that his eyesight wasn't good enough to require it – he was entirely surrounded by his friends.

Arnold came first, walking slowly and proudly, head in the air.

Then Connie was at Luke's right shoulder. Evelyn at his left. They were not to touch him, but when he stumbled involuntarily at the step between the pathway and the grass, both put out their hands to help him, and were allowed to keep them there.

Sé came next. Sé and Luke had stood face to face in the common room.

'I did not want this to end this way,' Sé had said stiffly.

'Neither did I,' Luke had replied. There had been a pause. 'Will you walk with me, Sé?'

'Yes. Yes I will walk with you.'

Beside him was Ranjit, crying and stumbling like an exhausted child.

He was led to the post at the end of the college lawn as the final rays of sun vanished from the mullioned windows above, in the rooms where Connie had sat and dreamed her nights away, of sailing in a star-tossed sea.

There they were motioned back by the men in the riot suits to the edge of the green, and Luke stepped on alone. Ranjit had started to wail.

Connie was the last to let him go, staring at his bent head, tears streaming down her face, soaking into the grass beneath her feet.

'My love,' she said. 'My darling. My Luke. Look at me. Look at me.'

He did so.

'Always,' he said simply.

And then he said her name.

'My Constance. My constant girl.'

'Don't call me Constance,' choked Connie. 'Just call me Hair.'

'Hair,' said Luke, so gently, as gently as if they were falling asleep. 'Farewell, Hair.'

She was shaking her head as he stroked her cheek one last time, and she closed her eyes and let her tears run down his fingers. Only Anyali, staring intently, noticed what happened next: Luke's hand moved down and passed *inside* Connie's hand. That for a moment they were totally merged; something like a little flicker seemed to pass between them and the terrible pain etched on Connie's face was erased – temporarily at least – as there was absolutely no way of telling where one of them ended and one began. Anyali's hand went to her mouth.

The uncomfortable static in the air crackled menacingly. There was no need to wonder what it was. They were here.

'It's time,' warned Nigel.

'No.'

'It's time.'

In the end he had to take hold of the backs of Connie's arms and lift her away as she reached out frantically, then collapsed, sobbing, into the others. They held her up.

'I can't look,' she said.

'You should,' said practical Evelyn. 'He needs to see you.'

The pressure now in the air had reached painful levels. Ears were starting to pop. It was very uncomfortable to stand.

The Prime Minister stepped forwards. He had been planning a few apposite words for the occasion but Anyali had persuaded him this was not the time. So instead, as the men took up their firing positions, he simply said, 'I hope the next time two great civilisations meet ... we can perhaps at least attempt to be civilised.'

He nodded to the general, who saluted, then said, 'Ready. Aim.'

It must have happened quickly, but it felt incredibly slow to the people who were there. Connie, unable to help herself, broke free of the group, and hurled herself across the lawn. Just as the general brought up his hand and said 'FIRE!', Sé charged across after her, pushing her out of the way of the rounds and rounds of ammunition.

The first of seventy-five expended bullets ripped through his shoulder as he was still flying through the air. The second hit his leg.

The next fourteen hit Luke over the top of Sé's collapsed form, as he landed on top of Connie, staining the grass bright red, as Connie screamed to wake the dead and rolled herself underneath him and onto her belly where she could see Luke – but there was no Luke. Or rather, there was the shape of him, still in the air, an outline as the first bullet had hit him and blown apart the control of his own shape that had held him as he was; threw him instead into the majestic, tall, clear figure only Connie knew, while the rest of the people watching gasped in horror, and Brian, immediately and without hesitation put down his gun. But his shape, against the twilight, stayed only a second, hovering in the air, and in the next second, it too disappeared and a wall of salt water, a fountain, crashed down and mingled with Sé's bright blood on the jewel-covered grass and washed it all away.

And the crackle and static in the air of the alien presence dispersed and disappeared, and suddenly, after the hot days and tempestuous nights, a soft, English summer rain began to fall.

Chapter Thirty-four

Eighteen months later

Arnold was fanning himself. He looked profoundly uncomfortable in a white embroidered shirt.

'How many people are here anyway?' he said. 'Thousands! I've never seen so many people. Canapés alone must cost them a FORTUNE.'

'Could you be quiet?' said Evelyn. 'I'm trying to be respectful.'

'Also all these GORGEOUS women here,' said Arnold. 'And seriously, I'm probably not allowed to talk to any of them. I bet I'd have been a good caste.'

He looked sullen.

'Seriously, shut up,' said Evelyn. 'If I have to answer one more question about whether we're married and where our children are I'll hit something.'

Arnold groaned.

'How long does this thing go on for?'

'Three days.'

'Well,' said Arnold, looking down at his shirt. 'If this doesn't make me drop a few pounds, I don't know what will.'

'Oh no,' said Evelyn. 'I think you're going to like the food.'

There was a rustle in the temple and, to general, good-natured awestruck noises from the many guests, Ranjit was brought in on a golden chair carried by six of his relations. He was wearing a golden brocade jacket lined with what looked like precious stones, and a matching hat. On his feet were Gucci loafers, and several garlands of flowers adorned his neck. He was beaming from ear to ear. He spotted them in the crowd (not, Evelyn pointed out later, difficult) and waved frantically at them, mouthing, 'Wait till you see her!'

Evelyn had already met her at the mehndi painting: little Rupi, twenty-one, petite and giggly, who thought Ranjit was the cleverest and funniest man she had ever seen in her life. Ranjit had taken up a professorship at University of M and neither of them could wait.

Evelyn settled back to enjoy the long, intricate ceremony. She gazed at her hands, decorated with the delicate mehndi that gave her a skin of lace. She turned to Arnold, pondering.

'You haven't heard from . . . ?'

Arnold started.

'Yes!' he said. 'Yes, I did!'

'And you were going to tell me when?'

'I have been VERY, VERY JET-LAGGED,' said Arnold, pulling up his shirt and feeling in the large bumbag tied around his waist.

'Hey, Homer Simpson, could you not do that?' said Evelyn, covering her eyes. But Arnold had already located the postcard, had pulled it out and handed it over.

The stamp was Russian and there was a picture of a few brightly coloured huts among the snow. Here in the stifling dusty heat of a Mumbai October it was hard to imagine, Evelyn thought, that somewhere out there in the world it was freezing – since the moon explosion too, the tides had started to fall, and there was some evidence that this was having a positive effect on the Gulf Stream. But it certainly meant the cold places were staying very cold.

'What's she doing?' she whispered, as the ceremony went on. 'How come you hear from her and not me?'

'I'm the one sending her work,' said Arnold. 'We're still deciphering it, you know.'

'Amazing.'

Evelyn had gone back to Cairo as soon as it had stabilised politically. She had had enough of the northern hemisphere. Arnold had stayed.

'What does she do up there all by herself?'

'Oh, she's not by herself,' said Arnold. 'She's got a Russian woman – Galine or something? Anyway, she lives with a woman.'

'She really is a broad-minded girl,' said Evelyn.

'No, someone she knows, who's sick. She's looking after her up there. I think it works out all right. She fishes a bit. Lives quietly.'

'I still can't believe she got off prison,' said Evelyn. 'I can't believe we all did.'

'We basically saved the world, man!' said Arnold. 'You know, eventually.'

'Hmm,' said Evelyn. Then, 'Ssh! This is the good bit.'

High above the Arctic Circle, just outside a tiny Russian fishing village called Tarana, sometimes the whales nest in the summertime. You have to be lucky, or patient, but in the long, white nights when sleep is difficult to come by, you can put on your Arctic down parka, take a steaming mug of something hot and a dog if you have one – possibly a stray rescued from an animal-testing facility – and go and sit by one of the many inlets where the ice has melted, and you wait.

And if you are patient, and lucky, then sometimes you will see a whale – sometimes even a school of them.

They plunge and turn in the freezing water, joyously at home in their environment, their great, heavy forms free and light and lithe in the cold, white light as they thrash and dive and swim, huge tails flicking back and forth, at home, happy, free, and the girl with the cloud of bright red hair sits by the side of the water, and she watches, a discarded wedding invitation by her side.

And in her palm she rolls a strange, thin filament of clear twinkling light, which does not dim.

Just as the ceremony was beginning, an elderly man limped up the temple aisle and stopped before them. Evelyn noticed he was missing two fingers on each hand.

'Excuse me,' he said in heavily accented English. 'I think I'm meant to sit here?'

They both leapt up.

'Mr Weearasinge, sir,' said Arnold. 'Ranjit is going to be so glad you could make it'

And there, right behind them, was Sé: only a slight stiffness in his shoulder and a limp betraying his injuries. He glanced around – still doing it; couldn't help it.

'She's not here,' said Arnold shortly, passing over the postcard.

In the end, Galina had changed Connie's mind.

The little taxi rickshaw had moved remarkably deftly through the insanely crowded and bustling city streets. Once upon a time Connie would have been frightened – or excited, maybe – by the experience.

The wiry man delivered her to the temple door with a grin and she tipped him lavishly.

'Why so sad, lovely lady?' he said, but Connie just smiled quietly at him. She didn't think he would really want to know.

Outside the temple doors she took a deep breath. The noise, the richness and colour and smells of Mumbai were almost overwhelming after the quiet of the life she led now. Once upon a time, she knew, she would have adored it. And Galina had absolutely urged her to come: to be there for her friends, who had been there for her, for her and Luke, who had never doubted them, who had never let them down even for a second, who had risked their lives for her. She would be with them. And she knew they would understand, they had been there; they would hug, and laugh and cry and talk about it, and at least for a short time, at least for the duration of her trip, she could remember.

She readjusted her cotton tunic, took a deep breath, turned the great handle of the temple, and pushed open the door.

Transcript of name: LUKE
BEITH message to Sen.1678
patrol vessel 6.4.8.556

I have one thing to say. I don't care what you do to me. I don't care about incitement or fomenting a revolution or being hailed as a saviour or being made an example of. I don't care about any of that. Whatever you tell me to do I will do. Anything you need for peace. Just leave the Earth. Leave. Save her. Whatever it takes to do it, whatever you want I will do willingly. I will submit. I shall not flee and I shall not challenge you. Just leave. Please. Leave. Save her. Whatever it takes.

/message ends

Connie and Luke's journey

latitude 52.2; longitude 0.11, longitude 4.13, longitude 21.01, longitude 29.26

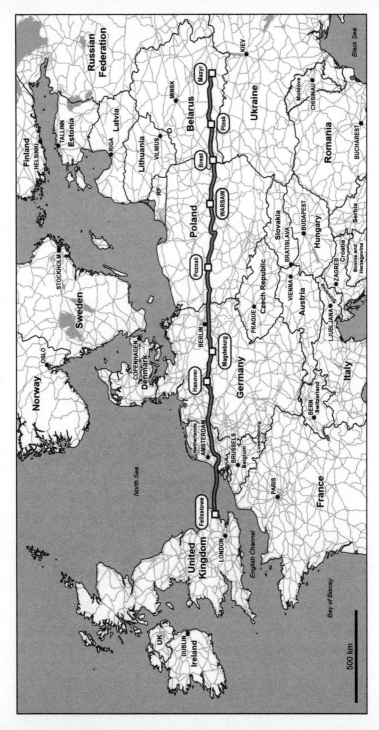

Acknowledgements

First and foremost, can I thank Edmund Harriss PhD, mathematician, artist and teacher at the University of Arkansas, and Alex Bellos for recommending him to me. Edmund has helped me immeasurably with his suggestions and work on this book. Any time the maths doesn't make sense, it will be because I have deviated from his path.

When Edmund was very busy in the summer (doing – are you ready for this? – he invented a new curve! I KNOW! Who does that? It is called the Harriss Spiral, and is extraordinary in both its mathematics and its beauty, and here it is:

(More at maxwelldemon.com)

Anyway, during that period we were also massively helped by the rather brilliant and talented Wren Robson, Consulting Mathematician, who also gave me a lot of the clever stuff. Thanks due also to the elfin James Harkin, who managed to take time off profoundly kicking arse on *Only Connect* to connect us up.

Tim Holman and his terrific team have made us feel so welcome at Orbit, and it has been a joy working with my wonderful editor Mrs Anna Jackson; Gemma Conley-Smith and Joanna Kramer too.

And the wider team of course at LB: Ursula McKenzie, David Shelley, Charlie King, Emma Williams, Victoria Gilder, the sales team, Hannah Wood and basically everyone who took up the challenge of me sidling up and saying, 'Well, I have something a little different.'

Also: the Bees, the board, Deborah Schneider and Mallory, D; Marcus Gipps; Tom Holland; chums, family and a special mention to the DW mob – Paul Cornell, Albert de Petrillo, Rob Shearman, Matthew Sweet, Lee Binding, Tom Spilsbury, Gareth Roberts, Justin Richards, Mark & Cav et al – for being so welcoming, and teaching me how to live safely in a science fictional universe.

And a very special thank you to the frankly marvellous Jo Unwin, to whom I might have erroneously suggested, when she very kindly took me on as a client, that I 'wasn't that much trouble'.

extras

about the author

Jenny T. Colgan is a pseudonymn for Jenny Colgan, the author of numerous bestselling novels, including *Christmas at the Cupcake Café* and *Little Beach Street Bakery*. *Meet Me at the Cupcake Café* won the 2012 Melissa Nathan Award for Comedy Romance and was a *Sunday Times* top ten bestseller, as was *Welcome to Rosie Hopkins' Sweetshop of Dreams*, which won the RNA Romantic Novel of the Year Award 2013. Under the J. T. Colgan pen name, Jenny has also written the *Doctor Who* tie-in novels, *Dark Horizons* and *The Legends of River Song*, and the *Doctor Who* short story 'Into the Nowhere'. Jenny is married with three children and lives in Scotland. For more about Jenny, visit her website and her Facebook page, or follow her on Twitter @jennycolgan.

Find out more about Jenny T. Colgan and other Orbit authors by registering for the free monthly newsletter at www.orbitbooks.net.

if you enjoyed

RESISTANCE IS FUTILE

look out for

WELCOME TO
NIGHT VALE

by

Joseph Fink and Jeffrey Cranor

The history of the town of Night Vale is long and complicated, reaching back thousands of years to the earliest indigenous people in the desert. We will cover none of it here.

Suffice it to say that it is a town like many towns, with a city hall, and a bowling alley (the Desert Flower Bowling Alley and Arcade Fun Complex), and a diner (the Moonlite All-Nite Diner), and a supermarket (Ralphs), and, of course, a community radio station reporting all the news that we are allowed to hear. On all sides it is surrounded by empty desert flatness. It is much like your town, perhaps. It might be more like your town than you'd like to admit.

It is a friendly desert community, where the sun is hot, the moon is beautiful, and mysterious lights pass overhead while we all pretend to sleep.

Welcome to Night Vale.

1

Pawnshops in Night Vale work like this.

First you need an item to pawn.

To get this, you need a lot of time behind you, years spent living and existing, until you've reached a point where you believe that you exist, and that a physical item exists, and that the concept of ownership exists, and that, improbable as all those are, these absurd beliefs line up in a way that results in you owning an item.

Good job. Nicely done.

Second, once you believe you own an item, you must reach a point where you need money more than you need the item. This is the easiest step. Just own an item and own a body with needs, and wait.

The only pawnshop in the town of Night Vale is run by the very young Jackie Fierro. It has no name, but if you need it, you will know where it is. This knowledge will come suddenly, often while you are in the shower. You will collapse, surrounded by a bright glowing blackness, and you will find yourself on your hands and knees, the warm water running over you, and you will know where the pawnshop is. You will smell must and soap, and feel a stab of panic about how alone you are. It will be like most showers you've taken.

Before you can offer Jackie your item, there will first be some hand washing, which is why there are bowls of purified water throughout the shop. You need to chant a little as you wash your hands. You, of course, should always chant when you wash your hands. It is only hygienic.

When you have been properly purified, you will lay the item on the counter, and Jackie will consider it.

Jackie will have her feet up on the counter. She will lean back.

"Eleven dollars," she will say. She will always say, "Eleven dollars." You will not respond. You are, ultimately, unnecessary to this process. You are, ultimately, unnecessary.

"No, no," she will say, waving her hand. And then she will name her actual price. Usually it is money. Sometimes it is other things. Sometimes it is dreams, experiences, visions.

Then you will die, but only for a little while.

The item will be given a price tag. Eleven dollars. Everything in the pawnshop is that price, no matter what she loaned you for it.

Once you are no longer dead, she will give you a ticket, which later you will be able to exchange for the item, or at any time you may look at the ticket and remember the item. Remembering the item is free.

You are leaving this story now. You were only an example, and it is probably safer for you not to be in this story anyway.

Jackie Fierro squinted out the window at the parking lot. There was no one coming. She was closing soon. Relatively speaking, she was always closing soon, and also always just opening.

Beyond the window was the parking lot and beyond that the desert, and beyond that the sky, mostly void, partially stars. Layered from her vantage, it was all distance, equally unreachable from her post at the counter.

She had recently turned nineteen. She had been recently nineteen for as long as she could remember. The pawnshop had been hers for a long time, centuries maybe. Clocks and calendars don't work in Night Vale. Time itself doesn't work.

For all her years as the newly nineteen owner of the pawnshop, she left the shop only when it was closed, and then only to her apartment, where she sat with her feet up on the coffee table, taking in the community radio and the local cable news. Based on what the news told her, the outside world seemed a dangerous place. There was always some world-ending cataclysm threatening Night Vale. Feral dogs. A sentient glowing cloud with the ability to control minds (although the Glow Cloud had become less threatening since its election to the local school board). Old oak doors that led to a strange desert otherworld where the current mayor had been trapped for months. It seemed safer to not have friends or hobbies. To sit at work, head down, doing her job, and then sit at home, glass after glass of orange juice, radio on, safe from anything that might disrupt her routine.

Her days were spent in silence, mostly void, partially thought. Some days she would recatalog her inventory. Other days she would clean the shelves. Every day she would sit and think. She would try to think about the day she took over the store. There must have been a day like that, but she could not think of the specifics. She had been doing this for decades. She was very young. Both of these were true at the same time.

She knew college was a thing nineteen-year-olds did. She knew being unemployed in a difficult job market and living at home was a thing other nineteen-year-olds did. She was content doing neither of those, so she continued on and on and on at the pawnshop.

She understood the world and her place in it. She understood nothing. The world and her place in it were nothing and she understood that.

Because of the lack of working time in Night Vale, she went off her gut feeling about when the shop should close. When the feeling came, it came, and the doors had to be locked, removed from their frames, and safely hidden.

The feeling came. She swung her feet off the counter. A decent day.

Old Woman Josie, who lived out by the car lot, had come in with a great number of cheap plastic flamingos. She had carried them in a large canvas sack and emptied them onto the counter like loose change.

"It is not for myself that I give up these little ones," said Old Woman Josie, addressing a bare wall several feet to the right of Jackie in a strong, formal voice, making the occasional sweeping gesture with her palm, "but for the future."

Josie stopped, her palm still out. Jackie decided the speech was over.

"All right, man, I'll give you eleven dollars," she said. Old Woman Josie tightened her eyes at the bare wall.

"Ah, okay"—Jackie softened, prodding at one of the flamingos and looking at its weak plastic belly—"tell you what, I'll give you a good night's sleep."

Old Woman Josie shrugged.

"I'll take it."

A good night's sleep was a wildly generous offer. The flamingos were worthless, but there were so many of them, and Jackie couldn't help herself. She never refused an item.

"Be careful not to touch those directly," Josie said, after she was finished being dead.

Using shop rags, Jackie laid the flamingos out side by side on a shelf, each one tagged with a single handwritten eleven-dollar price tag. Most things shouldn't be touched anyway, Jackie thought.

"Good-bye, dear," said Josie, taking the ticket that Jackie had filled out. "Come by sometime and talk to the angels. They've been asking about you."

The angels lived with Old Woman Josie, in her small tract

home whose tract no longer stood, leaving it alone at the edge of town. The angels did chores for her, and Josie made a modest income selling items they had touched. No one understood why the angels lived with her. Very little was understood about the angels. Some things were.

Of course, angels do not exist. It is illegal to consider their existence, or even to give them a dollar when they forget bus money and start hovering around the Ralphs asking for change. The great hierarchy of angels is a foolish dream, and anyway is forbidden knowledge to Night Vale citizens. All of the angels in Night Vale live with Josie out by the car lot. There are no angels in Night Vale.

Around the middle of the day, Jackie had acquired a car. It was a Mercedes, only a few years old, and offered with urgency by a young man wearing a gray pin-striped business suit stained with dirt. It was impressive how he got the car onto the counter, but there is a way these things are done, and it had to go on the counter. He washed his hands and chanted. The water went brown and red.

She settled on an offer of five dollars, talking him down from eleven, and he laughed as he took the money and the ticket.

"It's not funny at all," he explained, laughing.

And finally a woman named Diane Crayton arrived late in the afternoon—almost closing time according to Jackie's gut.

"Can I help you?" Jackie asked. She was unsure why she asked this, as Jackie rarely greeted people who came in the store.

Jackie knew who Diane was. She organized PTA fund-raisers. Diane sometimes came by to distribute flyers that said things like "Night Vale High School PTA Fund Drive! Help give kids the municipally approved education they deserve. Your support is mandatory and appreciated!"

Diane, in Jackie's mind, looked just like a woman who would

be an active PTA mom, with her kind face and comfortable clothing. She also thought Diane looked like a woman who would be a loan officer, with her conservative makeup choices and serious demeanor. She would look like a pharmacist if she ever were to wear the standard white coat, gas mask, and hip waders.

She looked like a lot of things to Jackie. Mostly she looked like a person lost in both a place and a moment.

Diane took a handkerchief from her purse. Without changing her upward, distant expression, she wept a single tear onto the cloth.

"I'd like to offer this," she said, finally looking at Jackie.

Jackie considered the handkerchief. The tear would dry soon.

"Eleven dollars. That's the deal," she said.

"I'll take it," Diane said. Her loose-hanging arms were now drawn up near her purse.

Jackie took the tear-dabbed handkerchief and gave Diane her ticket and the money.

After her brief death, Diane thanked her, and hurried out of the shop. Jackie tagged the tear with its eleven-dollar price tag and placed it on a shelf.

So a decent day. Jackie flipped the sign on the door to CLOSED, her hand touching the window, leaving its ghost upon the glass, a hand raised to say "Stop" or "Come here" or "Hello" or "Help" or maybe only "I am here. This hand, at least, is real."

She looked down to adjust the items on the counter, and when she looked up, the man was there.

He was wearing a tan jacket, and holding a deerskin suitcase. He had normal human features. He had arms and legs. He might have had hair, or maybe was wearing a hat. Everything was normal.

"Hello," he said. "My name is Everett."

Jackie screamed. The man was perfectly normal. She screamed.

"I'm sorry," he said. "Are you closed?"

"No, that's okay, no. Can I help you?"

"Yes, I hope so," he said. There was buzzing coming from somewhere. His mouth?

"I have an item I would very much like to pawn."

"I . . ." she said, and waved her hand to indicate everything she might have said next. He nodded at her hand.

"Thank you for your help. Have I introduced myself?"

"No."

"Ah, I apologize. My name is Emmett."

They shook hands. Her hand continued to shake after he let go.

"Yes, well," he said. "Here is the item."

He set a small slip of paper on the counter. On it, written in dull, smeared pencil, were the words "KING CITY." The handwriting was shaky and the pencil had been pressed down hard. She couldn't stop staring at it, although she didn't know what about it was interesting.

"Interesting," she said.

"No, not very," said the man in the tan jacket.

The man washed his hands and quietly chanted, and Jackie forced herself to lean back and put her feet on the counter. There is a way these things are done. She looked a few times at the man's face, but she found she forgot it the moment she stopped looking.

"Eleven dollars," she said. The man hummed, and other small voices joined him, apparently from within the deerskin suitcase.

"Where did this come from?" she asked. "Why are you offering it to me? What would I do with it?"

Her voice was high and cracked. It did not sound like her at all.

The man was now harmonizing with the voices from his suitcase. He did not seem to register her questions.

"No, no, I'm sorry," she said, fully aware of, but unable to stop, her poor negotiating technique. "My mistake. Thirty dollars and an idea about time."

"Done," he said, smiling. Was that a smile?

She gave him the thirty dollars and told him her idea about time.

"That is very interesting," he said. "I've never thought of it that way. Generally, I don't think at all."

Then he died. She usually used this time to finish up the paperwork, get the ticket ready. She did nothing. She clutched the slip of paper in her hand. He wasn't dead anymore.

"I'm sorry. Your ticket."

"There's no need," he said, still possibly smiling. She couldn't get a good enough look at his face to tell.

"No, your ticket. There is a way these things are done." She scrawled out a ticket, with the information tickets always had. A random number (12,739), the quality of light at time of transaction ("fine"), the general feeling of the weather outside ("looming"), her current thoughts on the future ("looming, but fine"), and a quick sketch of what she thought hearts should look like, instead of the pulsing lumps of straw and clay that grow, cancer-like, into our chests when we turn nine years old.

He took the ticket as she thrust it at him, and then, thanking her, turned to leave.

"Good-bye," she said.

"KING CITY," said the paper.

"Good-bye," waved the man, saying nothing.

"Wait," she said, "you never told me your name."

"Oh, you're right," he said, hand on door. "My name is Elliott. A pleasure to make your acquaintance."

The door swung open and shut. Jackie held the slip of paper in her hand, unsure for the first time in however long her life had been what to do next. She felt that her routine, unbroken for decades, had been disrupted, that something had gone differently. But she also had no idea why she felt that. It was just a slip of paper, just clutched in her hand, just that.

She finished her paperwork; on the line that said "pawned by," she stopped. She could not remember his name. She couldn't even remember his face. She looked down at the piece of paper. "KING CITY." She looked up to get a glimpse of him out the window, just to jostle her stuck memory.

From the counter, she could see the man in the tan jacket outside. He was running out to the desert. She could just barely see him at at the edge of the parking lot's radius of light. His arms were swinging wildly, his suitcase swinging along. His legs were flailing, great puffs of sand kicked up behind him, his head thrown back, sweat visible running down his neck even from where she sat. The kind of run that was from something and not toward. Then he left the faint edge of the light and was gone.

2

There's this house. It's not unlike many other houses. Imagine what a house looks like.

It is also quite unlike many other houses. Imagine this house again.

Given that it is simultaneously not unlike and unlike other houses, it is exactly like all houses.

One way it is not unlike other houses is its shape. It has a house-like shape. That's definitely a house, people might say if shown a picture of it.

One way it is unlike other houses is also its shape. It has a subtly unnatural shape. That's definitely a house, but there's something else, something beautiful, inside that house, people might say if shown a picture of it. I don't know if *beautiful* is the right word. It's more like . . . like . . . It's actually upsetting me now. Please stop showing me that picture. Please, those same people might beg a few moments later. It is a terrible, terrible beauty that I do not understand. Please stop.

Okay, the person showing the people the picture might reply, because that person might be good and caring. It is hard to say who is good and caring when you know nothing about a person except that they show other people pictures of houses, but there's no sense in going through life presuming awful things about people you do not know.

It would be safe to assume that the house is an enclosed structure owned and built by people.

It would be weird to assume that the house has a personality, a soul. Why would anyone assume that? It is true. It does. But that was weird to assume that. Never assume that kind of thing.

Another way it is unlike other houses is its thoughts. Most houses do not think. This house has thoughts. Those thoughts are not visible in a picture. Nor in person. But they find their way into the world. Through dreams mostly. While a person sleeps, the house might suddenly have a thought: Taupe is not an emotional catalyst. It's practical and bland. No one cries at any shade of taupe. Or another thought like OMG time! What is time even? And the sleeping person might experience that thought too.

These thoughts may also be shared in the shower. Grumpy thoughts. Angry thoughts. Thoughts that should be unthought before interacting with the public. Thoughts like [low guttural growl] or [knuckles crack, fists clench, teeth tighten, eyes stop letting in any new information, and water runs down a rigid face].

The thoughts are everywhere. Sometimes they are quite literal and utilitarian. There's a rodent chewing on some drywall behind the headboard could be one such thought.

Another way it is not unlike other houses is that it houses people. It houses a woman, for instance.

Imagine a woman.

Good work.

It also houses a boy, not quite a man. He's fifteen. You know how it is.

Imagine a fifteen-year-old boy.

Nope. That was not right at all. Try again.

No.

No.

Okay, stop.

He is tall. He's skinny, with short hair and long teeth that he deliberately hides when he smiles. He smiles more than he thinks he does.

Imagine a fifteen-year-old boy.

No. Again.

No. Not close.

He has fingers that move like they have no bones. He has eyes that move like he has no patience. He has a tongue that changes shape every day. He has a face that changes shape every day. He has a skeletal structure and coloring and hair that change every day. He seems different than you remember. He is always unlike he was before.

Imagine.

Good. That's actually pretty good.

His name is Josh Crayton.

Her name is Diane Crayton. She is Josh's mother. She sees herself in Josh.

Josh looks like a lot of things. He changes his physical form constantly. In this way he is unlike most boys his age. He thinks he is several things at once, many of them contradictory. In this way he is like most boys his age.

Sometimes Josh takes the form of a curve-billed thrasher, or a kangaroo, or a Victorian-era wardrobe. Sometimes he amalgamates his looks: fish head with ivory tusks and monarch wings.

"You have changed so much since I last saw you," people often say to him. People say that to all teenagers, but they mean it more with Josh.

Josh doesn't remember how he looked the last time each person saw him. Like most teenagers, he always was what he happens to be in that moment, until he never was that.

There was a girl Josh liked who only liked Josh when he was

bipedal. Josh does not like always being bipedal and found this news disappointing. There was a boy Josh liked who liked Josh when he was a cute animal. Josh always likes being a cute animal, but Josh's subjective sense of the word *cute* was different than the boy's. This was another disappointment for Josh, and also for the boy, who did not find giant centipedes cute at all.

Diane loved Josh for all of the things he appeared to be. She herself did not change forms, only showing the gradual differences that come with gradual changes of age.

Josh sometimes tried to fool Diane by taking the form of an alligator, or a cloud of bats, or a house fire.

Diane knew to be on guard at first, just in case there really was a dangerous reptile, or swarm of rabid flying mammals, or a house on fire. But once she understood the situation, she was calm, and she loved him for who he was and how he looked. No matter what he looked like. She was, after all, the mother of a teenager.

"Please stop shrieking and swarming into the cupboards," she would say. It was important to set boundaries.

Josh sometimes appears human. When he does, he is often short, chubby-cheeked, pudgy, wearing glasses.

"Is that how you see yourself, Josh?" Diane once asked.

"Sometimes," Josh replied.

"Do you like the way you look?" Diane once followed up.

"Sometimes," Josh replied.

Diane did not press Josh further. She felt his terse answers were a sign he did not want to talk much.

Josh wished his mother talked to him more. His short answers were a sign he didn't know how to socialize well.

"What?" Josh asked on a Tuesday evening. He had smooth violet skin, a pointed chin, angular thin shoulders.

The television was not on. A textbook was open but not

being read. A phone was lit up, a sharp thumb tapping across its keyboard.

"Come talk," Diane said from the cracked door. She did not want to open it all the way. It was not her room. She was trying very hard. She had sold a tear to Jackie that day. It had felt good to have someone explicitly value something that she did. Also, expenses had been higher than usual that month and she had needed the money. She was, after all, a single parent.

"About what?"

"Anything."

"I'm studying."

"Are you studying? I don't want to bother you if you are studying."

"Ping," the phone added.

"If you're studying, then I'll go," she said, pretending she did not hear the phone.

"What?" Josh asked on some other evening. It was a Tuesday, or it was not a Tuesday. His skin was a pale orange. Or it was deep navy. Or there were thick bristles that plumed from just below his eyes. Or his eyes were not visible at all because of the shade of his ram-like horns. This was most evenings. This was the incremental repetition of parenting.

The television was not on. A textbook was open but not being read. A phone was lit up.

"How are you doing?" Diane sometimes said.

Sometimes she said, "What's going on?"

Sometimes she said, "Just checking on you."

"Josh," Diane sometimes said, standing at his door, in the evening. Sometimes she knocked. "Josh," she sometimes repeated following a certain amount of silence. "Josh," she sometimes did not repeat following a second amount of silence.

"Dot dot dot," Josh sometimes replied. Not out loud, but like in a comic book speech-bubble. He pictured other things he could say, but did not know how.

For the most part, I do not like taffeta, the house thought, and Diane shared that thought.

"Josh," Diane said, sitting in the passenger seat of her burgundy Ford hatchback.

"What?" said the wolf spider in the driver's seat.

"If you're going to learn to drive, you're going to need to be able to reach the pedals."

The wolf spider elongated, and two of his middle legs extended to the floor of the vehicle, gently touching the pedals.

"And see the road too, Josh."

A human head with the face and hair of a fifteen-year-old boy emerged from the body of the spider, and the abdomen filled out into something of a primate-like torso. The legs remained spindly and long. He thought he looked cool driving a car as a wolf spider. He did look cool, although it was difficult to control the car. It was important to him that he look cool while driving, although he would not have been able to articulate why.

Diane stared him down. Josh took a fully human shape, save for a few feathers on his back and shoulders. Diane saw them poking out from underneath his shirtsleeves but decided that not all battles are worth fighting.

"Human form when driving the car."

Diane saw herself in Josh. She had been a teenager once. She understood emotions. She empathized. She didn't know with what, but she empathized.

Josh huffed, but Diane reminded him that if he wanted to drive her car, he would play by her rules, which involved not being a three-inch-long wolf spider. Diane reminded him of his bike and how that was a perfectly reasonable form of transportation.

Diane's task of teaching her son to drive took additional

patience, not just because of Josh's insistence on constant reassessment of his physical identity but also because the car was a manual transmission.

Imagine teaching a fifteen-year-old how to drive a car with manual transmission. First, you have to press down the clutch. Then you have to whisper a secret into one of the cup holders. In Diane's case, this was easy, as she was not a very social or public person, and most any mundane thing in her life could be a secret. In Josh's case this was hard, because for teenagers most every mundane thing in their lives is a secret that they do not like sharing in front of their parents.

Then, after the clutch and the secret, the driver has to grab the stick shift, which is a splintered wood stake wedged into the dashboard, and shake it until something happens—anything really—and then simultaneously type a series of code numbers into a keyboard on the steering wheel. All this while sunglasses-wearing agents from a vague yet menacing government agency sit in a heavily tinted black sedan across the street taking pictures (and occasionally waving). This is a lot of pressure on a first-time driver.

Josh often got frustrated with his mother. This was because Diane was not the best teacher. This was also because Josh was not the best student. There were other reasons as well.

"Josh, you need to listen to me," Diane would say.

"I get it. I get it, okay," Josh would say, not getting it at all.

Diane enjoyed arguing with Josh about driving, because it was time spent talking, having a relationship. It was not easy, being a mother to a teenager. Josh enjoyed this time too, but not consciously. On the surface, he was miserable. He just wanted to drive a car, not do all of the things it takes to be able to drive a car, like having a car and learning to drive it.

And sometimes he would say, "Why can't my dad come teach

me?" because he knew that question hurt her. Then he would feel bad about hurting her. Diane would feel bad too. They would sit in the car, feeling bad.

"You're doing a good job," Diane once said to Josh, in relation to nothing, only trying to fill a silence.

So every other time, I'm not doing a good job, Josh thought, because he didn't understand the context of her statement.

"Thanks," Josh said out loud, trying to fill the silence with graciousness.

"You still need to work on a lot of things," Diane did not say. "I'm sorry your father isn't here," she also did not say. "But I am trying so, so hard. I am, Josh. I am, I am, I am," she did not say. As far as things go, her self-control was pretty good.

I'm really good at driving, Josh often thought, even as he veered too close to highway barriers, rolled wheels up on curbs, and failed to yield to hooded figures, resulting in mandatory citywide ennui for hours. Night Vale's traffic laws are byzantine and kept on a need-to-know basis with civilian drivers.

Their driving lessons often ended in a "Good job" and a "Thanks" and a brief pause and a divergence into separate silent rooms. Later Diane would knock and say, "Josh," and Josh would or would not reply.

Diane hurt. She was not consciously aware that she hurt, but she hurt. "Josh," she said, so many times a day, for so many different reasons.

Josh loved his mother but he did not know why.

Diane loved her son and she did not care why.

Another way the house is unlike other houses is it has a faceless old woman secretly living in it, although that is not important to this story.

3

"KING CITY," said the paper.

Jackie had never felt fear in her entire life. She had felt caution, and unease, and sadness, and joy, which are all similar to fear. But she had never felt fear itself.

She did not feel it then.

She got to the work of closing: wiping down the bathroom sink, sweeping the floor, and adjusting the thick burlap covering up items that were forbidden or secret, like the time machine that Larry Leroy had stolen from the Museum of Forbidden Technologies, and the pens and pencils (writing utensils having long been outlawed in Night Vale for reasons of public well-being, although everyone still surreptitiously used them).

The paper was still in her hand. She hadn't realized it, had been going about everything without realizing, but there it was. Still there. Dull pencil. Smudged. Hurried handwriting. She put it down on the cracked glass of the countertop.

Now it was time to feed those items that were alive. Some of the items were alive. Some of them were dogs, and some weren't.

There were lights now, in the desert. Low bubbles of light coming and going. She had never seen them before. She ignored them, as she ignored all things that were not part of the small circle of her days.

There were always things she had never seen before in Night Vale. There was the man she passed in the desert using a pair of scissors on the top of a cactus, as if he were cutting its hair. There was the cactus that had a full head of hair. There was the day where the small crack that's always visible in the sky suddenly opened up, and several pterodactyls flew out. Later it was revealed they were just pteranodons, and all the panic was for nothing.

She finished her check of the inventory. The paper was in her hand.

"KING CITY," said the paper.

How did it get there?

"How did this get here?" she asked. The dogs did not respond, nor did anything less sentient.

She put the paper in a drawer in the back room, in the desk she did not use for the work she did not have.

There was nothing more to be done to close the shop. If she were honest, and she tried to be, she had been looking for excuses not to leave. If she were honest, and she tried to be, the floor had been clean enough to begin with. A glance out the window. The low bubbles of light in the desert were gone. Nothing there but a distant airplane crawling across the sky, red blinking lights, vulnerable in the vast empty, faint red beacons flashing the message HELLO. A SMALL ISLAND OF LIFE UP HERE, VERY CLOSE TO SPACE. PRAY FOR US. PRAY FOR US.

The paper was in her hand.

"KING CITY," the paper said.

Jackie felt fear for the first time, and she did not know what it was.

For the first time in a long time, she wished she had a friend to call. She had had friends in high school, she knew that, although the memory of high school was distant and vague. The rest of her friends hadn't stopped at nineteen. They had gotten older, living full lives. They had tried to stay in touch, but it was difficult as they moved on to adult careers and kids and retirement and Jackie just kept being nineteen years old.

"So, still nineteen?" Noelle Connolly had said, when they spoke on the phone for the final time. Her disapproval was clear in her voice. "Oh, Jackie, did you ever think of just turning twenty?"

They had been friends since sophomore Spanish class, but Noelle had been fifty-eight at the point she had finally asked Jackie that question, and spoke in tones that felt sickeningly parental to Jackie. Jackie had said so, and Noelle had become openly condescending, and they had both hung up, and she and Noelle had never spoken again. People who grow older think they are so wise, she thought. Like time means anything at all.

The radio came on by itself as she stood there, paper in hand. It always did at this time of night. Cecil Palmer, the host of Night Vale Community Radio, spoke to her. News, the community calendar, traffic.

She listened when she could to Cecil. Most of the town did. At home, Jackie had a small radio, only about two feet wide, a foot and a half tall. It was the lightweight portable edition ("under 14 lbs.!") with a mother-of-pearl handle and sharply angled, open-beaked eagles carved into the upper corners.

Her mother had gotten it for her whenever her sixteenth birthday was, however long ago that had been, and it was one of Jackie's favorite possessions, along with her record collection, which she never listened to because she didn't have a license to own a record player yet.

Cecil Palmer spoke of the horrors of everyday life. Nearly every broadcast told a story of impending doom or death, or worse: a long life lived in fruitless fear of doom or death. It wasn't that Jackie wanted to know all of the bad news of the world. It was that she loved sitting in the dark of her bedroom, swaddled in blankets and invisible radio waves.

Look, life is stressful. This is true everywhere. But life in Night Vale is more stressful. There are things lurking in the shadows. Not the projections of a worried mind, but literal Things, lurking, literally, in shadows. Conspiracies are hidden in every storefront, under every street, and floating in helicopters above. And with all that there is still the bland tragedy of life. Births, deaths, comings, goings, the gulf of subjectivity and bravado between us and everyone we care about. All is sorrow, as a man once said without really doing much about it.

But when Cecil talked it was possible to let some of that go. To let go of the worries. To let go of the questions. To let go of letting or going.

The slip of paper, however, Jackie could not let go of. She opened her hand, and watched it flutter to the floor. She stared at it. It was on the floor. "Dot dot dot," the blank back of the paper said, not literally, but like in a comic book speech-bubble. She stared and stared, and it sat and sat, and then she blinked her eyes and it was back in her hand.

"KING CITY," it said.

"This is getting me nowhere," she said, to no one, or to the dogs, or to the Thing that lurked in her corner.

She tried calling Cecil at the station, to see if he had heard anything about a man in a tan jacket, holding a deerskin suitcase. She couldn't remember Cecil ever mentioning a person by that description on his show, but it was worth a shot.

One of the station interns picked up, promising to take a message, but who knew if the poor kid would even survive long enough to deliver it?

"That's okay," Jackie said. "Hey, listen, I think the Arby's is hiring. Have you considered that? Their death rate is really low for the area."

But the kid was already hanging up. Oh well, not Jackie's job to worry about the life of someone foolhardy enough to be a community radio intern.

The shop was well and truly closed. At this point if she waited any longer she might as well lay out a sleeping bag and spend the night. Which, nope. So she stepped out into the parking lot, jumpy for sure.

There was a black sedan with tinted windows at the end of the lot—the windows cracked down enough for her to see two sunglassed agents of a vague yet menacing government agency watching her intently. One of them had a camera that kept going off, but the agent didn't seem to know how to deactivate the flash. The light against the tinted windows made the shots worthless, and the agent cursed and tried again and it flashed again. Jackie waved good night to them, as she always did.

Maybe she would take the Mercedes home. Drive with the roof down, see how fast she could make it go before the Sheriff's Secret Police stopped her. But she wouldn't, of course. She walked to her car, a blue Mazda coupe with double red stripes that had been washed, presumably, at some point before she owned it.

"King City," she said. The paper in her hand agreed.

It had been a mistake to accept what the man in the tan jacket had offered her. She didn't know what it was, or what it meant, or what information it was trying to convey and to whom. But she knew that it had changed something. The world was slipping into her life. And she had to push it out, starting with this slip of paper, and the man in the tan jacket.

She announced her intentions, as all Night Vale citizens must.

"I will find the man in the tan jacket, and I will make him take this piece of paper back," she announced. "If I could do that without having to learn anything about him or about what the paper means, that would be just ideal." The agents in the car, holding index fingers to earpieces, dutifully wrote this down.

Out in the desert, bubbles of light, low to the ground. The echo of a crowd arguing and then cheering. For a moment, a tall building, all glass and angles and business, where there had definitely been nothing but sand, and then it was gone, and there were more lights, shifting, warping the air around them. And the echo of crowds. And the lights.

She put the car in reverse, and pulled onto the highway, tossing the slip of paper out the window and watching with satisfaction as it fluttered into the night behind her, and then, snapping her fingers, caught the paper between them, where it was, where it had always been.